The Boxcar Kid

A Novel by

DICK MILLER

Copyright © 2008 by Dick Miller

ISBN(10): 1-59507-187-3
ISBN(13): 978-159507-187-3

ArcheBooks Publishing Incorporated
www.archebooks.com

Lyrics from "*Happy Days Are Here Again*"
Words and Music by JACK YELLEN and MILTON AGER
© 1929 (Renewed) WARNER BROS. INC.
All Rights Reserved. Used by Permission of ALFRED PUBLISHING CO., INC.

Second Edition: 2008

ArcheBooks Publishing

Dedication

This book is dedicated to the memory of

JOHN JOHNSON
Who inspired me to write this novel

December 4, 1924 - January 26, 2003

With Thanks

For those who encouraged, supported and stood by me...
My wife, Donna, who stood by me through the long years of my obsession with The Boxcar Kid; members of my immediate and extended family; members of Zion Lutheran Church in Fort Myers, Florida; my extended faith community; fellow members of the Gulf Coast Writer's Association and my Fiction Writing Group.

For those who mentored, read, critiqued and edited...
Betty Behrns
Marshall Chamberlain, author the unfolding ANCESTOR SERIES of Adventure-Thrillers, and Creative Self-Publishing in the World Marketplace.
Ruben Colon, author of Clarissa; Painted Eyes; Pat Middlekauff; Bob Miljus; Dan Miller; Errol Lincoln Uys, best-selling author of Brazil; Riding the Rails.

For those who provided computer and technical services, website design, maintenance...
Mike Behrns-Miller (http://blog.thedigitalmachine.com) and Dan Miller (http://hightechgeek.com)

For those who provided historical facts, personal stories...
Howard Brown, Harold Downey*, and Dick Rupert*—three friends who grew up together in Lima, Ohio during the Depression, who each related stories of riding the rails, infamous local railroad "bull", topography of railroad yard, Lima Locomotive Works, and other boyhood experiences.
John H. Danner—Director, Danner Funeral Home, York, Pennsylvania, former railroad brakeman. Reported stories of dangers and death on the rails.
Casimir Filipowicz—served four enlistments in Civilian Conservaton Corps; became CCC Supervisor; Supervisor of message center at office of Joint-Chief-of-Staff, Washington, D.C. during World War II.
Richard Griffiths—as a friend of railroad detective with Pennsylvania Railroad in Depression years, favored balanced view of detectives and trespassers on railroad property.
Ruth Griffiths—daughter of railroad engineer on Jersey Central Line during Depression.
Gustav Imm*—Aviator barnstormer in MN in late 1920's, '30's. Lived to be 102.

John Johnson*—Rode the rails at age 16 in Georgia. Responsible for initiating my interest in the subject matter.

Ruth Kinney—Resource on 1933 Century of Progress World's Fair in Chicago, Illinois. Extracted original Photogravure issues of Chicago Daily News, information on the Fair, and memorabilia from archives of deceased relative, who in her early 20's, visited the Fair.

Peter Krishana—Tour Director, son of former Ambassador from India. Resource material on diplomatic procedures, visas, education of diplomat children in US.

Georgia Kuhn—Reference librarian, Altoona Area Public Library, Altoona, Pennsylvania. Relative was railroad maintenance worker, reported violent death of brakeman confirmed by two other interviewees, also reported on Depression Era abusive mining practices.

Theresa McGinnes—Reference Librarian, Ft. Myers-Lee County Library.

Daniel L Parks, Holly Springs, N.C.—Appraiser, buyer, seller of coins. "Hobo nickel" resource.

Hermon ("Hop") Parsons—Left home in Pinesville, MO. to ride the rails at age 18. Shared his experiences from Joplin, MO to Sacramento, CA followed by military service in WW II.

John Paterson—Chamber of Commerce Visitor Center, York Pennsylvania, long time York resident, St. John the Baptist Episcopal Church, St. John's Boys Choir, extensive historical data on York.

Lawrence Pierce, Jr.*—Chairman, U.S. Board of Veterans Appeals (Ret.), Judge and legal adviser on 1930's legalese, courts and trial procedures.

Walter Prozialick—former mine worker, N.Y. Central railroad worker, Civilian Conservation Corps alumni, WPA worker, Reported Altoona, Pennsylvania and surrounding area history.

Richard Schweers—resource for bare-knuckle fighting and boxing in the 1930's

Cody Shelburne—Reference Librarian, Ft. Myers-Lee County Library, Ft. Myers, FL.

Eugene "Chip" Smith, P.A.—Legal adviser 1930's legalese, courts and trial procedures.

Robert Smith*, YMCA—switchboard operator and typesetter in New York City, in Depression years.

Kay Strommen*—Provided memoirs from childhood of the depression in St. Cloud, Minnesota, dairy industry practices, depression wages, and other related information.

Bruce Tiemann—Reported incident of a Depression Era woman's abortion with a knitting needle, a widespread practice by women of impoverished families in the Depression..

---

*In memorium.

INTRODUCTION

"…We also boast in our sufferings, knowing that suffering produces endurance, and endurance produces character, and character produces hope, and hope does not disappoint us, because God's love has been poured into our hearts through the Holy Spirit that has been given to us." – Saint Paul (Romans 5:3,4)

THE LONESOME WAIL OF A TRAIN WHISTLE – whether near or distant – carved itself into the memory of America's landscape through the 20s, 30s and 40s. Scarcely a person born during that period had escaped that plaintive and haunting sound.

Many teenagers growing up during the Great Depression transformed the sound into an imagined hope for freedom and opportunity. Thirteen-year-old Bucky Ellis, driven to riding the rails out of family tragedy, joined a quarter-million teenagers searching for a better life, but finding instead, only abuse, rejection, starvation and oftentimes, terrible death. Like the fabled pot of gold at the end of the rainbow, the lingering hope of profitable work and a better life ahead kept them from turning back.

From 1972 - 1980, I served as the pastor of a Lutheran church in Secaucus, New Jersey. Sometime during that period, John Johnson, a respected member of the congregation and community, made an offhand remark to me: "I was a hobo when I was a boy." Since I was raised with the notion that hobos were bums and unproductive members of society, my curiosity peaked. In my quest for further information, I learned that hobos, particularly those in their teens, represented a subculture that profoundly affected the course of American history.

Following their experience of hardship, sacrifice, hunger and abuse, America's youth found opportunity through restoration programs of the Franklin Delano Roosevelt administration to achieve their dreams of a better tomorrow. The Civilian Conservation Corps, for example, offered young men between 17 and 27 years of age a bridge to build character and gain productive skills. Under the supervision of the Army and the U.S, Forestry Service, the CCC provided discipline and work projects, including clearing fire trails, building dams, parks, roads and other public works. Lacking such beneficial government support, Depression-era youth in other parts of the world embraced revolutionary movements, such as Fascism.

Forged by hardship, sacrifice and government restoration programs, this generation of America's young people responded with patriotic pride and courageous service in defending the nation during World War II. Now dubbed "The Greatest Generation," these young men and women helped to win world-wide admiration and respect for America. We, who follow in the footsteps of those forbearers, owe them deepest gratitude for the legacy of their dedication and ideals.

Many stories in this book are gleaned from personal experiences of real people who permitted me to adapt them. The principal characters in the book are fictitious. Some situations involving actual historical persons may be true to their character but fictitious in details. In preparation, I immersed myself in research to weave an engaging and believable tale in the context of authentic history.

Dick Miller

The Boxcar Kid

PART ONE

CATCHIN' OUT

PROLOGUE

MARCH, 1930, Lima, Ohio

Labored breathing quickened in rhythm with the pounding heart of the scrawny fifteen-year-old. His feet blurred as he ran through night shadows, glancing back to see if his pursuers had spotted him. The beams of their flashlights bounced off surfaces in a frenzied dance to confound his escape. He shot another glance backwards. An immovable object stopped him cold. When the boy's vision cleared, he stared up at the huge form of the most feared railroad detective in Ohio. The snared youth's stare locked onto his captor's eyes as they pierced the shroud of darkness to fill the shaking boy with dread. With eyes stretched wide, the young pup's single word was scarcely a whisper.

"Cr...Cr...Crusher!"

The "bull," as hobos dubbed brutal railroad police officers, could have used his club, blackjack or the butt of his pistol to teach the squirt a lesson. Instead, he picked the boy up bodily, gripped his neck with huge hands and with a quick movement and audible crack, broke it.

The brute switched off his flashlight. Under the cover of darkness, he dragged the limp body past rolling stock until he came to an open top hopper. Slanted ends of the hopper container left room at each end of its platform for the bull to prop up his victim, leaving the boys legs to dangle on either side of the coupler.

The Boxcar Kid

Crusher inspected his work and smiled. *You won't be trespassing on railroad property any more, kid. This baby will be pulling out early in the morning. No telling where you'll end up Mr. No Name - just another addition to the casualty statistics. After all, everybody knows how dangerous it is to ride on the platform of a hopper car.*

1. THE BURIAL

MARCH 23, 1930 York, Pennsylvania

"My Gloria said Marcie did it with a knitting needle."

In the undercroft of St. Anne Episcopal Church, two men were re-lieving themselves in the rest room. A few moments ago, they had been among those who stood quietly against a chill March wind at the grave-site. The sight of the forlorn widowed father with his four children clustered around him had been unsettling to both.

The men stood side by side before the porcelain trough-style latrine.

"I heard talk that she'd done it twice before, but this time she got an infection," the second man said.

"It's a cryin' shame what's happenin' to families these days," the first one remarked.

"Yeah...too many kids, with nothin' to feed 'em and nothin' to put on their backs."

"I can't believe she was doin' it," the other said.

"Hell...I hear tell that plenty of other women have done it...or tried. These are hard times. It ain't surprisin' there's some that take des-perate measures."

"She was a beauty. Laid out like a princess, she was. I can see why Chuck couldn't keep 'is hands off her."

The two men buttoned their flies.

"That oldest kid seems to be a strappin' lad. How come he hangs around at home? Now with Marcie gone, Chuck oughta send him out to fend for himself."

"Yeah," the other agreed. "Chuck would be better off to kick 'is ass outa there...one less mouth to feed."

•

After the men left, thirteen-year-old Bucky Ellis cried as he rocked back and forth on the toilet in the stall. The men did not know he was there. Bucky had just lost his mother, and now it seemed like his whole world had collapsed as he realized his sweet mother had committed an unthinkable act, and, as one she had birthed, in confusion and grief, he made the illogical leap to blame himself, in part, for what she had done.

Bucky shuffled out of the lavatory into the room where the Ladies Auxiliary had served food. He had not tasted any of it, but had no stomach for food. At the burial service, he had steeled himself, repressing his emotions. He held Bud's hand tight to steady his younger brother, but inside, he felt his own painful digestive turmoil, and blood draining from his brain, leaving him light-headed. His brow and armpits felt wet with perspiration in spite of the cold wind. The only words he heard with clarity were those of the priest's dismissal: "This ends the committal service. Go in peace." Leaving Bud's side and slipping through the crowd, he dashed off to the toilet.

•

After all guests had gone, Chuck Ellis left the church grounds. Walking beside him, twelve-year-old Lena felt comfort in her father's protective arm around her, while the youngest, Lil, at nine, clasped his other hand tightly. Bud, who was two years younger than Bucky, followed with downcast eyes, scuffling his feet along the path, kicking at small rocks and pebbles in his path.

Looking up with sad eyes, Lil asked her father, "Daddy, where's Bucky?"

"Don't know, Lily. I haven't seen him."

"Shouldn't we find him, Daddy?"

"Don't worry, sweetheart. Bucky's old enough to take care of himself. He's probably at home waiting for us."

They walked in silence along the sidewalk. Chuck wondered how he

6

would take care of the children alone. *Marcie, I'll raise them right and give them all they need...I swear it.* Chuck was sincere, but had no clue as to how he would fulfill that promise. They were down to two milking cows, the harvest season was over and the planting season had not yet begun. At this moment, he had only the five one-dollar bills Father Griffin had pressed into his hand after the funeral.

"Take these, Chuck," the priest had said. "Some of your friends in the congregation want you to have it."

Assigned to St. Anne Episcopal Church upon his ordination nine months before, this young priest with blond hair and a boyish face, and his wife, Becky, received a warm reception from the devoted congregants. Addressed fondly by many simply as "Father Michael," the young cleric found the Ellises devout members of St. Anne's. Bucky and his younger brother sang in the Boy's Choir. For their talent, they received twenty-five cents each month. Father Griffin also provided ministry to Marcie Ellis during her illness before her death. She, in fact, confessed to him what she had done. He would not have counseled her to do what she did nor would he condone it, but he acted without hesitation, tending to her funeral with sensitivity. Though inexperienced, he had a heart for people, and responded readily to personal need with compassion rather than harsh judgment.

In the gathering shadows of dusk, Bucky walked home. He heard the wail of a train whistle in the distance. At school, he had heard about kids who left home to ride the rails. Nick, his best friend, had hopped a train a month ago. Buck had been with him the night he left. He had helped him roll a few belongings into a blanket.

Nick wanted Buck to go with him. "Come on, Bucky. Come with me. Everybody says there's plenty of action on the rails, and there's work and money waitin' to be had, too."

"Naw," Bucky said. "I got to stay home. My mom and dad need me to help with the kids and chores. Wood has got to be chopped, the chicken coop has to be cleaned, eggs gathered, me and the kids have to pick up coal dropped along the railroad tracks for the furnace in winter, and stuff like that."

Bucky tightened his belt, gritted his teeth and headed for home. *I was more of a burden than a help. Those guys were right. They'd all be better off without another kid to feed. I can take care of myself...get some work. How could I be such a blind jackass? I should've gone with Nick.*

Bucky knew what he had to do. His days of crying like a baby were over. Today he would become a man.

2. FAREWELL
TO BOYHOOD

Bucky quietly slipped out of the bed he shared with Bud, careful not to wake his little brother. He took a few things from a dresser and a blanket from a closet before leaving the room. Grabbing some other necessities, he tiptoed through the upstairs hall. Along the way, he saw light glowing under his father's bedroom door. *Papa is still awake. Should I knock on the door and go in?*

In his mind flashed a vision of a happier time when, at the age of six, he had burst into that room one early morning without knocking. He remembered the look of surprise on his parents' faces as they quickly separated under the covers. with giddy expressions on their faces. Now, in that same room, his father was inside alone.

Buck put his hand on the doorknob. His ears picked up the sound of deep sobs. He froze. Never in his life had he ever seen or heard his father cry. *What can I do, or what can I say to him? What will Papa think if I see him crying?*

Maybe he needs to be alone. I can't stand to listen or go in to see this. He backed away trembling.

At the open door to Lena and Lil's room, Bucky paused to ponder his decision. *What will they say when they wake up and find me gone? Who will help them get ready for school? How can I think of leaving them?*

Bucky tiptoed in, gently slipped to his knees at the bedside and

8

kissed each of them on the forehead. He stood and gazed at them. *I've made my decision, and I'd best stick to it. Goodbye. God bless you. I swear I'll be back with money in my pocket, and all will be well.* He slipped quietly out of the room and down the stairs. With a lump in his throat, Buck quickly moved toward the kitchen, picked up a few more necessities, wrapped them inside the blanket, and headed for the door.

Ready to exit, Bucky's eye caught sight of some items his father had left on a small table. Chuck Ellis habitually emptied his pockets onto this table at the front door whenever he came home. Bucky spotted the five one-dollar bills he had seen Father Griffin give his father. Instinctively, he grabbed the money. *I won't get far without any money – but they need it too.* He put three dollars back, and stashed the two he kept into his shoe where it would be safe. He looked at the items on the shelf again. *Ah...and what's this? Papa's penknife with his initials on it. That really would be handy. I need to take that.* Then his eyes fell upon a small pad with a pencil on it. For a moment, he stood transfixed. He lifted the pencil, leaned forward, as if to write. His hand poised to write, he stared at the blank pad. Then he shook his head, resolutely put the pencil down, and went out the door.

A dark sky hung low over the path along Codorus Creek. In the quiet of the night, Bucky heard only the gentle noise of the slow-flowing creek, as he walked the path to the freight yards. Trains from Harrisburg, Philadelphia and Baltimore regularly passed through York, and Bucky planned to follow Nick and other friends south to Baltimore, and then catch out to places that might offer a more promising future.

Walking slowly between the trains in the poorly lighted freight yard, his eyes darted nervously in search of any sign of movement. Fingers of distant lights reached through spaces between cars giving the appearance of formless, shadowy shapes ahead of him. *Geez...never thought this place could be so creepy at night...gives me the shivers. I wish Nick was here with me.*

A hand shot out from an open boxcar door. "Here, grab on to me, kid, and hop on up." Buck gasped and jumped back a few steps. Though he could not see his host, the voice sounded friendly. Bucky grabbed the hand and a strong arm pulled him up into the car. Inside, he could not see anything in the thick darkness.

"Name's K.O.," the rider said. "What's yours?"

"Buck."

"Where ya headed, kid?"

"No place special – wherever this crate is goin'." Bucky tried to project an air of cool self-confidence.

"Hey — you a gaycat?"

"What?" Buck asked.

"A gaycat — this is your first time ridin' the rails. I can tell, boy."

Bucky put his hands in his pockets, looked down and shifted his feet nervously.

"Relax, kid. Hobos got their own lingo. Most folks don't know it, but we're like a big family spread all across America. We're hooked together by railroad tracks, and we got our own ways of talkin' and doin' things. Wherever we go, we try to help each other out. I remember how I felt when I took my first ride. Don't worry kid. I'll show ya the ropes. Stick with K.O. here, and I'll teach ya what ya need to know!"

From his new friend's voice, Bucky thought he might be about his own age, but K.O.'s obvious experience on the rails made him sound more like an adult.

Bucky had never been inside a boxcar before. As his eyes adjusted to the darkness, he saw this one relatively empty except for some boxes stacked in corners. A few boxes were broken open with their ingredients scattered about the floor. Darkness prevented him from reading the labels on the boxes or identifying the spilled contents, which emitted a stagnant smoky odor that filled the car.

Bucky pulled his collar up to keep warm. At least it's warmer in here than it was outside. A cold front descending over eastern Pennsylvania had pushed the temperature down. It was not exactly what he had expected. As he took it all in, he wondered what lay ahead for him. *Maybe I should have waited to think things over before leaving home.*

The Maryland and Pennsylvania Railroad owned the line Bucky had boarded. A short line originating out of Baltimore, it continued north to its outpost at York. Baltimore lay only seventy-five miles to the south, but even the "Ma & Pa" line's crack passenger train took four hours to get from York to Baltimore. This freight would take even longer, since it was a "milk run," stopping to pick up and drop off milk cans at every town along the way.

Bucky thought about the stranger who had pulled him aboard. *Can I trust him? Will he try to harm me? He seems nice enough, but how can I know? I can still jump off if I want to...maybe I should.*

The "high ball," two short whistle blasts, signaled the train was about to depart. A series of quick bangs followed, as cars ahead of them took up the slack.

"Hang on, kid," K.O. said.

Then their car slammed to attention with a jerk and started moving. Buck had no idea how abrupt this jolt would be as he lost his footing, and would have hit the floorboards, had K.O. not caught him from behind. Gaining momentum, the train chugged out of the York yards. Soon the darkness intensified as the train snaked through hilly country along the banks of Muddy Creek.

The train slowly lumbered forward through the winding passage. Bucky thought about the people he had left behind...his family and friends. *That's it. It's too late now to turn back, and anyway, I'm not a little kid anymore. I'm gonna stick to my guns no matter what happens.*

Renewed confidence did not follow his resolve. His ambivalent mind exploded with despairing thoughts. *Jesus. What did I do? What will happen? I feel like I haven't seen Bud, Lil and Lena or Poppa for weeks. God I feel so alone. Don't cry Lil. I won't be gone long. Papa, I'm sorry. I'm sorry I took the money and your knife. Papa, don't be mad at me. I'll make it up to you, I swear.*

"What you mumblin' about, boy?" K.O. said.

Bucky tightened his lips. *Damn it, get with it. It's about time I stepped up to the plate. Whatever it takes, I can do it.* "I ain't mumbling," he said. "You must be hearing the creaking of this piece of shit we're riding in."

"Whatever you say, pal."

11

3. LESSONS BEGIN

Near the back of the train, Buck and K.O. sat in the boxcar and heard the noise of distant activity at each station whenever it paused to deliver or pick up goods. When they stopped at Bel Air, Maryland, they heard noise directly outside their boxcar.

The boxcar door slid open and Bucky and K.O. gave each other a wary look. In the dim light, they watched two hefty characters haul themselves up into the car and sit down at the opposite end. No one said a word.

A quick jolt, and the train was on its way again. Buck and K.O. picked places to sleep at their end of the car. The motion and repetitive clacking of the wheels made both boys drowsy and they quickly fell asleep.

Sometime in the night, Bucky felt probing hands on him, and his eyes snapped open. They fingered him. They poked everywhere. They rolled him before he knew what was happening. *They're pulling off my shoes. Shit...they're gonna pull my clothes off.* He froze in terror. With the sudden attack, and groggy from sleep, Bucky's attempts to fend them off were feeble.

Suddenly, he felt the weight of their bodies lifted from him. The action was quick. Bucky saw the form of his defender intervening. Strong hands pulled the attackers from their victim. The first assailant met with a smashing blow to his jaw and the clobbered man slumped to the floor. Buck realized the one who came to his rescue was K.O. Bucky saw the other lunging toward his protector. K.O. nimbly stepped aside and swiftly buried his fist in the other's stomach. The man buckled over only to receive a second blow that sent him flying into the wall with a thud. Sliding the door all the way open, K.O. grabbed the dazed men and flung them headlong out of the moving boxcar.

Bucky's blanket and other personal effects were scattered over the floor. He was relieved to see his father's penknife. *Maybe they just missed it...or maybe they left it because dad's initials are on it.*

K.O. knelt down beside him. "Are you okay, kid? Did they hurt you?"

"No," Bucky responded. "Thanks. They got the few bucks I had stashed in my shoe. It's all I had."

"Don't worry, kid. I ain't got much, but I still got some cash from work I did up in Harrisburg last week. It'll be enough to get both of us to Baltimore and a little beyond."

It was unusual for Bucky to rely on others to defend him. He was used to being self-reliant. As the oldest of four children, he learned to make his own way. His parents did not have much time for him, but expected a lot from him.

He demonstrated love for sports, excelling as an athlete. When boys played sandlot baseball at Bierman's Field, Buck stood tall as one of the leaders who picked players for his team. His dad taught him how to step into a pitch, putting the full weight of his body behind his swing. When he stepped up to the plate, the outfielders moved back toward the outer edges of the field. He exuded a maturity over his peers that sparked their admiration.

Buck had a way with younger children, as well. They idolized him, looking to him when they needed help. In the playground at school recess, he might rest on one knee to tie a shoe, wipe a runny nose, or button a coat on a cold, windy day. He played catch with them, teased them and had fun with them.

Now Buck sat in quiet reflection in the jostling boxcar. *I'm leaving so much behind me. God, will I ever see my friends and family again? What have I done?*

•

"Hey, kid, I've got somethin' here in my hand for ya," K.O. said.
"What is it?"

"It's a cigar. A pretty high class one at that. Must have been what they shipped in this here car. Some of the packin' boxes are broken open and cigars got spilled out all over. There's plenty of butts on the floor, too. The place stinks from tobacco. I'd guess whoever was in here before us was usin' the place for their own personal parlor car...without the fancy furnishin's of the Pullmans, of course."

"I wondered where that smoky smell was coming from," Bucky said.

"Here," K.O. said. "Take it and stick in y'r mouth. I got some matches here to light you up."

"I never smoked a cigar before."

"There's always a first time, kid. Here."

Bucky put it in his mouth and K.O. lit the match, which lit up Bucky's face...and K.O.'s as well. Bucky almost let the cigar drop from his mouth in surprise as he saw for the first time that K.O. was a Negro.

"Go on, take a good puff on it."

Buck remembered from the movies how big shots and wiseguy thugs puffed away on cigars. *No trick to this.* On his first drag, hot smoke seared the back of his throat and he broke into fits of coughing. K.O. laughed himself into near convulsion.

When the coughing passed and the laughing ended, K.O. said, "Let that be a lesson to ya, Bucky. Puffin' on a cigarette or a cigar may be good to relax you in certain times and places...but not inside a boxcar. Never, never, never, light matches inside any kind of car. You got a lot to learn about safety. Kid, if you're gonna ride the rails, then you better wise up. You got to know about the dangers, and how to stay safe. Don't worry. I'll teach ya everything."

Bucky was surprised to meet a Negro who was so self-assured. Although there were movements initiated by white activists to improve the status of Negroes in York, it had been the hotbed of Ku Klux Klan activity in York County. Negroes and whites attended separate schools, and lines of separation between the races were rigid.

"K.O.," Bucky asked, "how long ago did you start riding?"

"I been ridin' about a year...since I was fourteen."

"Where'd you learn to fight like that?" Bucky asked.

"My daddy...he was a fighter...I mean he was good and done it professionally. He was a prizefighter. He was even startin' to make lots of money for a while, and buildin' a reputation. He put a lotta fighters down. He taught me how to fight. That's how I got the name K.O. In the neighborhood, I didn't start bare knuckle fights, but I sometimes finished 'em. When bullies saw me fight and found out my daddy was a

14

big time fighter, they steered clear of me. I beat the crap out of 'em when they picked on the little guys."

K.O.'s disclosure of growing up in a Negro neighborhood where he gained respect provided Bucky with an explanation for his new friend's self-confident behavior. He felt at greater ease with his new companion, and his admiration for K.O. grew. "What happened to your daddy?"

K.O. lowered his head and with the resurgence of sad past memories stared at the floor. "He was always there for me and spent time teachin' me things. I loved those days. But it seemed as he became more success- ful, we didn't see him that much. He hung out with a lotta guys flashin' their money, and he got to drinkin' a lot with 'em. Sometimes he would come home late, all boozed up. He would get mean when he drank. It got so he couldn't lay off the bottle. I remember once I saw him hit mama and then, like a pitiful baby, he begged her to forgive him, prom- ising never to hurt her again. I cried myself to sleep that night and after that, nothin' was the same.

"One of daddy's friends later told me his promoter took all the prize money and deserted him. He said criminals took over and kinda 'pur- chased' my daddy. 'He was their property,'" he said. They forced him to fight dirty, like using the laces on his gloves to open a wound on an op- ponent's face, or to give him a double whammy wit' your elbow and break his jaw wit'out the ref seein' ya. Sometimes they took out the paddin' from the gloves to really hurt the fighter and break jaws. They opened a stitch in each glove and took a tweezers to pull out just enough padding where the knuckles would be. That way, the gloves kept their shape and nobody could tell. Daddy objected to these things, and when the drinking took over his senses, thugs beat him up and left him to rot. It was all over for him and he was out on the street.

"That's why I'm here. It ain't a good thing for a colored boy to be ridin' the rails...but the way things are at home, it's no place for me. Last I heard, mama took off wit' da kids and left my daddy. Six months ago, I lost track of 'em."

K.O. grew silent, and Bucky did not question him further.

After a few minutes, he said, "Don't worry, kid. We're gonna make it okay. My daddy taught me to box, and I can do a good job defendin' myself. There's bound to be somethin' good ahead if we keep on sear- chin'."

Bucky was grateful for this new friendship and the feeling of securi- ty it provided.

"Thanks, K.O., for whackin' those jerks for me back there."

4. BASIC TRAINING
FOR A "GAYCAT"

MARCH 24, 1930, Baltimore, Maryland

It was still dark when their train chugged along the tracks towards Baltimore.

"We're gettin' close to the yards, Bucky," K.O. said. "We better be hoppin' off before we get to where the bulls are patrolin'."

Bucky knew the term "bull" referred to detectives hired by the railroads to guard railroad property against trespassers. They had a reputation for being ruthless, especially toward kids who hopped onto trains.

When K.O. had pulled Bucky up into the motionless car back in York, it was relatively easy to swing up into it, but he had no experience when it came to hopping off. There were skills he still had to learn to avoid injury.

His experienced teacher dropped down smoothly from the slow moving train, like a pro. In contrast, on his first attempt to jump down, Buck fell stumbling to the ground like a puppet cut from its strings. Although unharmed, his blanket roll fell open onto the ground, strewing the contents about.

" Listen kid," K.O. said, "a lot of 'bo's tie up their crumb roll good, and then toss it off ahead of 'em before they jump. Then they go back and pick it up."

Bucky watched his tutor carefully, absorbing everything he said.

16

"But here's a better way. See the rope tied to my roll? That's my jump rope. I tie it around my roll so it serves as a carryin' rope. I double it over and tie knots to form a loop at each end. I can sling it over my shoulder and carry it like this."

He slipped the rope over Bucky's head and rested it on his shoulders.

"Now you have both your hands free. How's that feel?"

"That's a lot easier," Buck said. "What about jumping onto a moving train? Is there a trick to that?"

"It's not too hard once you get the trick, but you gotta be careful. You have to run alongside at about the same speed as the train. Never grab the ladder at the rear of a movin' car because if you lose your footin', you could swing back and end up under the next car and get crushed. Lots of 'bos are killed that way. Grab the ladder at the front of the car with your inside hand.

"When you jump off, hang back and drop off leadin wit' your back foot first. Be ready to hit the ground runnin'. And, shit, boy...watch where you're goin'. Once I seen a kid run headlong into a trackside signal pole. He nearly knocked himself cold and ended up with a big bloody gash on his head. If you're gonna stay alive, kid, you got a lot to learn."

•

A few days later, the two boys jumped off at an open area bordered by woods several hundred feet away from the tracks. Hunger pangs gnawed at Buck's stomach, and his mouth was dry. He had eaten nothing since yesterday morning before his mother's funeral.

"Don't see no place we can grab some grub, Buck," K.O. said. "Our best bet is to find the local jungle. There must be one nearby." Seeing the puzzled expression on Bucky's face, K.O. explained, "The *jungle* is where hobos hang out when they ain't ridin'. Most of the time, the jungle is a place where everybody shares what they got, and you can put together the makin's of something to eat. There's some good talkin', friendship to be had, and you can learn from each other about where the pickin's might be good. But sometimes, a jungle can be a bad place. I usually keep goin' back to the ones where I know the guys are okay. I ain't been around here before, but I know 'bo's who stayed in a jungle around here."

After a few minutes, K.O. spotted a path. "There's a path into the woods. Let's check it out."

As dawn approached, the first glimmer of light appeared through the top of the forest canopy, but below, it remained dark.

"Look there, Bucky. See through the trees?"

Buck could see the flickering of a fire in the distance. Moving closer, they saw five figures in an open clearing around the fire.

"Hold up, Bucky. Let's look the situation over." It only took a few seconds for K.O. to size up the situation. "Come on, Buck. I think we better hightail it outta here."

"How come, K.O.? What did you see?"

"Well, first thing I seen was them liftin' what looks like whiskey bottles to their mouths. Notice how they're movin' kinda funny...weavin' this way and that as they strut around? It ain't a good sign to find these guys drinkin' in the early mornin'. Don't know who they are, but it don't seem like the usual crowd. I wouldn't be surprised if this tough lookin' group is a bunch of locals who found a place to raise hell." After a brief pause and further observation, K.O. continued. "And see that fire! That ain't no campfire."

"It's big. It's more like a bonfire," Buck said.

"See those big timbers, Buck? Those are railroad ties. No doubt about it...and you can be sure the B & O didn't donate 'em."

"You mean they stole 'em?"

"That's for sure."

Bucky scrutinized the scene.

"And," K.O. continued, "by the way the flames are leapin' so high, I'll bet they broke into the lube boxes of the cars and stole the stuff they put in there to keep the wheels greased. I seen fires like this one before. When those rags are taken from the lube boxes, it could cause trouble with the wheels lockin' up."

"How do you know all this?" Buck asked.

"I've known some 'bo's to steal 'em to get a good fire goin'. Bucky, most of us are decent folks seekin' honest work and respectin' people's property. But not all are like that, and sometimes the local kids make trouble and the hobos get blamed. I know there are some 'bos who break in and steal liquor from the cars...I won't deny it...but there's word around that lots of stuff is stolen by the people who work for the railroads, and I've a mind to believe it. And guess who gets blamed for all that bad stuff? We end up gettin' the rap for it."

"Breakin' into the lube boxes sounds serious," Buck said.

"You bet." K.O. said. "I knew a guy who caught onto a car with a "flat" wheel that froze up. The ride nearly shook his brains and all his teeth out before he could get off. It made 'im so sick, he threw up all over the place. There's lots of things that can cause brakes to lock up. Sometimes a brakeman might set the brakes wrong. But I suspect no grease in the boxes could be a reason for a flat wheel, too."

Concentrating on the action at the camp, the boys failed to notice some of the motley band creeping up behind them.

"Well, well. What have we here? Looks like a filthy nigguh and a nigguh-lovin' white boy." They were brawny, about eighteen or nineteen, and their breath reeked from liquor. "Been ridin' the rails, eh? Well you ended up in the wrong place. This here place belongs to us now, and if ya have any doubts, ya can ask the twerps we booted outta here yesterday. But don't be in a hurry to leave. We aim to teach ya a lesson."

The drunken boy winked at his companion.

The second boy said, "Hal, which of these two assholes should we bust up first...'whitey'...or little Black Sambo here?"

The other spat out, "This one!" as he took a sudden swing at K.O.

K.O. responded like a flash of lightning. He blocked the punch with his arm, then delivered a stiff uppercut to his attacker's jaw with the other.

Buck stood close enough to feel the rush of disturbed air as K.O.'s fists flew. The kid fell to the ground like dead weight. Without stopping, K.O. pivoted and walloped the other in the head with a left hook, knocking him down into the dirt. Dazed, the scoundrel attempted to stand up, but Buck bashed the boozer's head with his fist, knocking him cold and putting him back down.

"That was a real flattener,'" K.O. said with a grin.

•

The action was quick, but caused enough commotion to attract the attention of the others. From their vantage point in the dim early morning light, the rowdies could not determine what had happened. Beset by confusion, and seeing the intruders had beaten their companions, they chucked their half-empty bottles into the woods and took off.

Putting a firm hand on Bucky's shoulder, K.O. gave him a reassuring smile. K.O. seemed to know how to roll with the punches, and Buck was glad they had teamed up.

Exhausted by their long night and ordeal, the two new friends left the camp area, found a clearing where they spread their rolls and collapsed for a welcome snooze before the full dawning of the day. Before drifting off to sleep, Bucky reflected upon the many unexpected and instructive experiences that had been crammed into one night. He had learned a lot, but realized his training had just begun.

5. A NEW AND
USEFUL SKILL

About mid-morning, a series of snapping sounds woke Bucky up. He saw K.O. jumping rope.

Buck recalled what K.O. had said earlier when referring to the carrying rope on his crumb-roll as his "jump rope." He didn't know how long K.O. had been at it, but beads of sweat popped out on K.O.'s brow as he jumped in unbroken rhythm. Several times, he would add some fancy footwork and arm crossings, swinging the rope over and under.

Seeing Buck awake, he stopped and handed him the rope. "Now you try, Champ." This was the first time he called Buck by this new nickname, and it was a clear indication of their growing camaraderie. It was not just a term of endearment, but also a title of respect. *Now here's a kid with spunk!*

Buck stood, took a deep breath, and started jumping. After a few minutes, K.O. gave appraisal. "That's good, kiddo." Buck stopped, as K.O. continued. "You know, I saw you slam that guy to the ground last night. Pretty quick action, Champ. Not bad form, either. I think I'd like to teach ya to box. What do ya say? Are ya up for it? "

"Hey, yeah!" Buck said. "Show me some stuff."

K.O. showed Buck how to be nimble on his feet and quick with his fists. He learned the difference between a jab, a hook and an uppercut, and how to pack more power into any kind of punch. In between instructions, they sparred.

Buck took to the sport like an avid street fighter. After their brief scrimmage, he said, "Can we do this each morning, K.O.? We can get our dukes up and practice until I get really good at this."

"Sure," K.O. said, "as long as we got the time and place to do it."

The two left the wooded area and made their way along the tracks towards the Baltimore yards. Maybe they would find a café, or some other place, to grab something to eat before they caught out again.

Bucky's excitement at his new lessons dispelled his thoughts of hunger. He had an energetic response to it all, and when they came to an innocent bush about his size, Buck started dancing around and punching out at it, defoliating the top of it. "Pow! Knocked his block off," Buck said.

"That's it, Champ! You're a natural. I like the way you're learnin' to pivot on your forward foot and swing your hip in as you bring your shoulder around to deliver the blow with a wallop...good job!"

"Com'on, Champ," K.O. said. "Let's see what's goin' on at the yards. We'll have to watch out for the bulls. I think we can pick up a train goin' south. It's the start of the growin' season, and we might find some work down there."

"Whatever you say, pal."

JUNE, 1930, Athens, Georgia

Bucky and K.O. sat on the grass outside a diner in Athens, Georgia, discussing their dilemma. They had picked up pocket money from work they did at a sugar mill up the line. Though they managed to survive by performing chores in exchange for food, this was the first money to pass into their hands for over a month. Now, with almost a dollar in change between them, they decided to splurge it on food at a short order café not far from the place they dropped down from a boxcar. Neither had eaten anything for the past few days.

Buck was salivating as he bound up the steps to the propped open doors on this warm day. "Holy mackerel, K.O.! I can't wait to park on a swivel stool and find something we can afford on a real menu."

"Hot diggety dog! Me too," K.O. said.

They barely made it through the entrance when a uniformed woman with a face creased with wrinkles and frown lines spoke from behind the counter, "We don't serve colored people in here."

"Can't we order something to take with us?" Buck asked.

"We don't do that."

"But..." Buck started to say.

"C'mon, let's just go, Buck. I ain't wantin' anythin' from here, anyways."

The two sat quietly on the grass peering through the doorway. Inside, they could see a smartly dressed young couple seated at the counter. With their backs to the door, the man and woman were engrossed in conversation and Buck felt a grain of relief that neither they nor any of the other patrons had paid much attention to what had happened.

K.O. said, "Buck, you go in and get something to eat. No reason why you should stay out here wit' me."

"Nothing doing, K.O. We stick together. You wouldn't get me back in that dive if they served free steak dinners."

As they spoke, a scrawny kid they had seen on the train walked up the steps and stood at the counter where the couple sat eating their breakfast. Without hesitation, he leaned over grabbing the attention of the pair next to him as well as the waitress. "Ma'am, is there any work here for me to earn a little lunch?"

This was not the woman that had rebuffed the boys earlier, but a more attractive younger woman. She had a sparkle in her eyes and a smile on her face. Winking at the boy, she glanced back over her shoulder and shouted "Jerry!"

A face popped out of the pass-through to the kitchen.

"What's up?" he answered.

"Kid here wants to work for a bite to eat. Anything he can do back there?"

"Sorry, kid, not today. Things are too slow. Get on your way, and come back when you got some money in your pocket."

Cocking her head, the waitress gave him a sympathetic glance.

Buck and K.O. could see the boy put on a sad face and stare down at the floor. The woman next to him gently jabbed her partner with her elbow.

"Did you see that, K.O.?"

"I sure did," he said with a sly grin.

Flashing a comprehending glance, the man said to the waitress, "Give the kid some lunch. I'll pay for it." Turning to the boy, he said, "Tell her what you want, kid...whatever you'd like."

The boy ordered a grilled cheese, some soup and a cup of coffee.

"Thank you, kindly," the boy said. "Can I pay you back by doing some chores?"

"Forget it, kid. Just enjoy it," the man said.

"God bless you on your way," the woman said before she and her companion left. Withdrawing it from her purse, she pressed what looked like an extra dollar into the boy's hand.

For Buck, it was another valuable lesson in his education as a hobo. He could tell by K.O.'s glance, he was familiar with the ploy.

The two rose to their feet and started down the road towards town. It was not long before they came to several stores on one side of the street across from a High School. Many schools throughout the nation had closed their doors due to the lack of funds, but here was a school with teachers and students. It was near the lunch hour, and some of the students came over to the store that sold candy, soda pop and cigarettes, and at lunchtime, a five-cent plate of beans.

None of the students took much notice of one among them who happened to be colored, and Buck and K.O. got their fill of beans, and raised and drained their bottles of soda pop without stirring up any trouble.

6. CAUGHT!

JULY, 1930, Memphis, Tennessee

"Buck," K.O. said, "There's a good place to catch out, but it's way on the other side of the yard. We got to go through this maze to get to it. We'll have to keep our eyes peeled for the bulls."

The boys were in the yards at Memphis, Tennessee, seeking a ride out. They faced a vast array of tracks, locomotives and long lines of rolling stock. Lying low, they scanned the yard catching glimpses of patrolling detectives.

In cities like Memphis, railroad yards covered so much territory that it was more practical for Buck and K.O. to risk walking through, rather than around them. K.O. dropped to the ground and shot glances both ways under the string of cars. About five tracks over, he saw a moving pair of legs with the stripe of a uniform on the pants.

"I see a bull patrolin' nearby. C'mon, let's go."

Together they cautiously made their way between the tracks. Near the center of the yard, a detective stepped out into their path. He drew a gun and had a bead on them.

"Stand right there, boys."

At that moment, there was a break in the string of cars on either side of them. Taking the opportunity, they instantly fled over the open track...in opposite directions.

The Boxcar Kid

"Stop, or I'll shoot," the bull shouted in the distance.

Buck kept on running, zigzagging between trains, equipment and structures. His legs moved like the uncoiling of a spring wound too tight, changing him into a blur, but there wasn't time to check where he was going or where the bulls might be found.

He heard a shot ring out in the distance. *Holy shit! They're really trying to kill us!*

He ran aimlessly in all directions. The bulls tightened their net around him. One of them jumped out in front of Bucky and popped his gun into the fleeing boy's ribs, almost knocking him down. Another bull stood on top of a car behind, gun raised with Bucky in his sights. There was no place to go. Bucky's captors led him to a clearing near the edge of the yards where the bulls had rounded up six others. Buck's heart sank when he saw K.O. among them. Officers piled them all into three police cars, and took them directly to the Shelby County jail.

The jail doors closing behind them sounded ominous. There were a dozen other boys crowded together in this small space. An overpowering odor immediately tweaked Buck's sense of smell. *This place reeks of "B.O." and pee. What do these guys do, piss on the floor?*

Some kids who had been in jail for some time took them aside and whispered, "You'd both be smart by keepin' your mouths shut and doin' as you're told, or 'Merciless' will have your asses."

"Who the hell's Merciless?" Buck asked.

"Pipe down, pretty boy," one said, pulling him aside. "That's the name we give 'im. He's a cruel monster placed in charge of all of us. The word is that he himself is servin' a long term for stabbin' a guy in a street fight."

Immediately after this warning, a tough looking punk came into the cell and said to Buck and one of the smaller boys, "Time for y'r 'nitiation." He led them to a cell occupied by Merciless and several of his cohorts. Apparently, the brute taunted the newest prisoners a few at a time.

Buck and the other boy stood alone before Merciless and two of his henchmen. The big man, probably in his early twenties, glared at them with an air of arrogant self-confidence. Without moving their heads, the two boys turned their eyes toward each other, each anxious about what might be coming.

The tyrant picked up on their glance. "Keep your eyes on me, you jackasses. How much money did the jailer lift from you little twerps?" Merciless barked.

Buck answered, "I had nothin' to give him." *He doesn't need to know about the money K.O. has stashed on him the jailer didn't find.*

Merciless eyeballed the other boy, who answered, "Five bucks."

"Five more will get you outta here, baby face," he said. "Do you have it?"

"The jailer took all I had," he answered.

"Is that so? Well maybe we better take a closer look to see if you boys are tellin' the truth, 'cause if you ain't, you're in for a little treat."

"Yeah..." said one of his goons, "a treat for us, but a treatment for you birds".

The three hoodlums laughed it up. Then they turned serious again.

"Strip down – both of you!"

The boys eyed each other in disbelief and then began removing their clothes. The strip search revealed Buck had told them the truth, but they found two dollars hidden in the belt of the other boy. They gave Buck his clothes, and Merciless said to him, "Y'r pretty cock sure of y'rself, aint you, kid. We're keepin' a sharp eye on you, so you better not try anythin'." They roughed Buck up a bit and then took him back to his cell. They detained the other naked boy.

In the cell, Buck and the other inmates could hear the boy left behind scream, "No, no! Don't do it...yeoow...ungh!" They heard blows landing, thuds and cries of pain. The ruckus continued for about ten minutes.

During the distraction, Buck seized the opportunity to forewarn K.O. what was in store for him. K.O. quickly took the small amount of cash he had held back from the jailer and gave it to Bucky. They made this exchange just in time, as one of Merciless' thugs returned the detained boy to the cell with the other hobos. The hapless victim appeared with his face bruised, his nose bleeding, and doubled over; he held his hands on his abdomen. He had his clothes on, but they were hanging off him, his belt unfastened, and his shirt torn. They all saw the boy had been crying and appeared badly shaken up. They could only guess about other abuses he may have endured.

Next, they took K.O. and a mousy kid, who shook with fear as the henchmen collared him and dragged him out of the jail. In the presence of Merciless, the trembling boy blurted out, "I seen this nigger give some money to the fella you had in here just before you come f'r us. I swear, they got money."

It was apparent to K.O. that by spilling the beans, the poor fellow hoped to gain favor with the hoodlums and make things easier for himself. The boy's plan backfired. Instead of unleashing abuse against K.O. and leaving the cowardly boy alone, Merciless stepped up to him and glared into his widened eyes.

"You know why I'm here, kid? I'll tell ya...because a squirt like you squealed on me."

Merciless turned to his henchmen. "Show 'im what we do wit' squealers."

K.O. could see the boy wetting his pants.

The two thugs moved in. One held him fast and the other began punching him. Merciless watched with a wide grin. He gave his full attention to the scene.

No one had an eye on K.O. *Here's my chance.* Seizing the moment, K.O. leaped upon Merciless. Grabbing him from behind and holding him around the neck, he twisted the villain's arm into a painful hammerlock.

The captors released their battered victim to attack K.O., but K.O. blocked their path, using Merciless as a shield. K.O. now stood in control.

"Tell your goons to turn around and open the door, or I'm gonna break your arm clean off!" K.O. demanded.

Merciless choked out the words, "Open it for 'em. Do it!"

They did this reluctantly, and brought the two boys back to their cell, shoving them through the door with a show of force, as if to demonstrate they had subjected them to the same humiliation as the others.

The next morning, after a meager breakfast of cold oatmeal, a piece of dry bread and coffee, the jailer released them and told them to move on. No one took the cash K.O. had given to Bucky.

Within the hour, they sat in a boxcar with a dozen other hobos on their way to points south.

The repetitive clickety-clack of the wheels over the tracks cast a sober atmosphere over the silent group. Bucky reflected on the unexpected abuse he suffered on his journey thus far. *Will we find more of the same ahead or is there really opportunity somewhere out there? Is it all a lie that there's money and work? I know there's something better ahead...there just has to be.*

7. HARD TIMES

AUGUST- SEPTEMBER, 1930

During the months following, Buck learned a great deal about how to survive the hardships of life on the rails. Things did not always turn out as anticipated. Instead of adventure and excitement, Buck and K.O. met up with poverty and hunger.

Jobs were scarce. Rumors about work available in other places did not materialize, or closed up before aspiring job seekers could apply. Farmers allowed fruit crops to fall to the ground and rot because the cost of picking, packing and freighting was more than the price of the commodity. Even when jobs existed, employers generally favored older men over boys, even if the boys were stronger and more able. K.O. had an additional strike against him in getting hired: he was a Negro.

Occasionally, Buck and K.O. found menial jobs washing dishes, harvesting strawberries, working in a tobacco warehouse, and chopping wood, but these were brief opportunities separated by long periods of poverty. Buck had left York on a bold quest for a better life. Instead, he now tasted the bitter shame of begging for food.

"It's hard at first," K.O. said, "but you'll get used to it."

He was right. Buck considered it an intolerable option, but several consecutive days without food are enough to convince any self-reliant boy to swallow his pride, knock on doors, and shamelessly plead for something to eat.

Still, hobos were not tramps simply wanting a handout. Most earnestly sought work in exchange for a meal. When they went from house to house, some residents responded kindly. Others called them "bums" and told them to get off their property and out of town.

K.O. taught Buck to recognize the common code markings made by hobos on fences and posts to identify residents as kind or abusive. In their subculture, hobos maintained a close network to keep each other informed and schooled in survival techniques. In the hobo jungle, the boys might get a taste of "Mulligan stew" usually consisting of such things as meat, potatoes, carrots, onions, or whatever they found available. Campers threw everything into a pot of water and boiled it.

Such acceptance and mutual support within the hobo community revived the hobo's hope in a world where they daily confronted rejection, abuse and life threatening dangers.

OCTOBER, 1930, Lynchburg, Virginia

Although nearly everyone suffered the consequences of the Depression to varying degrees, Buck and K.O. sometimes received unexpected kindness from people burdened with their own unmet needs.

In the town of Lynchburg, Virginia, Buck and K.O. saw a woman hanging out her laundry on a makeshift clothesline in her yard. They noticed a familiar marking on her front gate. The snowman-like figure with three small triangles to the right of it revealed a kind woman lived here.

The woman had been widowed several years earlier, and her only child, a girl of about six or seven, stood beside her holding the bag of clothespins. The clothesline was a fifty-foot rope tied between two trees. A balance pole with a "Y" at its top held the line up at its center. The rope had loosened, and some sheets and other items hanging on it were dusting the ground. The two boys noticed the woman's consternation over items in her basket still not hung, and paused for a brief dialogue.

"This could be an opening for some grub, Champ."

"Yeah, I'll say," Bucky said.

They proceeded towards the woman. "Excuse us, ma'am," Bucky began. "My friend and I were just making our way to your house to ask if we could work for food. But seeing as you may need help with your line, we figured we'd ask if we could tie it tighter for you, whether you can feed us or not."

The shy girl stepped closer to her mother. "Well," said the woman, "I know it should be pulled tighter, but I don't know how I and little Mary Jane here can do it."

"We can do it for you ma'am," Buck said.

"Oh, bless you. Why God himself must have sent you to my door!"

The two travelers had also noticed another marking next to the snowman and triangles: a cross, which marked the woman as religious.

"Do you boys think you can fix it for me?"

"I reckon so, ma'am. We don't get much to eat these days, but you can see that we are still a couple of strappin' boys. If K.O., here, can pull up on the line near that tree, I'll get enough slack to untie it and pull it up higher."

"And ma'am," K.O. added, "If we could help you take down those two sheets you just hung, I think we could get the line real tight without taking the other things down."

The woman removed the clothespins and put them in the bag held by her daughter. Then the boys took the sheets down and carefully put them in her basket. While fixing the line, K.O. noticed a clothesline already strung between pulley wheels hung on a second story window of the house and a backyard pole.

"Hey, Champ. See over there. She's already got a clothesline that seems fine and dandy to me."

"Hey, yeah," Buck said.

They asked the lady about it, and she told them the original line had slipped off the pulley on the pole and became jammed about six months ago. "The harder I pulled to free it, the more firmly it got stuck," she said. "I made the makeshift line as a temporary substitute, hoping that my brother-in-law, who's visiting next summer, might fix it for me."

Buck and K.O. held an on-the-spot conference to discuss a solution.

"Ma'am, let us have a try at it! I think we can free the line for you," Buck said.

"I'll take you up on your offer," the woman answered, "but only if you'll stay and have supper with us."

This hospitality surprised Bucky, and he could see by K.O.'s expression he shared the reaction.

"Ma'am, just to eat on your back doorstep will be fine," said Bucky. "We aren't cleaned up and don't think it would be right for us to come into your nice home."

"I insist," she said. "You can wash up inside. That's the condition. If you don't agree to come to our table, then I won't let you fix the line.

31

Honest work is worthy of payment. I haven't money to offer, but we've got some fresh picked corn and I'm making some stew. It wouldn't be right for you to eat that on the doorstep." Glancing down at her daughter, she said with a wink, "I think we can add a few extra things to the stew to make enough for all, don't you think, Mary Jane?" Mary Jane's answer came in the form of a big smile.

They exchanged glances and Buck could see the shared exuberance in K.O.'s eyes. This would be their first meal of the day.

"Thank you, ma'am," K.O. said.

"Thank you very much," Bucky said.

"You boys are a godsend," she said. "But mind you, I don't have a ladder."

"Don't worry, ma'am," Bucky said.

"No, ma'am, don't you worry. We'll find a way," K.O. echoed.

"You boys must be hungry. I'll get supper started as soon as I hang up all these clothes."

"Thank you, ma'am," they said again.

"Might we search in your shed to see if there's anything we could use to climb the pole?" K.O. asked.

"Certainly," she replied.

They found two empty rain barrels and turned them upside down. They laid some planks across the top for a scaffold. Boosting each other, K.O. stood on the platform with Bucky perched on his shoulders. K.O. placed his arms around the pole for stability and Buck used the pole to steady himself. Buck was still too far below the pulley to reach it. However, in their search for a useful tool in the shed, they had found a garden rake, which Buck extended to the rope jam. The situation was precarious and required a vigilant balancing act. Stretching to reach the pulley with the rake, Buck finally freed the rope and moved it back into the groove of the pulley. The clothesline was again operational...and just in time. The barrels started to tilt and Buck quickly discarded the rake as they both fell to the ground.

The woman ran from the house, the screen door slamming hard behind her.

"Are you all right? Oh dear, I hope you aren't hurt!"

"No, ma'am. Not a scratch," Bucky said, as they quickly sprang to their feet to demonstrate their bruises were really nothing at all.

When the boys came in, the appealing aroma of the food awakened their salivary glands. After washing hands and faces they sat down at the table and the woman offered a prayer of thanksgiving to God for the bounty the Lord had provided for them. She included a petition for the boys' safety and welfare.

The little girl, with her sweet disposition and smile, brightened their spirits. The woman and her daughter were so disarming in their welcome that the two boys felt completely at ease. Soon they were all laughing heartily, as Bucky and K.O. entertained Mary Jane by doing silly things and seeing who could make the best farm animal sounds. After supper, they all agreed that Mary Jane had produced the best animal sounds of all.

This loving demonstration of care and consideration overwhelmed the boys. Seldom in their travels had they found such hospitality, and as far as the boys were concerned, it had been the best meal they had ever eaten.

The woman invited the two boys to sleep in the house on a real bed. This time, however, Bucky and K.O. declined the invitation, insisting they would accept only the shelter of the outside shed and some warm blankets. She finally gave in to them and supplied them with a lantern, blankets and pillows.

That night, Bucky thought about Mary Jane. *Geez, the fun I had with Mary Jane reminded me of what fun I had at home with Bud and Lil and Lena. I wish I could be home. I wish I could go back to those days and see them again.*

Buck and K.O. left at daybreak. As the woman saw their bedclothes folded neatly on the back steps, she remembered how her neighbors had chided her for being too welcoming with the strangers who frequented her door.

Ellie Parks had said, "You should be careful about letting vagrant strangers come into your yard and to your door. How would you defend yourself if one of them 'no-goods' returned later to break into your house and rob you blind, woman?"

Another threatened, "What if they tried to hurt Mary Jane? I've heard some of these bums are perverts. You should be careful."

"They're lazy and useless and deserve to go hungry," Molly Hughes said.

Although she did not put much stock in their dire warnings, this was the first time she had permitted hobos inside her home to sit at her table. She was always welcoming, but careful to observe boundaries. These two boys seemed trustworthy. *Perhaps I should be more cautious, but I am convinced in my heart I am acting wisely, and these experiences will help Mary Jane to grow up to be a more caring and generous adult.*

8. LESSONS IN SURVIVAL

JANUARY, 1931

Winter brought falling temperatures, sometimes dropping below freezing, even in southern climates. One chilling night, Buck and K.O. were alone in a boxcar with no insulation. They wedged something in the door to keep it from locking on them, but the wind, blowing through the opening, made it feel even colder. During the night, the temperature dropped into the mid 30's. Bucky shivered under his blanket.

Suddenly, he felt another blanket thrown over him, and K.O. slipped his body under it and pressed up against him. Bucky flinched at this close physical contact.

"Easy, kiddo," K.O. said. "I ain't got any funny ideas. I just come to know that two bodies pressed up against each other under a double layer of blankets can keep a fella from freezin', that's all."

Bucky relaxed and felt the heat from K.O.'s body warm him enough to stop his shivering.

"Seems to me you must have done this before," Bucky said.

"Yeah," K.O. said. "I learned how to share blankets and body heat from a smart aleck white guy in California."

"No kidding?"

"Yeah. I was on a Southern Pacific goin' from Barstow to Bakersfield. We went over the mountains through freezin' temperatures. It was

34

when I was first ridin' and I didn't know much. The boxcars were all packed full wit' riders, so I jumped into an open gondola. Don't ever do that. It's a bad place to ride even if you don't need to keep warm."

"What happened?" Bucky asked.

"Damn! When I hopped inside, I seen this white guy sittin' at the other end of the car. When we hit the high ground, we both sat at each end freezin' our asses off. He had the better spot with his back to the wind. Then, as I sat shiverin', the white guy...he must have been around 18 or so...he says to me, 'Come here, nigger!' He looked tough, and was bigger than me. *This is a helluva time for the tough bigmouth to want to get his kicks,* I thought. I wasn't lookin' for trouble, so I kept my trap shut and just sat still."

"'I said 'Come over here.'...I mean now!' he demanded. I prob'ly could've whupped his ass, but I was stiff with cold and not in any mood to mix it up with 'im, so I done what he said. Soon as I stood up, the wind hit me smack in the kisser. The blast of freezin' air took my breath away and chilled me to the bone."

"'Get down on the floor and under both covers.' I felt him turn towards me, put his arms around me and pull me close to his body. "Oh, I see. He's a freakin' homo out to mess me up," I said to myslef. I was certain of it, and like you, I bolted and tried to pull away, but he held me firm and yelled over all the noise into my ear. 'Listen, bastard. Any other time or place, there's not a chance in a million I'd be found cozying up to a nigger. But if either of us is gonna make it over this mountain without freezin', we better stick together like goddamn glue, ya hear?'"

"He never laid a hand on me, and once we slipped past Tehachapi and over the top and began to go back down, we soon felt the warmth of the San Joachim Valley. The cold shook us up bad, but we made it alive. I'm damned sure he saved my life...and me...I saved his. But neither of us spoke a word. Each of us just picked up and went our separate ways. I never seen him again."

Though hobos met with kindness from some members of society, hardships and rejection far outweighed them. Facing poverty and near starvation, many hobos resorted to creative measures to survive.

Day-old bread from a bakery at closing time could help sustain homeless travelers.

The undertaker was a good source of used clothing.

Hardship also fueled clever schemes. A slice of bread picked from a garbage can and placed on a doorstep might evoke sympathy from a resident who came to the door. "Ma'am, is it all right if I take this piece of bread?" That kind of situation sometimes brought forth compassion from the resident, and often more nourishing food for the beggar.

One boy they met in the hobo jungle told them how he survived on a little bit of catsup, water and crackers. "I go into a diner and sit down. When the waitress comes, I make like I'm waitin' for someone to join me, and tell her I will order as soon as he comes. I ask her to bring me some water. After she leaves, I make a fancy cocktail outta catsup and water. Usually, there's other stuff on the table, like crackers and mustard, and other fixins. After a while, when I've eaten most everything I can, I get up and tell the waitress, 'I guess my friend isn't gonna show, so I'll be on my way.'"

"Cracker sandwiches spread with mustard...that doesn't sound too great," Bucky said.

"A little salt and pepper here and there does wonders," the boy said.

"It won't put much meat on your bones, skinny," K.O. added.

"What the hell," the resourceful boy said, "I'm here, ain't I? It kept me alive."

Others were not so subtle, and simply stole whatever they could get their hands on. Some pilfered food from markets. Bottles of milk left in the early morning hours on front steps might mysteriously disappear.

Buck and K.O. felt degrees of hunger and hardship they had never before experienced. Many people rejected and abused them, but they clung to their memories of kind people, who shared with them in spite of their own poverty.

APRIL – SEPTEMBER, 1931

During the spring and early summer, the two travelers managed to subsist on the charity of people and the meager work they found. In Spartanburg, South Carolina, they dug ditches for a pipeline for eight cents an hour. At Augusta, Georgia, they found work picking peaches. In Arkansas, they harvested strawberries, earning between fifty-five cents and two dollars a day.

In midsummer and into early fall, Buck and K.O. found some success working the wheat harvest. They followed the harvest through Kansas, Nebraska, the Dakotas and into Montana.

Harvest season ended, and Buck grew increasingly homesick. He missed his dad, his brother and his two sisters and longed to see them. He anguished over lingering thoughts of the possible pain his father endured over his hasty and unexplained departure. Now that he had money in his pocket, he was determined to return home to seek his father's forgiveness.

K.O. was also thinking of revisiting old friends in New York, where his father had once been well known and respected. The biggest obstacle in the plan was the separation they would face. By now, K.O. and the Champ had become inseparable.

K.O. said, "There's a YMCA in Harlem where I know I can get mail. Let me give you the address."

"And I can give you my address in York," Bucky said.

They resolved to reunite afterwards. They had become blood brothers for life.

SEPTEMBER, 1931, Cheyenne, Wyoming

At the end of the season, Buck and K.O. were in the middle of a Montana wheat field they had finished harvesting that afternoon. They had picked up their pay and sat cross-legged in the field, counting their accumulated earnings.

"How much you got, K.O.?"

"I got fifty smackeroos, Buck. How much you got?"

"Seventy bucks. That makes a hundred and twenty between us. I think we got our ticket home."

"Yeah, that ought to get us out of here and on our way."

From Billings, Montana, the boys hitched on and headed southeast to Cheyenne, Wyoming, and from there, hoped to do a straight shot east.

It was a plan, and with their combined earnings in hand, they both felt confident their future appeared brighter.

The two boys left the train some distance outside of Cheyenne and started walking. Few cars came by going their way. When one came along, the boys put their thumbs out in hopes of getting a ride. They ended up walking the three miles to the freight yards after six cars had passed them by. Two of them slowed as if to stop and then, observing the boys close up, sped up and shot by them.

"It's me, Buck. Nobody's stoppin' for a colored boy," K.O. said. "You know, you'll always do better wit'out me. Maybe we should split."

"Did I hear you right, bro? I ain't going anywhere without you, K.O., and you ain't going any place without me, either."

Buck turned, grabbed the front of K.O.'s shirt and pulled him forward so their noses almost touched. K.O. could see by the fire in Buck's eyes that he was hopping mad.

"Cut out that 'poor little old me' crap right now. So you're colored and I'm white. That doesn't mean shit. You and me...we're a pair, and nothing can break us up. Get that through your sorry head."

"Gotcha, Champ," K.O. said stepping back, cocking his head, and holding up his hands in feigned fear, betrayed by his famous wide grin.

Arriving at the Cheyenne yards early in the day, Buck and K.O. kept hidden as they scoped out the situation. They watched the bulls in their systematic surveillance of the territory. As trains slowly pulled out, one bull walked the catwalk, ferreting out hobos from between the cars, while two others patrolled the ground, one on either side of a train. The two companions watched 'bo's abandoning the train as a team of detectives moved from front to rear. They saw one boy between cars surprised by a topside bull who violently clubbed him off the train. As the caboose moved slowly by, the hidden boys saw a bull on its platform firing a shotgun at some fleeing target.

Later, under cover of darkness, Buck and K.O. were able to catch out unseen.

"Geez, Champ, I can't believe we made a clean getaway," K.O. said to Bucky.

"Yeah...the place was crawling with bulls earlier, but I didn't see a one when we made our move to catch on."

"Yeah...maybe the Lord is smilin' on us," K.O. said. "We still got our hundred and twenty dollars."

"Shoot, K.O. We got our money and we're going home...Whahoo!"

"Whahoo!" K.O. repeated, lifting his fist into the air in triumph.

"Hey, you guys...pipe down, will ya?" a nearby 'bo chided. "Shut up and get some sleep. You ain't home yet, boys."

•

On the previous afternoon, classes had ended and two cocky cadets swaggered along the sidewalk.

"Kill any of 'em yet, Herman?"

"No," the other cadet said, "but I'm having a great time watchin' their scared-shit faces when they're lyin' on the ground starin' up the barrels of my gun after I clobber 'em!"

At Cheyenne, a school for railroad detectives was thriving. Rookie

38

cadets gathered from near and far for hands-on training, with emphasis on delivering never-to-be-forgotten punishments against railroad property trespassers. Graduates from this school were renowned for their cruel tricks and brutality.

"Geez, I can't believe they booted me off the state police force for beatin' the crap out of miserable trouble makers, and now they train us to bash 'em up good. It's a great feelin' to have a callin' you can live up to!"

They both laughed as they headed to the local bar.

•

Later in the night, about five miles from the Nebraska border, the train slowed and stopped at a remote location. Three shadowy figures holding guns and clubs jumped from the train. Planted on the train were bulls from Cheyenne. In moments, they routed Buck, K.O. and nine other boys from the train and lined them up alongside the tracks.

"Peel off your clothes, boys," one of the cadets said, "every stitch. It's time to pay up your rail fare!"

The boys dropped every piece of clothing at their feet, including shoes and socks. Even though there were no other witnesses at that hour of the night, Buck felt more demoralized than at any other time in his life.

Buck and K.O. had hidden their money in their belts, and they dropped their pants with their belts still in their loops in the hope these rookies would not detect it. The bulls rifled through the discarded clothing.

One of them announced, "Now boys, we keep half of all we find as payment for riding on the Union Pacific."

When a bull found K.O.'s fifty dollars, he took a few steps back and ordered the muscled boxer to step forward from the line. With a disarmingly piercing gaze into the colored boy's dark eyes, he waved K.O.'s money in his face. "Niggers pay twice," he said and stuffed the fifty dollars into his shirt pocket. Then he turned around as if to walk away.Then he made a sudden turn and swung his club at K.O. hitting him in the abdomen. K.O. yelped and fell to the ground holding his stomach. He lay silent on the ground in a fetal position, resisting the urge to retaliate.

Buck started, and made a movement to help K.O., but the bull thrust his club into Bucky's stomach and shoved him back in line.

Then, as they kept their guns trained on the shivering band, the detectives hopped back on the train as it pulled away and disappeared into the darkness.

The boys scrambled for their clothes to get dressed, but Buck went straight to K.O. to examine him. Buck lifted him to his feet. K.O. managed a few steps, before falling to his knees and vomiting. A kid threw him a handkerchief to wipe his face.

"The god damn rookie bulls treated us like scum," K.O. said, his eyes narrowed and his teeth clenched together. "I'll never forget these bastards as long as I live."

"The lousy sons-of-bitches," Buck said. "We came into town with 120 bucks between us. They took half of my seventy and all of your fifty. Now all we got left is thirty-five dollars. What a heartbreaker. Are you okay? Will you be all right?"

"He hit me good, but I'll be okay. The bastard! Give him to me in a fair fight...I'll kill 'im...I swear it."

"Let it go," Buck said, "Let it go," as he helped K.O. to his feet and gave him his clothes. "Remember what you once told me, pal. 'They'll be better days ahead'...you'll see."

9. THE HOMECOMING

OCTOBER, 1931, York, Pennsylvania

At Harrisburg, Pennsylvania, Buck and K.O. parted ways.

"The good Lord will bring us together, Champ," K.O. said as they shook hands.

"Yeah," Buck said, "if He even knows who we are. Remember, we agreed to a reunion in New York at the Y four months from today – or sooner, if things don't work out for me at home. Then we can let each other know how things turned out and how we'll keep in touch after that."

"Yeah, Champ. I won't miss that. Geeze, I love ya, kid. We been through a lot."

Buck's face reddened at K.O.'s heartfelt words. "Hell, don't get mushy on me. I can't wait for when each of us gets married and we have families, and our kids will be friends and play together like cousins."

They gave each other a light punch to the shoulder and went their separate ways.

•

Bucky jumped from the train at his hometown with mixed feelings. It had been a year and a half since he had left York. Walking along the familiar streets, his anxiety heightened. He wondered about the reception he would receive.

The Boxcar Kid

It seemed to Buck not much had changed in York. He noticed some stores boarded up. When he walked by Feder's Cigar Store and Pool Room on George Street, he remembered the cigar K.O. had given him the night he left town. He turned up his collar and avoided an open route along the street, walking a maze close to buildings, through shadows and around street objects to remain inconspicuous. He was not ready to confront people who might recognize him and ask unsettling questions.

Outside of town, he saw his home down the road. Drawing closer, he found the scene strangely quiet. He noticed the yard had turned into a weed patch, and the house itself was dilapidated. Sections of the front porch railing had broken and fallen to the ground. Paint had flaked off the siding, and broken windowpanes gave evidence of abandonment. At the edge of the property, Buck's eyes picked up a sign posted on the grass. He had seen such signs before on residential properties. It said, "Sheriff's Sale." Someone once told him the sign meant the owners could not keep up payments for the land and the government took the property over to sell it. A warning stated that if anyone did anything to the sign or removed it, they could go to jail. Bucky did not know how long the sign had been there, but the house appeared as if it had been vacant for some time.

The house, a two-story farmhouse on a small tract of land, once belonged to his grandma and grandpa. It was set on a country road, just outside of town. Memories of the times spent here filled his mind: playing games, wrestling on the grass with his brother, teasing his sisters, eating and laughing with his family and sleeping in his own bed.

Seeing the sign, Bucky stopped in his tracks. His heart sank as a feeling of panic mounted within him. For a few moments, he stood frozen, staring at the sign and then at the house he had lived in as a child. Where was his family?

As his emotions peaked, he suddenly darted for the front door and banged on it. A padlock secured the front door, but to no purpose, as broken windows in the house allowed easy entrance. Buck did not go in.

Instead, he sat down on the front stoop, elbows on his knees and drooping head in his hands, trying to figure out what to do next. He flashed back to some of the good memories of his childhood...going fishing with Bud and his dad...the summer parades when Barnum and Bailey circus came to town...and skinny dipping with his friends where the willow trees hung over the creek on the hot summer days.

I wonder what Gary, Billy and my best friend, Nick, are doing now?

10. NICK

As Buck thought about this friendship, he wondered if Nick had come back to York. *Maybe I could stay at his house until I sort things out...maybe his folks know where I can find my dad.*

Buck hesitated a moment before pressing the doorbell of Nick Bradley's house. Mrs. Bradley opened the door.

"Why Bucky! What a surprise. Where have you been, and what brings you here?"

"I've been riding the rails, ma'am," he said. "When mom died, I thought my dad needed one less kid to worry about."

"Oh, Buck, how wrong could you have been? Your dad was beside himself with worry."

Buck hung his head in shame. He wanted to ask Mrs. Bradley if Nick had come home, or if she knew where he was, but he was afraid to raise the question in the event something bad had happened to him.

Just then, an adolescent boy came up behind Mrs. Bradley, and a grinning face popped out from over her shoulder.

"Buck! Bucky Ellis! Is that you? Well I'll be damned!"

"Nicolas Bradley!" his mother snapped in surprised amazement. "You watch your mouth!"

"I'm sorry, mother," he said sheepishly, and then bounded off the front porch with his friend, landing on the front lawn.

Buck learned Nick had returned home after a harrowing experience on the rails.

43

"Me and two other kids were kicked off a train," Nick said. "It was at an isolated spot up in the Canadian Rockies. The only way out was for us to follow the tracks, so that's what we did. We walked for miles and our feet were getting blisters walking over the goddamn rocks and ties. Then we came to the edge of a cliff and shot a nervous glance down into a deep ravine. Holy shit...was it scary! The tracks continued over the narrow trestle. We sure as hell weren't gonna turn around and go back, so we started walking out onto the trestle. It was the scariest thing you'd ever want to see. It made us all dizzy to look down. We could see a stream flowing under the bridge hundreds of feet below.

"We took it one tie at a time with our hands on the shoulders of the kid in front of us. I was in the middle. When we got about half way across, we felt braver and moved a little faster. That's when it happened. Behind us, we heard the sound of a train coming our way. I nearly crapped in my pants when I looked back and saw the locomotive comin' onto the bridge. You should've seen us. By God, we ran like the wind. Butch, the guy up ahead, jumped onto safe ground at the end just as the train was on top of us. I hit the ground safely, too. But Jimmy, behind me...the train with its horn blaring right behind him..."

His speech began to falter, as he related this traumatic experience.

"T...the...the train got him," he said, starting to tremble. "I know I'm here only because Jimmy...because Jimmy...gave me a big shove at the end. He saved me, but got killed because of it.

He remained silent for a few moments as if in a trance. Then he turned to Buck and said, "Buck, you're the first person I ever talked to about this. I haven't even told my parents. It feels good to get this off my chest. You're a great friend."

Bucky didn't know what to say, but wanted to give him some sign of encouragement. He put his arm around Nick's shoulders. He could tell by the way Nick turned his head and looked at him with soulful eyes and a weak smile that he appreciated the gesture.

After some moments, Bucky asked, "Do you know where my family is? What happened to them?"

"Things didn't work out for your dad," Nick said. "He tried hard to keep things together, but it was rough. I don't want to make you feel rotten, Buck, but I gotta say...your leavin' didn't help things. First, he lost your mom...then you. When he lost the farm, his whole life caved in, and he took the kids and left. We heard he went to Altoona to work for the Pennsy Railroad."

Buck cringed at hearing of his dad's misfortune. He had already been guilt ridden before he got to York. Now he was determined to find his family and make things right again.

The boys talked until dusk. Mrs. Bradley came out and told Nick it was time for him to come in for supper. Then, with an apologetic expression, she turned to Buck and handed him a bag.

"Bucky," she said, "In my heart I had planned to ask you for supper and to stay here with us. But Nick's daddy won't hear of it, so I fixed these sandwiches for you. Please don't think unkindly of him. He's stubborn and set in his ways. But really, he's only thinking of us and feels we can't afford to take you in."

"Thank you, kindly, Mrs. Bradley," Buck said. "Honestly, I would never think of busting in on you. I can take care of myself."

Buck knew from his long friendship with Nick that the father and son didn't get along. He knew a fight with his dad is what sent him out on the road. Now, it was his dear, sweet mother, whose heart was broken when he left, that kept Nick home.

Nick stood and put his hands on Buck. They said their "goodbyes," and Nick started for home."

Mrs. Bradley had not told Buck of Mr. Bradley's reaction: "So Chucky's son's come crawlin' back, has he? Does the little thief think he can grab more dough from his dad and take it on the lam again? Tell that little shit to stay out and stay away from here. Tell Nick he ain't to see 'im no more. The kid made his bed. Let him lie in it!"

Buck went back to his former home and sat on the back steps. He ate the food Mrs. Bradley had given him. It was a repeat performance of all the times during the past year when people had given him a handout and told him he could eat it on their back steps.

The old pump in the backyard still worked, and the cool well water was refreshing.

Halfway through his second sandwich, Nick appeared and sat next to him.

"Hey, did you get your supper already? What are you doin' here?" Buck asked.

"I lost my appetite," Nick said. "My dad said I wasn't to have anything to do with you and we got into a big fight, I told him to go to hell and left."

"You ought not have done that, Nick. He means well, and I know what it's like not to have a father to talk to. Go back and tell him you're sorry. Maybe we'll see each other again, and...maybe not, but you and your dad may not realize it now, but you both need each other."

11. A SHOCKING DISCOVERY

OCTOBER, 1931, Altoona, Pennsylvania

The Pennsylvania Railroad's choice to build locomotives and other industry-related products at the base of the Allegheny Mountains gave rise to the city of Altoona. The demand for workers brought thousands to this unpopulated area. The railroad hastily built housing for workers and their families and provided essential services. A paternalistic bond between shop laborers and railroad owners secured the loyalty of workers. Isolated in this place, employees were dependent upon the railroad for their livelihood.

In Altoona, innovation was the order of the day. It became the melting pot of immigrant laborers and industrial geniuses. The city soon boasted it had the largest group of railroad shops in the world. Here, the Pennsylvania Railroad engineered the ingenious track curvature known as the "horseshoe curve." Trains could traverse the mountains that had formerly been a barrier to westward expansion and commerce.

Surrounded by the ear-splitting noise of machinery and hammering, Chuck Ellis put in a hard day's work at the Erecting Shop in the Juniata Locomotive Shop located in the eastern "Juniata" section of Altoona. Workers stood in a line on either side of a track, performing repetitive tasks of assembling parts of a locomotive, and other rolling stock, as it moved before them to the line's end where it stood proudly as a completed unit.

Charles Ellis was part of a four man riveting team. With twenty-four riveting gangs on either side, a car could be completely riveted in about six minutes.

•

Bucky arrived in Altoona late in the afternoon. He immediately checked out the layout of the town. His search led him to the office of the Pennsylvania Railroad Locomotive Works. It was dusk. A light inside indicated someone was still there, and Bucky went in.

"Excuse me, sir," Buck said, trying to get the attention of the man behind the desk whose face was buried in paper work.

The man turned in his chair and said, "Hey, kid. Whatcha need?"

"I'm looking for my father. He works here."

"A lotta people do. What's 'is name?"

"Charles Ellis."

The man opened a file drawer and began perusing the employee records.

"Hmmm..." he said, flipping through the files. "Let's see...Ellis ...Ellis...yeah, here it is," as he pulled the file. After glancing through it, he said, "Second shift riveting crew. His shift ended a half hour ago. If he ain't at home maybe he stopped by Clancey's for a nip or two. Did his old lady send ya after him?"

"Sir, tell me where he lives. I need to find him." Bucky said.

"Wait a minute, buster. You claim to be his kid and you don't know where ya live?"

"Well, you see, sir," Bucky said, "I've been away from home for a while. We used to live over in York."

"Just a minute, son. I'm almost done here. He's in a rooming house up on Dutch Hill. I can go that way. I'll give ya a lift there."

The man drove Buck to another part of town where rows of two-story rooming houses on both sides of the street snaked up, over and between the steep hills. They stopped in front of one, and the driver said, "This is it kid. Number 256. Com'on, I'll walk you to the door."

The gentleman lifted his big hand and rapped on the door. The door opened a crack as the man inside peered through it.

"Chucky, this here kid says he belongs to you."

Glancing beyond the man before him, Chuck Ellis exclaimed, "Bucky! Bucky! Bucky! What the hell..."

"I guess he's tellin' the truth. I'll leave you two alone," the office manager said.

"Buck! My boy! Buck, you've come back!" Tears welled up in his father's eyes.

The door swung wide open as Charles Ellis extended his arm, clasped his son's hand and pulled him to him. "My God, what happened to you? I missed you so much. Let me look at you."

Then Bucky saw her. She was standing in a corner back by the bed in a slip with a strap hanging down from her shoulder. Bucky gasped and instinctively pushed his father away.

Chuck caught the drift right away. He tried to explain to his long-absent son how things were.

"Buck, it's not what you're thinking. You don't know what I've been through...not just me...but the kids, too. I missed your mama so much. Then you went off without a word. I couldn't bear it. I was so lonely. And I don't mind tellin' you Buck that I was scared. I didn't know how I was gonna raise Lena, Lil and Bud without your mom. How could I take care of 'em like she did? Everything slipped through my hands all at once, and I didn't know how I would go on. Then Helen came along and helped us all. She came and gave us what we needed..."

Helen had slipped on a dress and was nervously fixing her hair.

"She's a good woman, Buck...she loves us...and I care for her... don't you see? Please..."

"How could you do this to mama? She ain't been gone hardly a year! Don't you care about her anymore?"

He shoved his father back so hard Chuck had to brace himself against the dresser to keep from falling to the floor. Then Bucky lashed out with a devastating accusation. "You never cared about her. I know why she died! I know what you did to her!"

Buck raced out the door. He hardly cleared the doorway when he darted back into the room again. Taking his remaining eight dollars from the harvest work wages, he threw the cash on the floor.

"Here's what's left of the money I earned. I was bringing it to you and the kids. I was going to tell you how sorry I was for what I done and for takin' the two bucks. Now we're even. I hate you!" he said, as he ran out the door and raced down the street choking back sobs.

12. LITTLE BROTHER

Helen ran to the stricken father and tried to console him. The terrible effect of his son's rejection was immediate. He threw himself on the bed in silence and then broke out in an uncontrollable fit of crying.

"What have I done? My boy...my boy ..." he said.

Bucky hadn't noticed the children watching from the top of the stairway, silent and huddled together. Now they were near hysterics. The two girls ran down the steps and threw themselves on their father in confusion and despair.

•

Buck's 12-year-old brother, Bud, ran out and chased after Bucky. Bud kept crying for him to stop, but Buck kept running until he collapsed on a grassy knoll near the freight yards.

After Bud caught up to him, Buck stopped crying and pulled his brother close to him.

Buck said, "Take it easy, little Buddy. Things will turn out all right."

"Bucky, Bucky, take me with you," Bud wailed. "I want to go where you're going. I want to ride the trains and be like you."

Buck took Bud by the shoulders and locked eyes with him. "Not on your life," he said. "Stay away from the trains. It's no life for you. Believe me, if I had to do it over again...besides, you need to stay here and take care of our little sisters. What do you say? Listen to your big brother, you hear?"

"Okay Buck, I will." A moment later, he asked, "When will we see you again? Will you come home to us?"

"You know I will, little pal."

They sat in silence staring at the ground. Then Bud said, "Buck, you know Aunt Helen...that's what we call her...she isn't bad at all. Dad was so sad after mom died and you left. He was mean and ornery...until he met Aunt Helen. Then things changed. She's been good to dad, and is kind to all of us. She ain't our mama, but she cares about us. She really does, Bucky."

Buck began to regret the scene he had made and the things he had said and done. But it was too late to turn back now.

They both stood, hugged, and Bud turned and moped along towards home, his face toward the ground and his arm bent to wipe tears from his eyes. As Buck watched his brother disappear in the distance, he felt everything he cherished drop out of his life.

What a mess I've made of things. I came here wanting to say I was sorry and make things right, but I only made it worse.

He had chosen his path, and the unresolved remorse that invaded his heart left him devastated.

Soon, Buck sat against the inside wall of the boxcar as the speeding train raced toward New York City. His despair continued to overwhelm him. *Will I ever see Bud and my dad and family again? I'm sorry, but how can I go back? I've closed the door. I don't deserve their love.*

NOVEMBER, 1931, New York City, New York

K.O. was elated when Buck showed up at the "Y." He listened to Buck's tale of woe and regret.

"Buck, I ain't had a setback like yours. That's a tough break, Champ. But I ain't done too well here either. Things have changed. Some of the guys I knew are gone, and some I thought could help me find work were down on their luck. Shit, Champ, wit' all the people packed into this city, it can be the loneliest place on the planet."

"I think we should get out of here and move on. What do you think, K.O.?" Buck said.

"Yeah. This shit hole ain't my home no more. I guess you're the only real friend I got, Buck."

"Yeah," Buck said. "No families, no nothin', but we got each other, and that's enough for me."

13. A FATEFUL ENCOUNTER

FEBRUARY, 1932, Lima, Ohio

Lima, Ohio was a railroad town and the site of the Lima Locomotive Works. Regarded as the "Rolls Royce of steam builders," its powerful and fast steam locomotives were coveted prime rolling stock on major railroads. Lima was not only renowned as a major rail center, but as the base of operation for one of the most feared and brutal railroad "bulls" in the nation. Nicknamed "Crusher" for his widespread reputation of maiming and killing dozens of hobos, he unleashed havoc against young trespassers in particular. Hobos everywhere feared this assassin along with infamous bulls like "Denver Bob," "Texas Slim," and others. The United States may have been the land of the free where laws were upheld to protect its citizens, but on railroad property, frontier justice prevailed, and heinous crimes were commonly committed without redress.

A stretch of tracks between the local landmarks of Erie Hill and the Detroit, Toledo & Ironton (DT&I) tower presented an ideal place to catch out. Because of the convergence of many rail lines and crossover tracks, approaching trains slowed. Freights, in particular, likely slowed or stopped along this section, as passenger trains always had the right of way. Strands of rolling stock rested on sidings waiting for locomotives to move them to other destinations. A slowed or stopped train was an open invitation to hobos to climb aboard.

Local teens jumped on the trains to get to school, while their less daring counterparts walked along adjacent St. John's Road, just west of the tracks. Most knew to jump off before increased speed of the train made it too risky. Occasionally, a student who was afraid to jump off at the right spot ended up past his intended destination late or absent from school.

Occasionally, some incident might influence the young pupils to choose walking rather than riding. Such was the case, for example, after a boy's foot slipped through a ladder and brushed against the train wheels. Abstinence would be temporary, however, and soon plucky, spirited boys returned to the rails with renewed bravado.

•

Bucky and K.O. lay hidden in the tall grass. A slowing train approached.

"It's now or never," K.O. said. "Let's go!"

The boys catapulted out of the bushes with Bucky in the lead. Simultaneously, dozens of kids sprang from their hiding places and raced across the open area toward the train. Gun shots rang out and a big, brawny detective appeared from out of nowhere.

Running alongside the train like a flying arrow towards its mark, Buck and K.O. reached frantically for a ladder iron. Bucky caught a grip and gained his footing, but his relief was short lived. A quick glance backwards revealed the bull had K.O. locked in a death grip.

The bull appeared out of nowhere and Buck saw him grab K.O. and press the butt of his gun into his gut as if to shove it right through him.

Bucky's blood chilled as another rider cried out, "That's Crusher! That nigger's a goner!"

Many Lima residents, including local teens, were fully aware of Crusher and his ruthless tactics, and most parents gave their children stern warnings to stay away from trains. Some local kids had drawn fire from the bull's pistol. Sometimes, Crusher used his weapon to pistol whip young offenders to the ground.

Hobos recognized this area as Crusher's territory and the threat of running into him was real. Younger ones, not yet effected by the disillusionment of many long time hobos, had hope and determination that did not crumble in the face of threats or hardship.

As the train clacked through a section of curved track, Bucky had a more panoramic view of the scene. The long freight with its heavy load was gaining speed. Bucky could clearly see the detective's evil intent. K.O. had knocked the gun from Crusher's hand, but Crusher had brought K.O. to the ground with a punishing hold, pushing him closer to the tracks.

With every ounce of adrenalin pumping, Bucky jumped from the train, determined to go back and help his friend. It seemed hopeless. He hit the ground running in the same direction as the train. He skidded to a stop. His heart raced as he turned to see the two man conflict in the distance. Crusher and K.O. were barely visible, but Bucky could see clearly that K.O. could not withstand the driving force that would place him under the moving train. Crusher had gained the upper hand. He had at least fifty extra pounds over K.O. The Negro dug his shoes into the ground, but Crusher only made trenches with them, shoving the boy backwards with brute strength. A feeling of utter helplessness descended upon Buck as he realized he could not save his best friend.

Buck heard the noise of an approaching train coming from the opposite direction on the adjacent track. *Here's my ticket back!*

The train approaching the yards slowed its pace. Bucky started running alongside. The train still moved at a clip, and when Buck leaped and grabbed the iron, it nearly ripped his arm from its socket. He had caught onto the ladder, but his feet had not found their footing. His biceps strained as he pulled against the train's movement and the force of gravity. Just as he felt his grip slipping, he squeezed his fingers firmly around the rung and pulled himself up with all his might, first one foot and then the other. At that instant, he saw the two fighting men directly ahead.

K.O. struggled furiously and gained a little ground, trying to crawl back under Crusher's legs. Crusher was too powerful and held him fast. Once again, he had him to the tracks only seconds away from certain death.

With another burst of superhuman strength, Buck lunged from the train, hurling his 170 pounds against the villain. The impact sent Crusher over K.O. into the moving caboose.

Crusher's scream pierced the air as his face and body smashed against the platform of the caboose. The protruding iron railing ripped into him and hurled him through the air towards a catastrophic landing into the dirt and cinders.

Bucky stood stunned as he gazed upon the stricken man. The battered bull laboriously raised himself to his hands and knees, head hanging down, face bloodied, and an eye dangling from its socket by delicate strands of tissue.

K.O. grabbed Bucky and snapped him to attention. "Come on, pal. Let's get the hell outta here."

The image of the battered officer's macabre face emblazoned itself onto Bucky's mind as they fled.

•

Crusher could bear it no longer. His agitation skyrocketed these past weeks...the growing numbers of increasingly insolent youthful trespassers...wearing him down.

Crusher's reputation and news of his clash with Bucky spread through the hobo community like a herd of galloping antelopes. Although most never met Bucky, the exaggerated tales of what he did to Crusher elevated him to near god-like status: "Young Bucky was only half his size, but he picked Crusher up bodily and threw him against the side of the speeding train!" It became a David and Goliath story. Hobos from California to New York passed the story on as a cherished folk tale.

Bucky himself did not exult upon hearing these stories. What happened at Lima remained something he tried to push to the recesses of his mind. Not only did the memory of what happened bring him pain, it aroused fear that the authorities would hunt him down.

The knowledge of Crusher's scarred face and missing eye made him easily identifiable to hobos, who heeded warnings to avoid him. A few exceptions sought him out as an infamous spectacle, and taunted him as though he were a runaway from a freak show. Yet, those who did so did not escape Crusher's wrath, and some did not live to regret their underestimation of the raw brutality he could inflict.

Even if Crusher's dreadful appearance had been an effective deterrent to keep hobos away, he would have understood these events as a frustration of his goals. His passion had never been to keep them off the property, but to capture and punish these lawbreakers. A few of them foiled his attempts to lay hands on them, but any he captured regretted it. There were never any arrests. Instead, he sent survivors back to the hobo community after brutal blackjack beatings to demonstrate the consequences of his wrath. Because trespassers were subject to arrest, none of them dared report him to the authorities. Still, things now had spun out of control.

I must abandon the duties that confine me to this place and these petty hoodlums. I must free myself to focus on my main target...a single individual against whom I will unleash a steady stream of avenging retaliation that will bring him to his knees. That is the triumph I crave. Bucky Ellis must feel the weight of God's justice against those who disobey the law and run free. I will be your avenger, God. Give me opportunity!

Crusher had few friends, and those he had, began distancing themselves from him. Without any close companions, the only consolation Crusher received was the kind face of his dear mother. A religious woman, who read from her Bible regularly, she showered her affection on her only child, teaching and demonstrating to him the love of Jesus.

As a boy, Crusher had been a bully. His name was Billy, but the other children called him "Bully Boy Fuller." He loved to antagonize the girls by pulling their hair and knocking their books to the ground. He taunted and beat up younger and weaker boys.

The bully acted out the violence he had experienced in his own home. Billy and his mother often endured severe beatings at the hands of his drunken father. He sometimes escaped his father's rage only because his mother interceded for him, deflecting her husband's anger against herself. There were times when Billy witnessed his father beating his mother until she fell to the floor unconscious.

14. CRUSHER'S MOTHER

MARCH, 1932

Returning from work, Crusher entered the house and found it strangely quiet.

"Mother," he cried, "Where are you?"

Searching through the house, he entered her bedroom. He found her lying face down on the bed. He touched her forehead. It was cold. He took her wrist and searched for a pulse. He could not find any.

Crusher shook his mother in disbelief. "Mother...mother," he cried. When reality finally dawned, his grief turned to anger. Shaking his fist towards the sky, he expressed his rage with a piteous scream. "God," he screamed, "will you take away everything dear to me? Damn You, God!"

A week later, his employer told him he would receive a generous retirement package.

At thirty-seven years old, Crusher was smart enough to know his career as a police officer had ended. He had received several warnings about the growing tide of protest against his brutal tactics and these developments did not surprise him. They were giving him his walking papers.

To hell with the railroad. This could turn out to be a happy turn of events for me. I'm freed from chasing petty trespassers in this godforsaken place Good riddance! God, maybe this is your plan for justice to be done. With the only per-

son who really cared about me gone, my sole purpose and comfort will now be a single-minded pursuit to punish my quarry. My first task would be to locate my prey. I will need help...trustworthy stool pigeons who could gather information, ahh...and I know just where to find them.

15. A LOST BROTHER

APRIL, 1932, Flagstaff, Arizona

The train out of Albuquerque was a fast flying "red ball," identified by a white flag with a red circle in its center flying from the front of the locomotive. Hobos understood this flag meant the train would arrive at its destination directly, with no stops in between.

Riders jumped off one by one as the train pulled into Flagstaff, Arizona. Most scattered, making themselves scarce for fear of the bulls.

After jumping off, Bucky and K.O. saw a boy running frantically towards them alongside the slowing train. Every few yards, he dropped to one knee and shot quick glances under the moving cars. Buck and K.O. watched with curiosity, as the caboose reached the runner and rolled by. The boy stopped and gave a glance once more at the tracks behind him, then ran towards Buck and K.O.

Colliding with them with arms flailing, he practically knocked Buck and K.O down. "Help me, please," he cried.

The boy was perhaps sixteen or seventeen-years-old. Tears ran down his cheeks. His blond hair was matted and dirty, and grease and soot covered his clothes.

"What happened to you, boy?" K.O. asked. "Are you hurt?" From his appearance, K.O. suspected he had been "riding the rods."

The boy choked backed his tears.

Buck grabbed him by the shoulders and said, "Tell us how we can help you."

His distress caught the attention of others, and a small group gathered at the scene.

The boy cried in desperation, "My brother! He's not here! My God! Help me! Did anyone see him? He's got to be here!"

The hobos clustered around the distraught boy.

"Stand right where you are, and don't anyone move," a voice boomed over the noise.

The group turned to see three bulls spread out behind them, pistols drawn.

The one in the middle, Officer Mark Brady, commanded, "Stand clear, and let us through, and no one will get hurt."

Taken by surprise, the group separated to let the officer through. Instantly, Buck and K.O. planted themselves squarely between the bull and the boy, as if to protect him. To dispel the group's anxiety, the officer holstered his gun and motioned to the other detectives to do the same. No one ran, and responding to the man's less threatening manner, Buck and K.O. stepped aside.

The detective put his hand on the boy's shoulder, and said, "Don't be afraid, son." He handed him a clean, white handkerchief from his pocket and said, "Wipe your face and tell me about your brother. If he's hurt or lost, we may be able to help you."

The boy hesitated. Then he said in a faltering voice, "Me and my older brother...we got on this here train in Albuquerque..." He paused, blinked his teary eyes, and gave a few short sniffs to stop his runny nose.

"Go on," the detective urged. He suspected what might have happened, and said, "Tell me where you and your brother rode on the train."

"We rode...under the cars," the boy answered.

"On the rods...right?" officer Brady said. *Will they ever learn?*

K.O. and Buck knew the extreme danger of riding on the supporting struts that extended the length of some cars, about eighteen inches under the floor. A rider could hide there, but once they were moving, the noise of the rolling train became deafening. Gravel, dust and soot pelted the rider continuously, and there was no getting off while the train was moving. To make matters worse, there was little or nothing to hang on to, and if you fell asleep, you were likely to fall off and meet a sorry fate.

The detective turned to the crowd and said, "Leave the yards as quickly as you can and get out of town."

Recognizing the responsible role Buck and K.O. had taken with the

60

boy, he told them to remain. "I may need your help," he said.

Buck and K.O. nervously started shifting back and forth on their feet. They were apprehensive after their experience in the Shelby County jail.

"You will not be arrested or harmed," the detective assured them. "Wait here. I'll be right back."

He went to the other two detectives and spoke to them. The boys saw the two eyeball each other and then disburse to other parts of the yard. They recognized this man was different from the other bulls they had encountered, and they trusted him.

"I'm detective Mark Brady," he said, and led them to a small office. After they sat down, he asked the boy some further questions.

"What's your name and the name of your brother?"

"Willie Freedman, sir. My brother is Marvin."

"Why did you hop the train and come here?"

"Well, we saw other kids jumpin' on the train, and we'd never done it before. We heard a lot about it, and thought it would be fun to try. We knew we could be arrested if we were caught, and wanted to hide from the detectives. When I saw my brother duck under a car and hide there, I did the same thing a few cars behind. We thought we'd get right off at the next town and make our way back home. But the train never stopped, or slowed until we got here. It was hard to stay awake all that time, and I was really scared when the train crossed a bridge. It was at night, but I could sense we were pretty high up as we went over, and it seemed like the bridge was swaying back and forth."

He paused as detective Brady listened with a sober frown on his face.

"I know what we did was wrong, and I'm really sorry. Am I going to go to jail?" he asked.

Detective Brady said, "I think you've learned your lesson, Willie. I'm not planning on arresting any of you. But our big concern now is to find out what happened to your brother."

"Yes, sir," Willie said.

"Was there anything else about your ride you can tell me? Did anything unusual happen?"

"Another thing that happened was pretty scary, too. All of a sudden over all the noise of the train, I heard loud clanking noises nearer the front of the train, and I saw sparks flying up there."

Mark Brady's heart sank when he heard these words. By this time, Brady could guess what had happened to Marvin. *It's time to read them the riot act, not that I expect they'll take my advice...*

"Boys, riding trains is a dangerous business. The Interstate Commerce Commission keeps records on injuries and deaths of trespassers on railroad property. The numbers go higher every year. Kids like you are a big part of those numbers. Kids get hurt jumping on and off trains or falling from dangerous places. Trackside obstacles, signs and narrow bridges rip off legs hanging out doors of a moving train. Sad to say, many deaths and injuries go unreported." *If they only knew the whole of it...that security police and railroad employees plan deliberate accidents to kill these young riders.*

"In all earnestness I urge you to go home to your families and stay there. We can help you, Willie, to get back home. I only hope and pray your brother may be all right and be waiting for you at home."

K.O. had no home to go to, and Bucky thought, *If I only could...but it's easier said than done. Too much water has passed under the bridge of my life.*

Just then, a man rapped on the door and entered. Buck recognized him as one of the two detectives who had been with Mark Brady earlier.

"Sergeant Brady," the man said, "The police back in Winslow found a slain boy along the tracks near the town. I'm sorry, sir, but the boy was so mutilated...they said like someone cut him up with a machete...that it drew the attention of people near the site, and the local media has already picked up on it."

Willy's eyes bulged in anxious anticipation of what the detective would say next.

Mark Brady grimaced and shook his head in remorse. Then he said, "Any identification?"

"No sir, but the boy had blond hair, was slight in build and, oh, yes...on his wrist he had a scar from a prior injury."

Willie sprang to his feet, his arms spread at his sides, his jaw dropped and his eyes wide with alarm. "It's Marvin!" he exclaimed, and his knees began to wobble and he would have fallen to the floor had Buck and K.O. not stood and grabbed him. His body fell limp, and the boys helped him to a cot where he laid face down on it, sobbing convulsively.

Detective Brady remained seated and watched the two boys try to comfort the lad.

"Maybe it's not him at all," Buck said.

"Yeah," K.O. affirmed. "How can you be sure?"

With his teeth tightly clenched, and tears flowing freely, Willie choked out the words. "Mom and dad weren't home, and I was teasing him...he chased me and I ran out onto the front porch and slammed the door behind me...right in his face. He was running...and when the door closed, he hit it with his arms out to keep it open, and his hand broke right through the glass pane in the top part of the door..." A period of bitter sobbing followed, and then Willie said, "That's how he got the scar on his wrist...Marv...*oh, Marv!*"

Mark Brady knew all too well the terrible death Willie's brother suffered, but said not a word about it. The trick was common knowledge among railroad workers and bulls. The brutes tied a gigantic square nut to the end of a heavy hemp rope. They tied the other end to a part of the cab. When the train was on the move, a designated bull or worker would drop the nut onto the tracks, leaving it to drag and bounce, setting off an array of sparks and cutting to pieces any stray rider under the train. Brady had heard of this malevolent practice, and would hardly have believed it, had he not seen a pair of bulls up the line preparing the killing device with gleeful anticipation.

Under the train, Willie had seen the sparks and heard the action ahead of him, but could not see what was happening. If the rope had been longer, he might have learned first hand about the rancorous nature of these unrestrained bulls.

There was a time when Brady was hardened against hobos, but his experience with this kind of brutality evoked sympathy from him, especially when it involved teens close in age to his own children.

Now the task remained to return Willie safely back to his family, express condolences to them all for "an unfortunate accident," and hope his earlier lecture would deter them from repeating their actions.

16. CRUSHER'S EXPANDING SYNDICATE

Meanwhile, Crusher's resolve strengthened. *I must make that boy suffer as I did. It would be too good for him if I just killed him. No! He must live, but I will ruin his life. With my hands, I will reduce him to rubble.* He pushed forward his plans. Within months, he had picked up a cadre of homeless boys to do his bidding. None of them would ever be aware of Crusher's ultimate purpose to use them as pawns to find the boy who ruined his life.

There were many of them on the rails, and he was familiar with their ways. It was easy to win their loyalty with a little bread and something in their pocket…just enough to keep them yoked to him and his purposes. As further incentive, those who gained experience and Crusher's approval to go out on the road as part of his elite corps of informants enjoyed a position of honor and privilege among their ranks. Should any of them have any ideas of deserting, he used blackmail and threats to prevent defections.

Crusher reinforced his plan with tricks he had learned in his profession as a railroad detective. He had come across operations controlled by unscrupulous men, known as "yeggs," who drew vulnerable, hungry boys into a poisonous web of criminal activity and abuse. They snared and caged young boys into a life of servitude to the yegg who kept them from defection through petty rewards and threats. In most cases, they became fully dependant on their master for survival. Some yeggs were also "jockers," or homosexual men, who possessed their captives by the burden these boys carried resulting from shameful sexual activity.

Crusher, however, had no such inclinations. He had but one precisely defined purpose fixed in his mind. His skills and knowledge acquired in police work also served him well in this endeavor. Establishing a network of locations staffed by well-trained and trusted informants, Crusher accumulated a growing file of data on Buckingham Ellis. Now he knew his name, that he and "the nigger kid" traveled together, and both of them were formidable bare-knuckle fighters. He learned of places where they had been and was hot on their trail. Crusher richly rewarded the boys who gave him the most pertinent information, though they knew nothing of his hidden purpose.

17. INJURY IN
THE YARDS

SEPTEMBER, 1932, De Moines, Iowa

A sprawling array of tracks, equipment and structures filled the Des Moines yards. Bucky and K.O. dropped off the train without incident about a half-mile east of the yards.

"The best place to catch outta this town is on the other side of the yards," K.O. said, "but to get there, we need to cross through without getting caught."

"Can't we go around the yards?" Buck asked.

"It'll be winter before we'd get around this place. In these big cities, the yards stretch out in all directions."

They entered the yards and dropped to the ground to look under the trains for uniformed legs.

Bucky said, "Damn, K.O. There's a lotta bulls here. Listen, we got separated before when we were running from the bulls in Memphis. Why don't we make a plan, in case that happens here?"

"Good idea," K.O. responded. "I think it would be best for us to separate and meet somewhere at the other side."

"You've been here before, right K.O.? Is there a good spot we can meet?"

"Yeah...let me think." After a brief pause, K.O. said, "On the other side of the yard, there's a road that runs along the east side of the yards. Let's split up and move through this mess to the other side. When you get out of the yards, walk south, where you'll see more traffic and places

66

of business. You'll soon see a busy crossroad. Just beyond, up the hill on the left, there's an Esso gas station. That's where we'll meet. If one of us is still not there by sundown, whoever's there should go on.

Buck gave K.O. a blank stare and said nothing.

"I know what ya thinkin', Buck...we might never see each other again. We should have plenty of time to get to the place and I hope that won't happen. Do you have a better suggestion, Buck?"

Hesitatingly, Buck said, "I guess not, but let's break our butts to make sure we get there." He put his hands on K.O.'s shoulders and their eyes met. "God, don't let that happen," Buck said. "If we miss each other, it will be like losing a brother." He felt himself getting choked up.

"OK, Champ. Now get a move on," K.O. said quickly to end the tension.

"Watch you're ass, buddy," Buck said.

"You too, Champ. God willing, I'll see ya under the Esso sign."

Shaking hands and patting each other on the back, they separated.

About ten minutes into the yard, a break between cars gave Bucky a glimpse of K.O. streaking by about six tracks over. Seconds later, he saw a detective in hot pursuit. Buck dropped to the ground. "Jesus," he said under his breath, "get us out of here!"

As he lay there, he heard a faint moaning. Bucky observed his surroundings carefully before standing and moving towards the sound. It came from a gondola coupled to cars parked along a siding.

Keeping a sharp eye out, Buck approached the gondola car and slowly climbed the ladder. Peering over the side, he saw its cargo of steel pipes all askew. Jutting forth from a tangle of pipes, a black-skinned face creased by heavy stress lines emitted agonizing groans. Apparently, the load had shifted and fallen on top of this hapless rider. The boy appeared seriously injured. *He sounds delirious.*

With a bound, Bucky leaped onto the top and began removing the pipes. *Damn. This is a job. These pipes are heavy and there's not much space to pile them up.* He finally lifted the last pipe. From the boy's appearance, Bucky guessed he might be slightly older than he...maybe in his upper teens or early twenties.

The boy could not move. Bucky saw his right leg broken below the knee with the bone protruding.

The boy was hefty, and Buck had all he could do to lift him into his arms without injuring him further. He managed to get him to the side of the gondola, but lifting him over it and down to the ground seemed impossible.

"Boy!" he heard from behind him. Glancing back over his shoulder, he saw a man wearing the striped overalls and cap of a railroad worker. "You having trouble, son?" the man asked.

Buck turned with the injured boy in his arms and faced the man. He hesitated, not knowing what to expect.

"Looks like you can use a little help. Here, let me help you get him down."

Together, Buck and the railroad man managed to get the injured boy over the side and to the ground. Bucky's first instinct was to run as fast as he could, but the man now holding the boy blocked his way, and Bucky's sense of responsibility constrained him to remain rather than abandon the injured boy.

The squint of Bucky's eyes and his stiffened stance signaled to the man Bucky's distrust. The railroad worker said reassuringly, "This boy needs to get to a hospital. Some of the bulls have gone off duty, and I've been around here long enough to know the routines of them that's still here. God knows they're not only mean sons o' bitches, but lazy, as well. By this time, the few that's here are probably sittin' in some cozy place readin' the paper. While us brakemen work our butts off, they march around the place like peacocks shootin' it up and hurtin' people. Believe me, boy, we ain't got much love for each other."

Bucky took a deep breath. "Geez," he said, "Am I glad to see you."

"It's a good thing for both of us that I just finished my shift. We need to get this boy to the hospital."

He carried the dark-skinned boy to a small railroad shack, and turning on an outside spigot, washed the wound. A wooden stick served as a splint, and Bucky bared his chest and offered his shirt as a bandage to wrap the leg. Then the man carried the boy to his car and laid him across the back seat.

"Get in the back seat and watch him," he said to Bucky,

The man went inside the shanty and said to his fellow worker, "Contact Abby and let her know I'll be late getting home. Tell her I'm taking a seriously injured boy to Mercy Hospital. She'll understand."

At the hospital, Bucky and the railroad worker sat in a small visitors' area waiting for further word on the injured boy.

Willie Higgins, a long-time, hard-working railroad man possessed common sense and simple honesty that compensated for any perceived lack of education. A brakeman on the B&O line, he took pride in his work and brought the best he had to his labors. Buck appreciated Willie's thoughtfulness when, in exchange for Buck's donated shirt, he offered him the jacket the injured boy had with him, as protection against the chill. It was fleece lined and a bit large for him, but Buck was glad to feel the warmth it provided.

"Name's Willie Higgins. What's yours, son?"

"Buck. Most folks call me 'Bucky.'"

"How'd you come to be ridin' the rails, Bucky?"

The man seemed genuinely interested in him.

Buck told him about his mother's death and about his father and family. He did not mention the conversation between the two men after the burial service, but simply said. "I decided the manly thing to do was to go out and earn my own way in the world instead of being another mouth to feed at home."

He noticed Willie had two fingers missing from his left hand.

"Mr. Higgins," he said, "How'd you lose those two fingers?" After he said that, he felt his face redden, as he realized it might have been inappropriate to question a person so directly about a handicap.

Willie responded without any sign of offense or embarrassment.

"I'm a brakeman. Son, there are many dangerous jobs on the railroad, but I think a brakeman is one of the most risky. I lost my fingers in the hump yard while I was couplin' and uncouplin', cars. The hump yard is a place where we roll cars over a track with a high spot. When two cars are lifted at the hump, there's slack in the coupler so ya can pull out the lockin' pin. After cars are uncoupled, they're rolled onto different tracks where they hitch 'em up to other cars headin' for other places. Workin' the hump is pretty dangerous, especially when you have to drop the pin in. You have to get between the cars when pullin' or droppin' the pin. You can imagine what would happen if you weren't quick enough to get the pin in fast enough to get out of the way. Sometimes cars broke loose and rolled over the tracks."

"That sounds really dangerous," Buck said. "I can see how you lost fingers."

"Right, Bucky. But losin' a few fingers was nothin' compared to some of the horrible things that happened. I can tell you one story I've heard so many times that I believe it must be so. A fella got caught between two movin' cars and the coupler closed around his body jist about slicin' him in half...but the strange thing was he remained alive and could talk the whole time he was locked in the damn thing. People knew he was finished, but his mind was sharp and he could speak plainly. They went and got his wife. She was near hysterical and was cryin' her eyes out. Damn. They say the fella was so brave and tried to comfort his wife. They even called a priest, who performed last rites. They say that as soon as they got the coupler open he died right on the spot. It must have been the most awful thing anyone could've seen. And by God, I believe the story is true."

"Wow," Bucky said. "I never would want to be a brakeman doin' that...I don't care what they'd pay."

"That all happened a long time ago, Bucky. Nowadays, railroads are required by law to use the new Janney automatic couplers, and air brakes, too, but a lot of 'em don't abide by it. It takes money to convert the old stock, so some of the old link and pin style couplers are still bein' used.

"And now," Willie said, "I'd like to hear from you. Tell me about your friend. What happens to him when he gets out of here?"

Bucky realized Willie's inquiry applied to the injured boy, but the word "friend" immediately reminded him of K.O. His eyes shot from Willie to the clock on the wall. He leaped from his chair knocking it to the floor. "Shit! I forgot all about K.O. It's almost five thirty! How the hell am I gonna get to K.O. before sundown. I don't even know where the yards are, much less how to get to the gas station from here!"

18. THE TICKING CLOCK

"What's the matter son?" Willie said.

Ignoring Higgins' question, Buck spilled out words of distress, certain he would not be able to keep his appointment before the sun sank below the horizon. "How could I have forgotten...how could I let the time slip by?"

"What is it, son?"

"Willie!" Buck said. "Willie, you need to help me. You got to drive me back as fast as you can. I got to get to a place on the east side of the yards...please..."

"That's a bit of a distance, and it's gettin' late. That ain't the way I go home, and Abby ain't gonna be too pleased if I miss supper. Can't it wait till mornin'? You can come home with me and tomorrow I'll bring you back to the yards and help you find a hitch out..."

Frustrated he was getting nowhere with Willie, and panicked that K.O. would leave without him, Buck blurted out, "Godammit! Mr. Higgins, I'm really grateful for all you've done...really. But I got to get out of here," and he disappeared out the door and bounded down the stairway.

In the parking lot, he saw the sun low in the western sky. *Which way do I go? Geez, why didn't I pay attention when he was driving. Let's see...maybe I can remember...I think we came around that side of the building, and..."*

"The car's over there, Bucky," Mr. Higgins said. "Come on, I'll take you. You can tell me all about it as we drive to wherever it is you need to go. I don't know why I'm doin' this...it's crazy...I guess I just like ya, kid!"

When they arrived at the intersection, the sinking sun flung its rays out, illuminating the drifting clouds in an array of blazing colors, as if in a last ditch effort to go out in glory. At the crest of the hill, Buck pinpointed the Esso sign lit up against the western sky. He thanked Higgins, jumped out, and started running up the grade. His eyes strained to scan the station. It appeared deserted...no cars at the dimly lighted pumps, the Esso sign casting its glow over the pavement like a lone sentry. No K.O. A wooded area framing the side of the road blocked Bucky's full view of the station. *O shit...did I miss him?.* He started yelling as he ran closer

"K.O., K.O.! K.O., are you there?"

A mechanic's garage with two open doors came into view. One car sat over a bay. Buck's eyes picked up an attendant moving about in the front office, but no sign of K.O.

A movement in the garage caught Buck's eye. Out of the shadows, a silhouette arose from the back bumper of the parked car inside the garage. The form began moving toward him and then broke into a rapid stride.

"K.O.!" Buck yelled, quickening his pace.

"Champ!" the sprinting figure replied.

The light washed over K.O.'s face highlighting his signature smile...a wide grin that could punch a hole through the deepest darkness.

With open arms and complete abandon, they came together and embraced without shame or embarrassment.

The scene astounded and deeply moved Mr. Higgins, who watched this heartfelt reunion from the bottom of the hill. Neither Buck nor K.O. noticed Mr. Higgins driving slowly up the hill behind them as they walked to the gas station.

Like two cawing crows, the friends chattered noisily, overlaying their words:

"...And this bone was stickin' out of the kid's leg...and Mr. Higgins, with two missin' fingers...what a great guy..."

"...An' Buck, one time two bulls were on to me and almost got my ass, but I got through the yards without a scratch..."

They agreed they needed to leave Des Moines as soon as possible.

Just then, Mr. Higgins, his window rolled down, drove up beside them.

"Get in boys. I suspect you're wantin' a ride out. Tell me where you're goin', and I'll spot you a safe place on a train, where you can get a good night's rest. I think I can put you on a freight that will be movin' out early in the mornin'. There won't be any of them sneaky detectives until about eight o'clock tomorrow mornin', but they might not take kindly to you if you hang around for 'em to see ya."

True to his word, the switchman set them up in a boxcar with piles of cardboard inside, which would provide them with insulated warmth along the way.

"Mr. Higgins, the railroads can't be all bad if they got guys like you workin' for them. Hey, you're the greatest," Buck said.

"Don't forget," Higgins said, "the railroads give you free transportation to all kinds of places. The bulls and bosses don't favor you, but there's a lot of us workers who take pity on you guys and give you a break. Respect railroad property and have a good trip, boys."

Sometime later, as the cold night air set in, Bucky turned up the collar of the jacket he wore and thrust his hands in the pockets. Hardly thinking, he pulled from the pocket a wallet and a few other small items. Full realization unfolded before his eyes. *I'm still wearing the dark-skinned boy's jacket. Holy crap...there's money in here. What do I do now?*

19. THE WALLET

"Holy smokes! Take a look at this, K.O.!" Buck held the wallet open for K.O. to see. K.O.'s eyes popped wide when he saw the glut of cash. In addition, Buck found a student I.D. from Ursinus College in Collegeville, Pennsylvania, and a passport identifying the boy as a native of Tonga. His name was Tanoa Toupu and his birthdate put him at age nineteen. Look here, K.O."

K.O. read the I.D. "Whoa! This looks like he has some kind of high position in Tonga."

"Yeah, it sure does," Buck agreed. "I think this is some kind of special diplomatic visa."

"Where the hell's Tonga, anyhow?" K.O. asked.

"If I remember right from school geography, I think it's an island somewhere in the Pacific Ocean."

He examined the wallet contents more carefully. "This stuff is important. I've got to return this."

"What? But how?" K.O. asked.

"I've got to go back to the hospital right now. It's late, but maybe I can still get inside."

"But the brakeman has us all set up here. What about our plans to head south?"

"Forget that, K.O. I can't run off with this. I need to hoof it back to the hospital. Maybe I can get back here before you leave."

"And what if you're not back?"

74

"Go on without me."

"I don't like that choice. You know, Buck, we could go a long ways with that money."

"No way. It wouldn't be right. K.O., our friendship means a lot to me. I owe you plenty. You helped me from gettin' beat up by those thugs. You taught me the ropes and how to box. You treated me like I was your brother. Whatever happens, I'll never forget you. But I'll try my damnedest to get back before morning."

"I feel the same way about you.We make a great team, Champ. I think that's the way it's supposed to be."

"Hey, you've been around, right? Can you think of a good place we could meet if I don't get back in time? I could catch up, if I knew where you were."

"Now there's a 'Champ's plan'. I know a good place just outside of Davenport, Iowa, where Higgins said this train's goin'." K.O. tore a piece from the paper lining the boxcar walls.

"I'm drawing you a map on this paper. Take it with you. It ain't hard to find." He quickly scratched a rough map on the paper and gave it to Bucky. "This here's a good camp. I know the 'bos that go through there. It's well organized. Everybody pitches in. It's safe." Then he explained details of the map to Bucky. "But mind you, get your little white ass back here before morning if you can. I can wait for you at the jungle, if things are good there, for maybe a day or two, but not forever."

In this emotion charged moment they stood facing each other with hands on each other's shoulders, and could not find words to speak. In K.O.'s eyes, Buck saw his friend felt the same pain as he did. "K.O., come hell or high water, we can't go separate ways. I'll find you no matter what...I swear it."

It was 8:25 PM when Buck approached the reception desk. The woman at the desk was gathering her personal things as though to leave and said, "I'm sorry. Visiting hours are over."

"Look, lady," Buck barked. "See this jacket? It belongs to a person in this hospital who's in serious need of what I've got here."

He thrust the patient's I.D. cards under the nose of her bespectacled face.

Her eyes did not miss the signs of notable status of the patient.

"If you don't let me see someone in charge who can find Tanoa Toupu right now, there may be some serious consequences for you before morning."

The woman was stunned into silence by Bucky's brusque manner. She would not have believed he was only a boy of fifteen.

A staff person preparing to lock the front door heard the ruckus and walked over to the desk.

"Is this young man causing you difficulty Miss Millicent?"

"Oh, dear!" was the only response she could muster.

Bucky quickly explained the predicament to the well-dressed man who acted with an air of authority.

"Miss Millicent, get back behind that desk and check the hospital registry for this person."

"I have his I.D. here in my hands," Bucky stated. "You won't find him in your records. Would they have any general listings of...like...what's it called...John Doe listings?"

They pondered his question but said nothing.

Annoyed at their ineptness, he said, "Forget the listings. He's here with a broken leg. Where in this joint would they put patients with such injuries? The place isn't that big. We oughtta be able to find him. There must be nurses or somebody around to help us."

"The boy's right, Miss Millicent," the staff person said. "You can leave. Go now, so I can lock the doors and help find this boy." He grabbed some of the red-faced receptionist's things, escorted her to the exit, handed over her belongings, and politely guided her out the door.

"Follow me," the man said to Bucky, and they both sprang up the steps two at a time to the next level. The Charge Nurse on the floor turned her head toward the commotion as Buck and the hospital worker approached her. Buck poured out his story. More cooperative than Miss Millicent, she quickly examined the wallet and its contents, directed Bucky to a chair, thanked and told the worker to return to his duties, and went downstairs where members of the Hospital Board had gathered for a late evening meeting.

"Excuse me, gentlemen," she said.

Mr. Lockingham, the Hospital Administrator, chaired the meeting. "Yes, what is it?"

"There is a patient here who came with no identification and we have been treating him as though he were a vagrant, but we received information suggesting he is the son of a foreign diplomat. I thought you should be informed of this."

"Gentlemen, this is a serious situation that takes precedence over our agenda," the chairman said. "Let's close the meeting and reconvene tomorrow night at the same time. Can you all be here?" Everyone nodded in agreement.

"We'll need to issue new directives for this patient. Who is the physician assigned to him – never mind – get Dr. Jones – he's our top surgeon."

Mr. Lockingham went directly to Tanoa's ward. The disarray of bedclothes indicated the patient's restlessness. The medical personnel had made an effort to straighten the compound fracture by binding the leg with a new bandage wrap.

When Dr. Jones burst into the room, the nurses quickly stepped back to let him pass. His brow furrowed when he read the patient's chart. His gruff manner made it clear to all he was perturbed to have been called from his home at this hour. The scowl on his face grew more pronounced when he read the injured boy's chart.

"What is the planned procedure for this patient?" the doctor demanded.

One nurse ventured forth with a timid response. "He has a compound fracture of the tibia," she said.

"I already know that. I can read the chart. I asked about the scheduled procedure."

"He is scheduled for surgery in the morning, doctor," another said.

"What kind of surgery?" he asked.

The room was quiet. Then one of the nurses said almost in a whisper, "His leg is to be amputated, doctor."

Instead of remaining in the chair, Bucky had followed the procession to Tanoa's bedside. No one noticed him standing in the doorway. When he heard "amputated," his jaw dropped in disbelief. "What...what did you say?" he stammered, interrupting them. His remark met with abrupt silence and surprised expressions on the faces that stared at him.

A nurse stepped over, ushered Buck out of the room, and pointed to a place for him to sit on the floor of the hallway out of earshot.

Inside the room, the doctor started spitting out directives.

"This is a fiasco," he said, perusing the chart once more. "I don't know if I can trust these records. They lack sufficient detail. Tell me exactly what medications he's been given. Which doctor treated him?"

"Dr. Hawkins, sir."

"He is reassigned to me," he said. "I want the procedure revised. Unwrap that leg and make sure his bone has been set properly. And I do mean immediately!"

"Yes, doctor, right away."

"If that bone is not set right, the longer we leave it wrapped, the harder it will be to bring it in line properly."

Everyone scurried about performing respective tasks with the doctor supervising.

Later, as the doctor left the room, he saw Bucky sleeping on the floor in the hallway. "Who is this boy?" the doctor asked Mr. Lockingham.

"He's the boy who saved that patient's leg. He pushed his way into the hospital with the boy's wallet and papers. That's how we found out the patient was someone of importance."

"He looks exhausted," the doctor said. "Don't disturb him."

"You're right. I'll see that a nurse brings him a bed pillow and a blanket to throw over him."

While the doctor had spit out his directives to the medical staff, Mr. Lockingham contacted the Governor of Iowa. When the Governor answered in a groggy voice, Mr. Lockingham said, "Governor, this is Lockingham over at Des Moines Mercy Hospital. I know this is a late hour, but a situation has developed here that needs immediate attention."

After Lockingham explained the circumstances, the Governor responded, "I understand the gravity of the situation. I will alert people I know in the foreign services to uncover other information on the boy. You've given me the important statistics...it's a good start. I'll move on this first thing tomorrow morning. Be assured, Lockingham, it will all be done discreetly and kept under cover. We must avoid any scandal."

"Thank you, Governor."

The next morning, Buck sat up, rubbed his eyes, stretched and yawned. With his eyelids barely lifted, he scanned his surroundings. *What am I doing on the floor in this hallway? Oh yeah, now I remember. I'm at this hospital.*

A nurse came to him and said, "Good morning. I hope you weren't too uncomfortable sleeping on the floor. We didn't want to disturb you, but now that you're awake, would you please come with me?"

Buck rose to his feet and tucking his shirttail in, followed the nurse to Mr. Lockingham, seated behind a desk in a small office. He stood, extended his hand to Bucky and said, "This is the first opportunity I've had to thank you for bringing the vital information needed to appropriately treat Mr. Tanoa Toupu's injury. I've directed that patients in one of our wards be moved elsewhere so the boy can have a private room. You should be able to visit him shortly."

"Were you really going to take his leg off?" Bucky asked.

Mr. Lockingham's face reddened. "I know it is severe, but these days it's common procedure in most hospitals in our nation to choose the quickest and least expensive procedure if the person is a transient without any money. Times are hard these days, and hospitals are barely able to survive."

Buck reflected upon the fact that he himself was a "transient" with little money in his pocket and that could happen to him.

"Of course, his unsightly appearance and the fact he is colored didn't help. You can understand how the medical staff could easily mistake him for someone who merited little attention," Mr. Lockingham added.

Buck felt his temperature rising, and if his seething had been visible as fire, it would have scorched the ceiling above him. He might have exploded, but instead, stayed seated with his teeth clenched and his narrowed gaze shooting a piercing path towards Lockingham's face.

20. TANOA

"Good morning, Tanoa," Mr. Lockingham said. "I want you to meet the young man responsible for saving you. Tanoa Tapou, meet Bucky Ellis."

The boys greeted each other with a handshake.

"I'll leave you boys so you can get acquainted and talk."

The Tongan stared at this stranger in amazement. "I was told of your noble deed and how you saved me from suffering a great misfortune. I am humbled by your unselfish attention to my need. What can I say that would sufficiently show my gratitude?"

"It was nothin'," Buck answered. "A railroad man helped me to get you here. Without him, you'd probably be back in the train yard."

"Tell me, how did you find me?" Tanoa asked.

After Bucky explained the whole story, Tanoa asked, "Why did you stop to help me? Was it not a big risk for you to do this? Could you not have been arrested or injured? What can I do to repay you? I will never forget this."

"I just did what anyone would do. Forget it. You don't need to thank me."

The polished young boy said, "You are wrong. We are an honorable people, and we cannot allow such a noble act to go unrewarded. Just ask what you desire, and if it is within my power to grant, it will be done."

Bucky was feeling embarrassed over such gushing attention. "Aw, shucks, it was nothin'. I just did what anybody would do."

Just then, an attendant brought a steaming tray of food and set it before the patient. Tanoa noticed how the other boy eyed the food and appeared tired and hungry. He told the attendant who brought the food to wait a moment, then asked, "Master Buck, have you had anything to eat yet? Does this food seem to your liking?"

"Uhh...I haven't had anything...and, yeah! The food looks good."

"Bring another serving of food for my friend," Tanoa said to the attendant, who scurried off.

Bucky was impressed. *This fella seems accustomed to giving orders that are obeyed.*

The attendant came in shortly and served the same breakfast Tanoa received to Bucky. It was not the usual hospital fare. He stared at the hearty cheese omelet with bacon, sausage and toast. *I must be at The Ritz.* Milk, Cream of Wheat and coffee rounded out the meal. He felt his mouth salivating almost to the point of drooling, and would have devoured everything within a minute's time, but he remembered his manners and forced himself to eat at a leisurely pace, leaving the plates as if they had been tongue-licked clean.

"My American friends call me 'Tano'."

"And mine call me 'Bucky'. I can't believe I'm sitting here talking with a person of such high position. Tell me about your homeland. Tonga is in the Pacific Ocean, isn't it?" he said to show he was not a total jug head.

"That's right. Tonga is a monarchy that includes a cluster of one hundred and fifty islands. We are a protectorate of Great Britain, but are independent. We keep close ties with Great Britain, however. Ours is a constitutional government, but Queen Salote exerts great influence in Tongan affairs because of the deep devotion of the Tongan people for her."

"How are your people alike or different from Americans? What sort of beliefs and customs do they have?" Bucky asked.

"Before the missionaries came about a hundred years ago, my people followed the traditions of the ancestors and we still preserve them. They are important to our history and culture. Today, we are also devout Christians. Our laws, which prohibit work and certain activities on the Sabbath, embody the religious fervor of our people. Our faith in God is firm alongside our national pride. Queen Salote is determined to preserve our cultural roots and to continue the traditions along with our Christian beliefs. "

Tanoa's command of the language impressed Bucky. "Are you a

prince?" he asked. "Is the Queen your mother?"

"No, Master Buck, not quite. My father is Queen Salote's half-brother. In her kindness, she has shown favor towards my father. She sent him to Suva for training by the Fiji police. Upon his return, she appointed him as her Aide De Camp in the Royal Guard. Now he is Captain of the Royal Guard. As a result, my father is an insider who is present at most palace events. I have seven brothers and sisters, and we spend a lot of time playing in the palace garden with the princes and princesses. Prince Tu'ipelehake and Crown Prince Taufa'ahau and I are best friends."

"Tano...is it okay to call you that?"

"Most certainly," Tanoa said. "You are already becoming my closest friend in America."

"Well," Bucky continued, "Before the missionaries came, were any of your ancestors...uh...*cannibals?*"

Tanoa laughed heartily. "No, Master Bucky. It is true that in ancient times, cannibals inhabited the Fiji islands, but that is no longer the case. Even so, among the papalangi, that reputation hangs on."

"The who?" Bucky said with a puzzled expression.

"Oh, I'm sorry, Buck. 'Papalangi' is Tongan for white people of European or foreign ancestry. There have never been any cannibals on Tonga. Throughout our history, we have remained isolated from much of the world. Not many tourists make it to Tonga, and there are no hotel accommodations or restaurants. But if we had restaurants, the menus never would have included 'humanburgers'."

Buck laughed. *Tano's got a sense of humor. This guy's really down to earth...doesn't act like a highfalutin' royal person at all.*

"How did you end up in Des Moines, where I found you messed up?" Buck asked. "What happened?"

"My friend from school convinced me to go with him on a train riding adventure during our school break," Tanoa said. "He said it would be great fun, and I would learn a lot. My school, Ursinus College, is about twenty-five miles from Philadelphia. We hitchhiked to Philadelphia and then went west on the trains. Near Chicago, we climbed into the railroad car with those pipes. No one was there to see us, so we stood up on top of the pipes to watch what was going on. We did not expect the sudden lurch of our car when the train started moving. It knocked us off our feet. My companion fell over the side. As soon as I fell inside the car, all the pipes fell on top of me, crushing my leg under them. The train moved out and I did not see my friend again. I could not move.

The last thing I remember, my leg was throbbing and getting numb. Next thing I knew, I woke up in this hospital."

"How are you fitting in at your college...what's it called?"

"Ursinus. My father and I considered many colleges, and we liked this one the best because it is a small college with a pre-medical program. It is located in a rural setting, yet it remains close to Philadelphia."

"I'm from Pennsylvania," Buck said. "So you are studying to be a doctor," Bucky said.

"Yes. It's a hard road to travel, but I think I have what it takes to succeed."

"What kind of things are you involved in at college?"

Tanoa said, "I have some scholarships, but still must earn my support, so I serve tables in the college dining room. I love athletics and the outdoors. I was interested in your game of football, but am too unfamiliar with it to try out for the team...perhaps I will try in my later college years. I joined the wrestling team. In fact, they call me a 'star athlete' because in the middleweight category, I have never lost a match."

21. HARD QUESTIONS AND A GENEROUS ACT

Tanoa had questions for Bucky, too, about life in America. Once he started, his questions came in rapid succession. "Why do many white people treat dark-skinned people as though they are inferior to them? Why do your newspapers and citizens sometimes speak with such disrespect about your president and leaders? Are they free to say anything they please without fear of punishment? No one in Tonga would think of such a thing. For centuries, those who have authority over us have been spoken of only in terms of high respect."

"That's part of the freedom we have in a democracy," Buck said.

"I do not understand. My father sent me here to learn about freedom, but it is hard for me to see how you restrain people from doing wrong things. The behavior of some of my classmates offends me."

"What kind of behavior, Tano?"

"They use vulgar language and talk about women in a way that would be unspeakable in my country. Are there any forbidden things under your freedom?"

"I'm not sure I understand you, Tano. Can you give me an example of what you mean?"

"Well, when I asked my fellow classmates about going on a date with a young lady, they use disrespectful words. They talk of 'getting on' with a girl. What does that mean? When I asked my college friends what they did on dates, they laughed at me and said, 'Get laid, what else?' I think they are playing games with me. Their attitude toward women is disrespectful, and it seems to me the only thing some of them want to go to parties and get drunk.

Bucky felt his face flush. *He's getting an education, all right. He could probably tell this fifteen-year-old kid a few things.*

"Tano, I hardly know what to say. I can only say that in this brief time I've gained high respect for you and what you believe and think. Your character and honesty makes me proud to know you. Not everyone at your school is like those you describe. I'm sure there are many at your school who are respectful and caring. Those crude jerks who act stupid are immature. Forgive them, let them alone and give them time to grow up. Meanwhile, you'll make friends who are worthy of you. Stick to your studies and your interests and don't worry about girls. One day you'll find just the right one."

"I guess you are right, my friend. Besides, there is not one colored girl at my school, and it is not good that I get too involved with your white girls."

"Whether it's good or bad, I don't know, but I think you may be right about that."

"Master Bucky, you make me feel a lot better. In you I see someone who is wise and kind."

"I'm just a kid, Tano. Holy smokes, I don't know anything. But I think if you study hard and don't let the boneheads get your goat, you'll find your way to a great life."

"Now," Tanoa said, "It is time to tell me about yourself, your family, where you grew up and what you did when you were a boy."

Buck shared memories of his experiences, his friendship with K.O., the circumstances that brought him to Des Moines and his desire to one day be reunited with his father, his brother and his sisters.

In the early afternoon, Mr. Lockingham returned to the room and interrupted their talk.

"Tanoa, we are going to take you to surgery. Also, we have had contact with your guardian, and he will be here tomorrow. We assured him we will give you the best treatment and that our top surgeon will perform the operation."

Spying the clock on the wall, Bucky said, "Holy cow! Where did the time go?"

"Time moves swiftly when good things are happening," Tanoa said. "It is difficult for me to describe how I hold dear in my heart the time we have spent together. Bucky, if you believe in God, please pray I will be well, and that one day we might become the closest of friends."

"I do, I will, and we already are."

The attendants carefully moved Tanoa onto a gurney, but before leaving the room, Tanoa asked them to stop and hand him a small purse from his bedside table. He took out a twenty-dollar bill, and calling his new friend to him, opened Buck's hand and pressed the bill into his palm. They both said good-bye as the attendants wheeled Tanoa from the room.

Alone in the room with Bucky, Mr. Lockingham put his hand on his shoulder.

"Bucky, I want to talk to you. Let's go to my office."

Seated in Mr. Lockingham's office, the administrator continued. "Bucky, last night I spoke with Governor Turner, and through his office we were able to find information about our patient. A messenger hand delivered a letter with the governor's seal about an hour ago. It indicates Tanoa is in America with a guardian, a diplomat from the island kingdom of Tonga. The guardian demanded the boy receive the best care regardless of cost. He told the governor a firm schedule would prevent him from coming here immediately, but he would arrive tomorrow and said if there were any mishandling of the boy's medical needs, someone would answer for it. He expressed the desire to meet the young man who rescued his charge. Are you able to stay until tomorrow? Of course, we will make you comfortable. You won't have to sleep on the hallway floor."

"My friend is waiting to meet me outside of Davenport. I can't decide whether to get out of here as soon as possible or wait around. I'd like to make sure this kid will be treated as well as some of the rich white kids in this town."

Bucky regretted the slip, but Mr. Lockingham got his drift.

"Bucky, I feel as badly as you do about such policies, but that's the way things are. You can be sure if circumstances improve one day, I'll be the first to see each person gets the care he deserves, regardless of color."

"I'm sorry, Mr. Lockingham. I didn't mean to be impolite. I guess I can trust the people here to do what's right, especially since his guardian will be checking up on things. So I think it's best to head out right away."

"Bucky. You've done a commendable thing in not only bringing Tanoa here, but returning with what we needed. Your action just might change the way we do things around here."

They stood and Mr. Lockingham shook Bucky's hand. "Good luck," he said.

When Tanoa returned to his room, he saw the twenty-dollar bill he gave Buck on top of the bedside table. *My father will be angry with me when he learns I failed to give a reward to the boy who saved me.*

22. LIFE IN THE JUNGLE

Leaving Tanoa behind, Buck now gave full attention to catching up to K.O. At the yards, he hoped to come across Willie Higgins, who might help him find a safe ride out, but it was too risky to sneak around if any bulls were on the prowl. Gaining experience as a hobo, Buck knew how to get information about train times and destinations. Before long, he nestled down with a few other 'bos in a boxcar hooked onto a Red Ball freight heading directly to Davenport.

SEPTEMBER, 1932, Davenport, Iowa

He breathed a sigh of relief when the train pulled into Davenport and he jumped down feeling solid ground under his feet.

Consulting the clear directions K.O. had drawn, Bucky found the hobo jungle without difficulty. He stood at the outskirts of the camp scrutinizing the group assembled there. A few older hobos stood around talking, while others performed routine tasks like cleaning up, keeping the fire going, and other chores. Some boys intermingled with the older men. Bucky eyed each one of them and his heart sank when he saw K.O. was not among them.

As he stood there, several of the men who saw him came over.

"Look whut jist blew in," one of them said.

Another said, "You look like the young fella we been waitin' for."

"You named Buck?" the first one asked.

"Yeah," Buck answered, his spirit reviving with the hope these men could give him news about K.O.

"K.O.'s out workin'. He's got a job at a dairy farm. Should be back soon. He told us to watch out for ya, kid."

Smiling broadly, Bucky thrust his right arm through the air in a fisted uppercut and declared, "Hot-diggety dog!"

His smile was returned by a third man who thrust out his hand to offer him a hot cup of coffee. "Here, son. Bet you could use this." The rich aroma wafted up from the steaming tin cup. Buck couldn't wait to raise it to his lips, blowing across the hot surface before taking a sip.

"Thanks," Buck said, heartened by the friendly welcome he received. He took a sip. "Wow! This is the best coffee I ever tasted! What did you put in it?"

"Jist regula coffee, boy!"

"Oh, yeah...not quite," another corrected. "There's a few eggs broken in it, shells and all, and, o' course, a pinch of salt..."

"...and some walnuts thrown in for flavor," someone else added, and went on, "We jungle birds have our own recipe which none can duplicate!" as he lifted his tin can in a toast in feigned sophistication, his nose in the air and his pinky extended in a refined manner.

One of them gave him a light punch on the shoulder, spilling some of his coffee, as they laughed heartily. Then they led Bucky closer to the fire where others greeted him.

The group included several colored men. To Buck, it seemed they intermixed well with the white members of the group without any problem. *Hmm...maybe the common experiences of hardship shared by us hobos glue us together. Imagine that! I'm talking about myself here. I guess by now I'm a bona fide hobo at that. Geez...and I think I'm even feeling a sense of pride in that! I can see why K.O. said this was good place.*

Many of the hobos returning to the camp late in the day brought back ingredients for the Mulligan stew brewing on the fire.

"I got an onion and some carrots," one said.

"I bummed some scraps from the butcher," said another.

"I got me here some carrots and a few spuds," another offered.

The hobos cooperated to keep the place orderly and neat. They stored belongings for community use — tin cups for stew and coffee, a pot for dipping in the stew to divvy out the mulligan and assorted knives and spoons in a cigar box. A coffee can with a tight lid held grounds...some of them left over and used again, until the leeched-out flavor made it undrinkable. After using, they cleaned everything in the nearby brook. Buck saw a mirror suspended from a branch hobos used for shaving. Matches were preserved in a small tin box with the coffee can.

"Get yourself cleaned up, kid," one of them said with the voice of authority. "You're a mess. Go wash your face at the brook and comb your hair."

After cleaning up, Buck struck up a conversation with another boy around his age. "This is a pretty good place. Everybody seems friendly."

"Yeah," said the boy, "Most of 'em are all right. There's a few of 'em, like those two old buzzards who dip out the stew for us...they kinda run the camp. Ya better do as they say or they'll give ya trouble."

One of them had given Buck the order to clean himself up.

The boy continued, "If they take a likin' to ya, they'll dip deeper into the stew for ya to get the good stuff at the bottom. Then there's a few like that fella over there lyin' in the bushes. Don't get near 'im...the smell of whisky will knock ya dead. And that other one. He just sits over there by himself. All he does all day is cry. It's pitiful...a grown man cryin' like that. He ain't got nuttin', and he ain't goin' nowhere. You'll always find him sittin over there by that tree. I hope I never end up like him."

"Hey, Champ! You found your way!"

Hearing a familiar voice behind him, Buck turned and saw his friend. "K.O.! Hey, your directions were great,"

They sparred playfully for a few seconds, hugged and patted each other on the back.

K.O. had a long and tedious day, but felt gratified to see Bucky.

"How much you takin' in at the dairy farm?"

"I'm gittin' ten cents an hour."

"That ain't bad," Buck said. "How big a farm is it?"

"Pretty good size, I s'pose. They got about a hundred cows. Some of 'em ain't milkin' 'cause they're havin' calves."

"What do you have to do?"

"Well, it's a pretty stiff grind. I got to be there about 5:30 in the mornin', right after all the cows been milked. After they're milked, they pee and crap right there, so my first job is to shovel all the shit off the floor into wheelbarro's and dump 'em outside in a pile. Then we got to hose the place down."

"Geez, how can you stand it, K.O.?"

"Ain't no time to be choosy, Buck. I'd rather be with the crew at the milk house where they bottle the stuff. But it's a job and I do what I'm told. One of the best parts of workin' at the farm is the breakfast they give us after the milk's delivered. We get bacon 'n eggs, toast and butter and all the fixin's."

"Hey, think they could use another hand? I can shovel cow flops as good as anybody."

"Well I ain't told you the bad part yet," K.O. said. "It's a great job, and we might both settle down here and rack up some cash. I was gonna tell ya right off, but you asked questions, so I didn't say anythin'."

"What, K.O.? What happened?"

"The owner told some of us he didn't need us any more. It seems his brother, from Kansas, had some bad luck. He had a dairy farm, but there was a fire and the whole barn burned down. Things got really bad, and his brother sold off all his cows and lost his land. Yesterday, his whole family...I think there are ten of 'em...they showed up to help on the farm here. Our boss told us that with them helpin', they didn't need any more extra workers. So there you are, Buck. It seems just as we get somethin' goin' for us, somethin' happens. I don't see nothin' here for us. I think we should be movin' on. At least I got a little money in my pocket for both of us."

"That stinks," Buck said. "When we ever gonna get a break?"

"I know...but damn...here I am talkin' about what I been doin' and I ain't givin' you a chance to tell me about this foreign kid and what happened when you went back to the hospital."

Bucky had plenty to tell K.O. about his experiences in Des Moines. "You should have seen this prissy old maid who wouldn't let me in when I got to the hospital..."

When Bucky came to the part where Tanoa gave him twenty dollars, K.O.'s interest rose. He was not, however, happy to hear Bucky refused to take it.

"Wait a minute. You mean he gave you twenty dollars, and you just left it there?"

"Yeah. It didn't belong to me. It would be wrong for me to take it."

"Wrong? Are you crazy? How could it be wrong if he offered it to you?" K.O. grew agitated as he thought about what an extra twenty bucks could mean for both of them.

"I did what any person would have done. My folks taught me you don't get paid to do good deeds," Buck said.

"You're thinking like an ass. You ran all the way to the hospital,

91

you saved that boy's leg and spent all that time wit' 'im, and you think that's worth nothin'?"

In his mind, Bucky began to realize K.O. had a point, but he wasn't going to back down now. "I didn't deserve any reward. It wouldn't be right takin' money from a stranger, who got taken for a ride, broke his leg and ended up in the hospital. I just couldn't do it."

"I saw what was in that wallet," K.O. said. "The kid was loaded wit' dough."

"It doesn't matter. I don't care if he has a million bucks. It's just wrong. Just because you had a poor upbringing and can't understand right from wrong, that's no reason for you to dump on me for doing the right thing."

Frazzled after hours of hard work, K.O.'s muscles tightened, his face contorted in anger, and he started shouting, "I'm here breakin' my friggin' back shovelin' up shit for both of us...remember...we been splittin' our earnings, right? And you let money that could be our ticket out of here just sit!"

"Can't you see taking that money from Tanoa is stealing? Damn you, K.O. Don't you know the difference between taking and earning?"

"Listen, you self-righteous white ass! You think you're so good. Did you ever stop to think in that pea-sized brain of yours that this rich kid's offer might have been God's way of helping us to get a leg up? What if God wanted you to have it? Would it be wrong then?"

Bucky jumped to his feet. "Oh, I see," he said. "I thought you were my pal. But now I'm 'stupid'. So I'm a 'self-righteous white-ass'! The color of my skin never made any difference to you before. How come you come off calling me a white-ass? You're nothing but a black bastard and a greedy son-of-a bitch!"

K.O. smashed a fist into Bucky's face and knocked him down. Bucky leaped to his feet, made a dash for K.O. and tackled him, bringing him to the ground. They rolled over in the dust, each one gaining brief advantage over the other, pummeling each other with hard fists. Those in the camp watched the ruckus for a few moments, and then a few of them stepped in to stop it. "Come on, boys. Cut it out!" one of them said. They separated and dragged Buck and K.O. to opposite sides of the camp, where each sat down in silence.

Bucky used his arm to swipe his face and realized from the blood and dirt on his sleeve that his nose was bleeding. He saw the faces of those who glanced his way. *I must be a sorry sight.*

Bucky had never felt so isolated and alone as he did at this time…not even in those moments when he longed for the days when his family had been together.

What the hell is the matter with me? Maybe K.O. hit the nail on the head. God gave an answer to our prayers, and it was staring me in the face. I was too dumb to see it. I could've sent money home to dad, Helen and the kids. I could've shared it with K.O. so we could get on with our lives. Damn! All I ever do is mess up. There are things I better straighten out…things with my family…and this thing with K.O. And I better start tonight.

Later that evening, the group gathered in a close circle around the campfire. The sound of gurgling water in a nearby brook passing over the rock bed through a narrow channel, added to the idyllic character of this gathering of men clustered together under a brilliant starry sky.

Someone had a guitar. As he played, everyone joined in singing songs familiar to them all. Some songs were plaintive ballads about the rigors and trials of hobo life. In this life of deprivation, they drew comfort from fanciful lyrics of a land of peace and plenty.

The warmth and closeness of this scene made Bucky feel lonelier than ever. Late that night, he sat alone in the campfire light writing a letter to his dad, and the kids. From time to time, he would stop and gaze at the stars, reflecting on what he had written…trying to get the right words to describe deep feelings.

Dear Dad and Helen,

I'm writing this from Davenport, Iowa. I'm doing okay. Don't worry about me. Things are pretty good.

I'm sorry I ran off without saying anything. After mom was buried, I heard some of dad's friends say you'd all be better off if I left home and got on my own.

I'm sorry I took the money you had on the shelf at the front door. I put a couple of dollars in with this letter and I'll send more as soon as I can. I swear it.

Aunt Helen - Bud told me they call you that -- may I call you that? I didn't mean any of those bad things I said to you. When Bud chased after me, he told me how good you are to everyone. I hope you can forgive me. I know I don't deserve it after what I said.

Dad, I love you. I wish I could be with you, but I

know I don't deserve to come home, and I can't bring myself to ask. I'm sorry I brought so much trouble to you.

Tell Lil and Lena how sorry I am and that I love them. And Bud, too. Especially Bud, who came running after me and wanted to go with me. I told him to stay home and help out. I love that kid. I know he's gonna make it one day. We'll all be proud of him. Tell him that for me.

Bucky

For the first time since he spilled out his sorrow on the day of his mother's funeral, Buck lay down and cried before drifting off into a fitful sleep.

The next morning, Bucky talked to K.O. asking him to forgive him for words he did not mean, spoken in anger. Even as he spoke, K.O. interrupted him to own up to his own guilt, and to ask Bucky to renew their friendship. They both talked rapidly in a jumble of awkward words…not especially coherent to the ear, yet each understanding perfectly what the other meant. In an emotion-filled exchange, they stood facing one another and put their hands on each other's shoulders.

"I'm sorry, K.O."

"I'm sorry, too, Champ."

Bucky sniffed back a runny nose and quickly wiped his eyes as the group approached them and gathered around them.

A crisis had erupted in their relationship. Nevertheless, their friendship stood up under the test. In the crucible of discord, their friendship became purified and stronger than ever. They pledged never again to allow any differences between them to get in the way of their bond of friendship.

Before setting out for new horizons, the two friends faced the group and humbly offered their apologies. It felt like a fresh start with the hobos rallying around them, wishing them well, and pressing them to return when they came through Davenport again.

23. THE MYSTERIOUS STRANGER

MAY, 1933, Wichita, Kansas

The mysterious stranger appeared at the wooded edge of the hobo jungle. An unsettling feeling arose in the group gathered there, as they nervously milled around eyeing the stranger and then each other. It was hard to put a finger on the reason for their anxiety, but something in the manner of this hulking figure was foreboding. Maybe it was the cap he wore over his head with flaps turned down on the sides. Was it the patch over his eye some of them saw in the flickering light of the campfire?

His manner was commanding, and when he stepped toward the center, the 'bos parted to widen their circle for him.

"Don't be afraid," the man said in his coarse, husky voice. "Look what I brought with me." From beneath his coat, he pulled out a chicken, already de-feathered and ready for the stew. "My compliments...for your mulligan." He dropped it into the boiling pot.

One of the hobos spoke up. "You don't look like you belong here. Where ya from, and what's y'r business? Are you a cop? We ain't done nothin' wrong. Just mindin' our business, that's all."

"No, I'm not a cop. But I am a stranger to these gatherings. I'm here because I need your help. Listen carefully, because there's some big money for whoever can help me find a lost boy. He's the son of a rich family out east. He ran off and left to ride the rails, breakin' his dear mother's heart. She's a sweet woman and his dad is as kind as can be. They're both worried sick. So they hired me. I'm a private dick sent out by them to find him and bring him back."

All eyes were on him, and he had their full attention.

"He's a good lookin' kid and last he was seen, he was travelin' with a colored boy. They've been ridin' the rails together. They're both good bare-knuckle fighters. I'm told the two of 'em could punch their way through a brick wall."

"Sounds like Bucky and K.O.," one of the men blurted out.

"Shut up!" snapped the leader of the group, who now was standing directly in front of this intruder, as if to defy him. "How we know this guy's legit? Keep your traps shut. I don't trust him!"

"That's them," the big man responded. "Yeah...his name's Bucky! He was here? And the colored boy was with him? Where are they now?"

There was silence.

"I'm tellin' you the truth." He reached inside his coat, pulled out his old police detective's badge, and waved it in front of them. "See, here's my badge." He was careful to keep them from noticing it no longer was valid. "The boy's family's dyin' with grief, and his mom's going crazy with worry!"

"Why should we believe you?" the man facing him challenged. "You got anything to prove your story?"

The mysterious man, sensing they knew details about Bucky's whereabouts, answered, "Nothin' but my badge. Ain't that good enough for you?"

"For all we know you might've taken it off a dead man," the shrewd hobo said.

"I tell you, Bucky is the one I'm looking for, all right."

The hobo and the detective stood in silence staring each other down.

With frustration, the stranger blasted, "That's it! I'm through talking. I know they've been here and I'll find them sooner or later." Crusher waved some large bills in their faces. "There's a big reward for the one who tells me where I can find them. Here's the hotel and the room number where I'm stayin'." He threw a paper onto the ground. "I'll be there tonight. Whoever gets to me first with the information gets this fist full of money right on the spot...no questions asked."

At that, he promptly turned and walked off into the woods.

A cold chill came over the group as they silently looked at each other. They all sensed the stranger was somewhat less than noble in his intents. Each wondered who might betray the two friends they had come to know and admire.

The paper Crusher had thrown onto the ground lay untouched, but before the night was over, it disappeared.

•

Crusher lay on his bed in the dimly lit room. In response to a knock on the door, Crusher's face broadened into a sinister grin. He rose to his feet and went to the door. "Who's there?" he whispered.

"Open da door and show me da money, and I'll tell you what you wanna know," he heard from the other side of the door.

The door cracked open and a seedy-looking older man stood in the hallway.

Crusher said, "Come in."

The old codger stepped into the room and saw the detective's face clearly. The old hobo started, as he saw the stranger's drooping flesh and scars.

"Okay, what you got for me?" Crusher demanded.

Transfixed by his terrifying face, the man stood speechless for a moment. Then he said, "Uh...show me...show me da *dough* first!"

Crusher pulled out the cash.

Shifting his gaze from Crusher's face to the handful of cash, the old man's eyes widened. "Don't know the exact place where they is now, but I know where dey're goin'. I heerd 'em talkin' 'bout goin' to Chicaga to da big expo that's openin' dere. Dey figgerd dey'd get some woik dere and have fun at the same time."

Crusher had heard about Chicago's "Century of Progress" World's Fair scheduled to open in June. He slapped the money into the old jungle buzzard's hand, and the man left quickly.

Moments later, the former bull slipped out into the night. Sighting the informant in the distance, he started in his direction.

No one ever saw or heard from the old hobo again.

24. "CENTURY OF PROGRESS" WORLD'S FAIR

JUNE, 1933, Chicago, Illinois

On a hot Friday afternoon in June, Bucky and K.O. arrived on the outskirts of Chicago. Evening shadows deepened as the two friends trekked along Lake Shore Drive to the World's Fair. In the distance, resplendent dancing colors from Fair lights illuminated the night sky.

At Grant Park near the fairgrounds, Bucky said, "Let's bunk down here for the night. In the morning, we can find where we can apply for jobs."

After spreading his blanket on the grass, K.O. fell asleep in seconds, while Bucky lay for some time transfixed by the brilliant light show in the sky, his mind filled with thoughts of new and wonderful experiences inside the fairgrounds.

The next morning, the boys reached the personnel office. The World's Fair had opened its gates just one week ago and the Fair management still sought additional workers to fill open positions. Buck fudged about his age and landed work as a barker.

When K.O. approached, the personnel officer said, "I'm not sure we have any work here for you, boy."

Suspecting K.O.'s color was a factor, Buck said in a commanding, but polite manner, "Sir, the two of us are together. I won't work unless my friend here is hired."

It took courage for Buck to risk losing his own job by standing up for K.O., but it worked. The personnel director gave K.O. a job tending the elephants, which meant washing them down, feeding them and shoveling up their dung. They each received a wage of fifty-cents a day.

With a megaphone, and a platform to stand on, Buck urged people to enter the Musee de Horreurs, a wax museum on the "Streets of Paris." Buck hailed the spooky thrills awaiting visitors inside this "grotesque and gruesome gallery of horrifying sights and sounds." His working hours afforded him short breaks from time to time, and on Mondays, he enjoyed a day off.

One Monday, when Buck joined fairgoers walking the Midway, someone tapped him on the shoulder. Surprised, he turned to see who touched him, and saw a familiar face from the hobo community. "Tiny! You old buzzard! What ya doing here?"

"Remember you and K.O. was talkin' 'bout the World's Fair? Well, it seemed a good idea to me, too. They's lots of us here!"

Buck and K.O. had met Tiny, an aging hobo, in a jungle. A teller of stories, Tiny loved sharing tales of his escapades on the rails.

"I have the day off," Buck said. "I landed a job here barking outside the Museum of Horrors. Come on, Tiny. Let's go over to Eitel's Pastry Shop. I'll treat you to a cup of coffee and a piece of their 'Supreme Coconut Cake'. The coffee ain't the blend you been used to in the camps, but it's hot and it ain't bad."

It was an invitation Tiny happily accepted.

At Eitel's, Buck and Tiny exchanged stories. Buck told Tiny about the jobs he and K.O. had landed. "You ought to apply, Tiny. I'm sure there's some work here for you," Buck said.

"Nah!" Tiny responded. "I ain't gonna git nailed down to one spot. I gotta git goin'. I got my eye on the harvest. The wheat's high, and I'm good at doin' what I done before."

As Buck talked with his friend, he felt a real sense of pride at his ability to treat a visitor to coffee and cake in a nice restaurant like Eitel's.

While conversing, Tiny said, "Say, Bucky, I just thought of somethin' that happened that you might wanna know."

"What's that?"

"Remember back in Wichita?" Tiny began.

"Yeah. Good group of guys. That's where you heard K.O. and me talkin' about coming here to the World's Fair."

"That's right, but soon after you and K.O. left, this weird lookin' creep showed up askin' about ya. He gave us a story about your mom's broken heart over your leavin' home and your dad payin' him to go and find you."

"What a bunch of malarkey," Buck said.

"He offered a reward to anyone who knew where you was, but he looked suspicious, and none of us trusted 'im. He wore a patch over his eye."

"Don't remember anyone like that. Maybe he's some old pirate I met back when I used to sail the ocean blue!" Buck joked.

"It sure seemed like he was up to no good...big and scary. He even offered cash to anyone who could tell him where you was. But, of course, Buck, none of us said a word, and finally he left us alone. Do you know who it might've been, Buck?"

"I have no idea, Tiny, and I don't really care who he was."

They continued to chat for an hour before Tiny said he needed to be on his way.

The next day, when Buck told K.O. about Tiny's visit with him, it did not occur to him to share Tiny's report about the mysterious stranger.

K.O. was busy with the company of elephants, whose droppings piled up as fast as he shoveled the dung away. Their need for food, water and hosing down was hard work that kept him busy most of the day.

When their days off coincided, Buck and K.O. hung out together to watch the people at the fair. They especially found pleasure in watching the girls walking by on the Midway, picking out ones they fancied as best-looking chicks.

Their eyes often embraced a world they had not known before. They stared with wonder, as people freely spent money on ice cream, games and other indulgences for jubilant children.

"Geez, imagine if we had money like that to spend. Look at the fun those kids are having," Buck said.

"Now don't be greedy, Buck. You have to admit our situation has gotten a lot better than it was. I can just hear my grandma sayin', 'Now, Jeremiah, you be glad and thank God for all He's given you.'"

"Yeah," Buck said. "I suppose she's right."

"You know, Buck, this life ain't half bad. Maybe we can make somethin' of ourselves. At least we got a good place to sleep in hay in the elephant tent."

"Yeah, and the lake's a pretty big bath tub for the both of us," Buck said. "We've been getting good and honest money and plenty to eat. What else do we need?"

K.O. and Buck eyed each other and then came up with the same answer: "Girls!"

"We've seen plenty of pretty girls here," Buck said.

"Yeah, Champ," K.O. agreed. "but after all this time bein' on the road, even the ugly ones look good to me."

•

The Midway at the Century of Progress World's Fair formed the main thoroughfare, where a string of shops, concessions, exhibits, and other attractions lined this large, open promenade. Hundreds of hobos visited the fair. Buck and K.O. ran into another hobo they knew, whose name was Howie. Howie had an unusual talent and they found him demonstrating it at the fair. He used a pocketknife skillfully to carve portraits of famous people into the soft metal of the buffalo nickel. He offered these masterpieces as prized souvenirs. Sitting on a crate, he set up a sign describing his business proposition:

LEND ME A NICKEL. FOR THE PRICE OF TWO
NICKELS, I WILL CARVE A FINE PICTURE ON YOUR
NICKEL AND RETURN IT TO YOU.

Howie put samples of his work on display so people could examine his work. His unusual craft drew attention. People stopped to watch Howie carve each nickel. Some observers became his customers.

Several days after Buck and K.O. talked with Howie, they saw him involved in a commotion. Highly successful in his venture, Howie met up with opposition from the Fair management. K.O. and Bucky watched two Security Policemen confronting the boy.

"We're shutting you down, boy," one of them said. "Pack up your things and come with us."

Before leading him away, one of the security men turned to the crowd and apologized. "Sorry, but this boy does not have proper authorization to sell stuff on the Midway."

Some of the others expressed disappointment. One man said, "Give the kid a break. He's really good at his trade."

Ignoring the objections, the police led Howie away.

Over his shoulder, the brazen kid yelled, "I'll be parked right outside the gate. You can see and buy my stuff there."

"Shut up, kid," the burly guard said and picked him up off his feet by his collar and carried him away. Buck and K.O. followed to the main gate, where the police explained to Howie that in order to sell merchandise on the Midway, he'd need to submit an application. An officer assured him the competition was tough, and that some of his earnings would go into the coffers of the World's Fair.

Howie did not accept these terms, and the officers escorted him off the fairgrounds.

"You can come back as a visitor, but you'll have to pay the entrance fee to get in," said one of the officers.

"And don't think you can get away with hanging around the Main Gate, either. You're still on fairground property, so get on your way, boy."

With their employee passes, Buck and K.O. could leave and return to the fair at will. They caught up to Howie as he slowly walked away.

"Gee, we're sorry, Howie," Buck said.

"What ya gonna do now?" K.O. asked.

"It ain't so bad, guys," Howie said. "It's what I 'spected. I picked up some good money in the short time before they got on to me. I learned the trade from other hobos, who are experts at coin carvin'. Like some of 'em, I get by on the road by carvin' nickels for food. It ain't a bad life, so I'll be movin' on. Good to see both of ya. Hope you're doin' okay. Maybe we'll meet again. Good luck."

"God bless ya, Howie," K.O. said, and patted him on the shoulder. The hobo disappeared down Lake Shore Drive.

After that, whenever Buck and K.O walked by the spot where Howie had practiced his trade, they wondered what he might be doing and how he fared.

"Hey. K.O., do you think someday, those coins might be worth more than a nickel?"

"What do ya mean, Champ?"

"Well, sometimes, things get more priceless with age, especially if people want to collect them and there aren't many of them...you know, like antiques. I think of all the souvenirs saved from this World's Fair, Howie's nickel might be worth the most."

"I wonder how many of those coins are out there?" K.O. said.

"You wishin' you had one of those nickels?" Bucky said. "Think you might strike it rich some day?"

K.O. laughed. "I don't think I'll live long enough for that to happen, and if it does, I don't think it'll do Howie much good."

Dick Miller

•

A wide variety of attractions took place on the Midway. Always on the lookout for opportunity, one unusual spectacle gave Buck a bright idea...at least he thought so.

Bucky said, "Geez, look over there, K.O. Did you ever see anything like that?"

"No sir, Champ. A man wrestlin' an alligator...what else will they think of?" K.O. grew excited watching the match between man and reptile. He cheered them on with shouts and energetic actions. "Stomp 'im! Hold 'im down! Yeeaaah!"

The bout captured Bucky's interest, but he remained deep in thought. After the show, Bucky said, "K.O., I've got an idea. How popular do you think alligator wrestling is outside of the fairgrounds?"

"I dunno, Champ. It's probably not the most popular sport in the world. Why you askin'?"

"The Midway is filled with all kinds of sport related attractions, but there's one sport that gets more popular every day that isn't here."

"You mean..." K.O. said, and they both finished the sentence in unison: "boxing!"

"Hey, yeah," K.O. went on. "But wait a minute. You gotta be crazy if you're thinkin' that you and me can do any boxing here at the Fair."

"Why?" Buck countered. "From Howie we learned a little about how to get a spot on the midway. Why don't we give it a try?"

"But what about all the equipment and things we need to do that?"

"We don't need that much," Buck said. "We could bare knuckle fight if we had to. Such fights are going on in cities all over the country. I think if we could sell the idea to the people in charge here, they might just give us whatever we need. Do you think the alligator wrestler put up the fencing and all the other things he needed? What do you think?"

"All right," K.O. said. "Let's give it a go. Where do we start?"

"How about at the office where we got our jobs?"

The boys tried several times to speak with someone with authority to put some flesh on their bare bones idea. Because they were just two kids, no one took them seriously. Out of frustration, Bucky made a bold suggestion.

"I've got a plan," Buck said. "They gave me a megaphone. What could be a better set up to spark a response from the crowd? If the Fair managers won't listen to *us*, maybe they'll pay attention to *the people who come here.*"

The Boxcar Kid

That afternoon, Buck stood on the platform once again calling out to prospective patrons. This time he added something new to his pitch.

"Attention, ladeees and gentlemen," he said with flourish. "Gather round and let me tell you about one of the most exciting new attractions that will soon open here on the Midway."

People started to gather.

"It's boxing, folks, right here on the Midway! You'll see boxing at its best. There will be exhibitions and contests, and those of you who are game to try might win a prize! You'll see me paired with a first rate fighter...professionally trained by his father, the world famous Joe Franklin, who beat contenders in major cities in the country."

The gathering crowd gave Buck its ear.

"And he's with us here today. K.O.", he said, turning to his fighting partner, "come on up here and let's show them a little action."

Bounding up onto the platform, K.O. began prancing around and punching into the air against an imaginary opponent.

"Ladeees and gentlemen, I give you Jeremiah 'K.O.' Franklin."

K.O. peeled off his shirt and Buck followed suit. The crowd could see the boys' well-toned muscles and became enthusiastic. The sight of the two men stripped to the waist sparring with one another captured the attention of those out of earshot, and they came closer.

While they were showing off some fancy footwork and quick moves, out of the corner of his eye, Buck saw some uniformed police coming towards them through the crowd. Giving K.O. a sign to make a quick exit, he gave a final word to the crowd.

"Watch for this attraction, folks, coming soon to the Midway...and thank you for your kind attention!"

Buck and K.O. jumped to the ground and ran down an alley to the rear of the *Musee de Horreurs*. The fairgrounds police, enmeshed in the crowd, were foiled in their attempt to chase after them, and the boys escaped.

Sometime later, K.O. returned to tend to the elephants, and Buck was back at his post doing his promotional routine.

The day passed without incident, but on the following day, during Buck's megaphone blast to prospective customers near the Museum of Horrors, he saw two officers walking to the edge of the platform. This time, there was no place to run, so when the officers directed him to come down and follow them, Buck did not resist.

•

Dick Miller

The two boys sat opposite three men. One sat behind a desk while the others stood.

After preliminary introductions, the man sitting at the desk said, "Boys, you know you did a foolish thing yesterday. What you decided to do out there could have prompted plenty of confusion on the Midway. It was irresponsible. We can't let people come in here and set up whatever they please. We already have a few exhibitions that have sparked some controversy."

Buck wondered if he was referring to what he and K.O. encountered at the German Pavilion, where representatives approached them and urged them to embrace a new political philosophy called Fascism, as they distributed "friendship badges" bearing the Nazi party's swastika and the American flag.

One man, commanding the attention of those passing by, gave a fiery speech at the pavilion. "With Adolph Hitler as our new *Fuhrer*, Germany will come into its own. He will purge our land of impurities, and establish Aryan people as the master race in Germany, and throughout the world, as God in heaven ordained it. Let the people of the world join us in this venture to eliminate those who seek to dominate and oppress us. Join us to bring new economic hope to our land and to the world..."

"What the hell is this 'Aryan' thing?" Buck asked K.O. "Ever hear of that before?"

"No, but it doesn't sound too good to me. I think we heard enough."

"Me, too," Buck said. "Let's move on."

The man behind the desk continued, "Would you tell us, please, what prompted such behavior?"

Buck answered, "We didn't mean any harm, sir. We are both good boxers, and we saw that you've got all kinds of great things on the Midway, but there's nothing at all about boxing. It surprised us, since boxing is becoming such a popular sport. We tried to talk to someone in your offices, but no one would see us. We thought boxing was sure to be a great and exciting event for the people. Sir, we are sorry if we caused any trouble. We didn't mean to—"

The man interrupted, "You both understand, I suppose, you should be sent to spend a few days in jail. Have either of you a police record?"

Buck remembered their jail time in Memphis, and quickly answered, "No, sir." Without hesitation, K.O. echoed Bucky's reply.

Buck gave a quick glance at his pal sitting beside him. *Here goes our chance to make something of ourselves.*

"Boys," the man said, "You have been fortunate. Do you know why you're not sitting in a jail cell or wandering around the city without your jobs?

They stared speechless.

"It's because someone of influence saw what you did and thought it was daring of you. He admired your ingenuity. But the thing that worked most in your favor is that he is a fan of boxing and thinks it would be good to give it a try."

The boys sat up straight and flashed a look of surprise at each other, then gave their full attention to the man.

"Don't get too excited yet," the man said. "The whole idea needs plenty of consideration. The man who watched you is Mr. Clarence Gordon, a very generous benefactor and member of the Century of Progress Board. He was impressed with your spunk and ability.

"The fact is we also received other positive response to your demonstration. Our office has been receiving inquiries about the boxing exhibition prompting us for details and when it will start."

The boys eyed each other in stunned silence.

One of the men standing said, "Usually, concessions at the fair must be applied for and approved. Mr. Gordon, however, is considering sponsoring you in a boxing exhibition and, if he approves of your character, and terms can be agreed upon, he wants to start up as soon as possible."

Buck opened his mouth and stared at the man, flabbergasted. *Could this really be happening to us?*

"He wants to meet with you personally. What's more, he wants you to come to his home, and has invited you to dinner. If you satisfy his requirements, he is prepared to make a recommendation to the board on your behalf."

"Wow!" K.O. said. "You really mean it? You're not joshin' us?"

"No, K.O., we're not 'joshin'," the man said.

"The invitation to dinner is for tomorrow night at 6 P.M. There are things you need to do to get ready. Be back here at 3:30 for further instructions and we'll help get you prepared. If things go well, Mr. Gordon will approach Mr. Rufus Dawes, chairman of the board. If Mr. Dawes goes for the idea, Mr. Gordon will personally go to bat for you, and if the board approves, he will put up the funds to get you started. Now I think we better let you fellas go. You have your jobs to think about, you know."

"Thank you, sir," K.O. said first, with Bucky following.

Once outside, the boys abandoned their composed behavior.

Slapping Buck on the shoulder, K.O. said, "Well what do ya think about that?"

Buck punched him back. They whooped, hollered, jumped up and down with excitement and hugged each other.

25. AT THE GORDON ESTATE

A buzz of activity filled the afternoon of the dinner party. For the occasion, attendants groomed the boys and dressed them in neat, but casual clothes.

Mr. Gordon, the boys learned, had a reputation for promoting progressive ideas, and passionately committed himself to implementing innovations that would promote the success of the Century of Progress project. His desire to question the boys personally was extraordinary, and to invite them to be his guests at his home, elevated the matter to a higher level of consideration. The invitation demonstrated Mr. Gordon regarded this endeavor as significant. To interview them in such a setting would promote free flowing discussion without inhibition or distraction. It also provided a basis for building confidence and loyalty in those he recommended for employment.

In the evening, a chauffer picked them up in a limousine and drove them to the Gordon estate, past the entrance gate, and up the tree-lined drive to the front steps of the Georgian style mansion.

"This ain't your daddy's farm, Champ," K.O. said.

"It sure ain't the YMCA," Buck said.

The chauffer led them up to the front door set in the middle of the columned porch stretching across the front of the house. The two boys appeared diminutive as they stood in front of the great wooden doors adorned with intricate carvings. A butler opened the door, greeted them and ushered them to a sitting room where the two waited to meet their host.

Buck had never before been in a room paneled with mahogany, and he was certain K.O. had never seen the likes of this either. The dark wood of the walls and furniture, and penetrating stares from portraits on the walls cast a somber and unwelcoming pall over the room. The boys stood quietly, each shifting his weight nervously from one foot to the other.

The atmosphere brightened when Mr. and Mrs. Gordon entered with glowing smiles and kind greetings. Extending his hand to each of them, Mr. Gordon said, "Buck Ellis and Jeremiah Franklin, welcome. This is Mrs. Gordon."

"How do you do, ma'am," K.O. said as he took Mrs. Gordon's hand.

"Pleased to meet you, ma'am," Bucky added.

To his wife, Mr. Gordon noted, "Mr. Franklin has an interesting nickname: 'K.O.' Perhaps during dinner he can tell us how he received it."

The boys felt relieved to see Mr. Gordon dressed in slacks and an open collared shirt. Mrs. Gordon wore a simple print dress that reminded Bucky of a dress his mother used to wear to church.

Mr. Gordon turned on a switch producing light radiating from an overhead crystal chandelier, dispelling the room's somber appearance. Taking a seat in the overstuffed chairs, the room now seemed cozy. Still, Bucky and K.O. remained apprehensive about how they would respond to questions Mr. Gordon might ask.

At the start, Mr. Gordon's demeanor seemed ominous. "How did you feel about breaking the rules with your unauthorized display of showmanship?"

Bucky nervously repositioned himself in his chair at this direct question. He clasped his hands together on his knees, stared down at the floor and remained silent, not knowing what to say – an uncharacteristic response for the boy who usually did most of the talking for the two of them.

K.O. noticed this right away and quickly offered, "We know we done wrong, sir, and wish we hadn't done it."

Bucky regained some confidence and added, "Yes, sir. We're really sorry for the trouble we caused."

"Well," said Mr. Gordon, breaking into a wide smile, "I thought your action was ingenious and very thought-provoking...right on the mark, I'd say."

Mr. Gordon watched with a twinkle in his eye as the boys' jaws dropped and they regarded each with surprised faces.

"I dare say you boys have guts. You alerted us that the fair lacked something important, and you did it in a bold and masterful way. I like that."

"Really?" Bucky said. "You mean it?"

"When I realized your intent, I considered that you acted as I may have when I was your age."

The two sat in silence.

"Did you think I never got into trouble as a boy?" Mr. Gordon asked.

"No sir...I mean yes sir...uhh...I mean ..." Bucky blurted out.

Mr. Gordon laughed.

The ice had been broken, and the boys now breathed easy, relaxing their rigid posture.

"The fact is when I was a boy, it just seemed trouble came my way. Oh, mind you, I wasn't bad or anything like that. But things happened to me...innocent things...that sometimes put me in trouble with my teachers. I saw the inside of the principal's office more than once."

"Really? What kind of things happened to you?" Bucky asked.

"Oh, all kinds of things."

"Tell them your famous story about the penny, dear," Mrs. Gordon prompted.

"Oh, yes, of course. That's a good one. One time, in the classroom, I sat at my desk playing with a penny. After a while, I noticed it was missing. I searched all around my desk, but it was gone. So I went up to the teacher and told her I lost my penny. I thought she would ask the class if anyone had found it, but instead, she gave me an icy stare and said firmly, 'Sit down!' I was devastated. Completely confused, I cowered back to my seat and sat down. I hung my head and gazed at my desk. I knew all eyes were on me. It was then that the penny I had absent-mindedly stuck to my forehead fell to the desk with a loud noise. I had completely forgotten I had stuck it up there."

Everybody broke into hearty laughter, even Mrs. Gordon, who had heard this story many times.

Mr. Gordon told several additional stories about mishaps in his youth. Soon the tide turned, and the boys talked non-stop about themselves, which was Mr. Gordon's ultimate objective. Mr. Gordon found out all he needed to know about them, including the identity of K.O.'s father, and how K.O. received his nickname. The boys' determination

110

and simple honesty impressed him. Mr. Gordon could see they were hard workers who knew the meaning of sacrifice and loyalty. In their usual social circles, the Gordons had their fill of pompous, pretentious people. Mr Gordon relished this little parley with the boys as a refreshing change of pace.

In addition, Mrs. Gordon had great interest in the plight of young people, and, Mr. Gordon, as a boxing enthusiast, had much to say.

As they were ushered into the dining room, Buck whispered to K.O., "Did you ever think a wealthy big shot like Mr. Gordon would turn out to be such a regular guy?"

K.O. shook his head.

The two boys sat across the table from each other with Mr. and Mrs. Gordon taking places at opposite ends of the table. They followed Mr. Gordon's lead and bowed their heads reverently during the table prayer. Then Mr. Gordon reached over and pulled a nearby tasseled rope signaling the servants to enter and serve the food.

While one served soup from a tureen, another delivered a silver platter with a cover. When the servant lifted the cover, Buck and K.O.'s eyes lit up at the sight of juicy hamburgers and hot dogs piled high. They noticed as well that the two silver containers on the table contained ketchup and mustard. Beaming smiles replaced lines of tension on the boys' faces.

"Relax and enjoy yourselves, boys." Mr. Gordon said, as he passed the tray with the main course to K.O. "The only rule we have here is that you both eat heartily."

"Yes," said Mrs. Gordon, smiling. "We absolutely insist on that."

In the course of the meal, K.O. noticed the pert young Negro girl helping to serve the food. Mr. Gordon addressed her as "Estelle." She wore a smart looking black uniform with short sleeves trimmed with a white band, a simple white collar around the V-neckline and the strip at the top of her white apron tied into a bow in the back. K.O. stared at her, his eyes locked on her every movement, until she exited and he had noted the starched ends of her apron bow rocking back and forth, accenting her gait and shapely behind. If Mr. Gordon selected the uniform for modesty, he missed the mark from K.O.'s point of view. She looked downright sexy. *What a filly! She's a terrific knockout.* K.O. was determined to find out as much as he could about her, but he was not sure how to go about it.

Buck noticed K.O.'s distraction when Estelle entered the room. He saw K.O.'s hungry eyes feasting on Estelle's cleavage as she leaned forward to place things on the table. He gently kicked K.O. under the table and K.O. flinched. Catching Buck's prohibiting expression, he lowered his eyes in embarrassment.

Buck found it difficult to keep his own eyes off her. *K.O.'s in a trance. She's a great looking babe, alright!*

As Estelle started clearing the table, K.O. thought he found his chance to get her alone.

"Excuse me," he said. "Would it be okay for me to go to the bathroom?"

"Certainly," Mrs. Gordon replied. "Estelle, would you show Mr. Franklin where the bathroom is?"

"Yes, ma'am."

K.O. was ecstatic. *It worked! My timin' couldn't be better!*

Halfway down the hallway, K.O. stopped Estelle. He had little time to think about what he would say, so he blurted out, "Estelle, how can I see you again?"

Estelle looked at him in wide-eyed surprise.

"We are not permitted to talk with the guests, Mr. Franklin," she said, and cast her eyes down in modesty. Then, giving him a quick glance, she said abruptly, "The bathroom door is right behind you," and walked quickly through the hall to the kitchen.

K.O. scowled. *Damn, I muffed that up good!*

•

Before the meal was over, Mr. Gordon forged a framework for a contract to feature the boys in a new boxing event on the Midway. He planned to bring a proposal to the COP Board to start the exhibition on a trial basis. After the trial period and an assessment, the program could be continued, changed or abandoned. In addition to exhibitions and demonstrations, the attraction would include contests bringing amateur combatants to the ring. Contestants lasting the three rounds would receive prizes. The boys would receive a stipend and free passes to the food concessions. At least during the trial period, the boys would also continue in their respective jobs. If the enterprise succeeded, everything would be re-evaluated, including their stipends. But first, the approval of the COP Board must be secured.

•

Estelle's aloof manner disappeared when she was among her female friends employed in the household.

"K.O. was making eyes at me," she said, as her face blushed.

"You jivin' us, girl?"

"Mrs. Gordon asked me to show him to the bathroom, and in the hallway he asked me where we could meet later."

"Did he invite you into the bathroom?"

"Yeah," said another, "Did you see his you-know-what?"

"Girls!" Estelle said, flashing them a disapproving frown.

"I saw him," another said. "What a tomcat. He could tame me any day."

"What happens now?" someone asked.

"Yeah, how come you let 'im git away?" another said.

With a slight upturn of the corners of her mouth, Estelle displayed a sly smile and said, "Don't worry, girls. I listened in at their talkin' and I know just where to find him at the Fair."

"Where's dat?"

"On the Midway. He and the white boy are going to be part of a new thing Mr. Gordon wants to start. They'll be boxing...you know, with gloves and trunks and all."

"You mean the pretty white kid, too?"

"That's what she means, Brenda. But remember, he's white. You can look, but you can't touch."

26. A NEW EVENT
ON THE MIDWAY

JULY, 1933

The COP board unanimously approved the boxing venture. Workers constructed a rudimentary platform on the Midway in preparation for the new feature. The day arrived for the first exhibitions and tournaments to begin.

To minimize bruises and to extend their endurance, Buck and K.O. sometimes used a cavalier style of boxing consisting of defensive maneuvers. The biggest crowd pleasers were fast action slugfests between the two. K.O. had schooled Bucky in the art of "slap fighting." By delivering jabs and punches in rapid succession with open handed gloves, the boys fooled all but the most perceptive eye into thinking they were thrashing each other.

The two boxers took turns taking on contenders. Only amateurs were qualified to volunteer, but no one checked out anyone's level of experience. Occasionally, a good fighter brought Buck or K.O. to the mat, but in most instances, the champions prevailed. Unlike professional matches, where opponents fought for a prize with careers at stake, this Midway feature served primarily as entertainment. Showmanship was important to the COP Fair management, so appointed managers advised the fighters to give challengers an occasional opening to land some good punches. While bruises sustained by the champions heightened the excitement for the spectators, this policy placed Buck and K.O. at greater risk of injury.

In a month's time, crowds attracted to the boxing events overflowed the space allotted for the exhibition, interfering with the flow of traffic on the Midway. The COP board quickly approved continuing the spectacle and moved it to a better location accommodating a crowd of more than a hundred people. A work crew provided additional seating and constructed an open canopy overhead for protection against the weather.

Boxing primarily interested men, but in this case, the exhibitions drew a large complement of women. While most considered it indiscreet for women to stare at muscled, shirtless men in trunks, at the exhibitions, refined ladies could indulge themselves without risk of criticism. Large promotional photos of Buck and K.O. appeared posted throughout the fairgrounds together with a boxing events schedule.

Included among the women who gathered at the boxing ring was the young Negro beauty from Mr. Gordon's household, Estelle Simmons. K.O. first caught sight of her during a heated match with a challenger. The surprise of seeing her distracted him, and he left himself unguarded. His opponent struck a solid blow to K.O.'s head that made him see stars. K.O. quickly recovered, and mopped up the ring with his opponent, dashing the contestant's hope for the prize.

27. AN UNEXPECTED SURPRISE

The Sky Ride was, without question, the premier attraction at the fair. Since their arrival, Buck and K.O. aspired to go up the elevator and ride in a rocket car. Visitors rode in cars hung from cables that carried them from one tower to the other, giving them a panoramic vista of the fairgrounds and the city of Chicago.

Now they both stood staring at the printed ticket in Bucky's hand.

```
To all fair workers:

    The extraordinary success of the fair
since opening day has led the Century of
Progress board to express appreciation
for your service during that time. This
pass entitles you to one free admission
on the Sky Ride.
    To prevent the convergence of too many
workers at any given time and to avoid
crowds, we have scheduled a time for each
worker to use this privilege. Please
arrive at the East tower (on the island)
10 minutes after the fair closes. You
will be admitted only on the date
scheduled for you. Present this letter as
```

you board the elevator. The operator will
give you further instructions.
    Your scheduled date is <u>Tuesday, August
22nd</u>
    Thank you for your efforts to make the
1933 Century of Progress Fair the very
best it can be.
    Have fun!
    - The COP Management

A young man had hand delivered the passes to them. The boys delighted in what they held, and stood staring at the printed ticket in Bucky's hand.

"Hey, Buck, can you believe it? So many great things have happened to us. How can we be so lucky?"

"Yeah," Buck said. "I guess Mr. Gordon isn't the only generous guy on the Board."

•

Shortly before closing time, Buck and K.O. stood at the Sky Ride elevators. With the exit to the Fair located some distance from the East Tower of the Sky Ride, most of the people had already left the area. At midnight, all the lights shooting skyward, illuminating building facades and major areas automatically turned off. Except for a few scattered night-lights, the fairgrounds went dark. A bustling metropolis of sights and sounds moments ago, the grounds now resembled a place of silence and shadows.

One of the elevator doors opened. A young man in a uniform stood before them. Smiling, he said, "Greetings, Bucky and K.O. Come aboard."

They each handed their pass to the man.

Bucky asked, "Are we the only ones here?"

"Yeah, where is everybody?" K.O. echoed.

The elevator operator glanced at their passes, and said, "You are a little early, you know. Others should be arriving. But there's no reason to delay. I can bring you up and come back down for the others."

As the doors closed and the elevator rose, the boys stood in silence.

"The plan is to take you all the way to the top first," the operator explained.

Sky Ride visitors could go directly to the Otis Company's new high-speed Elevator Exhibit at the top, bypassing the rocket car stop at a lower level. On top, they could step up onto a raised platform with the elevator shaft opening at its center. At the guardrail, spectators could watch the operating machinery of the elevator.

"Be sure to see the elevator exhibit on the upper platform. The view of the machinery is something you won't want to miss...quite a sight. When everybody's ready, I'll come and bring all of you back down to the rocket cars. Then we'll all ride over to the other tower, I'll show you around and then we'll take the elevators down to end our tour."

"How high are the towers?" Buck asked.

"They're 628 feet high," the operator answered. "The rocket cars carry you over at the 210 foot level."

In "less than a minute," as Otis Elevator Company promotional ads claimed, they landed at the top of the tower. When the elevator doors closed behind them, it was dark at the top. Lights below illuminated the tower's frame, but lights on the platform itself were off. Cloaked in eerie darkness and solitude, the two stood as if cemented to the floor. Only the soft rush of the blowing wind disturbed the silence apart from distant sounds of the city.

"Geez, this place is spooky," Buck said.

"Yeah," K.O. said. Then he turned his head toward the west and reeled. Motioning to Buck to look toward the city, he whispered, "Look over there, Champ."

A man stood leaning against the guardrail with his back to them. As the man turned and faced them against the backlights of the city and streaming façade tower lights, K.O. and Buck saw only the silhouette of the man. The glint of a badge on his breast pocket, his official-looking hat, and a red stripe on his uniform sleeve identified him as an official guide. The attendant spoke in a coarse voice, but in a reassuring, friendly manner.

"Right on time," he said. "We keep the lights off up here so you can appreciate the beauty of the lighted city and the fairgrounds."

Pointing to the stairs to the upper platform, he said, "Why don't you start over there. You can get ahead of the crowd and be first to get an up-close view of the machinery. Take your time."

Relieved, the two partners bounded up the steps. A single overhead light illuminated the exposed machinery.

"Wow!" Bucky said. "How clean and shiny everything is. It's beautiful...not what I expected."

118

"Yeah...I thought we'd see a lotta grease and cables," said K.O.

Encased in a silver cylinder, the operating mechanism gleamed. It had oval cutouts for venting. Surrounding the cylinder in orderly fashion rested other polished accessories and equipment. Leaning far out over the open guardrail, the two boys could almost touch the machinery.

The machine was at rest, but suddenly emitted sounds of operation.

"Hey, Champ, it sounds like they're bringin' a group of folks up to join us."

"Yeah," Buck said.

"You think they hire someone to climb all over those machines and shine 'em bright each day?"

"Why of course, K.O. I can just see you and me crawlin' all over the works with rags, givin' everything a spit shine."

The machinery stopped. Engaged in conversation, the two didn't notice that no sound of disembarking elevator passengers came forth from the platform below.

Turning his face to look directly at Bucky, K.O. said, "Hey, buddy, you know something's bothering me."

"What's that, K.O.?"

"That elevator operator...how come he knew our names? We weren't wearin' our I.D. badges, and the passes we gave him didn't have our names on 'em."

"That's right. I never thought about that. He greeted us by name before he even got our passes."

Without any warning, the uniformed figure leaped out of the shadows and pounced on them. Before they could think, Buck and K.O. felt his big hands lift them bodily from the platform floor. In an instant, they found themselves over the rail, flying headlong into the machinery.

Moments later, Crusher stepped into the awaiting elevator and joined its sole occupant, his uniformed accomplice. The two men descended to the bottom of the tower.

28. OUT OF
THE SHADOWS

Since his arrival at the Fair, Crusher had been crafting his evil plans for weeks. A hat tilted forward and a pair of dark glasses worn over his eye patch was sufficient disguise to allow him to go freely wherever he wished without fear of recognition. While the image of a bloodied face with a dislodged eye hanging over the cheek burned itself into Bucky's memory, he retained no clear image of Crusher's features.

Mingling with the crowds around the two contenders in the ring, Crusher's rage burned hot. The young man in the ring was not the frightened, skinny kid he remembered from his encounter over a year ago in Lima, Ohio. As a Midway featured boxer, he had put meat on his bones, and stood confident and handsome as he danced sprightly around his opponents in the ring, popping them with jabs and punches before he floored them with a whopper punch.

Yet, as he meticulously brought his plans closer to completion, Crusher's attitude mellowed, his rage soon turning into elation in anticipation of his achieved goal.

Knowing they could defend themselves with their fists, Crusher concluded it vital to take each of them by surprise. *It should not be difficult. They are completely unsuspecting. I shall not kill, but maim, and I know the perfect place to see it done.*

Satisfied that the trap was set and ready, he visited the boxing tournament one more time. *Enjoy it all, glory boys. Soon you'll be beaten and*

Dick Miller

broken, and no one will give you the time of day. You won't be such a pretty sight when Crusher gets through with you.

At the end of the matches, Crusher summoned a nearby uniformed worker he saw sweeping up debris and depositing it in trash cans. Offering him a five dollar bill, he directed him to deliver two envelopes to the boxers. He watched from a distance as they received and opened the envelope and removed the contents. Their eager, approving faces brought him complete satisfaction. *The deed was as good as done.*

•

Making a quick exit from the elevator, Crusher and his aide left the public area headed for a vacant restroom. Approaching their destination, they heard distant cries of distress. Within the expanse of the fairground complex, any person hearing the sound would be hard-pressed to determine its source. Only the two men walking side by side knew the origin of the cries, and that brought a smile of satisfaction to Crusher's face.

After exchanging his uniform for his street clothes in the restroom, Crusher passed an envelope filled with a wad of cash to his helper and reminded the bribed operator of his agreement to leave the city and disappear immediately.

•

Early in the morning hours of the following day, several custodial crews entered an elevator of the east tower. One crew stepped off at the Rocket Car platform area, while a husband and wife team rode to the top. An hour before sunrise, the elevator door opened at the top, its interior light racing forward to strike a path through the darkness. Charles and Martha had worked here since the fair opened, always beginning their routine at the top of the east tower.

Charles turned on lights before they went about their work in this quiet place of solitude. Even the distant sounds of an awakening city blended into the mix that made the lofty tower their own private place of peace and comfort. Not churchgoers, the couple found spiritual enrichment each morning in this tower, feeling a closer connection to the God they believed created the universe...or at least, this small piece of it.

Almost finished with their tasks, Martha spotted two young boys lying together on the floor in a partially obscured part of the exhibit. The

121

sun brought greater brightness to the scene.

"Charles," she called to her husband, "Look here."

Charles turned and ambled closer. "Why it's two boys...one white boy and the other colored."

The boys stirred as the couple approached them.

The man, noticing the hands of these strangers were marred and swollen, stepped in front of his wife to protect her. There were other signs of possible roughhousing, including minor cuts and bruises and clothes stained with grease and dirt. A rip in the Negro boy's shirt left part of his chest and abdomen exposed.

"All right, you two, git up, and I mean now," Charles roared, "and don't you try anythin'. I got stuff in this here pail that I kin use to knock y'r brains from here to Toledo!"

Buck and K.O. stood up quickly. At the sight of someone who could get them out of this prison, they both jumped forward, voicing their pleas together, ignoring the old man's warnings.

"Help us, please..."

"Are we glad to see you..."

"...Tried to kill us last night..."

"...Threw us over into the machinery..."

"Please...get us out of here..."

Instead of defending himself with the cleaning implements, the man flinched at their sudden movement and dropped the tin bucket, which rolled across the floor spilling its contents.

As the man sputtered out incoherent words at the uproar, Martha drew him back and quieted him. "Just a minute, Charles. Calm down," she said like a schoolmarm correcting a child. "It sounds like these boys might be in trouble and need our help." Then, to the boys, she said, "Tell us exactly what happened."

"We came to the tower because we both got a pass that said workers at the Fair could get a free tour of the tower after it closed," Buck said. "But we were the only two to arrive, and the elevator operator left us off up here and said he was going down for the others."

"Now wait just a minute. You mean to say someone brought you up here after closing? Who do you think is going to believe that?" the old man barked.

"It's true, sir," K.O. said.

"Let me see that pass," the man demanded.

"We can't," Buck said. "We gave it to the elevator operator...and when he left us up here there was a guy in a guide's uniform who sent us to look at the elevator shaft and then he came up behind us a few minutes later, and threw us over the rail. Honest to God, mister…we ain't lying."

Wearing a stern visage, the man asked, "How'd you two get up here? I know what you kids are like…you were out for some kind of a thrill, weren't you!" The man grabbed each of them by the scruff of the neck and dragged them to the elevator. This time, the wife remained silent, not interfering, and Buck and K.O. did not try to overpower the old man, but Buck strongly protested the man's accusations.

"Mister, this crazy guy tried to kill us! We grabbed what we could and hung on for dear life! We screamed for help, but no one came. Finally, we struggled and helped each other back up onto the platform and fell down exhausted."

The man opened the elevator door. "Git in the elevator, and don't try anythin'," he ordered.

The couple took Bucky and K.O. down to the rocket car level, where the other members of the custodial crew were gathered.

"Found these two up at the top," the old man explained. "Seems like they were horsin' around with the elevator operations."

The old man's wife said gently, "They told us someone brought them up here after the tower was closed and tried to kill them."

The group observed them in silence. Then one of them, younger and more robust than the others, stared at them and said with a gruff voice, "What the hell kind of a cock-and-bull story is that? You stand here with torn clothes and filthy faces. We've seen your kind around here. Anyone can see you're a couple of hoodlums up to no good. How the hell did you get up there?"

Buck stammered, "We told them…we got this pass…it said – "

The young goliath, obvious supervisor of the custodial staff, stopped Bucky in mid sentence, shoved him back, and pinned him to the wall of the elevator shaft. "Shut up, you bastard!"

Two others grabbed K.O.'s arms and held him in their grip.

The brute shoved his knee between Buck's legs, clamped his arm across his neck and pressed him so hard against the wall with his massive hulk that Buck could hardly breathe.

With his face twisted with rage, the behemoth turned to the old couple. "Did they do any damage up there? Did you find any liquor or beer bottles?"

"No, nothing like that."

Someone said, "They could have thrown bottles over the side, Mr.

123

Gunner."

Just inches away from Gunner's face, Buck could distinctly smell liquor on the super's breath.

"Tim. Go up with Charles and check things out. Come back and tell us what you find."

Then, with a display of Herculean force, Gunner dragged Buck to the edge of the platform and bent his head and upper body over the rail, clamping a huge hand on his head, forcing him to look straight down at the ground. "Tell us the truth boy. There's nobody up here who is gonna keep me from turning you into a squashed ripe tomato on the pavement...which would give me great pleasure."

Martha stepped timidly toward the enraged supervisor. "Mr. Gunner, Mr. Gunner," she said trying to restrain him. "Don't you think we should call the police, Mr. Gunner?"

Gunner held a firm grip on Buck, and didn't answer.

"If we hurt them, we'll never know what happened. Mr. Gunner, the police can get the truth out of them. We need to get on with our work."

Gunner glanced at the others. No one disputed Martha, and every one on the platform stared at him with pleading eyes, as though they wanted the whole violent thing to end and get back to work.

Gunner took several deep breaths. Then he relaxed his hold on Buck. "Call the police," he said.

The group brought the two bedraggled boys down to the ground, and soon after, the authorities came to question the alleged intruders.

•

At the station, the police led Buck and K.O. into an interrogation room, where two officers stood waiting. "Sit down," one of them said, as he pulled up a chair and sat down on the other side of the table.

"Okay, boys," the officer said. "You're both in pretty big trouble. The best way to avoid serious consequences is to own up to the truth."

Buck's eyes glared through slits under brows contorted in anger. *Geez, they're treating us like criminals. They haven't even checked out our bruises. My hands are all torn up.* He squirmed in his chair as though he was sitting on a bed of sharp tacks.

"We already told you guys our story," Buck snapped. "You can see how beat up we are. What about the one who attacked us and tried to kill us? Is anybody trying to find him?"

Buck's sudden, atypical outburst towards an officer of the law took

K.O. by surprise, and he squirmed nervously in his chair as he watched Buck's face and heard his angry tirade.

The detective leaned forward, stuck his finger in Bucky's face and said, "I didn't ask for any of your lip, kid – just the *truth!*"

Buck swallowed hard and shut his mouth.

Gaining his composure, K.O. said, "Sir, a young man gave us an envelope. When we opened it, it had an invitation...written all fancy wit' nice letterin'. It said we done such a good job workin' at the fair that we could use the ticket for a free ride up the tower. We ain't got the ticket, 'cause we done gave it to the man who took us up the elevator."

"Look, fellas. Your story really seems bizarre...maybe too strange for you to have concocted it. That you went over the rail and were in the shaft seems evident. There are definite signs of that. But your claim someone else was up there with you to harm you...so far, it's not holding water."

"It's the truth," K.O. stated.

"Come on, fellas. Why don't you level with me? You guys climbed up there for kicks, right? Did somebody dare you to do it? We can understand, if that's what happened. Listen, I was a kid once. I know how easy it is to get into trouble. But it will go easier for you if you don't lie to me."

Buck felt the pressure building in him again. Finally, he said, "What if it's true? Then you guys are sitting on your duffs wasting your time trying to get us to confess to something we didn't do while you ought to be out there searching for the crazy son of a bitch who tried to murder us."

The detective shoved his chair back against the wall and stood. "That's it, cuff 'em, Willie, and take 'em down to the slammer. I've heard just about all I want from these roughnecks." Then, scorching the boys with his piercing eyes, he said with a voice laden with sarcasm, "Boys, this pad is free. You won't need any passes to get into our jail."

29. JAILBIRDS

"You've got a visitor."

Buck and K.O. went to the bars and strained their necks to see who came to visit them.

Estelle slipped through the partially opened door and walked to their cell.

She wore a simple blue dress falling to mid-calf length and belted at the waist. With a V neckline, short sleeves, and buttons down the front to the waist, it conformed perfectly to her figure. Over her hair, she wore a ribbon band with a bow fastened at one end, completing the ensemble. A stylish touch, the bow enhanced the natural beauty of her face.

As she approached them, K.O. fixed his eyes on Estelle. *She's every bit as beautiful in a simple dress as she was in that uniform.*

"You poor dears," she said. "When I found out you were arrested, I was so troubled. I just had to come down to see how you were."

K.O. held the bars tighter. She put her hand on his. He felt an immediate surge of arousal throughout his body. Fearing she might feel his throbbing pulse or hear the drumbeat of his pounding heart, his face turned hot with embarrassment.

Captivated with each other, Bucky's presence was oblivious to them. His concentration paralyzed, Estelle's comforting words blew right past the young boxer. The touch of her smooth hand and the fragrant smell of her body filled K.O.'s senses.

"How did this happen?" Estelle asked in a soft tone.

126

K.O. stammered, his tongue tied in a knot. Bucky explained their ordeal to her.

"That is an amazing story." Estelle said, "I believe it. What a terrible experience. I wanted to bring something to cheer you up," she said, "but the only things I could find were these two apples." She pressed one into each boy's hand.

"K.O.," she said, "Please forgive me for being short with you in the hallway that night. I wasn't free to talk about personal things."

Bucky felt his eyes widen in surprise at hearing that information. Remembering K.O. asked to take a bathroom break, he put the pieces together. *Well I'll be...I wonder what he said to her in the hall. That shrewd charmer.*

When Estelle put the apple into K.O.'s hand, she caressed his hand with both of hers. "I really am interested," she said softly. K.O. felt his heart racing, but his voice constricted, and he stood mute.

"You're both sweethearts," she said before she left.

"Thanks for the apples. They're great," Buck said after biting into it.

•

Early the next morning, the police met with managers and other Century of Progress workers, who supervised operations in the East Tower complex. It included Mr. Lowe, the general supervisor, as well as Mr. Clarence Gordon. Only an urgent concern would have brought Mr. Gordon to the fairgrounds before his usual reading of the morning paper over breakfast.

Peter Gassman, the police detective addressed them, "We think these boys were up to no good, but we're not sure what their precise intent may have been. There was no vandalism or sign of forced entry to the Sky Ride. Right now, our men are going over the place with a fine-toothed comb. Are there any other ways to get to the tower besides the elevator?"

Mr. Lowe said, "I alerted the officers earlier to other ways they may have gotten to the tower. But they found everything secured."

Detective Gassman said, "With no sign of a break in, it must be assumed they were on the inside before closing. The cleaning crew said the elevators were all at ground level when they arrived, so these intruders were stuck up there in the tower. Is there some place up there they could have hidden when the last elevator came down?"

A custodial supervisor said, "It is assumed the elevator operator makes certain no one is left behind. I suppose it's possible, if the operator fails to do that, one might seclude himself behind the raised platform of the Otis exhibit, but that seems unlikely."

"What do you think about their claim someone else was up there with them and pushed them over the guardrail?"

Mr. Lowe said, "It doesn't make any sense. It's surprising enough that two of them remained up there without anyone seeing them...but three? That doesn't seem possible."

One of the managers said, "If, as they say, the operator who brought them up went back down, wouldn't the one who assaulted them be stranded up there, too?"

"Maybe...unless the intruder had the cooperation of an accomplice who could have operated the elevator to bring him back down," Gassman said.

"Detective Gassman, surely you don't suspect one of our own operators. I can't believe any of them would be involved in such an undertaking. Of course they were all recently hired at the opening of the Fair, and it would seem unwieldy and unnecessary to conduct extensive background checks on such employees."

"At this point, we need to talk to all who may have been involved; especially the operator assigned to the last shift. We'll need your assistance to arrange that for us."

"Of course, you'll have our full cooperation," Mr. Lowe said.

Detective Gassman paused, as he gave further thought to the matter. Then he said, "Mr. Gordon. I understand you knew the boys somewhat. What's your impression?"

"That's correct, officer. I invited them to my home. I must say they impressed me with their creative ideas and their well-mannered behavior. I can't quite understand how they came into this situation. It seems out of character for them. But then, you never know, do you?"

Detective Gassman had a few theories of his own, but thought it premature to mention them. Since there was no vandalism or theft, he reasoned the two boys probably went up on a dare. It was simply a lust for adventure...not unusual for boys their age. *Certainly, such shenanigans cannot be tolerated. Perhaps a couple of days in the clinker would put an end to their mischief*

"That'll be it for now," Detective Gassman said. "No doubt I'll have more information and more questions for you as the investigation progresses. Meanwhile, we'll keep the two mischief-makers under lock and key for trespassing. Thank you, gentlemen, for your cooperation."

•

"Come on, boys," the jailer said as he unlocked their cell.

"Where are we going?" Bucky asked.

"Back to the fairgrounds. The management has a few things they need to say to you."

"Holy shit, our asses are cooked," Buck whispered to his comrade as they followed the jailer. K.O. flashed a worried glance back at him.

Several hours later, Buck and K.O. sat in an office facing Mr. Gordan, Detective Gassman and Mr. Lowe.

Bucky and K.O. cowered at the sight of Mr. Gordon, their heads hanging.

"That was some helluva tall tale you told about your experience on the tower," detective Gassman said.

"Yes, sir, I know. But it's true, sir," Buck said.

Buck saw K.O.'s hands trembling. *Geez, he can flatten a big guy in a minute in a street fight, but now he's shaking like a leaf!*

Mr. Gordon said, "When I heard what you did, I was very disappointed...after we did so much to build you up and promote you on the Midway."

Mr. Lowe put in a comment, as well, "You're lucky they locked you up in jail. If I had gotten my hands on you, you'd be a lot worse off."

A tightening in the back of Buck's throat constricted and he swallowed hard. He shifted his glance away from them. "I'm sorry," Detective Gassman said. "We didn't mean to be so harsh."

A slight grin appeared on Mr. Gordon's face, but the two detained boys were too scared to notice.

"The fact is we have reason to believe your story."

The boys lifted their heads.

"Wha...what did you say?" Buck asked.

"Take a look at this." Officer Gassman pulled a small printed card from his pocket and handed it to them.

"Holy smokes." Buck said.

K.O.'s eyes widened and his lips curled up, his teeth flashing in a wide smile.

"Someone found that on the elevator floor at the Sky Ride," Mr. Gordon said.

The boys could hardly believe what they saw as they recognized the pass they gave to the elevator operator on the night of their attack.

30. NEW EVIDENCE

"One of our custodians picked it up. He quickly read it and thought it was a free pass of some kind, so he put it in his pocket thinking it might be good for something. If he hadn't done that, it probably would have ended up in the trash.

"Doesn't that prove we were telling the truth, sir?"

"I'd say so, Buck. Giving further credibility to your story is the clean print of a thumb we think might match that of the elevator operator on duty that night who failed to show up for work the next night. If he has a criminal record, we may identify him. We think this was the work of at least two people. Our men are searching for the missing worker, but so far, he seems to have disappeared into nowhere."

"In the tower," Gassman said, "we found a discarded Guide's uniform in a nearby lavatory.

"Boys, we came to the conclusion that not only did someone want to harm you, but whoever it was went to great lengths to plan careful details. It was an intentional ambush. Do you know anyone that might do this?

The boys eyed each other with blank stares.

"I can't think of anyone," Bucky said.

"Me neither," K.O. agreed.

"Please forgive me, boys, but I must ask you this. Have either or both of you been involved in any kind of criminal activities?"

"No sir!" Buck said.

"Has anyone ever threatened you?"

"Not that we know of."

After a minute's reflection, Bucky said, "Sir, could it be a case of mistaken identity? Maybe it was someone else they intended to hurt."

"That's possible," Gassman said. "but not likely. It sounds like your attacker had plenty of time to notice if you were the wrong targets...unless your attacker was a stooge for someone else."

"I just thought of something," K.O. said. "Remember, Buck, how that elevator guy knew our names? We talked about that and wondered how he knew who we were."

"It confirms our suspicion your attacker was someone who knew you well," Gassman said.

The questions continued. Buck and K.O. once more recounted a full recollection of the events.

"No one is bringing charges against you, so you are free to go. But don't think about leaving town," Gassman said. "There will be further investigation, and more questions, to be sure. This incident is serious, and your lives may still be at risk. We want to get to the bottom of this."

Mr. Gordon said, "In the meantime, an important weekend is approaching, and we want you two to be up and ready for a good show on the Midway."

"We'll have some extra police patrolling the Midway, just in case," Gassman said.

Once outside, Buck and K.O. flashed broad grins of satisfaction at each other. Buck pictured himself back in the ring with a contender laid out before him and cheering fans shouting their acclamation. He glanced at K.O. again. His boxing partner stood dreamy eyed staring into space, totally distracted.

"Ha!" Buck exclaimed. "I can see where your thoughts are, stud."

Buck could tell by K.O.'s sheepish grin that he hit the mark.

"Yeah...," K.O. drawled, "Estelle. I got to see her again."

Neither of them gave any thought to their attacker still at large.

"I feel sure we weren't the intended victims," Buck told K.O. and he agreed. Their troubles were over, and the veiled warning Tiny had given Bucky about a mysterious stranger who searched for him remained a distant and unheeded memory.

•

In spite of the management's efforts to suppress publicity that might be unfavorable to the Fair, the incident on the Sky Ride appeared in the *Chicago Daily News*. The banner headline on the front page, "Trouble on the Sky Ride," brought little comfort to the administrators, who feared attendance at the Fair, and the Sky Ride, in particular, would plummet. A news photographer had captured some candid shots of Buck and K.O. in boxing poses that appeared along with the story. As feared, attendance at the Sky Ride dropped off for several weeks, particularly in the evening hours, and the park emptied earlier after dusk.

Attendance at the Fair, however, did not drop. Curiosity sparked an interest in the boxing attraction and especially, the two boys featured in it. They were survivors of a terrible experience, and people wanted to see them up close and in action.

Some weeks later, the management decided it would be to their advantage to promote the incident. Fear had subsided, and an increase occurred in visitors to the East Tower who wanted to see "where it all happened that night." Guides referred to the incident as "an unsolved mystery," and a story popularized at the time claimed a ghost inhabited the East Tower and assaulted the victims.

People treated Buck and K.O. as celebrities, recognized and greeted them. Although their attacker had overcome and subdued them, many regarded Buck and K.O. as courageous heroes. A group of young girls brought clipped photos from the pages of the Chicago Daily News and asked each to autograph them.

As time passed, the incident faded into the background, attendance at the boxing exhibition and the Sky Ride le-veled off, and the boxers returned to their normal routines. The police eventually abandoned their efforts to determine who attacked Buck and K.O., and closed the file.

During this time, a familiar figure continued to appear at the boxing exhibitions. Crusher cursed all the time and effort he spent on the Sky Ride preparations and his failure to damage his victims, who now occupied a position of even greater adulation by the people. His continued visits to the boxing matches cemented his determination to trap and slaughter them in the most cunning and brutal manner he could devise.

SEPTEMBER, 1933

An early riser, Buck had a practice of going for his morning preparations to a rest room located in a remote part of the fairgrounds. More accessible to fairground employees than visitors, the lavatory became his private grooming salon most of time. As finely appointed as those in the heart of the fairgrounds, the spacious room had white tiled walls and floors, bright lights, hot and cold water sinks with mirrors, and clean stalls.

As usual, Bucky saw no one inside and had his choice of sinks with mirrors. After washing his upper body, and brushing his teeth, Buck slipped on his new slick looking round necked short sleeved shirt with its *Century of Progress World's Fair* logo. Moving his head from side to side, he admired his reflection. He liked the way the shirt hugged his chest and torso, accentuating his sculpted assets, the result of regular workouts. Standing at an angle with his nose in the air in a haughty manner, he flexed his muscles in a Charles Atlas pose and admired himself in the mirror. Then he moved close to the mirror and from a back pocket, he whipped out his prized accessory...a comb...and raked it through his thick, luxurious black hair. Satisfied, he shoved the comb into his back pocket. He leaned forward for a close up view, his clear, grey eyes scoping out his face for blemishes. With his finger, he smoothed an eyebrow to mask a cut inflicted in a recent boxing match.

Suddenly, a face appeared behind him. Buck's comely mirror image changed into a mask, eyes widened with terror, gaping mouth and dropped jaw.

Buck gasped. A massive arm clamped around his neck, nearly crushing it, stifling any sound. Holding him firmly, the man moved his hideous face forward next to Bucky's and peered into the mirror at him. Filled with terror, Buck's eyes stretched wider as he saw the horrific image staring back at him. One side of the man's face drooped in a misshapen mass. Discoloration, random tufts of facial hair and scarring lent an inhuman quality to the image. The victim's eyes fixed on the vacant socket of the attacker's missing eye. The tormentor rolled his good eye around, activating tendons and muscle strands inside the empty socket into rapid movements in a macabre, but meaningless dance. Buck felt vomit fill his throat but his airway was blocked by a muscled arm. He shuddered, and struggled to free himself, but the creature shoved Buck's face closer to the mirror for a close-up view of the action in the socket.

"Remember me, champ?" the villain said in a hoarse voice. "The name is Crusher...that's Crusher, from Lima, Ohio! You fixed me good, little bastard, but now I've got you and I'm gonna break you in pieces."

An instant memory flashed into Buck's mind, recalling the incident.

With full realization of who held him, adrenalin shot through his body. He furiously battled to break free, but Crusher tightened his grip to the breaking point, and with his other hand, smothered the boy's nose and mouth with a wet handkerchief. Bucky's struggling weakened, and he felt his arms falling limp as the chloroform soaked cloth turned everything black.

Crusher made his way to the elephant tent, carrying Buck's limp body out of the rest room unseen. He lifted the flap of the tent and scanned the area. Except for the intrusion of daylight through a few openings in the tent, it was dark. *Good.*

Crusher entered, carried the unconscious boy to the designated spot, lifted Bucky from his shoulder and laid him on the ground next to K.O., who had already been subdued with chloroform and positioned here.

Some days before, Crusher had checked out the tent and noted the long chains securing the elephants to their stakes. *What a perfect setting for an accident. How convenient that God has provided these chains for me.*

Crusher suffered no pains of conscience in this matter. He was acting against those who broke the law, attacked a police officer and needed to pay for their crimes. He based his decision to become a police officer on his strong conviction that everyone should adhere to the letter of the law, and those who did not should suffer the full consequences for their deeds.

Careful not to disturb the elephants, Crusher laid out a long portion of a chain in a straight line. He placed the two unconscious forms face to face on their sides and taking a middle portion of the chain, led it around their necks, then down a back, through their legs, up the other's back and around their necks again. Then he pushed the duo into place with Bucky face down on top of K.O. The rest of the chain remained in a haphazard pattern between stake and animal.

It's taking longer than the fifteen minutes I planned. I've got to hurry.

Finishing his task, Crusher could not resist taking a few steps back to admire his handiwork. *Absolute perfection! This tactic cannot fail. If all goes as planned, they will survive, but adulation will turn into repulsion!* He felt confident their mutilated bodies would suggest the two boys had been inside the tent where they should not have been. Some sudden disturbance must have caused the elephants to scatter, snarling the victims in the chains. *Such an unfortunate accident.*

The trap had been set. Crusher lifted the tent flap, turned and reviewed the set up one more time. Satisfied, he took out a gun, pointed it toward the tent's top, tightened his finger around its trigger, and fired.

As he made his escape, he caught a glimpse of elephants rearing up onto their hind legs, trumpeting their alarm at the sound that had broken the serenity of their dwelling place.

31. CRUSHER SAVORS A VICTORY

SEPTEMBER, 1933, Chicago, Illinois

Crusher sat on the edge of his bed in his room at Windermere House. He took a deep breath, arched his back and extended his hands towards the ceiling in an energizing early morning stretch. *I think a stroll down Hyde Park Boulevard to the newspaper stand will be a good way for me to start the day.* He stood, relieved himself in the bathroom, splashed his hands and face, ran a toothbrush quickly over his teeth a few times, pulled on some pants, shirt and shoes and went out the door.

Located in the Hyde Park district of Chicago, Windermere House offered clean rooms, moderate prices, and a close proximity to the Fair. An early morning shower had washed the streets and sidewalks, leaving a clean, fresh aroma in the air. Crusher's ears picked up the sounds of mocking birds singing in the trees above him. Ordinarily, he paid little attention to such simple pleasures, but on this morning, for the first time in years, he felt carefree and exuberant.

He had reason to feel elated. His criminal network was growing and providing him with more than a decent income. With his operation expanding to major cities, it pleased him that the demise of Al Capone had cleared the way for him to establish a new cell for operations in Chicago. Unlike Capone's overt crimes, Crusher's discreet underground activities were not likely to incite the direct attention of the authorities.

He might have sought housing with some of his operatives, but he scrupulously maintained his policy of concealing his identity from any of his informants.

Another situation gave Crusher more reason for his elation. The night before, he had taken a giant step towards satisfying a long time issue of personal justice. Two lawbreakers ran free and unpunished for crimes in Lima, Ohio against the B&O Railroad and against him personally. His carefully crafted plan worked masterfully. Now, in all likelihood, the two offenders lay mangled and maimed...probably in a local hospital.

He purchased the paper, tucked it under his arm and began the walk back to Windermere. Tempted to tear open the pages immediately and read the account of their misfortune, he was determined instead to carry the paper unopened to the comfort and seclusion of his room, where he could savor the moment of the detailed report.

On the walk home, he thought about possible outcomes from an elephants' stampede. *Did they suffer broken limbs? Did the chains crush them? Maybe the chains pulled tight around their necks and decapitated them!* He laughed aloud at the thought, oblivious to a passing stranger who gave him a curious look. Then Crusher became reflective. *No...no...they must not be decapitated. That would be too severe, and too soon. I still have more destruction to unleash against them. Perhaps they are in a hospital. Yes...that's it. They must be hospitalized. I think I will visit them there.*

He thought about sending them flowers with a get-well card and a package, but feared the purchase might be traced back to him. *I must not risk leaving this to others. I will forget the flowers, and deliver the package and a card myself. It should not be difficult to find a private moment during regular visiting hours.* He imagined himself stealthily going to their bedsides while they slept and leaving a small wrapped present containing get-well wishes and his signature eye patch. Once again, he laughed loudly as he quickened his pace to get back to his room.

Where is it? I've searched the pages over and over. Nothing. Not a word. They could not have escaped. A feeling of panic gripped Crusher. Beads of perspiration appeared on his forehead. Once again, he paged through the paper, finding no report about any incident with the elephants.

Nothing appeared in any newspaper for the next two days. Finally, Crusher made a visit to the Fair to investigate. He went straight to the spot where the two boys took on contenders and found a group of workers dismantling everything associated with the boxing exhibition.

Unable to repress his desire to know what happened, he went directly to the Century of Progress general office. Claiming to be a friend of the boxers, Crusher asked what had happened to them.

"Truth is," the clerk told him, "they left without notice. Soon after, however, they contacted us and said they were called away on an urgent personal matter, and would not be back."

"Do you have an address?" Crusher asked. "I owe them some money."

"As a matter of fact, we do. They asked us to forward their paychecks to them." The clerk flipped through some employee files and then said, "Here it is. I'll write it down for you."

Crusher read the address. It was a P.O. Box in New York City. He smiled at the man and thanked him.

Before the day ended, Crusher was on his way to New York City with renewed resolve.

Dick Miller

32. THE CHICAGO
FAIR REVISITED

The sound of the gunshot ended the silence in the elephant tent. The elephants reared up, and the ground around them shook like an earthquake when their feet landed. Their natural response would have been to run from the spot where Crusher fired the gun, but the noise reverberated throughout the tent, masking the place of its origin.

Instead of bolting off in one or more directions, the elephants huddled closer together, bumping and scraping against one another. The chains moved haphazardly, spasmodically wrenching the boy's wrapped forms several times. With one jerk of the chain, Bucky fell from atop K.O. and clear of the action. Links of chain, however, remained dangerously wrapped around K.O. Bucky stirred. Then, bruised and dirty, and his head still pounding from the residual effects of chloroform, he weakly lifted it and peered at the carnage around him.

The elephants continued shrieking as they collided with each other. Through blurred vision, Buck tried to assess the scene. The last thing he remembered, Crusher had plastered a soaked cloth over his face. *Where the hell am I? What is this place? Elephants going wild!* One of the animals rushed toward him and he quickly rolled out of the way avoiding the crushing blows of trampling feet. The reality of Crusher's demonic plan unfolded: *Good God! The monster set us up to be mangled by the elephants!*

Buck lifted his head, and when his eyes fell upon K.O., he flinched

139

to attention. Still shaky, Buck stood and stumbled over to his unconscious friend.

"K.O.! Wake up, damn it!" Buck yelled. He slapped K.O.'s face to revive him, and struggled to pull the chains from his friend.

K.O. opened his eyes and blinked a few times, then gave Buck a blank stare.

"Ohm...my head!" he said. "What hit me?"

Half conscious, he rolled about grunting and moaning as Buck yanked the chains from under him.

"K.O., help me! Got to get you freed!"

K.O. feebly struggled, oblivious to what had happened. Liberating K.O. from his bonds, Bucky dragged him out of danger.

"What happened? Shit! I don't remember nuttin'," K.O. droned.

"Crusher...it was Crusher...the bull we bashed in Lima, Ohio! He tried to kill us!" Buck yelled.

Their movement rekindled the elephants' fear. This time, the animals ran haphazardly in all directions. One elephant ran so fiercely it snapped its stake from the ground. Running away from the boys, the elephant plowed into the side of the tent, nearly bringing the whole structure down on their heads.

Visibly shaken, but energized by imminent danger, the two ran stumbling away and ducked through a flap in the tent's side.

They barely managed to evacuate before others, alerted by the noise, came running to the scene. The first workers met with an appalling sight. The elephants were scattered; some up on their hind legs and trumpeting loudly; others stretching their chains to their limits; a few others ran free, their broken chains bouncing and striking at everything in the way. It took a full twenty- five minutes to calm the elephants and bring the situation under control. Officials had the presence of mind to keep would-be spectators away from the tent.

The cause of the disturbance remained a mystery. No evidence of the plot Crusher had devised was apparent. Anyone later detecting the small hole in the tent's top would not likely connect it to this happening.

Dick Miller

33. HARLEM Y.M.C.A.

SEPTEMBER, 1933, New York City, New York

When Buck and K.O. arrived in New York City, they made tracks for Harlem, where K.O. had friends from former days. In his heyday, K.O.'s father, "Fightin' Joe Franklin" was well known and admired as the local boy who made good. K.O. knew the territory and it felt good to be back on his own turf.

From the days when he lived in Harlem, K.O. remembered a cheap and clean flophouse. The Walker House on 128th St. offered them separate rooms, each big enough for a cot, a broken down dresser and a chair. Each room had one window to the street. A clean community washroom in the basement offered showers, a big sink for washing clothes, and racks to dry them – all for forty cents a night.

Through his contacts, K.O. landed a job at the YMCA on West 135th St. as a janitor and boxing instructor on weekdays for two dollars a day. A brand new facility, built the year before, it replaced the old YMCA located directly across the street. Even in these lean days, the popular YMCA organization found philanthropic support from well-to-do residents of the city.

Bucky was not as fortunate. Few jobs were available in the city and a white boy had little prospects of finding work in Harlem, so Buck scouted out other parts of the city. He claimed to be older than his 16

141

years, but to prospective employers, he was a kid, whatever his age, and they passed him by in favor of older boys or adults.

Buck dragged his feet one by one up the stairs to his room at the Walker House. Grabbing the doorframe, K.O. leaned out to watch Bucky's slow, methodical walk up the stairs. Buck came to the top, turned and walked down the narrow passage towards K.O.

"Hey, Champ. Did ya find anything today?"

Buck remained silent and pushed by K.O. and headed for his own cubicle.

"Hey...what the hell. What's up, Buck? You look like shit."

"Leave me alone."

K.O. put his hand on Buck as he passed to detain him. Buck brusquely removed his friend's hand from his shoulder and shoved him away.

"Whoa...this ain't like you, champ. What happened? You look like a truck ran over you."

Buck stopped. Slumped over with his head hung, eyes glued to the floor and drooping shoulders, Buck looked like a vacuum had sucked him dry. Then he leaned forward and collapsed in K.O.'s arms, clinging to him as though K.O. was a buoy afloat in a turbulent sea.

"What's got you down, pal? Are you feelin' this way 'cause you didn't find work?"

"It's not that, K.O."

"Tell me."

"It's...the *nightmares*. It's Crusher. I can't get him out of my head."

"What? Here? You think he'd come here. Hey, he hasn't a clue. He's miles away. By now he's forgotten you and me. You need to forget about him."

"You never saw him, K.O. He took you from behind. You didn't see him like I did...in the mirror. I can't describe him...his empty eye socket...and the other eye looking straight at me. I never saw anything like it. My heart must have stopped...and then he had me...his hand over my face. I wake up in the middle of the night and can't get back to sleep."

They talked for another hour before K.O. said, "Let's go down and hit the showers, champ. You'll feel better after that, you'll see. The old bastard could never find us here. Tomorrow come down to the gym and we'll do a little sparring. It will be like old times. You'll feel good."

"Yeah, I guess you're right. It's up to me to get him out of my head and my life. Thanks, K.O. for the kick in the ass. I needed that. You're the greatest, you know?"

"I'm da best there is. kid. Just come to me. I fix what's broken."

K.O.'s pep talk seemed to bring Buck back to his more self-assured state. He spent a lot of time sparring with K.O. and helping him with his pupils. Although the YMCA had a segregation policy based on the cultural make-up of its location, through K.O.'s influence, they accepted Buck as a visitor and friend at the all-Negro 135th St. location.

Of special interest to Bucky was the in-house printing operation to produce circulars and periodicals distributed by the Y. His interest derived from days as a youth in York, Pennsylvania, when he and his friend, Tim, spent a good deal of time in the printing room of The York Gazette, where Tim's father worked.

The typesetter at the Y was a fellow named Clyde. His reputation for producing clean, attractive, error-free copy was not sterling. Present one day with some members of the Y staff, Buck saw the Administrator rebuke the boy for a serious printing error that had angered some readers. No one at the Y discovered the error until after the distribution of the weekly circular. The text should have read as follows: *A priest will be present to say Mass in the chapel for Catholic residents on Sunday at 4:00 P.M.*

Instead following appeared: *A priest will be present to say ass in the chapel for Catholic presidents on Sunday at 4:00 P.M.*

On this day, Bucky stood nearby watching Clyde at work. He noticed the type case, with compartments for each character, propped up on Clyde's left, while the draft of the text lay flat on the table to his right. It seemed an awkward arrangement, which required Clyde to turn his head constantly from type case to text, increasing his margin for error. *A better arrangement of his tools would make the job more efficient.*

Then, a new distraction entered into the mix. A fly appeared and targeted Clyde's head as an item of special interest. Before long, the fly was giving the poor boy fits. Finally, Clyde folded the written draft into a weapon and waited for his chance to wallop the insect. His moment came as the fly lighted on top of the type case.

Swiftly, Clyde slammed the papers down on top of the fly.

Now that boy has a strong arm. He'd do better at boxing than type setting.

Clyde's action did not solve the problem, but instead produced a more disastrous dilemma. He missed the fly, which casually flew off as if to mock him. Even worse, the blow landed with such force it knocked the type case from its shaky moorings onto the floor. The case dropped with a terrible crash, spilling its characters everywhere.

Clyde stood frozen with disbelief at the carnage. He knew his job was on the line and trembled at the probable consequences of this fiasco.

He snapped out of his trance and fell to the floor, frantically trying to sort the disarray of letters. In a panic, he scattered the letters even more.

The noise brought spectators, some of which stifled giggles.

Amused, but feeling sorry for Clyde, Bucky went to help him. "Clyde, I assume you have a deadline to meet here. Forget about putting the letters back in order. Show me where you're at in the text, and I'll help you get it together."

Clyde nodded his response to this suggestion. "Some letters are still in their boxes," Buck said. "Let's try to separate the capital from the small letters. You get the capitals, and I'll go for the lower-case letters. Together we can move faster and get this thing back on track. Read the script a little at a time, and we can put the letters where they belong as we pick things up."

Together, they worked quickly and efficiently. Once the body of text was taking shape, Buck began to insert spacers into the text.

Clyde had never used the spacers before. "What are you doing?" he asked.

"I'm arranging the lines to make them easier to read. It takes more than letters to make the finished product easy on the eye. Since the characters are not all the same size, you need to put spacers between some to keep the words from bunching up. Do you know what I mean?"

The boy, Clyde, appeared puzzled.

"Your headline, for example, could use some shaping up. Some spacers will do the trick."

"I'm not sure I know what you mean," Clyde said.

"See the 'M' next to that 'I' in your headline. Can you see they are too close together?"

The boy observed what Bucky was doing and listened.

"Now watch what I'm doing here." Buck worked on the headline and made adjustments. "See, doesn't that look a lot better?"

Clyde's eyes beamed. "Yeah, it sure does. It really makes a difference."

"I think your boss will notice the change. You don't have to tell him I helped you." Buck addressed those who stood watching them. "I don't think anyone is going to tell your boss what happened here today, right guys?"

People standing around nodded in agreement. Some said, "Right."

Included in the gathering of spectators was a man from the New York Times who participated in a sponsorship program with a boy who worked out at the Y. He took Bucky aside and introduced himself.

"I'm Mr. Brad Quartermain, the executive foreman of the composing room at *The New York Times*. How did you pick up those skills?"

Bucky told him how he and his friend Tim spent hours in the printing room of *The York Gazette*.

"*The York Gazette?*" Mr. Quartermain repeated. "I've heard of the editor, 'Jess' Gitt. He's quite a controversial character."

"I know some people didn't like him and sometimes, letters came disagreeing with some of what he said. He had some strong opinions, and he stuck with them," Bucky said. "Me – I didn't understand politics and didn't much care to. I was just a kid, but I thought he was a fine man who knew what he was talking about."

"I agree with you," the man replied. "He was very progressive in his thinking. Before the Depression kicked in, he warned the public what was coming down the pike. While others were promoting a raging 'bull-market,' he had the guts to warn people about the signs of imminent economic collapse."

"But tell, me, how did you manage to learn so much just from hanging around the printing room?"

"Well, Tim's dad was a really nice guy," Bucky said. "I think he liked teaching us all about what he did. We were careful not to get in his way, of course. After a while, he let us help him set up the type. It was fun. I remember, though – my mom – she didn't like me going there so much, because I came home covered with ink."

Mr. Quartermain smiled knowingly.

"She never did forbid me from going there, though," Buck said. "One thing I really liked was that we got to read the paper before it hit the streets. I loved reading, and when you get used to checking for errors, you find yourself even reading the want ads."

Mr. Quartermain said, "I like what I saw and what I'm hearing from you. How old are you – I mean truthfully?"

"Sixteen," Buck confessed, but added eagerly, "but I'll be seventeen in January."

"Good. You're a sharp young man," Mr. Quartermain said. "Here's my business card. Come down to this address around eight-thirty in the morning, and ask for me. I'll have a job waiting for you in the composing room. Sound okay?"

"Okay." Buck said with a broad smile.

Buck read the card. The address was 229 West 43rd St. Buck went directly to K.O. and, with a gleam in his eye, flashed the calling card in front of his face. "Guess what?" he said.

34. 229 WEST 43RD STREET

Bucky saw the name on the front of the building: The New York Times Annex.

The people at the information desk directed him to the composing room. The noise grew louder as Buck walked up the stairs, and became deafening as he stood with wonder before the linotype machines.

"Hello, Bucky," he heard behind him over the noise. Bucky turned around and saw Mr. Quartermain, who reached out to shake his hand.

Another man stood at Mr. Quartermain's side. "Marty Jones, here, will work with you until you get the hang of it," Mr Quartermain said. "He will show you what you will be doing with these machines."

Marty Jones extended his hand and said, "Don't worry about the noise...you'll get used to it. Everything here is the very latest in the business."

"It's a far cry from *The York Gazette*," Buck said.

"Let me take you downstairs to our personnel office," Quartermain said. "We can discuss the details of your job and if you would like to work here, we can fill out and sign the forms, and we can start you right off. How does that sound, Buck?"

"Very good, sir."

Mr. Quartermain spoke to Marty. "I'll bring him back up here afterwards. Show him the ropes, Marty and stay with him. A week from today, I will want to meet with you to find out how our new employee

146

Dick Miller

is doing." He smiled at Bucky and led him to the personnel office.

Before the week ended, Bucky moved like an old hand with a team of workers who fed lines of letters on paper forms into the steaming hot machine that cast the letters into molten lead sentences.

"We produce fourteen lines per minute," Marty told Bucky. It was exciting to be a productive part of such a massive operation, even though the sound of the machines lingered in his head every night almost all the way home.

This is the best thing that's happened to me in my whole life! Buck concluded. His prospects for advancement were promising and his pay, at six dollars a week, seemed like a small fortune. Buck thought their search for a better tomorrow might be taking shape. Perhaps they could put down their roots and start life over again. *New York City! This is the place to be!*

That night, he wrote a long letter to his father and to Helen. He did not know the Altoona address, so he sent it in care of the Pennsylvania Railroad Altoona Locomotive Works, in the hope they would receive it. He told them about his friend, K.O., and some of the experiences they had on the road. He took care not to make riding the rails appear glamorous or safe, and urged Bud to stay put and help the family as much as he could. He missed his little brother the most, and could not forget how Bud had run after him when he left the house in Altoona. He closed his letter with well wishes.

> ...I hope you are all well. Give Lena and Lil a big hug for me, and tell Bud to keep his chin up. Maybe I'll be able to come home soon, but right now, I got a job and I need to stick to it. After I get a few paychecks, I'll send you some money.
>
> Missing you all and loving you,
>
> Bucky

In less than a week, Bucky had a reply from Helen. On behalf of them all, she expressed elation about his success. As he read on, he learned the family managed to make ends meet, but the work his father did, as breadwinner, was hard, and raising the kids in such circumstances was not easy.

147

Buck's job was also strenuous, and the noise of the workplace brought him back to the Walker House each night grateful for the peace and quiet he found there. Soon, he wrote another letter enclosing some cash from his first month's earnings and including some brief comments on his situation.

...Mr. Quartermain, my boss, says I'm doing well at my job. He told me he started off just as I am, and now he's the head of this whole department. I think there is a chance for me here to move up the ladder. The people here are great, and we get along pretty well, so I guess I'll be here for a while. As far as I'm concerned, New York City is the place to be.

Dick Miller

35. IN THE DEAD OF NIGHT

JANUARY, 1934

Sometime in the night, Bucky's eyes snapped open. There in the corner of his room loomed a huge, shadowy figure. As it leaned forward, a ray streaming in from a streetlight illuminated the face.

Crusher!

Crusher raised his hands into the light.

My God! He's got a rope…twisting it tight between his hands…

Bucky sprang from his cot spilling the bedclothes onto the floor. There was nowhere to go and the man was on him instantly. Crusher dropped the rope around his victim's neck and pulled it tight. It sliced into Bucky's neck. He couldn't breathe.

Choking me…can't get free…my arms…I can't move them…can't breathe …dragging me…to the window…can't resist. Migod! He's shoving me out the window!

Buck's fingers grabbed and tightened around the inside woodwork on the sides of the windows. Crusher dropped the rope. With a gasp, Buck sucked air into his lungs. Crusher used both hands to force Bucky out. He pried Bucky's fingers loose from one side, almost breaking them off. He grabbed Buck's leg, lifted it and forced it through the opening. Now Buck had one leg in and one outside the window, and held on with only one hand. He felt his grip slipping…then it was gone!

Buck felt himself flipped backwards out the window into a downward tumble. He wanted to scream, but his voice was mute.

149

He saw the street below much more distant than it should have been. He floated suspended...hanging in mid air...drifting so slowly to his death.

I won't look down. Turning his eyes upward, his heart stopped at the sight of Crusher's gleeful face staring down at him from the window. He looked down again. Now, incredibly, the street raced towards him with astounding speed and in the space of a millisecond, he saw in vivid clarity the texture of the pavement, and details of the debris that had blown against the curb.

Bucky bolted and sat straight up. Beads of cold sweat ballooned on his forehead and burst into rivulets. The bedclothes and his underpants were soaked from perspiration. His heart still pounded as if intent to leave it's chamber. The nightmare had ended...but the trembling and fear endured until daybreak. He suffered these symptoms whenever it happened. There were variations, but always the same recurring theme: *Crusher's final onslaught.*

Buck fell back and stared at the ceiling. *He couldn't be here. He could never find me in this city...not here.*

FEBRUARY 1934

Bucky arrived at work on schedule and headed for his station.

Louis, a co-worker approached him. "Hey, pal. Somebody's lookin' for ya. What's up, pal. You got a record or somethin'?"

Buck didn't say anything.

"That's him over there," Louie said, "talkin' to old man Quartermain. See?"

Buck saw an imposing, well-dressed man in a tailored overcoat, talking with his boss.

Just then, the two men turned toward them. Mr. Quartermain lifted his arm and pointed across the room at Bucky. Quartermain shot a hand signal for Buck to wait and they both began walking in his direction through the maze of machinery and workers.

Buck turned pale. *Holy shit. Sure as hell it's one of Crusher's goons...here in New York! Damn, he won't get me!*

Buck panicked. There was no time to think it out. He bolted like a wild stallion and took off.

"Wait," the man yelled over the din. "Buckingham Ellis! I need to talk to you."

•

Louis watched Bucky bolt out the door. He was only joking about Buck having a record, but when he saw how anxious Buck became he wondered if he had been right. The two men rushed over and stood near him. Louis heard some of their conversation over the noise. From bits and pieces he could hear, he fathomed that the man had asked for Bucky's address. He saw Mr. Quartermain write on a paper and give it to the man.

This all took place quickly, and as soon as the man had it in his hand, he scurried out of the room.

•

Coming up from the subway, Buck rounded a corner. Halfway down the block, Buck spied the man standing on the front steps of the Walker House.

How did he get here?

Buck darted off across the street, but he caught the eye of the stranger who started after him. The man was big, but could run fast. Sparked by a massive release of adrenalin, Buck raced down the street like a speeding comet.

With people at work at this hour of the morning, and streets relatively deserted, in no time at all, Buck reached the posh neighborhood on Manhattan's west side near the Hudson River. Here, stately oaks planted eons ago lined the streets. Lush potted plantings framed townhouse entrances distinguished by resplendent doors made of fine wood and etched glass.

Even though Buck was outpacing his stalker, the stranger kept him in his sights. Buck glanced behind him, still running like the wind. He ran through a park, but could not shake him. Leaving the park, he ran north on the sidewalk fronted by more residential town houses.

Hell, I can't shake him. He now ran on a long stretch of street between blocks. *Where can I go? An alley...that's it...an alley.* He took a quick turn, hoping he would elude his chaser, and ran. Ahead of him he saw a brick wall, but as he ran closer, he saw a space between the building and wall to the left and the right. Ducking behind the building to his left, he found himself smack up against a large locked entrance gate to one of the backyard gardens. Glancing quickly over his shoulder, he noted he would face the same situation if he'd gone to the right. The

151

space barely provided enough room for him to hide.

Trapped!

His breathing labored, Bucky pushed himself back against the gate. He stood as quietly as possible and listened.

Maybe he didn't see me come back here.

When Buck heard footsteps entering the alley, he broke into a sweat and rolled his eyes in disbelief. *Shit! My ass is cooked.*

As the footsteps came closer, he began to fumble for his dad's initialed pocketknife he still carried since the day he left home. His hands trembling, he managed to pull out the small blade. As he tried to position the knife in his sweaty hand, he dropped it and froze as it bounced noisily out into the alley. *Dammit!*

The man was coming straight for him. Buck clenched his fists. By the sound of the man's footsteps, he tried to gauge the moment when he would be just around the corner. He held his breath and stood perfectly still.

This is it!

Buck jumped out at him and landed a wild punch against the man's face. The stalker cried out in pain as he fell back. His head smashed hard against the wall of the other building and he slumped to the ground.

Bucky did not stick around to see what would happen next. Leaping over the fallen form, he bounded out of the alley and ran like a greyhound to the distant corner, where he disappeared down steps leading to the subway.

At nineteen, K.O. had gained a reputation in Harlem as an excellent tutor of young boys in the art of boxing. When Bucky stormed into the Y, he saw his partner dishing out lessons to a group of young fledglings. When K.O. spied Buck rushing in with furrowed brow and waving arms, he quickly stepped away from a punch thrown by a sparring student, and went to the edge of the ring. Leaning over the ropes, K.O.'s mouth dropped open and his eyes ballooned into big circles at Bucky's whispered words: "It's Crusher. He's here!"

K.O. turned to his trainees. "That's it for today, fellas." Then he jumped over the ropes and down onto the floor. "Buck, what are you saying?"

"K.O., Crusher's back. I barely escaped one of his goons. We got to get out...and I mean right now!"

"Hey, Champ, wait a minute. Slow down. You mean to say Crusher's here in New York?"

"I don't know if he's here himself, but it sure as hell looked like one of his hit men. He chased me from Harlem clear over to Morningside Park on the east side. He cornered me in a dead end alley and trapped me. I thought I was a dead duck."

"Holy crap! What happened?"

"I hid in a space behind the building, jumped out when he came close, whacked him and got the hell out of there."

"What we gonna do, Champ?"

"Listen, K.O., he knows where we live. He was looking for me at work and when I ran out and got home, there he was waiting for me. We can't go back to the flophouse. He's probably still searching for us right now. It ain't safe for us to stay here, either. Since he knew I worked at *The Times*, he must have a close watch on us. I say we clean out our lockers, forget what we got at the Walker House, and scram out of here."

Frantically, they grabbed up the few things stored in their lockers, lifted soap, towels and other items, threw them in bags and ran out the door without saying a word to anyone.

"Damn. Just as things were comin' together for us," K.O. said. He brutally kicked over a trashcan, spilling its contents into the street.

"Yeah," Buck said as they ran side by side. "This town's not big enough for us and Crusher and his stooges."

•

They hoofed it down to the freight yards along the Hudson.

"Hey, Champ, looky there," K.O. said pointing to a string of box cars. "See those orange-colored babies down the line? Those are reefers."

Buck could tell K.O. was in his element once again.

"Yeah," Buck said, "refrigerator cars. I know."

"It's like they're hooked up and ready to be loaded onto barges goin' over to Jersey," K.O. said. "They're sure to be headin' south. That's where we'll set ourselves up."

"What's the deal?" Buck asked. "Why a reefer?"

"Because it's empty and warm, Champ."

"How do you know that?" Buck asked.

"Coming from south to north, reefers are packed with frozen produce, and after they unpack 'em, they send 'em south again, empty."

"Empty," Buck repeated. "I see what you're saying. All the produce comes from the south in winter. There's no produce up here to ship back."

"Right," K.O. said.

By this time, the two had climbed on top of one of the reefers. K.O. opened a door to one of the bunkers located at each end of the cars.

"This is where they put the ice when they ship the goods. The compartment is insulated, so we'll be toasty warm in here, and it ain't likely the bulls will find us."

"Do all the 'bo's know this? What if someone who doesn't know gets in an empty one down south before it's loaded? Does that ever happen?" Buck asked.

"Yeah. Once I was in a yard in North Carolina and saw a big commotion where they were unloadin' the reefers. They had opened the plugged door and were taking off the goods, and someone noticed blood seeping from the bottom of one of the bunkers. Buck, you don't want to know what the guy in the bunker looked like after the ice dropped on him."

"And you're sure it's safe to ride in this one?" Buck asked.

"With it coolin' down again," K.O. said, "and us with nothin' warmer than the clothes we got on our backs, it's the best and safest place for us. Com'on, Champ. Let's get cozy and warm."

36. THE BERNARD SISTERS

FEBRUARY 1934, New York City, New York

Dr. Geoffrey Bernard, his wife, Agnes and two daughters, Emily and Nanette, lived across from Morningside Park on Morningside Avenue in an affluent neighborhood of upper Manhattan. On this warm summer day in February, Emily's mother thought it an opportunity to send the children outdoors for some fresh air.

"Girls, I want you to go outside. It's such a fine morning, and you've been cooped up inside now for weeks. Go out and play and get some sun."

"Oh, mama, do I have to play with Nan?" Emily said with a frown on her face.

"Of course, dear...you'll both have fun."

Agnes Bernard went to the secretary desk, opened a drawer and took out a small box.

"See what I have. I bought this a while ago and was saving it for you as a surprise when the weather turned nice."

"What is it mama?" Nanette asked.

It's a box of chalk. I know how much you like to play Hopscotch on the front sidewalk. Take a look. They're making chalk in different colors these days. See the variety?" She lifted the lid for them to see the rainbow of colors.

"Go get a sweater. It's still winter even though the sun is shining."

Emily rolled her eyes and reluctantly took the chalk from her mother while Nanette quickly retrieved her sweater, eager to make the first marks on the sidewalk with the new chalk. Emily slipped the sweater over her head, putting her arms in the sleeve, one at a time, as if mired in a tedious exercise. *Why do I always get stuck taking care of the brat? She's thirteen now, but I still have to play with her and watch her like she's a baby. Kid sisters are a pain.*

There was a time when Emily enjoyed playing Hopscotch with Nan and her friends, but now, as Emily approached her fifteenth birthday, her interests had changed. These days she gave more attention to boys on the street than to children's games. In fact, one boy in particular had captivated her with his slick behavior and good looks. As Emily led her sister out to the sidewalk, she reflected upon her obsession with the boy of her dreams.

Emily first encountered Josh last summer. She and her friends were jumping rope on the sidewalk. A group of boys lined up on the curb across the street watched them. With eyes locked on the girls and their mouths stretched into saucy grins, they postured like roosters, some with arms folded on their chest, others with hands on hips, some simply standing tall. For several minutes, they stood unnoticed, making bawdy comments to each other in whispered tones.

One of Emily's girlfriends gave a glance their way.

"Hey, girls," she said, "take a gander at that!"

"Are they watching us?" one asked.

"You bet your bottom dollar they are, Betsy, and they got hungry eyes.

For most of these girls, the brazen ogling by flirtatious boys was a new experience. Dropping the rope, they moved into a huddle for safety, taking quick glances over their shoulders at these young wolf cubs ready to pounce.

"What do they want?"

"What are they whispering?"

"Let's go on with our jumping and pretend like we didn't see them."

"Too late for that!"

"Girls, I'm not comfortable with this. Maybe we better pick up and leave."

"Don't be dumb. Pretend you don't see them," another said.

"If you stop all your fussing and take a good look, you might see something you like. What's so bad about boys messin' with us? I think I might like that," one said, immediately inciting shocked stares from the others.

Emily had already taken notice, especially of the tall alluring boy in the middle of the line. An air of impudent confidence exuded from his grinning face. This was Josh.

All the girls turned and gawked as Josh stepped off the curb and approached them. Emily felt her pulse quicken and temperature rise as Josh swaggered towards her, locking eyes with hers. Although his good looks attracted her, his brash behavior initially repulsed her. *Thinks he's pretty hot stuff, does he? He needs to be taken down a few rungs.*

She brazenly stepped off the curb and placed herself between him and the girls on the sidewalk. She stood fixed in a protective stance with her arms folded and her eyes glaring. That would have been enough to scare off most boys she knew, but not this one. Her message may have been clear, but, if so, it went unheeded. Josh continued to saunter over to her. The icy barrier she had erected began to melt as she stood only inches away from the bared chest of this shirtless smooth operator. His steely blue eyes fixed on her almost drew sparks. Emily's face flushed, she swallowed hard and took a breath. She stood motionless, transfixed at the sight of his ruddy appearance and tousled sandy hair framing eyes she felt burning a hole into her heart. Adjusting her position nervously, Emily lifted her arms and casually raked her long, slender fingers through her hair, sweeping it back over her shoulders, pretending to be immune to his brash behavior.

As Emily glanced down, Josh noted her long, thick lashes. Emily's advanced physical maturity had endowed her with well-proportioned curves that set her apart from her peers. A portion of her naturally curly blond hair, draped over her left eye, lent a provocative flair to her youthful innocence. Josh bathed her from head to toe with his eyes. *She's full bodied with a tight ass...best of the litter. I like the way she moved off the curb. The bitch has some moxie. I like that.*

Instead of deterring him, Emily's bold confrontation aroused a rush of excitement in this streetwise boy. He stood in front of her making no effort to conceal his intentions, continuing to scan her lustfully with his eyes.

Emily sensed herself coming unglued. With his thumbs hung by his belt, Josh's smug manner set her heart pounding. He gave his full attention to her, ignoring the other girls. She nervously crossed her arms again and glanced from side to side trying to appear uninterested. Her heart skipped a beat when Josh gave an approving glance to his pals on the curb and then turned and winked at her. She controlled her urge to flinch when he circled around her and slid his hand over her behind before returning to his comrades on the curb and the group sauntered off, shooting backward glances at the girls.

The girls pressed in around Emily.

"Holy cow," Mary Ann gasped.

They all began speaking excitedly.

"He's taken a shine to you, Emily."

"He's definitely got his eye on you, Em."

"He's a real heart throb."

Emily did not hear them. Only one thought filled her mind: *When will I see this boy again?*

•

"It's your turn, Emily," Nanette said.

Emily snapped out of her nostalgic reverie.

This beautiful Saturday afternoon lured droves of people outdoors. Across the street from the Bernard townhouse, Morningside Park teemed with activity. Lovers walked hand in hand. Others sprinted or rode over the bicycle paths, and men whacked balls out to players in the field. On the Bernard's side of the street, neighbors sat on their front steps, chatting or quietly observing people strolling by. Throughout the city, the warmth interjected a brief respite of peace and security in the midst of the nation's bleak economic climate.

In Dr. Geoffrey Bernard's neighborhood, there had been little evidence of the widespread poverty in the nation and the world. Except for trips downtown, when the two sisters saw destitute street venders selling apples on street corners, and rows of shoeshine boys lined up along the sidewalk, they had no comprehension of the severe hardships endured by millions of citizens. The aura of tranquility in their neighborhood offered no hint anything unsettling could ever occur in their unruffled lives.

While Emily took her turn, Nanette stood beside the chalked playing area, her back to the street. As Emily stooped to pick up a marker, Nanette could see beyond her into the alley that separated two townhouses.

"Emily! What's that way down in the back of the alley?"

Emily turned and her eyes followed the path of Nanette's stare. "It looks like a body," she said.

Nanette gasped. "Is it...is it a *dead* person?"

"How do I know? Come on, let's go see."

Emily took a few cautious steps into the alley.

"I'm not going there," Nan said, standing firm, but curiosity overcame her, and halfway into the alley, Emily felt her sister behind her grabbing her hand.

Trashcans and boxes stacked along the wall partially obscured the form from their view. Cautiously, they took several steps forward. Moving closer, the scene came into full view. Nanette gasped. For a moment, they stood petrified, Nanette clutching her sister's arm. Venturing farther into the alley, their eyes fell upon a man, lying face down with his arms askew. He lay silent and still. Turning in concert, they ran to the street and into their home.

•

During their investigation, the police identified the man quickly by his personal effects, including a wallet with full credentials and seventy-five dollars. A private detective, he bore the name, Bruce Reid. A big man dressed neatly in a dark pinstriped suit and tie under a stylish overcoat, his lifeless body lay in a pool of blood, formed around a wound on the left side of his head. The blood on the wall above suggested he died when his head hit the wall. His swollen face and jaw suggested a possible brawl with another person or persons. Money left in the wallet and other items of value remaining led the police to dismiss robbery as motive for the man's death.

Two items of possible evidence were uncovered: a penknife with the initials "C.V.E." embossed on it, and a letter stashed in the inside pocket of the dead man's suit. The return address on the envelope identified the sender as a prominent group of New York attorneys. The name "Buckingham Ellis" on the envelope front pinpointed the intended recipient.

The next day, Emily read the reported details in the newspapers. The name Buckingham Ellis fascinated her. *What a strange name. Could he be the murderer? What does he look like?*

37. EMILY AND JOSH

MARCH, 1934, New York City, New York

On Emily's fifteenth birthday, a group of well-to-do friends and relatives of the Bernard family gathered in a private room of a local restaurant for her debutante party.

Conspicuous to Emily alone was the absence of the boy with whom she spent more hours than her parents knew.

During the months since she met him, Emily always had a handy excuse for coming home late: she was detained to help a teacher with a project...she went to the library to do homework...she accidentally overstayed her time with girlfriends at the Sweet Shop. Emily could imagine what would happen if her parents knew about Josh. To her mind, they smothered her with over strict supervision. She despised their snooty friends, who would have been scandalized by the likes of Josh.

APRIL, 1934

"Hey, Josh," Emily said, "You're always talking about you and your boys, and the secret place where you stay. How about showing it to me?"

"I've been thinkin' about it," Josh said, "but you gotta keep your trap shut. Promise you won't tell anybody about it...even your best girl friend."

"I promise," Emily said, snuggling up to him in a display of excitement over a new and risky experience with this daring young stallion..

The hideaway, located behind an abandoned burnt-out storefront, did not approach any luxury, but provided Josh and his circle of felons with privacy and shelter. In this secret place, Josh schooled the members of the group in petty thievery, and took an accounting of stolen goods amassed each day.

Josh knew the boys would be working the neighborhood at that hour, and he and Emily would be alone.

"My boys sleep out here, but I have my private spot over there around the corner."

Emily surveyed it and was not impressed.

With a sly grin, Josh drew Emily close to him and started touching her. His hands stroked her slender neck and moved down over her shoulders as they traced the outline of her body. At first, Emily resisted the urge to respond to his advances, but Josh soon felt her breathing accelerate and detected an amorous glow in her eyes. She slipped her arms around Josh's neck and welcomed his kiss.

Twinges of erotic excitement washed through her body. Her hand pulled Josh's face closer. She pressed his full lips against hers, massaging them with her own. Then their lips parted and their tongues caressed. Their movements quickened. With panting breaths, Emily ran rapid fingers down Josh's body attacking buttons, belt buckle, and ripping pants open while positioning herself to accommodate Josh's swift action as he stripped off her clothes. Shirts, brassiere and pants dropped haphazardly to the floor. Josh pressed Emily to the wall ready to take her right there.

Like a tornado, two of Josh's boys stormed into the room and froze on the spot at the sight of the young girl pinned to the wall by Josh, her panties pulled down over her hips and Josh's briefs lowered.

"Josh...what...what are ya doin'?"

"What's she doin' in here?" the other said.

Josh's rage escalated as speedily as his arousal deflated. He pulled up his underpants and stepping back from Emily, Josh spat out his words, "Keep your noses out of my business and get your asses outta here."

One boy turned to go, but the other hesitated.

"What the hell ya doin, Josh?" he said. "We ain't never had a moll in here. Ya can't trust a female to keep her mouth shut, especially if ya get her knocked up! Next thing ya know, she'll yell 'rape' to the cops, and…"

A violent slap across the boy's face brought an abrupt end to his words. Josh picked him up bodily and riveted him to the boards on the wall. "Shut up, you bastard! You don't ever talk to me that way, understand? Never!"

"J…Josh, I only…"

"Shut up!" Josh dropped the boy to his feet and smashed his fist against his head, nearly bringing him to the floor. The first boy ran out of the door and the second leaped to his feet and followed quickly upon his heels.

Snatching up her clothes and hastily putting them back on, Emily watched in disbelief. She had never seen such blatant brutality. Though it frightened her, it also stirred her yearnings for Josh. *He knows how to treat a girl and is willing to fight for me. He's my honey-cooler for sure.*

At the same time, Emily felt the unsettling restraint of her conscience. Deep down inside, she knew she was treading on dangerous ground.

The mood broken, Josh got dressed and sent Emily home.

She breathed a deep sigh of relief as she returned to her familiar, safe home territory. Even so, in the days following, her desire for Josh flamed more intensely, and she found herself dreaming about a romantic life with him.

Motivated by rebellion against her parent's domination, she found Josh an irresistible alternative to her captivity and personal desire for excitement and freedom. Josh's character and roots were of little consequence to her.

But, if Emily knew a little more about Josh and his background, she might not have found him so attractive.

Josh was a bad seed. A year and a half ago, Josh had been in Duluth, Minnesota, where a friend recruited him into Crusher's operation. Josh already had a few skirmishes with the law, and seemed a prime candidate for participation in these criminal activities.

At that time, Crusher gave personal training to many new recruits. No one knew him, however, as "the Mastermind," the name by which he would be known to keep his identity as the organization's head hidden from his followers. In local training sessions, he was but one of a larger staff, each of whom was addressed as "Teacher."

In this band of petty thieves, Josh quickly mastered the art of the trade and moved up in the ranks as a competent member of the organization. More savvy and resourceful than the others, he scrupulously safeguarded his reputation by covering all traces of his involvement in criminal activity. Josh witnessed how operatives in the organization threatened with criminal exposure those who tried to leave or prove disloyal. *These saps break their balls for the creep and get no place for their trouble. Not me. I'll steal the old bastard blind and give 'im what he's got comin' to him.* At the opportune time, under Crusher's tutelage, Josh lifted the stolen loot his "Teacher" reserved for sustaining the group and slipped away.

When Crusher returned the next day for a training session and found Josh missing, he managed to hide the rage that seethed inside with a calm exterior. *To think I let this young squirt beat me at my own game. I could snuff out his life like he was an insect, and I would, if it would not distract me from my flaming obsession. I will say nothing to the others. It may give them ideas. As far as they are concerned, the prick just fled the coop. I'll never forget his face, and if I ever run into the little bastard, I'll put him in his grave!*

Josh fled to New York City, where he soon emerged as a master yegg himself, commandeering a tightly knit band of young felons. He made sure he had plenty of cigarettes and booze for his boys. In addition to the same enticements Crusher had offered, Josh charmed his followers with his personal charisma, presenting them with a model to admire and mimic as a daredevil soldier of fortune.

38. HOSPITAL BOARD MEETING

MAY, 1934, Springfield, Illinois

A group of hospital board members gathered in a room at Springfield Memorial Hospital in Springfield, Illinois. They assembled to take appropriate action on a recommendation to expand hospital staff.

Founded in 1897 by a group of dedicated Lutheran pastors, the hospital had a long, and at times, an uncertain history. A decision in 1931 to transform the hospital into a general non-denominational institution established a new governing board that brought representation from prominent members of the community. The introduction and growing popularity of voluntary group medical and hospital insurance, along with responsible fiscal management through the first years under the new board, brought about a dramatic reversal of accumulating debt and declining patient occupancy. Early in 1934, the hospital superintendent announced that the hospital could report "the largest number of patients and the best collections for a long period of time."

Hospital administrators now embarked on a program of expansion of hospital facilities and staff. The board initiated a nationwide search for progressive physicians of high competence, and the search had narrowed to a group of five candidates. Included on the list was Dr. Geoffrey Bernard, a prominent New York City physician and a member of the American College of Surgeons.

After much discussion and consideration, one member said, "It is clear to me Dr. Geoffrey Bernard stands head and shoulders over the other candidates. I make a motion we select him as the candidate for our position."

Someone seconded the motion and all unanimously gave approval. More hotly debated, however, was the salary they would offer. The package the finance committee proposed was generous by local standards.

"The hospital can't afford a stipend like that," one said.

"We know the pay scale in New York City is higher than what we can offer here," someone said.

Another said, "That package isn't commensurate with the present salaries of other staff members. We must consider that issue. Are we proposing to raise other staff salaries? I think that would be quite impossible."

Finally, a female member of the board voiced her opinion. "The information we received on Dr. Bernard indicates Mrs. Bernard was born and raised here in Springfield. That may be a factor in his acceptance. I think he will accept the finance committee's modest proposal. If not, we can negotiate further."

Her statement carried the day, and they unanimously adopted the proposed package.

MAY, 1934, New York City, New York

Dr. Bernard responded quickly to the overture from Springfield Memorial. Mrs. Bernard's yearnings to return to the place she knew and loved played a major part. In addition, Geoffrey and Agnes Bernard shared increasing apprehension over changes in their neighborhood that threatened the wholesome development of their girls. Disenchanted youth poured into the city in droves seeking work. Only days ago Mrs. Bernard heard the mayor make a plea over the airwaves for young people leaving their homes not to come to New York City, because jobs were not available. In their opinion, the Bernards believed these young vagrants brought a bad element to the city, and they found their presence threatening.

In contrast, the mid-western flavor of Springfield seemed safe and secure for them and their children. Springfield Hospital had all the earmarks of a successful medical institution with a promising future. They would make the move as soon as possible.

39. RUNAWAY

JUNE, 1934

It was 3 A.M. when Emily entered Josh's secret place at the rear of the abandoned building. She saw Josh's boys spread about communal style, sleeping on their cots. She knew where to find Josh in his private cubicle. Her eyes adjusting to the darkness, she stepped quietly through the array of sleeping felons. She carried a bag with a drawstring at its top, in which she had placed some of her belongings, and set it on the floor next to Josh's bed. She began removing her clothes, slowly, quietly.

Wearing only her panties, she slipped under Josh's covers and nestled up against his warm flesh. Josh stirred. Emily gently brushed her fingers through his hair and over his face, and then downward, over his body. At this sudden, intimate invasion, Josh bolted and instinctively tried to withdraw. Emily turned him towards her and quickly put a finger to his lips to quiet him. Seeing her, he abandoned his resistance. She moved partially over him and she felt him responding. Moving a hand below his waist, Emily found that unlike his young kittens, this tomcat slept in the nude. Slipping on top of him, she caressed his head with her hands and pressed her lips to his. It excited and pleased her to feel the steely hardness of his arousal against her.

•

Dick Miller

Josh had run a tight ship with his boys. At the beginning of each day, he sent them out to work the crowd on the street. Sometimes he gave special assignments based on tips he received. For petty thieves, special public events in parks and other places attracted crowds of unsuspecting prospects.

His absence from his "den" the next morning raised troubling questions among his band of young recruits.

"Where'd he go?"

"Maybe the cops got 'im."

"Naw, he took all his stuff, and if da cops wuz here, we'd all know it."

"Yeah. He left nothin' for us but some useless goods stashed in the joint and a few packs of cigarettes. We all know he hid the cash he doled out to us someplace other than here."

One of the boys who had been hanging back came forward. He had bruises on his face and a half closed blackened eye. He trembled as he spoke in a low voice. "I think I know what happened...but I ain't sayin' nothin' about it."

"Shut you're trap, Pete. He'll cream ya if ya don't," said another, who appeared to have knowledge of the information Pete was about to divulge.

"He looks scared shitless," someone said.

Just then, spunky Spike Biggs stepped out of Josh's den. "I think I know what Petey and Fuzz are tryin' to tell us. Take a look at dis." He held up a pair of women's panties. "Dis wuz in da Big Guy's bed. Da friggin' ratfink got laid and flew the coop...probably took off wit' his bitch fr greener pastures. Damn 'im to hell."

The boys' faces resembled those of crewmen who had just discovered their captain abandoned them and left them in a sinking ship. A few of the younger boys sat on the floor and started to cry.

By the end of the day, all the members of the group had scattered.

•

Josh walked briskly toward the rail yards with Emily trailing behind. *What the hell was I thinking? The last thing I need is a moll hangin' around. She's a great piece of ass, but that's about all she's good for.*

An intense argument with her father over her refusal to move to Illinois brought Emily to Josh's bed.

"I won't go! I won't, I won't, I won't!" she screamed at her mother

167

when she heard the news of the move. Later, when her father came home, he found her closeted in her room.

"Baby," he said, "The city is changing, and you'll like our new home. We'll be living in the country where there are woods and birds and lots of places to play."

"No, daddy, I'm not a little girl, and I have all my friends here. I'm not leaving...I don't care what you say or do to me. I'm staying here."

"That's impossible. You can't stay here in the city alone. What will you do? Why are you acting this way?"

"I just don't want to move."

"I think I know why, and it's exactly why we're moving. Who are you hanging around with? Some of your friends told their parents they don't see much of you anymore. Is there something you're not telling us?"

Emily clamped up and said nothing.

"One of them said you've been seeing a boy. What's this all about?"

Silence followed. Emily's eyes glared at her father with her lips drawn into at thin line.

"All right, young lady!" her father roared. "You are not going out of this house until you tell me who you're seeing and exactly what's going on. This rebelliousness will not be tolerated."

Emily's suggestion to Josh that they run off together came at an appropriate time. He had already been considering a change in his situation. *I'm damn tired of wiping their asses and noses. The little creeps. Somebody's always messin' up. There's been too many close calls with the cops. It's only a matter of time before they get wise and bust up my operation. It's getting' too risky and I can't afford to get caught and end up in the slammer.*

Josh was ready for a change, but he didn't count on Emily being part of the mix, nor did he harbor any deep feelings for her. Beyond their sexual escapades, they had little in common. Nevertheless, in the heat of passion, she had taken him hostage and he agreed to catch out that night with her in tow.

40. DISOWNED

AUGUST, 1934, Springfield, Illinois

"Come, Nanette, let's tell your father."

Mother and daughter walked into the living room where Geoffrey Bernard sat in his favorite chair reading the newspaper.

"Dear, we have something to tell you," his wife said. "Go ahead, Nanette. Tell your father about the letter."

"Daddy, my friend, Rosemary...you know my friend from back in New York...well I got a letter from her this morning."

"And..." Dr. Bernard said.

"Well, she talked about Emily. She said her sister told her Emily was seeing a boy named Josh, and her sister thinks she ran off with him."

"So?" her father said.

"So maybe we could find her. Maybe we could get her to come home."

"That's not an option, sweetheart. Emily made a choice. She's going to have to live with it."

Mrs. Bernard tried to intervene. "Geoffrey, dear, why don't you at least consider..."

"That girl is no longer my daughter," Geoffrey Bernard snapped. "I don't ever want to hear her name mentioned around here again."

The Boxcar Kid

Agnes Bernard stood stunned; her face a mask of pity and sorrow, not only for her wayward daughter, but for her unforgiving husband. As Mrs. Bernard stood rigidly silent, Nanette regarded her father with pleading eyes.

"Daddy, daddy, " Nanette implored, "Emily is my sister...please, daddy!"

"Didn't you hear me? I don't want to hear her name again!" Then, in a consoling gesture, he said, "Come here baby."

Nanette walked to his chair. Geoffrey Bernard reached out his arm and pulled her to him. "You're the only daughter I have now, sweetheart, and I'll always love you." He kissed her on the forehead as Mrs. Bernard lowered her eyes to hide her tears.

41. SEX FOR SALE

OCTOBER, 1934, The Deep South

With loud repetitive clanks and thumps, bumping freight cars signaled the slowing of the train.

Buck and K.O. eyed each other with puzzled looks, wondering where they were. Fifteen others in the car mimicked their swaying movement as the car bumped to a stop.

"I think we're at the Smithville water tower," a veteran hobo said. "We'll be here for a short spell while they give the old workhorse up front a drink."

Some members of the group shifted positions, while others stayed put. One old codger stood up, loosened his belt and tucked his shirt in neatly before tightening it again. Buck stood up and stretched his muscles. Someone carefully slid the door open to get some fresh air.

A moment later, two would-be passengers appeared at the opening. A 'bo reached out his hand to give them an assist. The smaller of the two grabbed it and the hobo pulled him aboard. Bucky noticed the boy had soft features and a black eye.

The other, a more robust and agile boy, grabbed a quick hold and swung up without anyone's help. His sandy hair clipped into a straw scarecrow cut framed his handsome face, as he flicked some road dust from his leather jacket with his fingers. When the newcomer lifted his arm to see the time, Bucky saw the gleam of a fine gold wristwatch.

Shying away from the group, the smaller boy moved closer to his companion's side. Almost instinctively, the larger boy shoved him away. The shunned companion cowered with downcast eyes, and shrank back into a corner like an animal with its tail between its legs.

Buck watched. *This is a strange twosome.*

The train remained at a standstill on the siding.

The cocky boy in the leather jacket said, "Listen up, fellas. I got a proposition to make."

All eyes focused on this impudent newcomer.

"Two bits 'll git ya the services of my pal here."

"Whadaya mean, 'services'?" someone said.

He stepped closer to the smaller boy. "Take a peek, fellas."

"No, Josh..." the frightened boy pleaded, "please ..."

"Shut ya mouth, bitch!" he shot back, silencing him. Then he ripped off the boy's cap, releasing an array of soft, blond curls that fell to the shoulders.

"Why, he's...she's...a girl!" someone said amidst gasps from the others. "Meet my sidekick, Emily," Josh said. "She might seem a bit shy, but she's got a fire inside her that will light you up!"

Josh grabbed the collar of her coat and pulled it off. Underneath she wore a man's shirt too big for her, and dungarees. Like a store window mannequin, she stood rigid, not attempting to resist. Even so, Josh bent her arm up behind her in a painful hammerlock to ensure her compliance.

Buck glared at the malicious tyrant. *What the hell is he doing to her?*

With his free hand, the rough boy pulled open the front of her shirt. She wore no brassiere, and the opened shirt fully exposed her breasts. Buck had never seen the bare breasts of a woman this close before. Once, at school, he saw a photograph of a lusty woman naked from the waist up that his friend bought for a nickel from a dispensing machine at an amusement park.

In spite of his mounting rage, Bucky could not help but notice her ample breasts that seemed too firm and full for such a young girl. The girl arched her back in a futile effort to relieve the pain of the brute's hold on her, and Buck felt an erotic twinge at the sight of her firm, up-lifted bosom.

Her captor applied greater pressure, bringing a painful grimace to the girl's face. Tears flowed from her eyes.

"Two bits...and ain't she lovely," Josh said. "You can have her right here and now. Who wants her first? Step right up. You won't get another chance like this one." A few old geezers, whose hopes for pleasure in this life had long ago disintegrated, walked over with their two bits.

Buck thought of his sister Lena, about the same age as this unfortunate girl, imagining what he would do if anyone tried to touch his kid sister.

What a bastard! Every muscle in his body tensed.

Several crotchety hobos pressed her into the corner. That they would molest her in full view of the others, who stood stunned and motionless, spoke clearly of their depravity and thirst for lust.

Bucky felt his temperature skyrocket in the presence of this contemptible rogue. He could no longer contain himself. An invisible switch clicked on inside him, and he leaped to his feet and dove at the men fondling the girl, as she struggled to keep them away. A couple of well-placed punches sent two of them reeling. Two others quickly backed away.

"Get back, all of you!" Buck ordered as the molesters shrank back into the ranks. "Anyone who tries to manhandle her will have to deal with me!" he announced.

K.O. saw Josh approaching Bucky from the side with a shovel in hand, raised to smash Bucky's head.

K.O. sprung from his spot and hit Josh like a bulldozer before the young hellion could clobber Bucky. The shovel knocked from his hand, Josh backed away with his teeth grinding and his eyes glaring.

Bucky turned around, and K.O. stepped back.

"Okay, Champ. It's your shot," he said.

Growing up in the streets, Josh knew how to use his fists. Bucky could see right away Josh was quick on his feet. Beneath his open leather jacket, Josh appeared well built and he had a few inches on Bucky. Josh appeared as if he would gain the advantage, but Buck's rage and pumping adrenalin evened things out.

The two opponents clashed. Josh delivered the first blow with a fist to Bucky's jaw. Buck fell back a couple of steps in a daze. Josh wasted no time and landed another blow that spun Bucky around into the wall. Buck leaned back against the wall getting his wind.

"You're done, hero boy," Josh bragged, and he moved in to finish off his opponent.

Bucky stepped aside as Josh's fist hit the boxcar wall, and with a grimace on his face, shook his fist throbbing with pain. Josh's boast had been premature. Buck grabbed his attacker and slammed him against the wall. His fist smacked Josh's head so quick and hard that Josh's body reeled sideways and he landed on the floor.

"I ain't never seen a punch like dat!" one hobo said to another.

K.O. grinned from ear to ear.

With a groan, Josh lifted himself onto his elbows, shaking his head back and forth. K.O. picked him up bodily and someone yelled, "Scumbag," as K.O. flung him headlong out the door into the tall grass beside the tracks and the hobos watched Josh get to his feet and run towards the back of the train.

All the men in the car cheered and gathered around Bucky and patted him on the back. Hobos who gave their two bits to Josh hung their heads shamefully and stood apart.

Buck ignored the accolades. He pushed through the circle and went to Emily.

"Don't be afraid," he said to her. "I'll see that nothin' like that will ever happen to you again."

Visibly exhausted, Emily fell asleep with her head on Bucky's lap. Buck stroked her silky blond curls. The vision of loveliness he saw the moment Josh removed her boyish guise remained to beguile him.

With a *clunk, clunk, clunk*, the protesting couplers signaled the train was starting to move. Long hours spent riding freight trains provided plenty of time to think. That night, Bucky lay next to the girl he vowed to protect, deep in thought. He wondered about the men who had quickly responded to Josh's proposition.

He knew these old men. He had seen them before...oh, not these men in particular, but others just like them. Bucky could easily identify them by the vacant stare in their eyes. They sat alone in silence staring into space. *What had brought them to such a state? What had happened to them to bring them down so far?* Buck already had a taste of this life of hard knocks. Yet, in his heart, he was determined he would never become like them. He would not compromise his morals. He had more determination than that. *I wonder how this will all end for me. Will I ever be like them? No, never!*

Dick Miller

42. ALL THE WAY

"Emily...is that your real name?"

"Yes," she said, "Emily Bernard."

"Where are you from?"

"New York."

"What were you doin' with that knucklehead?"

She started hesitantly, but little by little, she told Buck the circumstances that brought her to such a state.

"I got into a fight with my father because my father took a new position and wanted us to move from New York to Springfield, Illinois. I refused to go because of my involvement with Josh. At the time, Josh meant everything to me. My parents didn't know I was seeing him. I was such a fool. I let him take me down and ended up like this. I tried to get away from him once, but he caught me and beat me up."

"The bastard," Buck said.

"I don't know what to do. I'm so ashamed, and I can't go home," she said as her tears welled up. "Do you still want to stay with me? I wouldn't blame you if you didn't want to get mixed up with a girl like me. I'd understand if you went on and left me behind. It would be all right, really."

"Don't say things like that. I'm not goin' anywhere without you. I'm with you all the way, and 'K.O. is too, right K.O.?"

"Right," K.O. said.

Buck and K.O. related their experiences to Emily and told how they came to be fast friends. As they continued traveling, K.O. provided Emily with tips that would help her to know what to expect and how to handle situations that would arise on the rails.

Buck became her protector and guardian. She had been reluctant to tell much about herself, and details of how she came to the situation with Josh remained a mystery. The boys knew she had been through a lot, so they did not press her for more information.

As night came, travelers in the car found their spots and began to fall asleep. Emily and Buck slept alone in each other's arms. K.O. slept with the other hobos.

As time passed, Emily told Buck about how she came to meet Josh and how he took her to his hideout and tried to seduce her. "After that terrible fight with my father, I went to Josh...oh, Bucky...I...I went to his bed. I went to his bed," she repeated more emphatically, tears welling up in her eyes. "I begged him to take me away with him, and we went that night after I let him have me. I was so mad at my father I wanted to do anything to hurt him. I tried to blame everything on my father, but it was no one's fault but my own. I deserved everything Josh did to me."

"Don't say that," Bucky said. "No one deserves the kind of hell he gave you. We'll make things right, you'll see."

"Bucky, you don't understand. I'm pregnant. I'm going to have his baby."

Buck stood still for a moment with his hands on her shoulders. "Are you sure, Emily? How can you be sure?"

"I've missed my period...I have all the signs...I've been sick every morning. Bucky, I'm so scared. The child will remind me of him. I'm so afraid. What if I end up hating my child? How will I feel when it's born? I don't want this baby. I want to get rid of it."

"No!" Buck said. "You don't know what you're saying. I won't stand by and let you do that."

"But you don't know what can happen. What about Josh? What if he follows me and tries to take, or harm the baby?"

He won't have that chance," Bucky said. "I won't let him lay a hand on you or the child."

"No, Bucky. You must stay away from me. I'm a terrible girl...I've done a terrible thing. Thank you from the bottom of my heart for saving me from him, but I can't let you get mixed up in this any further. I'll drag you down. Dump me somewhere down the line and leave me be."

The tears poured forth like water through a lifted floodgate."

"Not on your life. I'm no prize, Emily, and someday I'll tell you how I got in this fix myself. Just get it straight...we're both in this for the long run, and I'm not going to desert you."

"You mean you still want to stay with me?"

"All the way."

"I thought having my first baby would be the happiest time in my life," Emily said. "Now I wish I was dead."

As they sat down on the boxcar floor, Buck took both of her hands and looked her straight in the eye. "I'm sticking with you, Emily. Don't worry. If I have anything to do with this, your baby's birth will be the happiest day of your life."

Damn! I don't know how I'll do it, but there's no way I'll let this sweet girl go the way that my mom did.

43. A PAINFUL SEPARATION

OCTOBER, 1934, Somewhere in Alabama

Several days later, in the late hours of the night, the freight train loaded with hobos in, on top, between and under moving cars started to slow on its trek from Montgomery to Mobile, Alabama. Some riders slept at this late hour of the night, while others were winding down. Moments later, everyone was awake after the noise and jostling of cars pulled onto a siding where the train stopped.

In a boxcar near the caboose, Buck, K.O., Emily and seven others regarded each other with questioning eyes.

"What now?" one of them said.

"Don't know. What time is it?"

"Almost midnight," someone answered.

Except for the distant sigh of the pent-up steam from the engine up front, it was silent. A moment later, their ears picked up the crunch of footsteps coming closer outside their car. As the noise stopped, they could see some light bleeding through the edges of the door. The door opened, and a man lifted a lantern and peered in. He moved it around to illuminate all the faces, and hesitated when he saw K.O. The man stretched his arm closer, blinding K.O. The man wore the clothes of a railroad worker, not a bull.

"You there, colored boy. Where was you last night. Was you off the train anywhere between here and Montgomery?"

178

"No, sir," K.O. said. He felt himself trembling. He recalled the stories he'd heard about atrocities committed in the south by white people against colored folks.

"Well, boy, you better get off the train quickly, before someone sees you."

"Here in this godforsaken place?" Bucky asked. "Why?"

The man swung the lantern to get a better look at this boy who had the audacity to raise a question.

"A girl back in Greenville says she was molested by a colored boy, who got on this here train."

"But he's been with us the whole time. We've been together since we left Montgomery."

"That's right," some of the others confirmed.

"Listen, kids. Whether he done it or not, there's a lynchin' party searchin' the train, and if they find ya, and the noose fits over ya head, you're done for. I ain't yet heard of a trial that took place before a lynchin'. You'll be swingin' from a tree, boy, you can bet on it."

K.O. and Buck stared at each other in panic, their eyes wide and their mouths open and gasping, Emily put her hands to her cheeks.

"I gotta go, Buck." K.O. said.

Buck pulled him away from the group and grabbed his collar. "Listen to me, K.O., there's nothin' but swamps and snakes out there in these parts. You can't just hightail it out of here."

"I got to." K.O. said.

"I'll go with you."

"Oh no you won't." K.O. said, breaking Buck's grip on his collar and scalding him with flaming eyes. "You ain't goin' nowhere!"

"What'll I do if you leave? You're my main man," Buck pleaded.

"No, you're the main man, Champ. You don't need me...at least not here...and now."

"No...no," Buck said. "I won't let you go alone."

The fireman and group of companions stood watching them, picking up on a few words, but not understanding what they said.

"No you listen up, Champ. You got a little lady over there who needs you. That's what you'll do. You'll take care of her...maybe help her get back to her home. Think, pal. What'll she do if you leave with me?"

That was the end of the conversation. K.O. grabbed his stuff and jumped out the door. Buck hung out the door and watched his friend trudge through the wet marsh and disappear into the night. Buck stood there staring into the darkness for the longest time, until he felt someone touch his arm. It was Emily. She regarded him with consoling eyes. Before turning to her, he quickly wiped his eyes. Now his path was clear.

I gave her my promise. K.O. is right. I can't desert her.

Dick Miller

44. BUCKY AND EMILY

Moments later, another man with a lantern approached from the front of the train. The fireman yelled back, "Checked everythin' out. Nothin' back here."

It seemed like an eternity before the train moved ahead. Emily watched Buck sitting in silence against the boxcar side, staring into space. She moved close and sat beside him, brushing his face with her hand and smoothing his hair. Up to now, she had needed Bucky's help, but realized at this moment, he was the needy one, and she was his only mainstay. They fell asleep in each other's arms.

A week later, they still had not heard anything about K.O. The two of them lingered around the yards watching for trains coming from the east.

"Hey," Buck would say to those jumping off, "have you seen a colored fellow a little taller than me?"

No one had seen him. Buck and Emily hoped and prayed K.O. had escaped without harm. A day did not pass when Buck didn't think about him, and he continued to question everyone he met about his friend.

During these days, Bucky and Emily drew close. She revealed more of her personal life to him, and Buck began to put the pieces of her story together. At first, he spent a good portion of time listening quietly to her. As her confidence grew and she shared more, Buck felt prompted to

181

reveal details of his own background.

During the night, Bucky thought more about Emily's separation from her family. He remembered how impulsive he had been with his father on that fateful night in Altoona. How he regretted that moment. The more thought he gave to the situation, the more convinced he became that he must do everything possible to bring Emily and her family together. As a homeless young girl on the rails, soon to give birth, she would be especially defenseless against dangers of the road, including possible sexual predators and abuse.

Emily's relationship with Buck grew deeper when he affirmed his commitment to stay with her until she reunited with her family. She feared the consequences of confronting her father in particular, but knew in her heart Buck was right. She needed to return home. His support was the prescription she needed to force her decision. She trusted Bucky, who had amply demonstrated his devotion to her in his swift action against Josh, and she agreed to his plan without reservation.

Dick Miller

45. ST. BARTHOLOMEW'S SOUP KITCHEN

NOVEMBER, 1934, St. Louis, Missouri

Bucky and Emily arrived at St. Louis destitute. Under overcast skies, Emily shivered in the blustery wind. At a used clothing distribution center in Memphis, Tennessee, operated by St. James Catholic Church, she acquired a gabardine coat with two large top buttons, above a missing third button evidenced by a few remaining unyielding pieces of thread. Pleated under his belt fastened at its last notch, Bucky wore oversized pin striped woolen pants. In anticipation of colder weather, Buck picked up a red and black plaid woolen jacket with double thick sleeves and side pockets that he wore over a cotton white shirt. The jacket had a six-inch tear in one sleeve, but still provided some warmth on this windy November day.

In the last month, Buck's weight had dropped to 154 pounds. With whatever food they managed to scrounge, he always gave the greater portion to Emily. When she sometimes protested, he said, "Take it for the baby. There's more than two of us to feed."

As they trudged along close to the buildings along the sidewalk, they stopped to catch their breath after a blast of cold air blew hard against them. The wind blew open the lower part of Emily's coat. Keeping their distance at the outer edge of the sidewalk, an elderly couple with the wind at their backs were about to walk past them.

With Emily approaching her third trimester, her pregnancy caught the woman's eye. Like a braking car suddenly turning to avoid a collision, she turned, walked directly toward Bucky and Emily dragging her startled husband by the arm. With a scowl and a furious gesture the woman pointed and shook her finger at Bucky and said, "How could you do such a thing to this poor girl? Why, you are both mere children. Such a young girl. Shame on both of you. God is punishing you for your sin, young man!"

Buck stood in silence as they walked away. He clamped his teeth together and felt his temperature rising. He muttered for Emily's ears only, "She's a friggin' blackheart in her mink coat and flashy jewels. What does she know about God...about anything?"

Emily took his hand and pressed it tenderly. "Buck, she just doesn't understand. I'm proud to be here next to you, and I wouldn't trade places with that bitch for a million dollars."

At her blatant assessment, Buck turned his eyes to her. His anger instantly dispersed, like air released from a popped balloon, and on the edge of laughter, his grimace fled and he smiled broadly. *God bless her. She's just what I need at a time like this.*

•

Winter had arrived early and Buck could see Emily's dispirited sorrow. *Damn it. I feel like shit. I thought I could help her improve her situation, but I can't even take care of myself, much less her with a baby on the way. Getting by in the city is like swimming upstream with a bowling ball in each hand.*

"Em, I don't want you to worry. We're going to find a way out of this friggin' town and get you home."

"I know you're feeling bad, Buck, but we still have each other. We've been in situations like this before, and God always gets us through."

A cold drizzle fell from the gray skies, so they retreated into the shelter of a recessed entranceway of a haberdashery.

An old man in tattered clothes had been watching. He approached them. "Come with me," he said. "A few streets down there's a soup kitchen. I'm headin' there meself. Come on. You'll find warmth and free grub. It appears your lady needs to eat for two."

They followed him to a storefront with a sign over the entrance: "St. Bartholomew's Kitchen."

"This here's the place," the old man said, and led them through the door.

The long rectangular room was clean, but stark. A few religious pictures broke the monotony of the gray walls. Two rows of tables lined with plain, wooden chairs ran the length of the room. Bare light bulbs hanging from the ceiling by their electrical cords provided illumination. Several rows of old church pews positioned near the entrance provided a waiting area for arriving street people to check in.

Buck and Emily sat and waited as their eyes feasted on rising steam and the aroma from food being prepared at the front of the room. Hot food of any kind would be a welcome change from the scraps and handouts they received on the street.

While they waited, a young girl came over to them, smiled pleasantly, and asked, "Do you believe in Jesus? Are you saved?"

Bucky avoided the question, "Ma'am," he said, "this kind man sitting next to me saw us freezing and hungry and brought us here."

The girl saw their wet clothes and hair. She noted how Emily, still chilled, held the top of her coat closed tight around her neck. The girl quickly glanced around to see if anyone watched them, came closer and whispered, "I am supposed to give you a tract and ask you about Jesus before you get into the line at the serving table."

"We both know Jesus, ma'am," Bucky said, not knowing if Emily had any religious training at all.

"Follow me," the girl said. Before directing them to the food line, she led them to a washroom where clean washcloths and towels had been set out. Other arrivals were already washing hands and faces. With dainty dips into the water-filled basin, Emily wiped gently around her eyes and mouth before cleaning the whole face. Buck, on the other hand, leaned into the basin and splashed water liberally onto his face.

"Bucky, what's the matter with you? You're splashing all over me."

Lifting his head from the basin, he arched his back, stretched his arms up as though ready to chin himself, and shook his doused mane like a dog coming up out of the creek back home.

"Boy, is that refreshing. I needed that."

A faint smile appeared on Emily's face. She doused her hands, tilted her head back and ran her fingers through her hair, lifting it and straightening out the tangles.

Buck's eyes locked on her with her arms up, her back arched, her uplifted bust, and her eyes closed in refreshing pleasure. *I'd almost forgotten how lovely she is.*

The girl, who had spoken to them, met them as they came out and directed them to the end of the serving line, dutifully advising them,

"Mind you, now, when you sit down to eat, bow your heads and say a 'Thank you' to Jesus.'" She placed a tract into Bucky's pocket.

At the serving table, the smell of the food drew their eyes to the steaming pot. The satisfying aroma of mixed vegetables cooked in a beefy stock sent Bucky's olfactory glands into a frenzy. "Uummm..," he said.

"That sure smells good," Emily said, completing his sentence.

A slice of bread and butter came with the soup. The couple hovered over the serving table as though it were the heavenly banquet.

"Bucky?"

The voice came from someone on the other side of the serving table.

46. INTERSECTING
PATHWAYS

Bucky raised his head to see who had spoken to him. His black hair was straggly under his newsboy cap. Though he had washed his face, he still appeared haggard and tired.

"Bucky Ellis...isn't that your name?" the man with the clerical collar asked. "You're Charles and Marcie's boy. You sang in St.Ann's boy's choir. I'm Father Michael Griffin. I officiated at your mother's funeral back in York. Do you remember me?"

Buck's jaw dropped and his eyes turned round and wide, as the memory of the priest he had known some four or five years ago surfaced in his mind.

"George," Father Griffin called, beckoning to a man nearby, "Will you stand in for me in the line? I've just met an old friend."

"Sure, Father."

The priest's face lit up and with an animated step, he rounded the serving table, put his hand on Bucky's shoulder and beckoned him to take his food and sit with him at a nearby table. "Come on, boy, we need to talk."

Once seated, the priest fired questions at him. "Why did you skip out on us up in York? Tell me what happened to you. Where have you been all this time? I can't believe you're here in St. Louis."

Father Griffin did not realize Emily and Bucky were together. Emily stood at the serving table and hesitated when Buck and Father Griffin went to sit down. She followed, lagging behind them.

Buck saw Emily standing idle after he and Father Griffin sat down. He stood and reached out his hand to her. Pulling her closer, he said, "This is Emily. She's with me," and he pulled out the chair next to him to seat her.

Father Griffin could not avoid noting her condition, but called no attention to it. "Hello, Emily. Welcome to St. Bartholomew's Soup Kitchen."

As Buck and Emily launched into their food, they listened intently, as the priest recounted how he and his wife, Becky, had left the parish in York six months earlier to take a position at St. Bartholomew Episcopal Church in St. Louis. The Vicar assigned the young cleric the responsibility of overseeing the operation of this storefront ministry among other duties commensurate with his office of Assistant Pastor.

With an expression of genuine concern, Father Michael passionately related the grief and sorrow suffered by Bucky's father and family at the eldest son's departure.

"Those in the parish and others who knew you were saddened by your father's grief, but when you left without notice at such a critical time, the whole community was deeply touched by your father's devastation. For a while, he isolated himself and did not attend church. Two of his friends at church visited him and brought him whatever comfort they could. They noticed your dad had gathered all the pictures he could find of your mother...and of you. Bucky, it was as if you had died, as well as your mother."

Bucky's temperature rose as a feeling of sorrow and shame gripped him. He sat quietly with his fists clenched. Then he said, "Father Griffin...I...I...it never occurred to me that anybody cared that much about me. I didn't mean to hurt my dad or Bud, or Lil or Lena. I swear, Father, thirty minutes out I almost jumped off the train to go back...I don't know why I didn't. It was just too late, and I couldn't burden my family any more."

As Emily watched and listened, Father Griffin put his hand on Bucky's. They talked across the table in rapid, broken sentences, passionately breaking in over the other's pleadings. Buck opened up and told Father Griffin what he heard said in the church lavatory after his mother's burial service, and his reaction to it. With the exception of K.O., he had not told another person about the two men whose comments convinced him that leaving home was the right thing to do.

Hearing this poignant story for the first time, Emily stroked

Bucky's arm gently, as if to soothe his troubled mind. Father Griffin observed the tender way they cast eyes on each other. He could see their feelings ran deep.

"Those two men opened my eyes to what a burden I'd been to the family," Buck explained. "In a way, I was part of the reason my mom did...well...you know.

Father Griffin was saddened this incident had clouded Bucky's judgment. *The boy thought he was doing the right thing, but nothing could have been so wrong. With his dear mother resting in her grave, his brokenhearted father needed his oldest boy more than ever. How tragic Buck could not see this. I must help this couple and get Bucky on the right track. I am determined to set the record straight and get Buck back home with his loved ones.*

At this point, he knew nothing about Emily, but could not dismiss the tender feelings he had seen demonstrated between them. *How did they come upon each other? What were her circumstances?*

Father Michael did not press for any immediate answer to these important questions. It seemed both inopportune and futile to intrude upon Bucky's convictions or probe into this young girl's past. His priority now was to get this couple's self-confidence restored and their situation turned around.

47. SAFE HARBOR

The warmth and comfort Bucky felt in the Griffin home stirred memories of childhood days almost forgotten.

Michael and Becky Griffin lived in a parsonage owned by the parish, furnished with used furniture donated by members and friends. Still, they heartily welcomed Bucky and Emily into their home, providing two small bedrooms for them.

"We always have enough. The Lord always provides for us," Becky Griffin affirmed.

Bucky insisted he take on household or other duties to help, in exchange for their kindness. Responding, Father Griffin brought him to the Soup Kitchen, to assist with maintenance and other duties.

Emily remained at home with Mrs. Griffin and helped with household chores. Coming from a family of wealth, Emily had not learned much about basic homemaking. In New York, her mother had servants to undertake household tasks. For Emily, this was a change of lifestyle. Yet, she took a liking to learning new skills such as baking, cooking and sewing. She took pride in tips Becky related, such as the "hospital corners" technique in tucking in the sheets at the foot of the bed. Never before had she seen or heard of using a wooden bulb to darn socks with holes in them.

Emily also helped at the mission when Becky took her to assist in the kitchen and pantry. Feeling useful and needed in this participation, Emily's confidence blossomed.

Soon, knowledge of the newest members of the Griffin household spread through the congregation. Some assumed Bucky fathered the child Emily carried and spoke disparagingly about them. Some referred to their "wantonness," Emily's "unfortunate condition," and "their sin." On the other hand, many took kindly to them and expressed special interest in their welfare. They acted compassionately, offering help with whatever the young couple needed. A doctor in the congregation offered his services to prepare Emily for childbirth and deliver her baby without cost when the time came. Emily cherished such friends who bolstered her spirit.

48. BUCKY AND BUTCH

At the mission, Father Michael noticed the outstanding abilities in this bright young boy. He first took note of Bucky's leadership potential on a day when a worker encountered difficulty in handling a particular disheveled man. Butch, a husky volunteer, grew impatient with the man's reluctance to follow simple directives. He began speaking to him in a brusque manner.

"Go to the table over there, pick up some silver and sit down at the end of that bench."

The man did not appear to pay any attention to Butch. Instead, he stood motionless, regarding Butch with a blank stare, as if intending to stand his ground in defiance.

Butch leaned into him and pushed him in the proper direction as he raised his voice to repeat, "Over there...over there, ya hear?"

The man moved backwards on an erratic path, and instead of following the orders, slinked away and stood near the wall, his eyes lowered and his trembling hands folded in front of him. Irritated, Butch shoved him, bounced him off the wall, grabbed his shoulders on the rebound, and shook him so violently that the man's hat fell off and his hair flew in every direction.

"Don't you know how to follow simple orders, idiot?" he yelled.

The man appeared utterly terrified. Everyone in the room grew silent as they watched.

Bucky stepped between them. In a calm and controlled manner, he said, "Butch, step back a little. Step back a little," he said again in a gentle voice. "Let me see what we can do here."

Buck took the man aside, led him to the bench, and sat him down. Then he knelt on the floor next to him to meet him eye to eye. He put his hands on his own ears and then touched the man's ears as he turned his head back and forth in a "no" gesture. The man watched Buck make the motion a second time, and then touched his own ears and then Bucky's as he imitated his head movement.

Buck gave the man a reassuring tap on his shoulders and stood. "This man can't hear. He is deaf," he said to Butch. "When you want to tell him something, make sure he's watching you, and put a smile on your face. Take his hand and show him where you want him to go. Understand?"

"*Uhhh*...yeah...I think so, Bucky. I'm sorry if I was mean to 'im."

"You meant well," Buck said, smiling. "Just don't be so rough with people."

"OK, Bucky. Thanks for helpin' me. You're not mad at me are ya?"

"No, not at all, Butch. You go help the others. I'll take it from here."

Bucky mimicked the gesture of eating from a bowl and then took the man directly to get utensils, brought him to the serving table and helped him with the food. Then Buck led him to the table and sat down across from him.

The man regarded Buck. His soulful eyes clearly reflected deep gratitude. Picking up his fork, he began eating.

Emily had been at the mission that day and had watched what happened.

"Buck, you certainly handled that well," she said. "How did you know the man was deaf?"

"I saw him when he first came into the mission. When he walked across the room, a fellow behind him dropped a tray of food on the floor."

"Oh, yes, I remember seeing that. It made quite a clatter," Emily said.

"The commotion got everyone's attention, but I saw the man who had entered keep walking as if nothing had happened. I could see he did not hear."

"Butch really jumped all over the poor man."

"Yeah. He's sometimes gruff in his behavior, but I think he has a tender heart. Look at him now."

The Boxcar Kid

Butch had picked up his tray and sat next to the deaf mute. Before long, they were communicating with signs and gestures. People could not resist smiling as they watched Butch fawning all over the man, trying to demonstrate his remorse for the way he had treated him.

Father Michael saw other occasions when Bucky took charge and solved problems. *It's time to channel Bucky's abilities into more challenging areas of service.*

The priest and Bucky picked up and swept the room before leaving one Sunday evening.

"Bucky, have you noticed there are mothers and families with children who come to the mission on Sunday mornings?"

"Yeah, I guess that's right, Father," Buck said.

"Our Sunday School at St. Bart's is conducted at the same time. I think some of the people who come here have no church home. I'm thinking we could start a second Sunday School at the Soup Kitchen."

Bucky cast his eyes to the side and appeared thoughtful.

"I've been thinking about this for some time. Can I explain it to you, Buck?"

"Yeah, OK."

Buck turned a chair around and sat down, straddling it with his elbows resting on the chair back.

"Buck, I've been watching how you handle yourself, and I think you could be a big help on a special project I want to start at the mission."

Father Griffin felt encouraged when he saw Buck's eyes brighten with interest.

"I know some people I can ask to help teach and do some other tasks. I've seen how you work with people and especially with children. You're a natural. When I saw you on your knees tying a little girl's shoes at the mission, you smiled at her and she beamed with admiration. It reminded me of a time in York, when I saw you strapping ice skates onto your little brother's feet. You caught my attention, and I couldn't take my eyes off of you while you taught him to skate."

"You were there? I remember that. That was the first time he ice-skated."

"Remember, I knew you way back then. I wasn't at St. Ann's very long before your mother died, but I saw how you took charge of things and watched out for your brother and sisters. I know you've never taught Sunday School before, but I think if I teamed you with an experienced teacher, you'd be a great asset to the program."

"Do you mean it?" Buck asked, his face now beaming.

"Yes, Buck. You're just the right age to set a good example for these impressionable young learners. Well, what do you think?"

"I love workin' with the kids. I want to do something useful. I think I can do this. I want to try!"

Not long after, Sunday patrons arriving at the soup kitchen found the room rearranged to accommodate several teaching areas separate from the dining tables. Food service ceased between ten and eleven o'clock and leaders encouraged people to join in the educational hour.

Under Father Griffin's supervision, leaders planned an agenda including devotions and two teaching group sessions with Bucky teamed up with Mrs. Bankoff. Sometimes the program varied to give opportunity for story related crafts for the children. Supplementing the children's Sunday School, Father Michael offered a Bible study class for adults, so that activities involved everyone who wished to participate.

Becky and Emily worshiped at the eight o'clock service and then accompanied Father Griffin to the mission where they participated in the Bible study.

Initially, a degree of chaos erupted under the new program. Some people were confused about the new procedures. Some elected not to participate, but remained, sometimes distracting program participants. Occasionally, children became unruly and noisy, which prompted some leaders to add loud and scolding directives to the din.

In the midst of one situation, in which leaders lost control of unruly children and vocal adults, Bucky jumped up on a chair where everyone could see him. "Hey, everyone, look up here," he said. When he had everyone's attention, he said in a clear, loud voice, "Everyone hold your finger up like this." He stretched out his arm and pointed to the ceiling. "Now put the finger of your other hand over your lips and keep silent." As one by one, the group assumed the posture, he said more softly, "Let's see how quiet we can make this room."

In a moment, every person in the room had their finger in the air and their lips sealed. The resulting silence impressed leaders and attendees alike. From henceforth, this became the method to restore order, and in time, the wrinkles in other procedures smoothed out as well.

"Buck, where did you learn to do that?" Father Michael asked later.

"When I was a kid, I saw the principal of our school do it to quiet a noisy assembly hall."

In a short time the new venture became so successful, the Church Council decided to conduct a study on how the program and facilities might be expanded.

49. A DEFINING MOMENT

Buck had attended worship services since childhood, and, as a teenager, he began to listen to sermons with greater interest. There were times when his mind would wander when a crying baby commanded more attention than the pastor's preaching, or when he would watch Emily and get lost in the beauty of her face, her eyes locked on the man in the pulpit she so profoundly admired.

On this Sunday, the message of Father Griffin struck a resonant chord. Bucky listened intently as Father Michael spoke about "The Providence of God" using as a model subject, Joseph, who had been separated from his father and family when his brothers sold him into slavery.

The preacher declared, "Joseph must have thought his life was over when the merchants who bought him took him to Egypt, a foreign land, where he was sold again to Potiphar, captain of the guard in Pharoah's army. Joseph was only about seventeen when this happened."

The last sentence hit Bucky's ears and flashed an instant alert to his brain.

Holy smokes, that's my age!

As the preacher continued, he chronicled the many abuses Joseph suffered and how God rescued him from each unfortunate predicament.

His story's just like mine. Geez, I can't believe it. I never realized that before.

Of all he took in from the message, the most astonishing revelation

196

he heard related to Joseph's response to his brothers when they stood defenseless before him in Egypt.

"Years later," the preacher explained, "when Joseph's eleven brothers were forced to go to Egypt to buy grain during a famine, they came face to face with Joseph, but did not recognize him.

"Was this not the moment Joseph had been waiting for? At last...here was his chance to exact full retribution for what his brothers had done to him. Now it was their turn to rot in prison. Now they would taste the suffering he had borne by their evil deed."

Father Michael leaned forward and scanned the congregation with piercing eyes. "Isn't that what they deserved? Wouldn't Joseph be acting justly by condemning and sentencing them to their fate? Of course! And now, God, by His providence, had delivered the brothers into Joseph's hand.

"What if it were you?" the priest posited. "Wouldn't you relish the chance to give them their just desserts? Isn't that how every good story should end...the good guy is rewarded and the bad guys get what's coming to them?

"But that's not what Joseph did. He passed up his chance to get revenge.

"When Joseph revealed his identity to them, they were terrified. They fell on their faces fully acknowledging their guilt. They realized he had the power to avenge himself. In utter remorse, the brothers threw themselves down before Joseph and said, 'We are your servants.'

"But Joseph said to them, 'Fear not, for am I in the place of God? As for you, you meant evil against me; but God meant it for good, to bring it about that many people should be kept alive, as they are today. So do not fear; I will provide for you and your little ones.'

"Hundreds of years later, the one prophesied to come as the Messiah of Israel died on a cross to atone for Israel's sins, and the sins of the whole world. Though he was innocent of any crime, he was unjustly sentenced to death.

"His tormenters threatened him. They shouted, 'Jesus, if you are the son of God, then come down from the cross.'

"How tempting that must have been for Jesus. He could have summoned thousands of angels to bring fire down upon his adversaries. Instead, he said, 'Father, forgive them. For they know not what they do.'

"In the prayer he gave us, we say, 'Forgive us our trespasses, as we forgive those who trespass against us.'

"Joseph was a prototype of Jesus. In him we get a foretaste of Jesus.

You are His followers…disciples who mirror Christ's image to others…can others see Jesus in you?

"The world is a mean-spirited place. People are quick to demand their just rights…quick to get even with those who hurt them. My friends, you have been freed from walking down that unsatisfying path of pain. Walk the way of Jesus. Forgive, as he has forgiven you."

Buck had heard plenty of sermons before, but never had a sermon stirred him more deeply than this one. Joseph met with abuse in prison. Bucky remembered the Shelby County jail and the bulls from Cheyenne. He knew the abuse Joseph felt.

Can I ever walk the path that Joseph did? Can I ever be like Jesus? How I long for justice for the bulls who lined us up naked in front of them! Could I let Crusher escape what he has coming to him? If I had the chance to rid him from my life, would I let him live? Mercy, instead of justice? Not today, Jesus. It's too much to ask of me. Maybe someday. Maybe never!

50. PRESSING CONCERNS

In spite of this nurturing setting, Bucky and Emily could not rid themselves of the cloud of melancholy hanging over them because of the separation from their families.

This was evident to the Griffins, and while these newest additions to their family brought great blessing to them, Bucky's and Emily's estrangement from their families weighed heavy upon the cleric and his wife..

Alone one evening, Becky said to Michael, "Bucky and Emily seem to be doing well with us, Michael,"

"Yes, they both seem to have recovered their confidence. I remember that night they came to the Soup Kitchen. Bucky was as skinny as a scarecrow and Emily seemed like a lost child. There's been a complete turn-around."

"I don't know," Becky continued, "there have been so many changes in our lives...and theirs...and so many issues that need to be considered. Maybe it's time for us to have a talk with them."

"Yes, darling, I agree. I think we need to do that, but the holidays are almost upon us, and you know what that means for a pastor and his family."

"Yes, dear...our heads will be in a spin with all the planning and activities, and there will be little time to think and talk about this. I understand, but can we do it early in the new year?"

"Yes, let's make a point of that."

Michael pulled her close and put his arms around her. "I think God has a plan for them...and us. I think something will happen to bring them together, sweetheart...in His time."

"I guess I just wanted to talk with you about it. Sometimes, even though there is no clear answer, it's comforting to talk," Becky said.

That night in their bedtime evening devotions, Michael and Becky asked God to give them the guidance they needed to lead their beloved Buck and Emily along the right path.

51. A CHRISTMAS
TO REMEMBER

DECEMBER, 1934

Resplendent with candles, evergreens and red and white poinsettias, the Christmas sanctuary and service at St. Bartholomew's sparkled with radiance. Real lighted candles adorned the Christmas tree positioned prominently beside the altar. On this Christmas Eve, fully opened stops on the great organ could not quell the voices of the congregation singing familiar carols. Vocal and handbell choirs and, at the end of the service, a string quintet to accompany the serene singing of "Silent Night," all added up to an inspiring experience. Buck and Emily felt transported to an enchanted, heavenly world. It was a night to remember.

The Thanksgiving and Christmas holidays cast joy over congregations and beyond, but the season also placed additional demands on a cleric and his family. White space on St. Bartholomew's church calendar disappeared, replaced by competing events, added services and celebrations. Activity at the Soup Kitchen also intensified, as patrons flocked to the mission for traditional holiday feasts. This annual whirlwind of seasonal activity resulted in some disruption of the regular pattern of life in the home of Father Michael and his family.

JANUARY, 1935

With the holidays over, life in the Griffin home took on a more relaxed tone that Buck and Emily had not witnessed since their arrival in early November.

When the dust settled after the rigorous chain of seasonal events, a semblance of normalcy returned to the household, and patterns of family life fell into place. In the quiet day-to-day demonstration of their faith, Father Michael and Becky provided strong building blocks for the spiritual underpinnings of their young protégés.

The gathering of the family around the supper table was an opportune time for devotional moments. On this evening, the supper Becky had prepared with Emily's help had been satisfying. They had consumed every morsel of baked chicken, turnip greens and boiled potatoes seasoned with butter and chives. Father Griffin had eaten his share. Buck noticed Father Michael had put on a few pounds since he had been a young assistant at St. Ann's in York. His blond hair had receded and thinned, but he had not lost his boyish good looks. On the other hand, Becky had changed little since Buck had seen her as a young pastor's wife, with the exception of her sandy hair, now flecked with gray strands, and cut to shoulder length. The five-foot-two-inch woman seemed as trim as ever as she flitted about performing household tasks.

Bucky had brought his own hearty appetite to the table, and if Becky thought he had not taken his fill, she would gently prod him to "Finish up the leftovers."

At the meal's end, Father Michael picked up the family Bible and handed it to Emily.

"Emily, it's your turn to read."

Emily smiled as she took the Bible from him, already opened to the appointed reading.

"The reading is from the prophet Isaiah, chapter 53, the first two verses," Father Michael said.

Emily read the passage:

> Surely he hath borne our griefs, and carried our sorrows: yet we did esteem him stricken, smitten of God, and afflicted. But he was wounded for our transgressions, he was bruised for our iniquities: the chastisement of our peace was upon him; and with his stripes we are healed. All we like sheep have gone as-

tray; we have turned every one to his own way; and the
Lord hath laid on him the iniquity of us all

Becky had the devotional booklet and read day's devotion based on
the Bible reading and, written by one of the denomination's pastors.
The devotion centered on the person of the Messiah, who would come
like a suffering servant to die on the cross for the sins of the world. The
writer of the devotion reminded readers that salvation is not a reward for
what we do but an unconditional, undeserved gift of God, won for all
people when Jesus died for the sins of the world.

Father Griffin ended the devotion with the prayer included in the
booklet: *"Dear heavenly Father, Thank you for giving us what we don't deserve. Thank you for sending Jesus to pay for our sins. Help us to know we are
God's children by faith and that He will never abandon or forsake us. Amen."*

Later in the evening, Buck and Emily had opportunity to spend
time alone, and to talk. "Bucky, how do you feel about the Griffins and
living in the parsonage?"

"Well," Buck said, "I think they adore each other and have a wonderful home life that I admire. They're such great people. I love them."

"Yes, I feel the same way. They would be wonderful with children. I
wonder why they never had any of their own."

"I've wondered the same thing. I can tell they're pleased we are part
of their family."

"But you know, Buck, even though they are both dear to me and I
would miss the warmth and happiness I find here, I long to be back
home. I miss my parents and my sister, Nan."

"Yeah...I'm grateful to be here, and in a way, I hope a lot of what
Father Michael and Becky are and do will rub off on me. But I'd give
my right arm to see both our families get together some day." Buck put
his hands on her shoulders and gazed deeply into her misty eyes. "Em, I
want to be with my family, but I couldn't bear to be away from you."

Bucky felt his face flush hot as he lowered his eyes realizing the intimate truth he blurted out that he had kept hidden in his heart. *Geez,
now she knows. I didn't mean to tell her like that...but I can't help it...that's
the way I feel.*

52. STIRRINGS

Not far into the New Year, a special celebration was in order. On January 12th, Bucky would be eighteen. Emily's time drew near, and the soon-to-be-mother's condition appeared healthy. Life for Bucky and Emily was changing for the better.

Now that Bucky had put some meat back onto his bones, he turned his attention to physical exercise. He ran, jumped rope, played basketball and did push-ups and sit-ups. On his birthday, the Griffins gave Buck a pair of boxing gloves...a generous gift, considering their limited finances. This thrilled Buck, and he quickly put the gloves to good use belting the life out of the punching bag at St. Bartholomew's Youth & Recreation Center.

Bucky and Emily were maturing and their feelings for each other now expanded beyond that of a boy and girl friend relationship. Though still clinging to the innocence of childhood, Emily's full feminine figure and alluring behavior did not fail to stir starry-eyed gazes from the boy whose hormones flamed hot. *There's something about her that draws me to her. She's irresistible...the way she looks at me. I'm tempted to touch her when we are alone, but I'm afraid it will set off fireworks that might blow my head off. I promised her I'd bring her home to her parents, but I want her for myself...I could not bear it if we ever became separated.*

One night, after the Griffins had retired to their bedroom, Emily, in her room, had prepared for bed, undressed and donned her nightgown.

204

Meanwhile, in his separate room, Buck had stripped to his underwear and had his pajamas on the bed. In the act of pulling his sleeveless ribbed undershirt over his head, Emily came into the room for a good-night kiss. Tossing his undershirt onto the bed, Bucky heard her and turned towards her. The moonlight streamed in through the window of the darkened room, casting its glow on Bucky's hardened abdomen, honed solid from his workout at the recreation center. At the same time, Buck saw Emily's backlighted silhouette through the sheer fabric of her nightgown. Emily stepped forward and placed Buck's hand on her midriff.

"The baby just gave me a kick. Bucky, feel it. Can you feel it?"

He felt a movement. "Sure enough!" His eyes lit up.

"Emily, let me touch you on your skin."

Emily lifted the gown so Buck could reach under it. Buck put his hand on her bare midriff. His pulse quickened. He felt his hormones coming to attention. He put his other arm around Emily and pulled her close.

"You are absolutely beautiful," he said, as he gazed into her soft brown eyes, her enlarged pupils almost eclipsing the surrounding color. Leaning forward, he gave her a tender kiss. Within moments, the kiss turned passionate. Bucky's hand slid upwards under her gown, touching her breast, tracing the curve of it with his hand and moving to her nipple.

Emily started. She stepped back, gripped Buck's probing hand firmly and moved it away from her.

Buck's face reddened, he lowered his head and froze in his position. Like a popped balloon, he went limp. "Oh, Em..." he said, "I shouldn't have done that. I'm really sorry. I didn't mean to..."

"We can't do this, Buck," she said, breathing heavily. After a brief silence, she added,"the Griffins...they've done so much for us...we can't break their trust."

"You're right...I know...it's just that it's so hard...being so close to you all the time and never being able to touch you...not without being afraid of what would happen if we did it."

"Oh, Bucky, I love you so much, but it's not right for us now. We both have to stick to the plan. You know God will help us get our lives in order."

"Yeah," Buck said, "You're right. I'm sorry. It's just that I can't imagine what my life would be if you were not a part of it...forever."

"Bucky, what are you saying?"

"I think we both know, Em. I guess it's about time I say to you what's in my heart."

Bucky got down on one knee and took her hand.

"Emily, you know I love you. In another month, I'll be eighteen. If you'll have me, I want to marry you after my birthday. After we're married, I want to officially adopt our baby, like I told you before. Please say yes."

Emily put her hands to her mouth and her eyes immediately started tearing up.

"Oh, Bucky. Oh, Bucky! Of course my answer is yes. But there's one loose end that I wish could be tied—"

Buck stood, still holding her hand. "I think I know what you're going to say, my darling. You're thinking about the other promise...the one about finding your parents."

"Oh, Bucky, you knew and remembered. Yes, if we could find my parents and they could be with us when we marry—"

"I want to ask for your father's blessing. It's the right thing to do. Em, let's talk to Father Michael and Becky tomorrow and see what they say. Meanwhile, I think we can consider ourselves to be engaged, right here and now!"

Standing at the window, they kissed in the light of the moon.

•

This romantic development did not escape the notice of Michael and Becky, and reminded them both of their unfulfilled commitment to discuss what would happen when the baby was born. "With the baby near at hand, we haven't much time to address this problem of their changing relationship, and what will happen when the child comes," Becky reminded Michael.

"You're right, and I didn't count on the escalation of their romantic inclinations. I've seen how they look at each other."

"Yes, I have too," Becky said. "Buck watches her every move. I catch him just staring at her in ordinary situations, as if he were transfixed. His growing attentiveness to her every wish worries me."

"You're right. We need to talk about this," Michael agreed.

53. DECISIONS

Holding hands, Bucky and Emily entered the parlor and stood before Father Michael and Becky.

"We want to get married," Buck said.

It was a Sunday afternoon, and the four had decided this would be the time to come together to talk about the coming baby and related issues.

Michael folded his paper, put it on the floor and glanced over at Becky, who returned his gesture.

"Not right away, though," Emily added.

"Sit down, and let's talk," Michael said.

The couple sat on the couch.

Emily began. "Father Michael, could you start us off with a prayer?"

"That's a good idea, Emily," he said leaning forward with bowed head and folded hands.

"Lord, how blessed Becky and I have been since Buck and Emily came into our lives. We love them dearly and they are an integral part of our family. Now, as another tiny addition to our lives is on the way, we need your guidance. Bless the child that is to be born, and Emily and Buck as they receive it as a precious gift from you. Lord, you desire the best for your children. Help us to make the decisions that would please you. Lord. Be with us and bless us to that end in your name. Amen."

The others echoed the "Amen," then all eyes turned to Father Michael, who straddled his left leg over his right knee in a relaxed manner.

"Let's start with your proposal to marry. Tell me what you're thinking about that."

Emily looked at Bucky, as if passing the baton to him.

"We have both talked on other occasions about a commitment to each other. We've pledged our love to each other, and now that the baby is going to be born, it seems to me that the right thing for me to do is to marry Emily and adopt the child...but there are other considerations. As soon as I learned Emily's story and about her separation from her family, I made a promise to her that I would help her to find and reunite with her parents."

"I was afraid of facing my father," Emily said, "but Bucky felt it was the right thing to do, and his promise to stay with me to make it happen convinced me."

"But when we reached St. Louis, we knew we'd never make it to Springfield in the state we were in...and...well, I guess you know the rest," Buck said.

Michael and Becky exchanged knowing glances as they remembered their own conversatons about this issue.

"We can't thank you enough for what you've done for us. You became our family, took us in and loved and helped us," Emily affirmed

"We've talked about that goal, too," Buck said. "I think we should find her family, and I should ask her father for her hand. Besides, it would be our greatest joy for me to meet Emily's parents and sister and to have them celebrate with us at our wedding."

"I can envision that as a wonderful experience and a laudable goal," Michael said.

"I agree," Becky said. "I must say, I'm proud of the way you've thought about these things, and Bucky, you're devotion to Emily...and to the unborn child is commendable."

"If we kind of got engaged at this time, and postponed the wedding until after the holidays, we thought that would be better. I'll be eighteen in January, and maybe be in a good position to find a job and support a family."

"That's a good goal...well thought out...but you know that you can stay here with us as long as you want to or need to," Becky said.

Emily said, "I know I could put the baby out for adoption...but I would never do that...besides, where could we find a better family to help raise the child besides both of you?"

Becky's face beamed at those words. She had always wanted children, but could not have any, and her imagination ballooned with thoughts of holding and caring for a baby and a family life that would fulfill her dreams.

Father Michael also was pleased, with some concerns, however. *I'm sure most of the congregation will stand behind this decision, but there will be some who will oppose it, firm in their belief that an unwed mother should put the child up for adoption. I'll explain this to the Church Council members...they're an outstanding group of leaders...and can field complaints...and the rumor mill? Well Becky will be able to address that with her personal contacts through the women's groups. Even so, there may be some fall out. So be it.*

54. A DISQUIETING INTRUSION

FEBRUARY, 1935

The news could not have come at a more inopportune time. A member of Father Griffin's former parish in York sent a clipping to him from the York Dispatch.

LOCAL MAN ARRESTED FOR MURDER

Police questioned and subsequently arrested Charles V. Ellis, of Altoona, charging him with the murder of Bruce Reid, a New York City detective. In February of this year, Reid was found dead in an alley in an uptown neighborhood of Manhattan. Police would offer little information, but did say that some items recovered at the scene tied Charles Ellis to the incident, including a letter found on Reid's person addressed to Ellis' son, Buckingham, whose whereabouts is unknown. Charles Ellis, employed at the Altoona Locomotive Works of the Pennsylvania Railroad remains in jail without bond as he awaits trial in New York City.

"This can't be true," Bucky protested. "There's no way my father could have done anything like that. What would he be doing in New York City, anyway?"

Confusion clouded Bucky's mind. In a daze, he walked to a chair and slumped down in it, with his head hanging.

As he sorted things out and pieced things together, Buck arrived at the horrifying realization that the detective could be the man who stalked him in New York City. Bucky remembered the man had fallen to the ground as he ran from the alley, but he had no idea the man was dead. There was no date on the clipped article, so Buck did not know how much time passed since his father had been arrested.

This must have been the man who was following me. What did the letter say? Did Crusher write it? Was it a letter of bitter triumph to be read to me before I met some terrible fate at the hands of this man?

Suddenly, Emily blurted out, "I know that man. I know the man who was killed!"

Buck, Becky and Michael Griffin looked at each other with raised brows and staring eyes.

"You knew this man?" Father Griffin asked.

"Not personally...but from the description, he is surely the man my sister, Nanette, and I found in the alley next door to our house! It was a nice, sunny winter day last year and we were playing on the sidewalk that morning, when we saw him in the back of the alley. We told our parents, and they called the police. The police questioned us, but we were both so frightened that we really couldn't tell them anything. We only got a glimpse of the body before we both ran out of there."

As Buck considered the implications of all this, a wave of panic anxiety swept over him. *I couldn't possibly have hit the man that hard. How did it happen? I'm a murderer! And my own father is the accused! How can this be? I've got to find out what happened.*

Father Griffin knelt beside Bucky. Putting a comforting hand on the boy's knee, he said, "Are you all right?"

Buck stared at him with apprehensive eyes and said, "I have to talk to you...in private."

Buck and Father Michael went into the kitchen and sat down at the table. Bucky told him everything that happened on the day the stalker followed and cornered him in the alley.

"Do you think it was the letter addressed to you that linked your dad to the man's death?" Father Michael asked.

"Maybe so...that, and the penknife I dropped, as well."

"What penknife?"

"The one I took the night I left home. It was my father's penknife and had his initials on it. I pulled it out of my pocket to defend myself, but dropped it into the alley before I could use it. When I ran out, I left it there."

"Wait a minute!" Father Michael said, trying to take it all in.

Bucky recalled how he impulsively took the penknife the night he left, an act he now regretted.

Buck and Father Michael went back into the parlor to explain the situation to the others.

Open mouthed and with eyes wide with amazement, Emily put her hands to her face. "Buck, I can hardly believe we shared in such a horrifying event long before we both met!"

They tried to think of plausible explanations for detective Reid's pursuit of Bucky.

"I am convinced he was sent by Crusher, but why the letter, and what did it say?" Bucky said.

"Is it possible," Becky postulated, "the detective had nothing to do with this 'Crusher'?"

Bucky was struck silent, and reflected on Emily's words. "But if...how could that be...if he wasn't Crusher's man...then who...? It's all a complete mystery." Then he announced, "One thing is clear: my father has been falsely accused of murder. I know what I must do. I must go to New York as soon as possible. I can't let my dad take the rap for something he didn't do!"

There were objections, but nothing any of them said, not even Emily's tearful pleading, could change his resolve. Buck assured her he would settle the matter and return as quickly as possible. He was equally resolved to be back in St. Louis in time for the birth of the new baby.

55. BACK ON
THE RAILS

The urgency of the situation and Buck's desire to return before the baby's birth demanded immediate departure, with little time for preparations. The Griffins quickly gathered some supplies. Concerned about his traveling needs, they urged him to take more than he could carry. Becky Griffin, in a motherly manner, offered snacks, and items for comfort along the way. Buck rejected the bulk of what they brought and packed only bare essentials in his small suitcase he would carry. "No self respecting hobo would be caught carrying such a stash of goods," he joked with a grin.

They all accompanied him to the tracks where he could catch on to a train heading east. To support him in hopping a train compromised Becky's better judgment. Her heart caught in her throat as the roar of the big engine and the hiss of steam raked her eardrums as it rumbled by while she watched Bucky's silhouette grabbing for a ladder. Although Emily assured her Bucky would be all right, Becky could not dispel thoughts of the many dangers from her own mind. She found some comfort in the pocket Bible she knew Father Michael had given him as well as the little cash they managed to gather for his trip. *May the Lord be with him.*

Buck caught on as the train came out of the yards, and now it moved at a rapid pace. He had no chance to climb down to a safer place, so he lashed himself to the catwalk with his belt and said a prayer he would arrive in New York before freezing to death. He felt grateful the Griffins insisted he wear warm clothing and gloves.

Although Buck did not get much sleep on his catwalk mattress, the trip proved uneventful until they reached the mountains. Bucky had not anticipated what would happen when the train raced through tunnels under the Appalachian mountains.

The train suddenly plunged into the black tunnel, the smoke from the steam engine belching out through the entrance hitting Buck squarely in the face.

Bucky gasped to get his breath. *Good God! What the hell is this?*

Heavy smoke and a shower of glowing cinders washed over him. "Eeeyaaa," he screamed. *The cinders are burning my face. Can't breathe!*

Farther into the tunnel, the onslaught intensified. *My sleeve! Omigod! It's catching fire!* Secured by his belt to the catwalk, he squirmed, twisted and swung his arms wildly to snuff out glowing cinders with his gloved hands. The heavy debris and fire continued to sweep over him for ten agonizing minutes before he emerged from the tunnel. He breathed a sight of relief. *Holy shit! I made it through, but I must be a sorry sight.* He swiped black soot from his face with his hand, his lungs seared from the inhaled smoke, and his clothing gave evidence of burns from igniting cinders. *I'm alive! Oh, Jesus, thank you. If I'd been closer to the engine, I'd be a goner for sure!*

Once in New York City, Buck darted off into a subway entrance in search of a public restroom. He entered the first he came upon. At this late hour, the rest room was deserted. He immediately removed his coat, gloves and some of his clothes to clean up. As he was washing his face and hands in a sink, an older man, who had followed him into the rest room, moved up behind him. Bucky flinched when he felt the man's hand sliding up the inseam of his pants, as the pervert leaned forward and whispered, "You're a little beat up, pretty boy. Need a friend...and maybe some money in y'r pocket?"

In an instant reaction, Buck turned and knocked the man onto the floor. He grabbed his suitcase and the clothes he'd removed and made a quick exit, taking the steps two at a time and running into the street. The hair on the back of his neck stood erect, and drops of perspiration popped out on his forehead. For the second time, he felt the inhospitable climate of this big metropolitan city where he could never feel safe and secure.

Early the next morning, Bucky headed for the police station and presented himself to the authorities.

He went to the reception desk and said to the uniformed officer, "I read about the man who was killed in the paper...he was a detective named Bruce Reid. I'm Bucky Ellis and I'm the one who killed him."

Those words brought prompt attention to those at the station house, and Bucky was ushered into a room for further questioning.

"OK, boy, give us your name and tell us your story. So you claim to have murdered Detective Bruce Reid?"

"Well, yes...and no, not exactly. It wasn't murder. The man you arrested is my father. He didn't kill the man...I did...but it was an accident. I never met the man, but he was stalking me and he chased me into that alley. I hit him to get away and ran like the devil. But I didn't know he died. That's the truth."

"Boy, your father is no longer in custody. We checked out his story and he had an ironclad alibi. He could not have been here in the city at the time of the crime."

Bucky's heart lifted and they could see his elation in his face, but his joy, scorched by the heat of their barrage of hammered questions, ended rapidly. In the process, Buck learned that after his father's release, authorities had issued an all-points warrant for the arrest of Buckingham Ellis. Having failed to locate him thus far, they considered it a fortunate turn of events that he had unwittingly placed himself into their hands. In the interrogation room, detectives pummeled him with questions and pointed accusing fingers at him. They would have been pleased to extract a confession that Bucky had intentionally murdered the victim. Buck consistently denied any malicious intent and stuck to his story, and following his conscience, confessed everything.

The clank of the jail cell door closing was like a lightning strike of remembrance of the terror and abuse he and K.O. had endured in past incarcerations. The police allowed him to contact Father Griffin, and Buck related the sad details over the phone.

Michael Griffin acted quickly, immediately dispatching to New York authorities a written character reference for Bucky, noting his participation in the Soup Kitchen and other church activities.

Father Michael also made contact with the archdiocese of the Episcopal Church in New York City. As a result, Bucky received visits from a priest, who gave him Holy Communion and brought a change of clothes to make him presentable at his trial. Two women from the church also accompanied the cleric and offered cupcakes they had baked and assurance that members of their congregation were praying for him.

One particularly fortunate consequence of Father Griffin's networking was the procurement of an experienced lawyer to represent the accused boy. The archdiocese approached Louis Grotto, a prominent attorney and a member of an Episcopal church in upper Manhattan. Attorney Grotto met with Bucky, and having a heart for the boy, he took up his defense on a pro bono basis.

Louis Grotto examined the available facts. He had obtained general knowledge of the situation, and had seen Bucky's testimony recorded in the police record. He asked Bucky specific questions related to the case, limiting them with intent to focus only on information that would strengthen his case.

"Bucky, I already know from Reverend Griffin that he and his wife took you into his home from the streets. Lawyers are required to answer truthfully about any information surfacing at a trial that might have a negative influence on the jury...or even incriminate you. For that reason, I don't want you to tell me anything about things you may have done when you were out on the streets...or riding the rails. Just answer my questions and tell me what I need to know to defend you. Sometimes ignorance of details is the best defense your lawyer can prepare. Do you understand?"

"Yes, Mr. Grotto. I'm grateful for your help."

In explaining his dread of Crusher, Buck wisely made no mention of the circumstances that led to Crusher's marred appearance.

"Crusher tried to kill me and my friend several times, and sometimes used other people to help him do it. I knew the man stalking me wasn't Crusher, but I was sure he was sent by him to hurt me. I thought only of escaping when he trapped me in the alley. I hit him and ran out of the alley without looking back. I didn't even know that he was dead." Buck added he had recurring nightmares about Crusher's pursuit of him.

Before they ended their interview, Louis said to Bucky, "Reverend Griffin's written character reference is hearsay and not admissible as evidence, but his mention of your work in the church and at the soup kitchen is a fact that can influence the jury's impression of your character. On that basis, I will offer Reverend Griffin's letter as evidence."

56. THE TRIAL

Louis Grotto decided against putting Bucky on the stand, in the event the prosecuting attorney might uncover questionable details about Bucky's past. Instead, he based his primary defense on the premise that Bruce Reid intentionally pursued Bucky, who had every reason to defend himself when this stranger cornered him in an alley.

The prosecuting attorney argued that in Bucky's recorded statement to the police, he had placed himself at the scene by his own admission.

"He openly admitted inflicting injury upon the man. It was entirely without provocation," he told the jury. "No concrete evidence even suggests detective Reid had any other intention than to deliver that letter to Mr. Ellis. In fact, if he had completed his mission, Mr. Ellis would have gained a considerable reward. Unfortunately, he misjudged the man's intentions and acted with foolish bravado. The boy exhibited the behavior of a reckless bully who settles things with his fists just for the thrill of it."

"I object!" Bucky's lawyer declared. "No evidence has been presented that would remotely suggest Mr. Ellis is a young man of such character. It is a complete fabrication straight from the mind of the prosecution, and from nowhere else."

"His brutal blow was enough to kill the victim!" the prosecutor shot back.

The judge slammed his gavel. "That's enough, gentlemen! Objection sustained." He directed the jury to disregard the prosecutor's character assessment and ordered his words to be stricken from the record.

The time came for each lawyer to present his closing argument. The prosecutor presented his argument first, in which he concluded, "Although you may sympathize with the defendant, his impulsive and foolish act resulted in the death of an innocent man, and that act must be reckoned with in full accord with the law."

Louis Grotto rose and walked calmly with an air of cool confidence and faced the jurors.

"Members of the jury, the prosecution has attempted to malign this young man's character, but we have ample evidence of the outstanding moral character of Mr. Ellis, which cannot be questioned. The letter from his pastor not only gives us the reverend's general opinion, but cites real situations substantiated by fact that confirm the defendant gave much time to serving others. It is interesting, and even ironic, that the prosecution cited the undelivered letter carried by the deceased as evidence against the defendant. In fact, it offers a reward from Queen Salote of the Pacific island kingdom of Tonga for Mr. Ellis having saved her nephew in an act of heroism...a tremendous testimony of this boy's outstanding character.

"If Buckingham Ellis had not perceived Bruce Reid as a significant threat to him, what possible motive could there be for his actions? According to the coroner's report, he had landed but one blow to the head. The only other mark of injury, and the one that proved fatal, was at his left temple, where his head hit the wall. There had been no vicious beating. We have seen that robbery was not the motive, since there was a significant sum of money on Mr. Reid's person.

"Ladies and gentlemen of the jury, this boy's story fits the circumstances perfectly. This young man felt his life threatened, was cornered in the alley, and sought only to defend himself. I ask you, in such a circumstance, would any reasonable person react differently?

"The prosecution has failed to present sufficient evidence that Buckingham Ellis is guilty of any wrongdoing. The jury should therefore heed the directive the judge will give you, that when such is the case, a judgment of 'Not Guilty' should be forthcoming."

After receiving their instructions from the judge, the jury filed out to deliberate. An hour passed. Inside, the discussion was intense. As disagreements over the evidence surfaced, the conversation heated up.

One of the jurors, a laborer in his 40's, sparked the discord by introducing a personal factor.

"He's just a kid. I got a boy his age. It got me thinking." With increased passion, he continued. "What if some stranger chased my son across the city and got 'im trapped in the back of an alley? If my kid remembered anything I ever taught 'im, I hope he'd remember to beat the crap out of 'im...er...pardon my language."

Another juror agreed. "I got kids, too. And if it were me, I'd defend myself and then make tracks to get out of there!"

"Yeah, this is a mean city full of nutty characters," another said. "Kids walkin' the streets are in danger."

A few of the women were clearly sympathetic.

One of them, a younger woman, decided the moment she set eyes on Bucky that he was innocent. *He's so cute. How could a sweet kid like that kill anybody?*

Another juror, a devout Jewish man, and a leader in a local synagogue, associated Bucky's act with that of Moses, who, in an act of rage, killed an Egyptian who had beaten a Hebrew slave. This story had a powerful influence on this juror, who reasoned, "If God could accept and even choose Moses to lead Israel to the promised land in spite of what he did, it is the godly thing to favor mercy over retribution for this boy who innocently defended himself against a supposed attacker."

Another man, just as firm in his conviction, countered, "Your judgment should not be based on emotion. Our job is to stick to the law. Is there any reasonable doubt he was the one who slugged the man, and he was the one who killed him? That's all there is to it."

"Yeah, that's right. He should take the rap for what he did," another man said. "We don't need any sentimental softies who'll let 'im git away with murder just because he's a kid!"

Someone else unleashed a brief tirade against all teenagers, branding them as "kids who run wild on the streets and are nothing but trouble."

As debate went on, the division between the jurors became more rigid. Everyone was talking at once, and no one listened to anyone else. The jury foreman lost control of the deliberations.

After the jury had returned, the judge asked, "Has the jury reached a verdict?"

"We have not, your honor."

The judge dismissed them to their hotel for the night. "We will reconvene back here at nine in the morning."

•

Back in the jury room the next morning, the dialogue continued as if it had never ended. The arguing cemented the jurors in their respective positions. Only two jurors changed their positions, but the final tally was the same, as each had been on opposing sides. The judge brought them back into the courtroom. Tension filled the room as the sober-faced group filed back into the jury box.

"Have you now reached a unanimous verdict?" the judge asked.

"We have not, your honor."

"Mr. Foreman, do you see a way for the jury to reach a verdict?"

"I do not, your honor."

"Then I am declaring a mistrial," the judge said.

The prosecutor had not been pleased with the case from the beginning. He was young and ambitious, and did not conceive of any way this case, win or lose, would further his career. The case was not high profile, and the media had given it no significant attention. He had no plans to take the matter any further. Therefore, he immediately advised the court the state would not be retrying Mr. Ellis and moved the court for dismissal. To the defense's relief, the court quickly granted the motion, and the judge told Bucky he was free to go.

The decision evoked an explosion of noisy exchanges as people voiced their mixed reactions.

57. THE ATTORNEY'S LETTER

At his departure, the prosecutor gave Bucky the letter held in evidence the deceased had on his person. While portions of the letter had been referenced at the trial, Buck had not seen the letter's complete content.

"Here, Mr. Ellis. Since this letter is addressed to you, it now belongs to you."

Buck ran his hand over the engraved letterhead, noting the fine stationery as he read:

> Hush, Lombardo & Westwood
> Attorneys at Law
> 201 Broadway
> New York City, New York
>
> January 24, 1933
> Mr. Buckingham Ellis
>
> Dear Mr. Ellis:
>
> The enclosed letter from Queen Salote Toupou of Tonga has been forwarded to us with instructions to ascertain your whereabouts and deliver it to you in person.

I believe you will find the letter self-explanatory. At the directive of Queen Salote, our firm is holding the sum of $2000 in escrow until such time as you contact us and provide us with satisfactory proof of your identity.

When you have met the above conditions, a certified check for that amount will be placed in your hands.

I trust you will contact us at your earliest convenience. We look forward to meeting you and completing the directive of Queen Salote as soon as possible.

Sincerely,

Marshall T. Hush, Esq.

Buck unfolded the enclosed letter carefully. As he glanced at the first paragraph, he blinked, reread the same words again, and sat down to steady himself.

January 14, 1933

Dear Buckingham Ellis,

I am deeply indebted to you for saving my dear nephew, Tanoa, from a terrible fate at the hands of uninformed surgeons.

Tanoa has told me of your fine character and how you unselfishly gave of your time and energy to prevent the amputation of his leg while his unfortunate injuries were being addressed in the hospital in Des Moine, Iowa.

In returning his wallet with everything in it, revealing his identity to the hospital officials, you changed the course of their procedure.

I am requesting that you contact a law firm in New York City, which our Tongan Government has retained to implement this matter. Their address is on the enclosed card. The matter necessitates a direct contact from you to verify your identity, and then you will receive the sum of $2,000 as an expression of gratitude on behalf of the royal family and the people of Tonga.

It is my hope that locating you will allow us opportunity to express our gratitude in a more personal way. Perhaps we may meet at some future time in Tonga, if it can be arranged for you to come here as our guest of honor.

For the present, I hope this reward will convey in some small way our sincere appreciation for your unselfish assistance to my dear nephew.

Yours truly,
Queen Salote

58. SOME PIECES COME TOGETHER

Upon Bucky's release, Attorney Mark Grotto's congregation presented him with enough money for transportation back to St. Louis. Some decent traveling clothes also arrived for him from a neighborhood Episcopal Church Used Clothing Depot.

Bucky knew he could remain in New York for only a limited time before he rode back to St. Louis for the birth of the new baby. Eager to accomplish the tasks he set out to do, he hurried on his way. First, there was the matter of the reward. *I sure wouldn't want to leave and have to return to this icy town later. It makes sense to hunt down the address of the law firm and get the $2,000 waiting for me.* Now Buck's thoughts fixed on the large sum of money, sending his head spinning.

The second issue arose upon Buck's remembrance of K.O.'s abrupt expulsion from the train in Alabama almost six months before. No news of him had surfaced since that time. *Maybe some of his friends at the Harlem YMCA may know something about where he is. Maybe he's there!*

Bucky decided to make his first stop the offices of Hush, Lombardo and Westwood, located along his route to Harlem.

His visit to the law firm ended in disappointment. The attorneys had apparently relocated long ago, and no one kept track of them.

"There are a lot of tenants in this building, and they come and go," a worker on the premises told him. "This place is like a revolving door.

Some have moved since we been here, and there are some vacant offices on this floor. Maybe you can find 'em in the phone directory. Sorry, kiddo, can't give ya anything more."

Reflecting on that comment as he left, it struck a chord. *Geez...I forgot...it's been over two years since Queen Salote wrote the letter.* Buck noted the time on the clock on the wall. *It may not be so easy to find these guys. I wish Father Michael were here to tell me what to do. Geez, I miss them so much, especially Em. I've got to get out of here. I want to get home. I'll head up to the Y, see what I can find about K.O., and then head on back to St. Louis. Father Michael will know what to do about the letter.*

•

Heading for Harlem, Bucky bounced briskly down the steps to the Lexington Avenue Express subway train, arriving just in time to slip into a crowded car before the doors closed, and the train departed. At four o'clock in the afternoon, passengers squeezed together on every seat. Bucky and other late comers remained standing, some clinging to upright poles as the cars squealed and rocked from side to side in a mad rush to deliver its occupants uptown. Buck joined others compressed into a small circle, claiming his space on the pole with a firm grip.

In this rhythmical sway of standing passengers, moving as though fused into one body, riders accepted without question the close physical contact with their neighbor. The soft leather from the gloved hand on top of Buck's naked hand drew no special attention from him to the boy who wore it. Perhaps a year or two older than Bucky, this fashionably dressed boy in a dark satin-collared overcoat and a brown felt snap-brim hat with a feather in its band cocked forward on his head would have stood out anywhere but here. No one noticed the stark contrast between this boy's finery in contrast to Bucky's outfit of corduroy pants, red plaid flannel shirt under a thinly lined jacket with its turned-up collar. Even when their eyes occasionally met, Bucky gave no thought to the furtive glances the boy repeatedly gave him.

When the doors opened and Buck exited onto the platform, the boy matched his pace and stepped lively at Buck's heels. When the crowd thinned, the boy hung back. He watched him when Bucky went through the doors at the Harlem YMCA. He glanced at his watch. It read 4:55 P.M. It's getting pretty dark. *It ain't good for a well-dressed white boy like me to be in Harlem at this hour.* He headed for the lights of a drug store on a nearby corner, where he might find a phone.

•

The place was at once familiar, but inside, Buck saw no one he knew. *I wonder if I have any friends left here.*

The thought had hardly passed when he spotted Clyde, the typesetter he had befriended.

Taking long strides, Clyde ran to him and declared, "I remember you. You helped me when I spilled all that type. Do ya remember that mess I made? Watcha doin' here?"

"Clyde" Bucky said, "How are you? Are you still spilling stuff onto the floor?"

Clyde laughed and said, "They got someone else settin' the type now, but I'm his helper...an' I'm the janitor now, too!"

"That's great," Buck said. He noticed a group of his old friends gathering around him.

"Where ya been, Bucky?"

"Wot happened to ya?"

"Yeah, you two were out of here like a bullet," another said.

Another added, "K.O. told us something complicated came up the day you guys left and you were forced to leave New York."

Buck's face lit up. "You heard from K.O.?" His heart started to pound, his voice charged with excitement. "Where is he? Is he here? What happened to him?"

"Why he's livin' in Chicago...you know, the 'windy city'. He's gotten himself a filly. He's married, ya know."

"What?" Buck said, "You mean it? Oh, no...hey...is her name Estelle...do you know?"

"Yeah, dat's right, Buck. Dat's her name. Would ya like deir address? I kin give it to ya."

"By God, yes...yes!"

"Wait here. I'll go git it."

A grin as wide as the Hudson River stretched across Bucky's face. "Well I'll be damned," he said.

"Hey, what brings you here, and where are you headed?" one of his friends asked.

"It's a long story, and now I'm headed home. Someone and something great is waiting for me back in St. Louis."

"Listen, Buck, don't be in a rush," someone said. "It's late. Why don't you bed down here? There's some space here for you, and you can take off fresh as a daisy in the morning."

"Yeah, Buck, come on. Then you can tell us what happened."

" Well...OK, it sounds like a good idea. I don't have much with me, but where should I park my stuff?"

•

In the drug store, the boy tailing Bucky put the phone to his ear.

"Hey, dis is 'Finguhs' here. Tell the *Mastermind* I been followin' 'is mark all day. I don't know when he got here or how long ago it wuz, but he's here in New Yawk City...yeah..., it's da kid, all right...it's Ellis, and he's bunked in at the Y on West A-hundred 'n-toidy-fifth Street...Yeah, I'm sure dat's where he's stayin'. I been here for two hours...no way, I ain't waitin' any more...I'm gonna hafta leave. It's colder than an iceberg, and my friggin' balls are frozen solid. Besides, I got a date an' I'm all dressed up pretty snazzy. Ya should see me...Yeah, I hope the job's done now. If so, I'll be waitin' fr my usual reward, but"—Fingers added with a nervous chuckle—"don't tell the *Mastermind* I said dat."

59. HOMEWARD BOUND

Bucky had come to New York City twice before under more humble circumstances. Each time he abandoned the train before it arrived at the station.

Now, inside Penn Station, Buck saw it for the first time. He craned his neck taking in the visage of the gigantic vaulted steel and glass ceiling as rays of sunlight streamed down over him. The sheer expanse of the open space left him open-mouthed, gaping. He had never imagined anyone creating a place of such grandeur for people to get on and off trains.

"One way to St. Louis, please," Bucky said to the ticketing agent, handing over money for the fare. He would not be traveling on the much-touted Pennsylvania Railroad's new passenger line, the *Broadway Limited*, with its plush accommodations for sleeping and dining, but in coach class on a less opulent train. Even so, he had never before ridden "the cushions," and to him it represented the pinnacle of luxury.

Jumping on board, he chose a seat next to a window. As he brushed his hand along the molded seat," a gray-haired middle-aged woman sat next to him along the aisle. Buck smiled. *This is nothin' like the iron platforms and wooden planks I had to ride on.*

The train tunneled under the Hudson River and sped farther from the city. Bucky watched dairy farms and gentle hills stream by outside the windows. He felt euphoric. *Things are finally coming together. Emily's baby is on the way, and she's the love of my life. I know someday we'll marry, and our country has a new president who sounds like he may turn things around for the better. Yes, sir, things are starting to look up.*

As the outside scenery faded away under the darkness of night, Bucky felt drowsy at the end of this rigorous, long day. The train now accelerated through open country. Only an occasional trackside lamp or a few distant lights interrupted the darkness outside. Buck's eyes started glazing over at the monotony of it all and his head drooped. Finding a comfortable resting place for his head, he dozed.

The woman sitting next to him rose from her seat and left. A few seconds later, a man sat down and occupied her seat. The man slid backwards into the seat, with his face towards the aisle. Not quite asleep, with lids barely raised, Buck watched the man's reflection on the window pane of the dimly lighted coach. The man turned his face with an unnatural slowness toward the window. As the window mirrored the man's face , Bucky gasped in terror at the sight of his eye patch.

Flinching, Bucky kicked the seat in front of him and slammed against the side of the car with a jerk. "What's he doing here? How did he find me?" he blurted out. "Where...where am I?"

"Sshh...there, there," the woman said as she gently restrained him. "You dear boy...you must be having quite a dream."

Bucky opened his eyes to see a sweet, motherly face with a faint smile on it. Relief washed over him when he realized she was the same woman who sat next to him. With Crusher's presence a mere fantasy, Buck breathed deeply, but the vision of his dream remained vivid.

"You seemed restless the whole time," she said, "but I didn't think I should wake you...until you started talking in your sleep."

Cowering a bit, Bucky said, "I'm sorry, ma'am. I hope I didn't disturb you. I'm really sorry."

"That's quite all right. You just get a comfortable position and go back to sleep. Think of pleasant things. We'll be in St. Louis in the morning, and everything will be fine." She smiled.

As the hours passed, the other passengers in the coach soon slept soundly. Only one person in the car remained awake. Eyes wide open, body restless, afraid to fall asleep, Bucky wrestled with one question:

Is Crusher lying in wait in St. Louis?

PART TWO

THE MAKING OF A MAN

Dick Miller

1. WELCOME HOME

FEBRUARY, 1935, St. Louis, Missouri

Standing on the Pullman steps and holding the handrail, Bucky craned his neck to scan the platform that appeared to slide by as the train docked. *There they are waiting to greet me—Emily, Father Michael and Becky. It must have been the hand of God that Father Michael was transferred to St. Barthlomew's here in St. Louis, and our paths crossed.* As the train slowed to a stop, Bucky flung his bag to the side and sprang with outstretched arms from the steps.

Michael and Becky almost lost their footing as Bucky landed and pulled them all into his embrace. "*Whoa!* Hey, you nearly knocked me down!" "Bucky!" "It's sure good to have you back!" "Welcome home." "Take it easy, Buck..."

Taking a step back, Bucky saw Emily's fullness and said, "Look at you, Em. Geeze, looks like I got back just in time!"

"Oh, you silly goose, you've only been gone about four weeks."

"Four weeks! It seemed more like a year!"

Michael picked up Bucky's valise. "Come on, let's go home. Buck, we want to hear everything that happened in New York City...your arrest...the trial...everything."

Later, relaxing in the parlor of the parsonage, Buck said, "I can't be-

231

lieve I'm here. It's so great to be with all of you. New York was awful. When they brought me into the jail, after each door slammed behind me my heart sank, and I really thought I might never see any of you again."

"I can't imagine what you've been through," Becky Griffin said.

"The lawyer prosecuting me turned me inside out. I was scared. He tried to make everyone think I was a kid looking for trouble. I shook when he stuck a finger out at me and called me 'a killer'. He acted like some kind of a monster. Everybody got upset, and my lawyer shouted his objections, and the judge said to take that remark out of the record."

"The man sounds like Crusher," Emily said, with a frown.

"Not quite," Bucky said. "Yet it wouldn't surprise me if he moonlighted as a bull down at the Hudson River freight yards."

Even Buck had to smile at the ripple of laughter caused by his unintended humor.

"Speaking of Crusher," he added, "The best part of this whole mess is that even though I felt terrible about accidentally killing that detective, I was relieved to know he had nothing to do with Crusher. It's a good bet that he doesn't know where I am. Maybe he's out of my life forever."

Emily smiled and hugged Buck. The two stared dreamily into each other's eyes.

"And the second best thing is the news I heard at the Y that K.O. is fine, married to Estelle, is living in Chicago, and I have his address. It's the first I heard anything about him since he left the train in Alabama to avoid getting lynched by a search party. First chance I get, I want to write him a letter. I'll do that first thing in the morning."

In bed that night, Bucky thought about his future. *After her baby comes, we'll get ourselves on track. We'll find Emily's parents. They're sure to welcome back their daughter and their new grandchild. And Crusher...is he out of my life...or not?. And then there's Josh. The baby is his. Is he still riding the rails? Could he be coming our way for his child? I hope we never see him again.*

Even though he had tried to convince Emily and the others that Crusher was not likely to be a threat anymore, he himself was not entirely convinced and a chill crawled up his spine. He closed his eyes. *Crusher. There he is again. I can see him as if it were yesterday...his eye hanging from its bloody socket by fragile strands of God knows what...Jesus, why does he haunt me so? Why can't I get him out of my head?*

Bucky followed through and wrote his letter to K.O. Within a week's time, he received a reply, which reported in part:

Dear Champ...

...Had nothing but good luck since I bin here. Chicago is the place for me. I got me a good job working for Mr. Gordon as a shofer and butler. Even get to wear a uniform. I also do odd jobs for him – he's a great boss...Me and Estelle have our own place over the garage. We can make love and be at our job a few minutes later. How bout that? Just a few of us at the wedding. Wish I new where you was. I wood have asked you to be my best man. I know you cud kech a ride to Chicago. Instead, Estelle's brother stood up for me...

Mr. Gordon let us stay at a place he owns on Lake Michigan for our hunnymoon. It was great...

If you ever come to this city, we got a place for you.

Your best pal,
KO

Buck showed Father Michael the letter. He also showed him the letter he had tucked away from Queen Salote, and described his failure to locate the attorneys who held a reward for him from the Tongan royal family for saving Tanoa's life in Des Moines, Iowa.

"Buck, this letter is outstanding," Father Griffin said. "There must be a way to find these attorneys. We should act on this as soon as possible. In fact, I'll make some calls right now."

It took Michael several hours connecting with contacts he had in New York City to piece things together. He learned the firm had moved their offices to the nineteenth floor of the Flatiron building located at 175 Fifth Avenue and Broadway in midtown Manhattan. He helped Buck compose a letter including his St. Louis address, requesting the steps he needed to follow to claim the reward.

"Bucky, all we can do now is wait," Father Michael said.

"And pray," Bucky said with a smile. "Don't forget that. Thanks for helping me write the letter."

Within the week, Father Michael reported to Bucky, "Our letter to the law firm came back. They have moved out of the Flat Iron Building and left no forwarding address. I'll keep Queen Salote's letter in case something turns up. Bucky, I'm sorry. I don't know what else we can do, but I'll work on it. Maybe some of my priest buddies in New York can find out something, so hang on."

2. MICHELLE REBECCA BERNARD

MARCH 8, 1935

As Emily's pregnancy progressed, Becky Griffin assumed the role of director of operations. Like a mother hen scurrying about and hovering over her chicks, Becky moved into the position with unrestrained determination. For weeks, she had been gathering a small library of books and articles about baby care and nutrition.

Becky had always wanted children, but after unsuccessful attempts to conceive, the priest and his wife had accepted the reality they were unable to have children. She welcomed this chance to direct her maternal instincts toward Emily and the baby waiting to be born.

Michael already had mastered the art of being Bucky's paternal mentor. Bucky's own father had always taken a special interest in his eldest boy, and although the backgrounds of the two men were different, Bucky found elements of resemblance between Michael Griffin and Chuck Ellis. A man of integrity, his father taught his children honesty, responsibility and respect for their elders. His demonstrated love for Bucky's mother laid a firm foundation for relationships they would form as adults.

Everything was in place when the new baby, a beautiful girl, was born on March 8, 1935. Emily decided to name the child Michelle Rebecca Bernard, after both Michael and Becky Griffin.

The Boxcar Kid

At eighteen, Bucky felt ecstatic about his new responsibility as custodian and protector of Emily and the baby. When he held Michelle, cuddling and cooing over her, any observer would have thought Bucky was the bona fide proud father.

Announced in the church's newsletter to parishioners, Michelle's arrival sent a stir of excitement through the congregation. A capacity crowd filled the church on the day of her baptism, and many people responded with gifts and congratulations. The kindness and loving behavior of their priest and his wife wielded a strong, positive influence on the members of St. Bartholomew Church, and most warmly embraced and supported them.

Meanwhile, the hope of receiving the $2,000 reward offered by Queen Salote seemed diminished, as a notice from the attorneys' firm claimed that because of the lack of response within a reasonable time period, the reward was no longer available. Efforts to dispute this met with frustration due to Father Michael's and Bucky's inability to confront the attorneys directly in New York City. Finally, they reluctantly abandoned their efforts.

During this time, Bucky felt a growing uneasiness about his dependence upon the Griffins. In spite of their limited means, the cleric and his wife willingly endured any sacrifice to provide for whatever Bucky, Emily and Michelle needed. Bucky still helped out at the Soup Kitchen, but without a real job and source of income, his volunteered service did not match what he and Emily received from the Griffins *How can I allow myself to burden them when I couldn't bear to do that to my dad? But I can't bring Emily and Michelle into a homeless future. Shoot. What the hell am I gonna do? Maybe I should just leave by myself.*

It soon became evident to Buck that Emily also shared these feelings.

"Bucky, have you ever thought about the way the Griffins do so much for us without asking for anything in return? Sometimes I can't bear it...we're taking food from their table when they have hardly enough for themselves."

"I know," Buck said. "I think about that all the time."

"I think we should leave and go our own way," Emily said.

"I thought about that," he said, "but the more I considered it, the more I came to recognize it as a bad idea. What do you think would happen if I took you and Michelle out on the road? Remember when we saw that fella and his wife with the crying baby in her arms trying to get a ride? They were just kids, like us, and nobody would stop to pick them up. Geez, I bet they're still standing there on the side of the road."

Emily's face went blank for a moment while she became lost in thought. Then she confessed, "I can't even say it...oh, Buck...do you know, I was so upset about this...once I even thought about going away myself and leaving Michelle with the Griffins. Michelle would be better off with them. I'm afraid to go home and face my father after the big blow-up we had...but I even thought of trying to get to Springfield...to look for them...I'm so confused about all this...and Bucky..." She began stifling her tears. "...I know you'd do better without me...I'm pulling you down, too."

The two sat on the bed next to each other as they talked, but when Buck heard these words, he jumped to his feet like a popping cork from a champagne bottle. He bent over and spoke directly to her, shaking his finger in front of her nose. "Holy mackerel, Em! Geez, how could you think that? Geez, without you and Michelle, my life would be worth nothing. You're everything to me. There's no way you'll ever get rid of me. I'm sticking no matter what, you hear me?"

"Oh, Bucky...I love you so...what can we do?"

"I know one thing, Em. We aren't going anywhere until we figure things out, Promise me you won't do anything dumb. Promise."

"I promise."

"Tomorrow I'm gonna talk to Father Michael. I think he needs to know how we feel. Maybe he can help us find a way."

"That's a good idea," Emily said. "I'll go with you."

Their eyes met, and Emily stood as Bucky pulled her into his arms. With a gentle wipe of his thumb, he swept away a tear from her cheek and moved his fingers back through her hair, brushing it from her face. Her thick lashes framing her soft brown eyes caught his full attention. As Buck stood embracing Emily as her strong protector, he felt an irresistible erotic urge charge through his body like lightning. With his hand behind her head, he brought Emily's face close until their lips met.

3. THE CIVILIAN CONSERVATION CORPS (CCC)

Becky and Michael Griffin had long harbored a concern over the future of these beloved guests in their home. With a baby in the mix, Michael and Becky knew the strain on them to support this expanded family without future prospects seemed an unhealthy situation. Yet, at eighteen in the continuing context of the Depression, Bucky would find little opportunity to assume responsibility of providing support for Emily and Michelle by means of an income of his own.

One day, a glimmer of hope sparked in Father Michael as he read in the *St. Louis Post Dispatch* an updated story regarding the Civilian Conservation Corps. The article announced a change in the age limit for recruits, extending it through age 27. Father Griffin knew about the program, established in 1933 under the Federal Unemployment Relief Act, and even though the change in upper age boundaries would not affect Bucky's eligibility, the story captured Michael Griffin's attention and started him thinking.

Under the auspices of the Army and the U.S. Forestry Service, the CCC offered discipline and practical working skills for those enrolled. The administration of President Franklin Delano Roosevelt intended the program as relief for the country's impoverished families and unemployed young people. Each recruit received a cash allowance of $30 dollars a month, $25 of which went home to his family. Enrollees without a family would have the money held in escrow for them.

Michael Griffin recognized this program as tailor-made for Bucky. Recruits had to be unmarried, and although all agreed the avowed intent of Bucky and Emily to marry should wait until Emily found her family and reconciliation came, enrollment in the CCC might further extend the time before they could join in holy matrimony.

The Griffins had no legal guardian status under the law, nor would they profit directly from Buck's CCC earnings, but with Buck receiving housing and living expenses from the government, the indirect benefits of this arrangement became evident.

Father Griffin wondered how he was going to tell Bucky about the CCC, and now, when the couple expressed their concern about the burden, it appeared that God had dropped the opportunity into his lap.

Bucky, who longed for a more adventuresome life in contrast to the domestic and dependent existence he experienced in the Griffin home, responded with exuberance.

"This is a chance for me to step up and make something of myself. It would be fun, but more than that, it would give me a brighter future, and not just for me, but for you, Emily and Shelly," he said, directing his last words to Emily.

"Buck," Father Michael replied, "It would be hard work, and you'd be under some heavy discipline. I understand that life in the camps is not all fun and games."

"I'm not afraid of that. I'm more than up for it. How do I get into the program?"

Emily expressed greater reluctance.

She asked, "How long would he be away? I know it would be good for all of us, but I don't know how I could get by with you away, Buck. I depend on you so much."

"We would be here for you, Emily," Becky affirmed.

"That's right, Em," Buck said. "Look, I know I'll pretty much go crazy without you and Shelly, but it will be a chance for us both to mature and be ready for a life together on a firm footing when I get back."

Father Michael quickly responded, "Buck, I agree with you. I think you'd be making a wise decision." To Emily and Becky he said, "As a man, I can understand Bucky's desire to establish a strong foundation before considering taking on the responsibility of a family."

After some further discussion, they all came to a consensus that the plan would greatly benefit everyone, even though the separation of Buck from the family…and Emily and Shelly in particular…would be difficult.

As Bucky continued to ponder the decision, his excitement grew. In his mind, the prospect for rough and ready adventure conjured up memories of riding the rails with K.O.

Geez, do I miss K.O. If he joined the CCC with me and we went to the same camp, it would be just like old times. K.O. and me...what a blast.

He also knew that could not happen because K.O. did not qualify for enrollment in the CCC on two counts—he was married and gainfully employed. *Damn. But how can I not be happy for him? The lucky son of a gun!*

Buck penned a letter to K.O. and Estelle, telling them about his plans to hook up with the CCC.

•

Crusher sat wringing his hands in frustration. *That bungling idiot. How could he let him slip away? My regional operative in New York City reports the stoolie was more interested in a fast time with the girls than he was over the assignment I gave him. It would have been simple enough for him to stick with Bucky to see what train he boarded and where he was headed. So close...yet he failed this simple task. He crossed the line and is no longer useful to me. I will take care of him.*

And where do I go from here? Where would the little bastard go? Hmmm...perhaps he would go to his home. I have some information on his family in Pennsylvania. Yes. That's where I will place a new and more responsible operative. There is no way I will let the unpunished get away. I will find him.

Dick Miller

4. MC DOWELL COUNTY COURTHOUSE

APRIL, 1935, Morgantown, North Carolina

After receiving his acceptance, Bucky traveled to North Carolina for his preliminary examination. At the McDowell County courthouse, he joined other boys in a room where they had to strip, form a line, and pass by medical personnel for a complete physical.

Bucky passed and at the end of the line was happy to don a new set of government issued clothes including a modified World War I uniform. He admired himself in a mirror as he fastened the belt of his pants. *Ha, K.O. So you think you're the only one who looks good in a uniform, eh?* He lifted the pants of his blue denim work clothes and looked at his shoes. *Not bad. I think they fit my feet. Wow!*

The government kept in escrow Buck's $25 monthly allowance normally sent to the enrollee's family. During the past year, he had written some letters to his family in Altoona, and Helen sent back chatty replies with news about his dad, Bud, Lily and Lena. The last letter he sent, however, came back with "moved - no forwarding address" stamped on the envelope. Buck was determined to try to locate them, but his rigorous schedule at the camp left him little time to pursue this goal immediately.

After an initial period of training and conditioning, Buck was assigned to Company 2348 at Norton, Virginia with about fifty other boys, all transported in decent passenger trains.

241

The Boxcar Kid

The camp, occupied by a supervised army of about 200 boys, was nestled in the mountains of western Virginia. Part of a forestry division, Buck joined enrollees assigned to clear fire trails with saws and axes. Few of the boys had handled such tools, but Buck had chopped wood on the farm in York.

When they first set out for training, Buck saw the forestry supervisor slam the blade of the ax against a stone before handing it to each crewmember. *What the hell is that for? He's deliberately dulling the blade.* Later, he recognized this as the supervisor's method to strengthen the boys' muscles and swing. Once well-seasoned in their forestry skills, they gave the boys axes with sharp blades, and they proved to be the best trailblazers in the camp.

Buck reached the top of his unit for proficiency and skill, and he knew his forestry supervisor had kept a sharp eye on him. On the trail, they divided the boys into two groups with separate assignments. The supervisor placed Bucky in charge of one group.

At work on the trail one day, Buck decided to divide them further into two separate groups.

"I'm marking this spot as a starting point. Victor, you take your group to the east and I'll go west with the other. We'll have a race to see who moves the fastest. The forestry supervisor placed markings so you can see where the trail goes. At the two-mile point, each of you will find a special yellow marker where you'll turn around and head back here. The group back here first will be the winner."

The kids picked up their tools, eager to start.

"But don't do any half-assed job. I'll be moving between groups on the trail to make sure each is doing it right. Everybody understand?"

The boys nodded.

"Okay, let's go."

Joining the group moving west, Buck did his share of the work. After about an hour, he left the group to check out the other's progress. As he approached, he listened for the sound of axes splitting wood. Instead, he heard the sound of laughter and kids hollering. Arriving at their location, he stumbled upon an unsettling sight. He stopped short. "What the...?

The boys had come upon a whiskey still in the forest. Although prohibition had been repealed about a year ago, someone continued to use this still to produce whiskey. One of the boys had found a bucket and filled it with the brew. They were hot and thirsty after working hard. One by one, down went the whiskey and off came their shirts.

Some were crazy drunk when Buck found them. He saw one kid buckled over vomiting. Another had passed out on the ground. Enraged, Buck kicked over the bucket, spilling its contents.

"Get your asses up to the trail and line up," he demanded. "Get Roberts off the ground and help Clarkson to his feet."

Victor, who Buck had chosen as their group leader, also had imbibed. "Victor. Not you!"

Victor responded with a sheepish smile as he struggled to stand straight.

Nobody moved. Each was waiting for someone else to be the first to comply with the orders.

Then one of them, giving Buck a cocky look and pointing at him said, "Hey, hotshot, how's y'r butt hole for rats?"

Then a big hulking kid standing a little to the side of Bucky grabbed him and flung him across the clearing against a tree trunk.

For a moment, Buck was dazed and shook his head, as someone yelled, "Com'on, guys, let's beat the shit out of hero-boy!"

Meanwhile, the workers from the west end of the trail had finished and returned to the central location to wait for the other group. Mr. Foster, the supervisor arrived and joined them.

On his way to join those on the eastern part of the trail, Bucky had passed this point only moments before, and learning about his plan for the group to divide, the supervisor said, "Wait here while I check on the progress of the others."

Hearing the noise ahead of him, the supervisor arrived on the trail above the fracas in the woods below just as Bucky started admonishing the group. From his vantage point, he had a clear view of the group while remaining unseen. He quickly sized up the situation as he watched in silence.

•

Buck stood straight as the ring of boys closed in on him. He jumped back and took a defensive stance, fists clenched, legs spread and feet planted firmly.

"Okay, that's it. Come and get it, if you think you're up to it!"

A couple of the agitators lunged at him. Buck moved like a slippery eel, avoiding the blow of the first assailant. The next aggressor doubled over with a loud grunt after Buck landed his fist solidly into the boy's stomach. Another, already wobbly on his feet from booze, flew sideways from Bucky's blow to his head.

These plastered jackasses couldn't fight their way out of a paper bag.

Not wanting to put any more of them down, Bucky avoided the attempts of those still wildly swinging at him, while the rest of the pack took steps backwards in retreat.

Instead of stopping the fight, the supervisor watched Buck continue to thrash the boys until he had them all subdued and under control. Then the supervisor made his appearance and said, "Okay, boys, on your feet. Start marching in as straight a line as you can. We're going back to the camp."

The next day, Bucky learned that the whole camp buzzed about the incident. A report circulated through the camp claimed Bucky had "single handedly beaten the crap out of the kids" in the rebellious group.

Later that morning, the supervisor summoned Buck to his quarters under a large tent. Buck reluctantly faced Mr. Foster, the forestry supervisor and Captain Adams, the camp supervisor from the Army.

"Ellis, I guess you had a pretty tough situation on your hands yesterday," Captain Adams said.

"Yes, sir."

"I understand you handled yourself quite well."

Bucky hesitated before replying. He had expected to receive a reprimand rather than a commendation.

"Thank you, sir."

"Even some of the more sober boys in your unruly group spoke of your bravado in the face of so many opponents. I think you have won their respect and admiration."

Buck was silent.

"And Mr. Foster, here, told me of your fighting ability."

"Where did you learn to fight like that?" Mr. Foster asked.

"My friend, who we call K.O., taught me. His father was a prize-fighter. We practiced sparring every day, and at the World's Fair in Chicago we put on an exhibition attraction on the Midway. In New York City, we had a boxing program at the YMCA to teach kids how to box."

The captain raised his eyebrows. *This kid is a find!*

Mr. Foster conveyed a look of satisfaction to Captain Adams.

"Ellis," Adams continued, "even before the happening last night, we've been watching you. You stay cool in a hot situation, and you conduct yourself in a confident manner. We've been looking for someone like you. We'd like to transfer you up to a camp at Prince William Forest Park up near Dumfries, Virginia where there is interest in expanding recreational activities. We would make you an Assistant Leader. This would be a nice promotion for you. As an Assistant Leader, your pay would increase another eight dollars each month."

Mr. Foster spoke, "To be more specific, Mr. Ellis, there is talk up there of setting up some kind of physical recreation activity for the boys to help build discipline and healthy bodies. An organized boxing program may be just the ticket. There are camps that have baseball teams and other sporting events where they have formed leagues with camp teams competing against each other. Boxing is a growing phenomenon. Company 3383 needs a boost, and we have a benefactor who is offering to donate equipment and whatever else needed to start such a program. Do you think you could pull it off? Why don't you take a little time to think about it?"

Bucky shook himself out of his awed stupor. *The extra money would be a godsend for Emily and the Griffins. And I couldn't think of anything I'd want to do more.* He answered, "I just thought about it, and I'm your man. When do I leave?"

"We'll check things out and let you know."

5. FIRE!

JUNE, 1935

"Hey Buck, look over to the west. Do you see that?"

Buck looked towards the horizon. "Uh-oh...looks like smoke."

"You know what that means," his buddy, Ted Staddle, said.

A moment later, the Company Commander, Frank Shawnburg, made his appearance and directed everyone to grab fire-fighting gear and get into the truck to be dispatched to the fire.

"The fire is up at High Knob," he said.

They dropped off teams at various locations to join enrollees from other camps who were making fire lines. Buck and Ted, among those dropped off last, joined a team closest to the fires.

For four consecutive days, the teams fought the fires without a break. Supplies were meager and the work difficult. Some slopes were rocky and nearly vertical, requiring tools for climbing.

Windy conditions whipped the fire out of control as it kept expanding. Fire fighters in another team they reached declared, "Are we glad to see you. Shake a leg. We're losing ground and the fire has already jumped our fire lanes and is coming this way."

By the fifth day, everyone was exhausted. Filth and grime covered Buck and Ted. Food that reached them sporadically was cold, but they devoured it like starving refugees. For the last two days, they had nothing to quench their rising thirst.

"I ate better when I was riding the rails and begging," Buck said.

"Give me yours if you ain't satisfied, and quit bitchin'," Ted said as they stuffed the food into their mouths while racing to the next spot. They both could have fallen asleep standing up, but there was no time to rest.

Now the fire suddenly loomed closer.

"Move back, move back," someone yelled. "Move the hell out of here!"

They raced to another spot and started helping a group already making a fire line, but the fire pursued them, licking at their heels. Now they stood at the fire's edge furiously working to establish the fire line.

Then a gale force wind drove the flames downward into the canyon. Crowns of the trees exploded as fire engulfed them. Producing showers of sparks and burning debris, the fire moved swiftly down into the canyon, where it separated the team into two groups. Suddenly, Ted, Bucky and others in their group found themselves surrounded by fiery walls. Struck by terror, they dropped their gear and ran. "Move your goddamn asses!" someone yelled. Then the roar of the fire smothered their screams as some ran and others dropped to the ground. There was no way to break through the ring of fire.

Two days later, after the fires subsided, the enrollees of Company 2348 filled the screened mess hall for the evening meal. Seven of the boys would not be present.

After supper, when Commander Shawnburg stood to address the group, the silence and somber faces told him they already knew and dreaded what he would say to them.

"I'm sure you all know, some of our boys are not here today. The party sent to search and investigate reported that a fire swept down into a low-lying pocket near the north ridge and trapped a group of our boys. The inferno overtook them so quickly none could escape. Rescue crews recovered four bodies, which they have now identified. The crews didn't find the three others known to be part of that team, and it's feared they tried to escape through the circle of flames which would have disintegrated their bodies."

Every boy in the group sat still as petrified wood. Some stared wide-eyed. Some lowered their heads as eyes glistened over.

"I now ask you to observe a respectful silence while I read the names of the deceased. I am going to read the names of those brought in first followed by the names of those whose bodies were not retrieved."

Pin-drop silence filled the room when Commander Shawnburg read the names: *"Thomas Boye...William Burke...Grant Murdock...Dean Tarnigan...*and then, *Bucky Ellis...Louis Nochlieber...Ted Staddle."*

Before he finished, the sound of a few boys choking back tears broke the silence, which prompted tears from other misty eyes.

Commander Shawnburg continued, "Arrangements for services and burial are left with the respective families. May God bless us all and comfort the bereaved families. Now please return to your tents. Try to get a good night's sleep and be back here at seven in the morning."

Outside, the group huddled close together consoling one another in soft whispers. Some put their arms around each other. Gradually, each retreated to his bunk and the group dispersed, leaving only dancing shadows under swaying branches of sycamore trees where the group had gathered in the light of the full moon. Darkness came early in the valley where the sweep of surrounding mountains block the rays of the setting sun.

A cloud of melancholy hung heavy over the enrollees the following day. At supper, the hushed sound of murmuring voices replaced the usual raucous chow-down. Appetites waned and diners picked at their food. Many eyes shifted back and forth to the empty places of the missing.

The squeal of a coiled spring stretched to its limit followed by the bang of the screen door against its frame riveted everyone's attention to the mess hall entrance. There stood three weary travelers, swaying on shaky legs holding each other up, their faces and bodies black with soot, dirt and bruises, their clothes ripped, and two of them shirtless.

One great gasp arose from the group. One boy dropped his tray of dirty dishes while others hastily deposited their trays onto the nearest tabletop.

"It's Louis, Bucky and Ted!"

With cheers and shouts, the group moved toward the three as though they were earth's center of gravity. Exuberant noise erupting from the mess hall instantly brought every person on the grounds to the scene. The three exhausted survivors stood wavering, jostled about and held up by the press of their rejoicing companions.

"Boys," Commander Shawnburg shouted, "Give them some breathing space. Some of you get into the kitchen and rustle up some food. Help Buck, Louis and Ted to a table. They must be starving. The rest of you leave. You'll all have plenty of time to talk to these boys after they're fed, rested and cleaned up. Now get out of here...all of you."

Before the boys retired to bed, Commander Shawnburg summoned them all back to the mess hall for a report.

"Medical personnel have checked the boys out. Ted, Buck and Louis are a little worse for wear, but would be fine."

The group erupted with applause, cheers and whistles.

"All right...hold it down," Shawnburg said.

Voices went mute, but the boys' exuberance—demonstrated by fun-poking, back slapping and smiles — could not be subdued.

"They will need plenty of rest," Commander Shawnburg advised, "so do not disturb them. You can talk to them tomorrow.

"Quiet down and I'll tell you the story of their survival."

Those who rose to their feet to cheer sat down.

"When the flames engulfed them, Bucky and Ted hit the ground and immediately saw a small opening along the canyon wall that led into a cave. Ted went in first with Buck following. Buck turned around and went back out to see if he could rescue others. Louis ran by a few feet from Buck, who managed to tackle him and pull him into the cave. Buck felt certain that a second or two later, both of them would have been overcome by the fire. The heat was intense, but they pushed back deeper into the shallow cave where the cool ground protected them. Instead of entering the cave, the smoke rose up towards the skies. When it was safe to venture out, they made their way back here by foot. It was an incredible stroke of good fortune they found that cave. God be praised!"

"I know we all have mixed feelings about this. Our spirits are high because of the three saved boys, but our hearts are heavy at the loss of the other four. I know we will remember them as true heroes who gave their lives for a valiant cause.

"When you first came here, many of you were greenhorns, and some of you even a bit rowdy."

A ripple of light laughter arose.

"But you have now developed into a team of fine young men of character. Though we will continue our daily work together in the days to follow, I want to take this time to commend all of you and to wish you well on your journey of life. God bless us all. Thanks to all of you. And now, return to your bunks and have a quiet night's rest."

When Shawnburg believed Buck had perished, he knew he needed to notify camp personnel at Company 3383 that Buck would not arrive to assist them in establishing a boxing recreation project, but he postponed the task. He also postponed contacting the families of the three missing boys, although he did not know why. Perhaps a glimmer of hope sparked within him.

During the time when Commander Shawnberg addressed the enrollees, the three survivors remained apart to get some rest. Bucky found a quiet spot in his barracks and wrote a letter to Emily and the Griffins. The letter grew longer as Bucky described details of the encounter.

When the boys from the barracks returned, Bucky lay fast asleep on the bed fully clothed, his arm hanging down over the written pages he had dropped on the floor.

With Buck back to full health and vigor, plans for his transfer could now proceed. The evening before their departure, Commander Shawnburg arranged a farewell party to honor Buck and six others ready to leave the next morning for Prince William Forest Park near Dumfries, Virginia. The cook surprised them by bringing forth a special baked Alaska dessert, the capstone of his culinary efforts.

Back in their barracks, the boys talked long into the night.

"Buck, how you gonna go about startin' that boxin' thing they want you to do?"

"I think I've got people there to help, so I just have to find out what they have in mind. I'm hoping it will be a program not just for the Prince William Forest guys, but maybe we can have some bouts with kids from other camps."

"What's it gonna be like there?"

"Pretty nice, I heard. The town of Dumfries is nearby and it's not far from Washington."

They talked about supervisors, facilities, the nearby larger towns and cities, activities, recreation, work projects and the girls of Dumfries.

"How about the kids there? Are they new, or do they know the ropes like us?"

"Hey, you guys, nobody can measure up to you. We're going to miss you."

They shook hands all around and exchanged names and addresses with a firm covenant they would always keep in contact.

JUNE, 1935, Company 3383, Prince William Forest Park, Dumfries, Virginia

Unlike the mountainous terrain Bucky had left in Norton, Prince William Forest Park was a vast area of natural forests and waterways on the Piedmont plateau between the Appalachian Mountain chain and the eastern coastal plain. Though the forested area of the park seemed remote from populated areas, it was only thirty miles from the nation's capital, and enrollees could visit small towns and villages nearby.

Once there, Buck spent a good deal of time with Company Commander Keith Little and a team of supervisors planning and building the boxing program. Bucky's importance to the project gave him a feeling of confidence.

Accustomed to makeshift quarters in Norton, Buck and his company happily welcomed the accommodations here, at Company 3383, where they resided in barracks surrounded by other, more permanent structures, including a large mess hall, and recreation and administrative areas. As Bucky toured the area, some of the terrain, particularly the forests where Quantico Creek ran through them, reminded him of rural areas along the banks of Codorus Creek near his home in York, Pennsylvania. *Yeah, I'm really gonna like it here.*

6. THE NOOSE TIGHTENS

MAY, 1934, Altoona, Pennsylvania

Crusher smiled, rubbing his hands together. *Soon, very soon, I will be able to put my finger on the exact location of the Ellis family. My operative in Pennsylvania has proved himself one of the best!*

This retired railroad "bull," infamously known throughout the hobo community at the time as Crusher, had now developed a loosely organized criminal network of informants. He amply rewarded them for delivering information to "the Mastermind", as those who did his bidding knew him. These well-paid emissaries directed operations in distant cities and towns. Typically, the hands-on work of pilfering goods and obtaining information fell on many of Crusher's moles, streetwise young boys from broken homes, or orphans. Crusher communicated with his field representatives through telegrams and other means, and promoted hirelings who completed their assignments with skill, giving them more challenging responsibilities.

Initial information Crusher received located the Ellis family at York, Pennsylvania. Recently, his operative in that district reported the family had moved to Altoona, Pennsylvania, and Crusher ordered him to go immediately to Altoona.

"Report the whereabouts and the activities of each family member to me," Crusher directed. The Mastermind always supplied a post office box address, which constantly changed, to ensure his anonymity.

In Altoona, Crusher's underling continued to gather data on each family member, but could not find much of anything about the missing oldest boy named Buckingham, except that he did not live at home. This young informant did not need to know why the Mastermind focused his interests on this particular family. He would carry out his directives, knowing if he pleased the Mastermind, he would enjoy rewards that could land him on Easy Street.

In the summer of 1934, when the family moved again, this time to the mining town of Sunbury, Pennsylvania, Crusher's operative followed in quick pursuit.

7. BARROOM BRAWL

JULY, 1934, Altoona, Pennsylvania

Chuck Ellis had found his niche when he moved with Helen and his children, Lena, Lionel ("Bud"), and Lily to Altoona, where he found work on the assembly line of the Twelfth Street Erecting Shop of the Pennsylvania Railroad. Helen, endowed with a kind heart and a love for the children, appeared at a critical time after the death of his wife, Marcie, to lift Chuck out of a deep depression. Before her arrival, he moped about and erupted, shouting reprimands at his children's slightest infractions. Aunt Helen, as the three children called her, brought a noticeable calm stability to the family.

Chuck not only felt gratitude towards Helen, but loved her and intended to ask her to marry him. The accusation, rejection and immediate departure of his son brought Chuck to the realization that he should not delay his proposal. She accepted, and the Rector of St. Luke's Episcopal Church in Altoona married them in a quiet ceremony.

•

Employees of the Twelfth Street Erecting Shop customarily frequented the bars after work. Chuck, with a family waiting at home for him, stopped only occasionally with his friends. Helen understood his need to spend time with his co-worker friends, and on such occasions

254

expected him home around 10:30 P.M.

One night, while Chuck drank a few beers and played poker with some fellow workers, "Lucky," a hard drinking section leader at the Locomotive Works, swaggered over and put his hands on Chuck's shoulders. Stooping down, he whispered in Chuck's ear, "How's it goin' wit' dat whore you got at home, Chucky boy?"

Lucky, like Chuck's other co-workers, did not know he had married Helen.

Chuck ignored him and fingered his cards, arranging them for his next play.

"You got you one sweet-lookin' honey pot, Chucky baby."

Lucky's raucous voice towered over the noise in the barroom.

"How you two getting' on? Wouldn't think a squirt like you could handle a piece like her!"

Chuck carefully folded his cards and placed them on the table, eyeing his agitator. Heads turned towards them, while Lucky continued to goad his target with repeated insults laced with profanities. Some pushed their chairs back for a better view while others moved to get out of harm's way.

Chuck's body stiffened and he gritted his teeth. Steely-eyed, he stared straight ahead.

"Ya eat shit, Ellis. Ya must know...or maybe you're the only one who doesn't...that while y'r soppin' it up here at O'Malley's, y'r lady's runnin' around. Word's out that she's the best lay in town...a fine piece of..."

Before he could finish, a switch snapped on in Chuck's brain. He leaped from his chair and, with a good crack at Lucky's jaw, knocked him to the floor. Lucky regained his feet and started slugging it out with Chuck. Onlookers fueled the blowup with shouts and cheers.

"Git 'im, Lucky. Beat the livin' crap out of 'im!"

"C'mon, Chuck...you can take him..."

"Break 'is goddamn neck!"

The place exploded. Chuck had Lucky on the floor and was getting the best of him when police arrived and dragged them both out the door and hauled them to jail.

For Chuck, the humiliation of the arrest was not the worst of it. Nepotism at the Locomotive Works ran rampant. Controlling family members filled high positions. Lucky held the position of Section Leader and had power to blackball anyone he disliked from a job.

Before being pulled to his feet and dragged off to jail, Lucky looked

255

Chuck straight in the eye and said through clenched teeth, "You're finished in Altoona, you son of a bitch. You better get the hell out of town fast if you know what's good for ya."

8. LIFE IN A COAL MINING TOWN

JULY, 1934, Sunbury, Pennsylvania

Down on his luck, Chuck sought work in the coalmines at nearby Sunbury. Unsafe and oppressive working conditions characterized the mining community. The large number of workers required for mining forced mining companies to construct living quarters in these unpopulated locations as quickly as possible, resulting in dilapidated housing and squalid conditions. In keeping with common practice of the day, the mining company at Sunbury paid workers in scrip coupons redeemable only at the Company Store, where prices were inflated. Typically, borrowing from the Company Store ensnared workers in a hopeless cycle of increasing debt.

Chuck accepted this job intending to leave as soon as the family established a footing that would allow them to move on. Helen's devotion to Chuck and the children was evident in that she remained with them during this difficult period.

"Charles, Bud asked me again to speak to you about letting him work." Whenever Helen approached Chuck on a serious matter, she always addressed him as "Charles."

"I know. He keeps coming to me about it. He's fifteen now, and ever since we moved here he's had a hankering to work in the mines, but he has no idea how terrible the conditions are. Some of his older friends have been lured into working in the "Breakers," where they sit all day before bins, chipping and separating slate from the rocks. Some parents send their boys to work there just to get extra scrip coupons. He's over fourteen, so it's legal for him to be hired, but Helen, it's a dangerous place for a boy his age to be, and it ain't setting right with me to let him do it."

"Yes," Helen said. "Some of his friends have been working in the mines since they were ten with written permission from their parents who falsified their ages."

"Yeah," Chuck said. "Forget the legal reforms about age and prohibitions against awful conditions...no one observes them."

"Chuck, dear, what will you do?"

"I don't think I have a choice. I have to let go of him. I can't prevent him from working much longer. But, by God, I'll make him follow my rules to stay out of trouble. I won't have him joining in with the rowdy trouble-makers who think they can do as they please. Some of those kids are young thugs...getting into all kinds of mischief. I won't let that happen to my kid."

The unhealthy environment in which these boys worked did little to instill high moral character in them. The boys quickly learned to manipulate, steal and promote their own interests by any devious means. The longer Bud worked with them the more he became like them. By the age of sixteen, Bud had learned the tricks of the trade.

Lording over the younger children and making sport of them brought great satisfaction to these bullies. When they tormented a tyke to the point of tears, they felt grand gratification for their efforts.

One day, Bud sat with his pals on the edge of a storage-shed platform. Forming a row at the platform's edge, they stared the kids down and blew puffs of smoke into the air from cigarettes like proud veterans of the habit.

The punk next to Bud eyed a particular young boy of about eight or nine. Pointing a finger at him, he directed, "Come over here, brat."

The group of younger boys all stood rigidly still.

Shaking his pointed finger and contorting his face in threatening anger, the lout said, "I mean you, ya little turd! Get your ass over here!"

The boy looked to his companions on each side of him, but found no sign of protection offered. He timidly stepped closer to the group and stood trembling before them.

"Okay, fellas," the ringleader said to his pals. "On the count of three. One...two...."

They all took a big drag on their cigarettes as he counted *"three!"*

Releasing their inhaled smoke in unison, they blew it directly into the face of the bewildered boy. An uproar of laughter arose, as the tyke stumbled back coughing and hacking before he turned and ran away crying.

As the boy ran away, a young girl ran up to the group of rowdies, appearing out of nowhere.

"You ought to be ashamed of yourselves, you big bullies, picking on a little fellow like that." Then the fourteen-year-old girl took a few steps over to Bud, and pointing a finger straight at her sixteen-year-old brother, looked him in the eye and said for everyone to hear, "You wait until you get home, smarty pants. I'm telling daddy. You're gonna get the strap when you get home. You wait and see!"

Then she bounded off down the street to the shack where the Ellis family lived.

Mortified by this chastisement, Bud felt his face turn red hot, and his head drooped in shame. As his peers locked their eyes on him, he glanced back and forth at them with embarrassment.

"Aw," he said, "that's just my dumb sister, Lil. She don't mean nuttin'. I ain't worried about her. She don't know nuttin'. She's just a busybody who thinks she oughtta run the world." He tried to laugh it off, but could only muster a nervous halfhearted chuckle.

"She needs her ass kicked up to her nose," an older boy said.

"Don't talk about her that way," Bud snapped. "I'll take care of her!"

Bud headed for home and acted as though he had nothing to fear. He tried to look as if he was off to a good time. He skipped along non-chalantly, occasionally pausing to throw rocks into the drainage ditches.

When he reached home, his heart stuck in his mouth. He tried to enter quietly without anyone seeing him. Once inside, he spied his father out of the corner of his eye. Pretending not to see his dad, he walked quickly through the room to another part of the house.

"Lionel!" his father said, sternly. It had been some time since his father addressed him by his given name. Bud stopped in his tracks. *Damn that Lily. Damn her to hell.* Bud turned, casting the most innocent look he could feign at his father.

"What do you have to say for yourself?" Chuck barked.

"About what?" He saw the veins pop up on his father's neck. *O, shit. I shouldn't have said that. Now I'm in for it.*

"About what your sister reported to me!"

"Well, dad, I...I only...I didn't mean to..."

"Were you smoking cigarettes?"

Bud lowered his head. "Yes, sir."

"Did you blow the smoke in the boy's face?"

"Yes," he replied again. He said it so meekly Chuck could barely hear him.

"What was that?" his father said sternly.

"Yes, sir." he said louder with a look of remorse that belied his thoughts. *That Lil. Wait 'til I get my hands on her. I'll kill her, I swear.*

"To the bedroom, right now!"

As Bud went slowly into the bedroom in the back of the shack, Lily and her younger sister, Lena, sat quietly in the front room. After father and son went to the bedroom, they could hear their father's belt snapping through his pant loops as he unbuckled and yanked it off. Lily looked at her sister and wondered if she too pictured Bud lying face down on the bed with his bare behind fully exposed. The sound of leather snapping across his flesh confirmed what her vivid imagination portrayed.

Lily felt a tinge of guilt, but consoled herself. *He deserved what he got. I was right to tell Daddy. He should have known better than to tease the little children again. Daddy will be proud of me that I told on him.*

Three swipes with the "strap" were sufficient. Then the bawling started. The boy had tried to put up a brave front, but his conviction that he had done a terrible thing gripped him. He could no longer restrain his tears.

"You stay away from that pack of hooligans!" his father roared. "I don't want you to end up like them. Stay away from them, you hear. And don't let me catch you teasing the little kids any more!"

"I'm sorry, sir," he sobbed. "I'll stay away from them...and I'll leave the little kids alone. I promise." This time, his remorse was real, and he meant to keep his vow.

Helen stood in silence nearby with her arms folded, not interfering. Her heart went out to Bud, but she knew how Chuck felt about discipline.

"A good lickin' is good for the character," he once told her. "No hemmin' or hawin'. A few wallops with the belt so the kid knows what he done. Then he's sorry and you can forgive 'im. Then it's all over and there ain't no need to bring it up again. Then he'll toe the line. That's just the way it is."

Bud tried to keep his promise, and for about a month, he managed to resist joining in with his unsavory friends. He stood firm against their constant prodding to join in their rank horseplay.

260

The pain of separation from the in-group of his peers proved difficult for Bud to handle. Inevitably, he once again joined them in a pattern of troublesome behavior succumbing to an irresistible urge and rite of passage every boy in this community had to endure.

9. AUNT HELEN'S LETTER

AUGUST 8, 1935

She had put it off long enough. Everyone had left the house. She would do it now. She sat at the table and picked up the pen, and dipped it into the inkwell. Aunt Helen felt tears welling in her eyes. She knew they betrayed her heavy heart. She wiped her eyes with a tattered hankie, its lace edges threadbare. It was not a letter written cautiously with pauses to ponder each word. Instead, the flame of deep emotion brought forth a continuous torrent of words spilling onto the page.

Dearest Buck

Writing this letter is the hardest thing I've ever done. I been putting it off for some time. Your father cant bring himself to write this. He's too upset. But he loves you and knows you should know what I got to tell you.

Did you know your father lost his job in Altoona? After that we moved here to Sunbury where your father started working in the coalmines. Your brother, Bud, worked in the mines too. Children can work there when parents give their permission. There are lots of boys working in the breakers. They sit before bins filled with rock and chip away the slate from each rock all day long. We knew it was a hard condishun for a young boy but did not know how terrible it was when we first sent him. Then we saw Bud change.

Around his 15th birthday, he left the children his own age and started hanging out with the older boys. Your father gave him a wipping after learning he was smoking with some ruffians and doing bad things. Later, we found out he wasn't going to the Company Store much, where he used to spend his money on candy. Instead, he was drinking beer bought by the older boys. We found out when he was caught drinking from a small flask he brought with him to the breakers.

Oh, Bucky! How can I tell you what happened next? I wish I could put my arms around you and hold you close and wipe away your tears.

Bucky, your brother fell into one of the deep mine shafts and smothered to death before anyone could get him out. I cant stop crying and your father will never get over it.

Bucky, he was really a good boy. He always looked up to you. If you had only been here...but it's not your fault, its ours. Your father blames himself for everything and his grief grew worser by his guilt in losing you. Its almost unbearable for both of us. We would do anything to get you to come back home, Buck.

I know it's a lot to ask, but if you could forgive us and come back home, we would find ways to make it up to you.

I wish you could have been here for the funeral. So many came. Our little church was overflowing with more people than you could ever imagine. All the people working here at Sunbury came out to pay their respects, and some folks from York and Altoona came, too.

I cried my eyes out when I looked at Bud all dressed up in the one Sunday suit he hated to wear to church, but he

looked so handsome and grown up in it...like a man. His hair
was combed so neatly and even had a bowtie. I can't
believe he isn't here anymore.

Helen paused and placed the pen back into its well. Tear drops started falling on the letter blurring the words. She felt convulsions erupting inside her and with her hands, she gripped the edge of the table. Taking a breath, she reached for a handkerchief, wiped her eyes and calmed herself. Blotting the moisture on the letter, she picked up the pen and continued to write.

Dear Buck, pray for us all, and God keep you safe. Your
father loves you more than you know, and would welcome
you home with open arms.

With all my love,
Aunt Helen.

10. THE CUNNING THIEF

Crusher's sixteen-year-old operative in Sunbury had no difficulty in finding the exact location of the Ellis family.

After reporting the absence of the oldest boy, he received instructions that this boy and his whereabouts were of particular interest to the Mastermind. Crusher's stooge initiated a strict surveillance of all members of the household.

When Helen left the family's shanty with a determined look on her face and a letter in her hand, the young snoop's body tensed to immediate alert. She headed for the Company Store with the boy close behind her. He had his eye on that letter. Pretending to look over some items on the store shelves, he watched Helen go to the clerk behind the counter, where customers paid for their purchases. He watched the man take the letter and drop it in an open sack on the floor next to him. *Hot dog. The letter sits in an open mailbag. This will be a cinch.*

The quick-thinking operative waited until the clerk was busy with several customers and then went to the counter and stood near those at the cash drawer. Taking a small purse from his pocket, he untied its string and turned it upside down to empty it into his palm. He fumbled a bit and dropped the coins on the countertop, making sure some of them spilled over the counter onto the floor behind it. The noise drew the attention and sympathy of the customers waiting to pay for their items with company store scrip. Exhibiting distress, the shrewd boy ran around the end of the counter and said, "Please, sir, may I come back and pick up my coins?"

"Git 'em, if ya must. C'mon in and be quick about it. I'm pretty busy here wit dese folks, or I'd h'ep ya."

The wily boy rushed in and fell to his knees on the floor. In a pretense of nervousness and haste, he knocked over the mailbag, spilling out mail from the top of the bag. The clever thief had positioned himself between the mailbag and the customers to block their view. Righting the fallen bag gave him opportunity to spy the coveted envelope with the Ellis return address, scoop it up and tuck it inside his shirt. With his coins retrieved, he moved out from behind the counter and out of the store without anyone noticing anything unusual. He grinned. *The Mastermind would be proud. That went smooth as silk. Let's see, now, what we have here.* He looked at the address in the center of the envelope:

Master Buckingham Ellis
C/o Rev. Michael Griffin
4201 S. Jefferson Ave
St. Louis, Missouri

In some obscure location, Crusher sat in a plush easy chair and looked at the name and address on the envelope. *Pay dirt!* He laughed aloud and then gave a whoop and a holler. Then he laughed again. *It's time to give some directives to Kritchner and his boys in St. Louis. It should be lovely there this time of year. As soon as I get more precise information from Kritchner, I shall be on my way.*

In his excitement to get the exact address of Bucky's location, Crusher stuffed the envelope in his pocket and threw the letter into the trash.

11. A VISIT FROM JOSH

AUGUST, 1935, St. Louis, Missouri

Father Griffin and Becky attended a pastor's conference in the Ozarks while Emily and Michelle remained alone in the parsonage. Emily had put Michelle in the downstairs basinet in the dining room, a central location accessible quickly from all parts of the house. Michelle slept soundly affording Emily some time for herself.

The bright rays of the morning sun permeated the room through a bay window that extended out towards the side street. Bathed in sunlight, the room exuded an airy spaciousness. Before the middle window stood a small accent table on which rested a full blooming potted amaryllis Mrs. Griffin had carefully cultivated.

Emily headed for an easy chair, but before she could be seated, she heard the familiar sound of the postman dropping mail through the slot in the front door. At this morning hour, Emily wore only a short sleeve pajama top buttoned down the front, and a pair of white panties. In bare feet, she walked briskly to the door, picked up the mail and shuffled through it. *Just what I was waiting for...another letter from Bucky.* Emily carried it back to the bassinet, checked to make sure Michelle slept calmly, then opened the envelope and took out the letter.

The Boxcar Kid

Dear Em,

Great things keep happening here to keep us all hopping (never a dull moment). We been busy beavers building cabins and doing roadwork around here. We're making new trails into the woods too.

Everything that happens here is super. They give us plenty of good food. Yesterday, Rustan, a Swedish kid who never ate pancakes before, downed 35 in one sitting! We all went wild watching him. We all clapped and shouted the number of each pancake he ate.

Last night we went roller-skating in town. It was fun. One thing I forgot to ask you - can you skate? I could use a pretty partner.

Actually, some guys who come here can't skate at all. They come just looking for girls. One of my buddies skates pretty swell, but made out like he couldn't skate at all to get a cute gal to teach him.

But there's no gal here as pretty as you, Em. Besides, I only have eyes for you. I love you.

I miss you and Michelle more than I can say. I can't believe she's almost five months. Does she walk yet_running...doing cartwheels? Ha! Well, maybe she's started crawling. Tell me more about what she's learning to do.

I can't wait to get your letters. Tell the Griffins to keep writing, too.

I love you,
Bucky

When Emily read the part about the pancakes, she smiled.

Before she could finish the letter, a voice behind her said, "Hey, baby. How are ya?"

Emily spun around. Her eyes opened wide when they met a familiar face. She let out a gasp and dropped the letter.

"Josh! *What*…how did you get in here? What are you doing here?"

"The back door was unlocked. I just walked in."

Emily froze as she saw Josh standing in all his arrogance before her, his face only inches from hers.

"So, how the hell are ya? Did ya miss me?"

To avoid waking Michelle, she said in a venomous whisper, "You got a helluva nerve coming here. Are you crazy?"

Josh chuckled, dismissing her protest.

"Get your ass out," she hissed. "The Griffins are away and there's no one else here." *Why did I tell him that? Now he knows I'm alone. What the hell is the matter with me?*

"I knew they was gone. I been watchin' you."

"You animal. How did you find me?"

"When that little gutless boyfriend of yours threw a lucky punch and knocked me off the train, I jist hopped on again a few cars behind." With a sinister grin and glint in his eye, Josh declared, "I bin wit' ya all along, baby. Remember the creep who took ya to dat soup place? He goes there all the time and hears a lot. We had friendly little chats. Everybody there knew you and your pretty boy pantywaist. It was easy to find out where ya was stayin'. I had business elsewhere and couldn't come right away, but I came back and here I am...in the flesh!"

Emily stood frozen. Josh started to move toward Michelle. "Gotta see my kid."

"Get away from Michelle!" Emily said, stepping between Josh and the baby and putting her hands on him to restrain him. "Don't lay a hand on her."

"I like your hands on me, baby. You c'n put 'em anywhere you want. Besides, I ain't interested in her. It's *you* I want." He grabbed her around her waist and pulled her closer. She struggled to break free. She beat his chest with her fists. Josh shoved her back toward the bay window. The sunlight streaming through the windows cast elongated shadows of the contending figures onto the wooden floor. Emily swiped his face with her nails opening several cuts.

Josh released a hand and put it to his face, removing it to see blood on his fingers, and cursed, "You little bitch!" He forced her back towards the bay window, overturning the table and sending the amaryllis plant to the floor, shattering the pot and leaving the floor littered by shards of clay, dirt and the naked bulb with its stem and blooms.

Emily's widened eyes glimpsed movements of the basinet as Josh pushed her back. Michelle stirred, but made no sound.

Emily clenched her fists and let them fly, but Josh caught her wrists and pinned her against the window frame.

"Let me go, you bastard."

"Bastard? That ain't me…that's your brat sleepin' over there."

Emily fought furiously to break free from her one…time-lover. "You goddamned…let me go!"

She rammed her knee into his crotch.

Josh buckled over with pain, then recovered quickly flashing Emily a sinister sneer. "Keep up your fightin', bitch. It's just makin' me horny as hell."

Like the snap of a mousetrap, Josh leaped at her pinning her against the window. Putting his hand behind her head, he wrenched her face to his, forcing a kiss. Emily struggled to free herself, upsetting their balance, sending them both to the floor.

Filled with rage, Josh climbed on top of her. His hand clamped her arm to the floor. Using his arm and legs, pushing and shoving, Josh gained advantage. Emily' efforts became feeble. Afraid to frighten Michelle, who continued to sleep, Emily stifled her screams.

Emily's heart pounded and her lungs heaved from exhaustion. Josh had her in his grip and she could not move. She trembled as she felt Josh thrust his hand under her pajama top and grip her panties. With brute force, he tore them from her. In a whirlwind of movement, Josh had opened his shirt unbuckled his belt, opened his pants and pulled them down. His bare flesh pressed against hers. She had little resistance left. Tears flowed from her eyes and down her cheeks. *My God, help me, I can't stop him.*

The doorbell pealed, cutting into the struggle like a razor. Josh froze and looked towards the front door. Emily seized the opportunity. With every ounce of strength she could muster, she swung her fist in a wide circle, bashing the side of Josh's head and sending him rolling on the floor. Energized by adrenalin, she rose to her feet.

Dazed, Josh shook his head, stumbled to his feet and cowered towards the back door.

In a low tone dripping with contempt, almost under her breath, Emily called him a name that was not part of her everyday vocabulary. "If you ever come back here, I'll shove a kitchen knife through your heart, and by God, I mean it."

Recovered, Josh pulled up his pants, zipped himself up and went out the back door like a dog with its tail between its legs. In a low voice, now devoid of the cocky impudence displayed earlier, he growled, "I'll be back to finish up," and left.

Emily quickly groomed her hair with her hands, gave a quick glance to the still sleeping Michelle, and rushed to the front door, picking up and throwing on a housecoat along the way. Keeping herself partially hidden behind the door, Emily saw before her a woman she recognized from the church.

"Hello, Mrs. Dawson," she said in a timid voice.

"Hello, dear," the visitor said. "Am I disturbing you?"

"Oh, no," Emily said. "I just put Shelly in for a nap and thought of taking one myself," she lied.

Although she did not know how close she was to the sleeping child, Mrs. Dawson instinctively whispered her words. "Oh, such a lovely child, in fact, she's why I'm here, dear. The Ladies Guild routinely collects clothes from families in the congregation. I have some pretty things here for Michelle the ladies thought you could use. Some of the clothes are like new."

"Why Mrs. Dawson, how sweet of them," Emily said with a forced smile. *Did she see or hear what was going on when she came to the door?* Trembling, Emily forced herself to mask her emotions in the face of this woman's cheerful errand.

"I...I don't know how to thank you. What a kind thing to do. Thank you...thank you so much."

"Oh," the woman said, "don't mention it. That's what we do...help one another. We have a center for used clothing. The ladies want me to ask you if there are any special needs you may have. One couple has offered to babysit if you and young Mr. Buck want to go out when he comes home...or for any other reason. You can let us know, dear. I know you must be busy, so I won't keep you any longer."

Emily took Mrs. Dawson's hand and thanked her, and took a quiet breath of relief as the woman turned and walked down the steps and out to the sidewalk.

Returning to Michelle, she gazed at her sleeping baby. She stood there for a long time with tears welling up in her eyes. Then she sat down in the rocking chair. She contemplated the awful consequences of what Josh would have done to her. *If only I could turn my life back to that awful night we slept together and ran off. I'd be home, safe and sound with my family. O God...but then I would never have met Bucky...and Michelle would not be here. Oh, Buck...I wish you were here.*

She sat quietly in the rocker looking at sweet Michelle in her bassinette. Emily folded her hands onto her lap.

"You intervened, Lord, just as you always do. Thank you, dear God.

Keep Bucky, Michelle and the Griffins in Your safe hands." With the memory of Josh's brutal attack burned into her mind, she prayed for herself. "Dear Jesus, I'm so frightened. Stay with me and give me peace and comfort. Amen."

Then she stood, locked all the doors of the house, sat down and read the remainder of Bucky's letter. Tears rolled down her cheeks.

12. MURDER AT
THE PARSONAGE

SEPTEMBER, 1935, St. Louis, Missouri

Crusher's plane slowly taxied to its place on the tarmac at Lambert-St. Louis Municipal Airport. In his shirt pocket, he carried revealing information in a letter from operative Kritchner, an educated man to whom Crusher entrusted broad responsibilities for a handsome price.

Crusher:

Buck Ellis lives with Rev. Michael Griffin, an Episcopal priest, and his wife. A young girl, about Buck's age, and a baby are also living in the house. I presume the girl is the mother, and Bucky may be the father, but I have not been able to confirm their precise relationship.

The best way for an intruder to enter the house appears to be by the back door, located a few steps up an enclosed stairway. As far as I can determine, there is no lock on the outer door.

I do not know your intentions, nor should I, but I thought it might interest you to know that the enclosed stairway provides an excellent hiding place to surprise anyone arriving or leaving by the back door.

K

As the plane landed, Crusher patted his breast pocket and smiled as he reviewed his plan to capture his quarry.

The Boxcar Kid

The parsonage was located on a corner facing a main thoroughfare bordered by a less-traveled side street. A break in the hedge that ran along the side street property permitted entrance to the property near the rear door through a latched iron gate.

From a parked car across the street, Crusher observed the house on this night. He watched the silhouette of the girl as she passed by an upstairs window several times. At one point, he saw her with the child in her arms. Shortly, the girl's room turned dark, but lights remained on in a downstairs room. Observing lights turning on and off, Crusher could follow the movements of remaining occupants as they went through the house, from the first to the second floor. Crusher waited patiently. A man appeared and closed the shades of the last lighted room upstairs. *Aha! That must be the good Reverend.* A moment later, darkness filled the house.

Crusher eased out of his car, walked to the back gate and quietly lifted the latch. Opening the outer door, he slipped in noiselessly, turned on a thin flashlight and assessed his surroundings. To his left, a few steps led down into the coal bin. A small window near the ceiling provided coal delivery access via the insertion of a chute. A single unlit light bulb with a pull chain hung from the ceiling of the coal bin.

Crusher took his flashlight, the sole source of light in this space, and aimed it straight ahead. He guided the beam up four steps leading to a platform before the inside back door. Moving the beam further up to the doorknob, he saw the keyhole. *Perfect. A mere skeleton key will get me in.*

Seeing his plans falling into place so perfectly, the rush of excitement filled Crusher like an intoxicating drug. Inserting his own skeleton key, he dislodged the inside key and heard it fall to the floor with a clink.

An unexpected noise from outside alerted his ears. Someone had unlatched the yard gate. Shuffling footsteps moved towards the door. Alarmed, Crusher quickly removed his key, quietly stepped back down the stairs into the coal bin and crouched out of sight in a corner.

Crusher had assumed Bucky was inside the house. It had not occurred to him his quarry might be outside at that hour.

At first, the thought of an intruder unnerved him, but as his mind grasped his advantage of Buck's presence already outside the house, his excitement grew. *I can ambush him and sack my victim without breaking in. How perfect.*

The sound of a great belch just outside the door tickled his ears. When opened, the door admitted enough light from a nearby streetlight for Crusher to see the shadow of the swaying boy on the inside floor. The odor of alcohol wafted into Crusher's space leaving no doubt about his victim's condition.

Crusher felt exhilarated. *The fates have smiled on me. Not only has the fly come to the spider, but the stupid bastard is as drunk as a loon. I could not have planned it better!*

Crusher lifted an amber bottle of chloroform from his pocket. *It worked for me once, it can work for me again.* In his haste, Crusher dropped the container and it fell away from him down the incline of stacked coal. He could not use the penlight without alerting his target.

The outer door closed shutting out the light from the street lamp outside. With eyes growing accustomed to the dark, Crusher saw the boy's form stumble up the steps to the back door. He swiftly and noiselessly crept up behind him and clamped his two arms around his neck in a stranglehold. Drunk as he was, the boy struggled fiercely, causing Crusher unwanted resistance and noise. Crusher became agitated.

"Keep quiet, you little prick!"

He had intended only to bring Bucky to an unconscious state, kidnap him and take him to a desolate place to do his dirty work. His grip grew tighter as his victim kicked and flailed his arms. Crusher held him fast and froze in his position, ever tightening his grip. His ears caught the sound of an abrupt snap. The form in his arms went limp.

I've broken his neck. I killed him. He released his burden letting it fall to the steps. *I did not intend for him to die so quickly. Damn my fumbling hands...if I had the chloroform.* He stood in silence, scarcely believing what he had done. *I've got to get him out of here.*

He dragged the body to the bottom of the steps and pushed the door open a crack. A ray of light from the streetlamp fell across the boy's face. The killer gasped. He could not believe his eyes. He had agonized over his hasty demise of his victim. That misery now paled compared to this. How could it be possible?

God in heaven! This is not Bucky!

Crusher stared at the illuminated face. Even in death, this boy had a look of confidence with his ruddy complexion, sandy tousled hair and strong jaw. His victim's eyes were closed, but Crusher knew their color...steely blue.

How can this be? I...I know this boy. He was one of my own...that little shit who flew the coop and took the money purse with him. What was his name...Josh...that was it! God, it's Josh. What twist of fate brought him here tonight?

275

Crusher took a few steps down into the coal bin to retrieve the bottle of chloroform. Of no use to him now, he nevertheless wanted to remove any evidence of his presence. He lifted the lifeless form and placed it over his shoulder. He cautiously peered outside. The streetlight brightened the path from the door to the hedge. He took a quick trot into the shadows behind the tall hedge and moved a few steps parallel to the street towards the gate. The foliage from a large maple tree shrouded the gate, the sidewalk and Crusher's car in deep shadows. With the swiftness of a gazelle, the hulking figure scurried through the darkness, deposited his load in the back, slipped into the driver's seat and sped off. He headed towards the river. As he drove away in a stupor, he could only wonder about the strange sequence of events that brought this boy to this place on this night.

•

The next morning, as Father Griffin walked down the stairs, the aroma of crackling bacon and frying eggs brought him to the kitchen.

"Morning, dear," he said to Becky who stood at the stove with her back to him.

"Good morning." She flipped the eggs over and turned to her husband and said, "Michael, were you up during the night? Did you come down to the back door for any reason?"

"No. Why do you ask?"

"Well I found the key on the floor. Someone on the other side of the door must have pushed it out. I think someone may have tried to break in here last night."

Michael Griffin had poured himself some coffee and placed it on the table, and then walked to the back door to investigate.

"Hmm...you may be right. I know the key was in the door when we went to bed."

He picked up the key and tried the door. "The door is still locked."

Unlocking the door, he walked down the steps. In a few moments, he returned.

"There are signs someone was in the coal bin and at the door," he said. "Something must have scared him away before he could open it."

"Remember last year when we found the key on the kitchen floor?" Becky said. "The same thing may have happened then. Maybe we should get a more secure lock for this door, dear."

"I'll tell the church elders to see that one is put in place."

Emily entered the kitchen with Michelle in her arms.

"Emily, someone tried to get into the house last night," Father Michael said. "We found the key pushed out onto the floor."

"Oh?" she said as she shuddered within, while maintaining a calm exterior. She suspected the stranger might have been Josh. She had kept Josh's earlier arrival to herself, and said nothing to anyone about his unannounced visit.

Once they installed a deadbolt lock, everyone forgot the incident, and no one bothered to mention it to Bucky in their letters to him at the CCC camp in Virginia.

•

When Crusher's snitch in Pennsylvania intercepted Helen's letter and sent it with Bucky's St. Louis address, the Mastermind had passed word to Kritchner. Ignorant of Buck's location in Virginia, Kritchner mistakenly identified Josh as Bucky when he saw him initially enter the house with ease and then interact with Emily. Through the bay window, he gained only glimpses of what was happening inside. To him, the situation represented a passionate encounter, and when he saw Emily and Josh drop to the floor, his vivid imagination supplied what went unseen. When Kritchner noticed the woman from the church arriving at the front door, he changed his position. His next sight of Emily put her at the front door conversing with the woman. His attention focused on this scene, he failed to see Josh leave by the back door. The assumptions he had made formed the basis for his flawed report to Crusher.

When Crusher arrived at his headquarters, he found a brief letter from another informant stating Bucky was an enrollee at a CCC Camp in Prince William Forest Park in Virginia.

Crusher looked at the postmark. If he had delayed another day before leaving for St. Louis, he would have saved himself a lot of trouble.

Somewhere in the depths of a broad and murky river lay a body secured to the bottom by heavy weights. The deceased had no friend or relative to report a missing person to authorities. No one would miss this boy, murdered in the prime of his youth...least of all Emily...or Crusher.

13. FRANKLIN DELANO ROOSEVELT

AUGUST, 1935, Prince William Forest Park, Dumfries, Virginia

The staff and boys of Company 3383 moved about frantically to get everything in order. Excitement grew as word spread through the camp of the imminent arrival of President Franklin Delano Roosevelt. The President customarily visited CCC camps and other restoration projects. Eleanor, the First Lady, also frequented the sites, sometimes with her husband, sometimes without him, accompanied by her own entourage. Bucky knew of Mrs. Roosevelt's recent visit to the coalmines in Bellaire, Ohio. Her presence lifted the spirits of the common people, even as she offended the nation's aristocratic society by her unconventional behavior and activism.

The ensuing frenzy to prepare, clean and polish everything in sight for the presidential visit included the refurbishing of the boxing ring. A team of camp supervisors, with Bucky's help, completed arrangements to schedule an inter-camp boxing match featuring Bucky and an opponent trucked over from another nearby CCC camp. Boys from the contender's camp had arrived to cheer their champion.

Around mid-morning, Bucky heard shouting. Looking over his shoulder, he saw enrollee Jake Hawkins racing up the hill like a deer with its tail on fire. "He's coming, he's coming!" Jake yelled. Capturing the attention of the boys at the top of the hill, he turned and ran back down shouting, "Come on, he's coming." One by one, the boys kicked up the dirt and ran after him like a herd of stampeding buffalos. Bucky caught up to the boys and sprinted past some of them, arriving at the road near the head of the pack. Jake stood pointing to the east as enrollees gathered around him.

"He's coming. I saw him."

The boys stared into the distance.

"Where...where?" one of the boys said, as another chimed in, "I don't see him."

Then expressions of exuberance appeared on faces when a motor car slipped over the crest of a distant hill and the glint of the sun's reflection from the chromed limousine struck their eyes. Visible for a moment, it slid down a dip in the road and disappeared.

Buck looked around, and then, with quick reflexes, ran across the road to a telephone pole. In an instant, he shimmied up to the utility rungs and climbed to its top. Seeing Bucky's action, a few of the others scattered towards remaining poles, intent on getting their own bird's-eye view.

The President sat alone in the back seat behind the driver. Seeing the boy's welcoming party, he leaned forward and waved out the window as his car passed by, followed by another carrying several men in dark suits. Bucky's heart pounded when the president glanced his way, adjusted his pince-nez spectacles, looked straight at him, smiled and waved. *Geeze, it's the man himself. He waved at me. He's really coming to see us.*

One boy near the top of a pole became so excited he lost his footing and would have fallen to the ground had his pocket not caught on a rung, ripping his pants, holding him long enough for him to get a better grip.

Once on the grounds, a tour of the camp and its facilities brought the President to the top of a hill, from which he noted a large group of boisterous fellows below around a boxing ring. Two boys in trunks and boxing gloves were mixing it up.

"What's this?" the president asked.

"It's a boxing match, sir," Keith Little explained. "We bring in champions from other camps and have tournaments. The boy with the black hair, Bucky Ellis, is a boy we moved here from a camp in Norton to help us set it up. His supervisors there noticed he had really great boxing skills."

"Is that so?" he said. The president appeared energized as he leaned forward and squinted to take in the sight. "It looks like Ellis is getting the best of the blonde fellow. May we pause and watch the match?"

"It's several rounds in, but certainly, Mr. President."

At first, no one noticed the president watching from the hilltop. Then someone spotted him and a buzz spread through the audience, and heads turned one by one to their president perched on the hill.

When the boxers themselves noted Roosevelt's observation, the climate changed for them. Buck felt edgy, but kept focused. He noticed his opponent broke his concentration with frequent side-glances. Appearing uneasy, Karl, his ash blonde opponent left himself wide open. Taking advantage, Buck launched a strong offensive. With hard blows, he pushed the other boy back into the ropes, bouncing him back for a heavy thrashing.

In the sixth round, Buck put Karl down to the mat while those of Buck's company cheered wildly. Karl did not stay down for the count.

Before the fight ended, Karl put in his share of punches, but at the bout's end, judges from each camp declared a perspiration-soaked Bucky the winner and held up his hand to the wild cheering of his fellow camp enrollees.

While on the campgrounds, President Roosevelt elected to dine with the boys in the mess hall. Bucky felt glowing pride burning inside him when the President told them, "I wish I could take a couple of months off from the White House and come down here and live with you because I know I'd get full of health as they have. The only difference is that they've put on an average of about twelve pounds apiece since they've been here and I'm trying to take off twelve pounds."

His comments brought smiles to their faces and a ripple of laughter.

After supper, Commander Little came to Bucky and said with a glowing smile, "Come with me, Buck. The president wants to speak to you."

"Mr. President, this is the young man responsible for putting together our recreational boxing and body building program and arranging the inter-camp matches. This is enrollee Buckingham Ellis."

Bucky shook the hand of the president firmly and said, "It's an honor to meet you, Mr. President. Welcome to Company 3383."

"Well done, young man," said the president. "Did you manage these competitions single handed?"

"Oh, no sir. I had plenty of help. We now have a sporting commission made up mostly of boys like me. Sergeant Harrison works with us as a supervisor, and we have some community volunteers helping us.

One of them is an athletic coach."

"It sounds well organized," said the President.

"It was Commander Little who suggested we form groups of our boys to take on specific tasks, Mr. President. Working as a team is an important principle he teaches us."

Out of the corner of his eye, Buck saw Commander Little lower his eyes and adopt a modest demeanor at this compliment.

"One group takes care of maintaining the ring and all the equipment. Another group arranges competitions with other camps. I serve as a Junior Supervisor, but it's the fellas themselves who do most of the work."

"How old are you, Bucky?

"Eighteen."

"Did you hear about the new world heavyweight boxing champ who won the title from Max Baer just a few months ago? His name is James Braddock," the President said.

"Yes, sir, I heard how he beat Max Baer," Buck replied. "I read all about it in the newspapers...I read every word. It lasted 15 rounds. I wish I could have seen it."

"Yes," the President said, "It was quite an upset. They figured Braddock to lose to Baer on 10 to 1 odds. You know, Mr. Ellis, you remind me of Braddock. Commander Little told me a little about your background. He came from a poor family and through tough times just like you. Did you ever think of a boxing career, my boy?"

"Bucky pondered a moment before answering. "I like boxing," he said, "but I don't think I want to make a living at it."

"Well, Bucky, I think you will do well in whatever vocation you choose."

The president stretched out his arm from his wheelchair, put his hand firmly on Bucky's shoulder and fixed his eyes on him.

"Bucky. Our country needs young men like you. Keep up the fine work."

"Thank you, Mr. President. Whatever I do, I want my life to count for something. I hope I get a chance to do something important one day."

"Well," said the president, "you sound like you have the makings for it, but I'm not quite ready to give you *my job* yet."

Bucky felt his face flush and his heart hammer inside his chest as everyone else shot him glowing smiles.

14. COMPANY COMMANDER KEITH LITTLE

AUGUST, 1935, Company 3383, Dumfries, Virginia

"Hey Bucky, Commander Little wants to see you right now!"

Moments later, Bucky sat before a desk across from Company Commander Keith Little.

"Buck, in reviewing the record of your experiences and activities since you first came into the CCC, and especially seeing what you've done here in 3383 Company, it is apparent that you possess gifts that characterize you as a capable leader. I decided to look further into your background when President Roosevelt mentioned how impressed he was with what you have done here."

Not knowing what to say, Bucky remained silent.

"Have you ever considered a military career, Buck? I think you have the makings of a good officer."

Bucky thought for a moment. Then he said, "Ever since I was a young boy, sir, I've wanted to be a pilot."

"*Hmm*. What prompted your interest?"

"I don't know. It seems as far back as I can remember I wanted to fly an airplane."

"What do you think your chances are of becoming a pilot?" Commander Little asked.

"Pretty slim, I guess. If I ever had the chance, I'd jump at it."

Keith Little stared at his desktop and folded his hands. He appeared pensive. Then he eyed Buck and said, "I have a friend who's a Navy pilot. He graduated from Annapolis. I could talk to him about the avenues that might be open to you for such a career. I think you have potential to go places and do things. You know, military service presents many opportunities for gifted young men like you. Maybe you should think about enlisting."

"Thank you, I'll think about that, sir," Buck said.

Bucky often felt uncertain about his future. He relished the camaraderie and active life the CCC provided, but knew it would end. Besides, he could never imagine a future without Emily. Commander Little's suggestion came unexpectedly and sparked a new vision he never imagined. *Could I really be a pilot? Geez...I'd go crazy with excitement. Emily would be so proud of me. What a blast!*

SEPTEMBER, 1935, Dumfries, Virginia

People turned their eyes to the skies in August to watch a barnstormer who flew over nearby towns on the Piedmont plateau in a bright yellow Piper Cub. Attracting attention with life-threatening daredevil flying, barnstormers earned their living by staging air shows and selling rides afterwards.

In the Fall, aviator Wendell "Windy" Boggs flew his plane out of a cow pasture near Dumfries, presenting air shows that drew customers clamoring for the chance to experience this new thrill.

When Buck learned about Boggs, he eagerly jumped aboard the camp truck with a few of his friends to seek out the location of the field where the flyer offered rides. The boys of Company 3383 had weekends free, and the camp truck dropped off enrollees in Dumfries, about two miles from the reported field. From there, Buck and his pals hitchhiked or walked to the spot. Each week, Buck forked over most of his stipend for rides. Boggs noted Bucky's special interest in aviation and before long, he and Buck struck up a friendship.

One day, after the last flight of the day, Windy said to Buck, "Say, lad, how would you like to learn to fly?"

"Are you kidding, Mr. Boggs? Do you really mean it?"

"Sure enough. I could start you next Sunday. But you'll have to come early, before my first customers. We'll give it a try and see how you do and then go from there...and don't call me 'Mr. Boggs.' It's 'Windy.' That's what my friends call me. You can call me Windy."

Buck thought for a moment about the offer before answering. "Aw, gee," he said. "You must know I don't have the cash to pay for lessons."

"Look, kid. You heard what I said...you get your first lesson free and then we go on from there. We'll work somethin' out."

Elated, Buck thrust his fist into the air and cheered, "Hot diggety-dog!"

The next week, Bucky returned to the field accompanied by Keith Little.

"This is Commander Little," Buck said. "He's our Supervisor at the camp. He wants to talk with you. "

"Hey," Boggs replied extending his hand, "Glad to meet the kid's boss. Tell me whatcha want to know, pard."

Keith Little shook Bogg's hand and said, "Hello...uh...Windy. I'm entrusted with the welfare of the boys in my company. If Buck has serious aspirations about learning to fly with you, I want to check out you and your operation to ensure it's legit and safe. Do you have a license to fly in this state?"

Windy pulled out some papers from the pocket of his beat-up aviator's jacket.

Little flipped through the papers.

"Well look at this. I see you were a flight trainer in New York."

"You got it," Windy said.

"Looks good. Mind taking me up for a ride?"

The Piper Cub had a fore and aft cockpit. Windy opened the door to the second seat. Keith Little started to pay him the fee.

"This one's on the house, Gen'ral. Jump up and strap yourself in. Strap yourself in good."

Commander Little noticed the set of controls in front of him. *Well, what do you know? This is an open cockpit training plane.*

From his veiwpoint beside the runway, Bucky watched the plane bump down the field and lift off. Windy made a few passes over the field. Then he initiated a series of fancy moves involving sideslips, sashays and flying low to the ground between trees and structures. After a few minutes of this, he landed.

Windy jumped out and opened the rear cockpit door for the Commander. Little stumbled out and hit the ground feeling shaky. His face paled from Windy's high jinks, he said, "Okay, Boggs, you made your point. I guess you know how to fly this damned thing." He sat down on a pile of rocks, then, with a concentrated stare, gave the flight instructor the eye.

"Boggs, I'd like to make you a serious proposition. Would you agree to be part of our CCC program? Could you provide some flying lessons for a select group of boys? I am sure we could make it worth your while, and you would be an asset to our program. We seek to offer a variety of career opportunities for the boys. I have been talking to Buck here about a military career and he has told me of his interest in aviation. There's also a prominent person involved here who has taken a special interest in this young man."

Buck's hearing sparked at these words and he gave a surprised look at Commander Little. No one had mentioned anything about any special person, and Commander Little seemed to deliberately avoid mentioning the interested party's name.

Commander Little continued. "Our major goal in the CCC is to prepare our boys for a productive life. We have fixed rules, but when special opportunities arise, we have the flexibility to make exceptions in the interest of our goals. So, what do you say?"

"I'll think some on it and let ya know," Boggs replied.

"Take a few days, and if you think something can be done here, make your way over to the camp and we can meet to work out the details."

The next day it rained, and Windy could not fly. Usually, he cursed the rain, but this day he was grateful to have the opportunity to sit across a desk from Commander Little.

By his demeanor, Windy did not appear to Commander Little as a highly educated man. By the time they had finished their discussion, Little recognized the barnstormer's ability to forge a well thought out plan.

"I figur' at first I'll keep the kids on the ground and teach 'em the rules. Later, when we get to the flying, I'll have to take 'em one at a time, since I got just the one plane. The learnin' don't take that long…maybe an hour and a half each session…but to get them all up will take time. I ain't lookin' to get rich, but since I won't be flyin' any payin' customers when I'm workin' wit' the boys, I think it would be fair to charge a fee for each boy. I'll take up to five boys, and I want your Bucky to be one of 'em."

The two men struck a deal for Windy to provide ten sessions on consecutive Sunday afternoons. Commander Little handed Boggs a list of five names gleaned from a longer list of candidates he had already selected, and they shook hands on it.

Keith Little had been inspired by Bucky's spunky spirit, and their relationship had much to do with his decision to accept Little's offer. Boggs would receive an ample fee, plus a bonus upon completion of their contract.

Surrounded by the four other boys chosen for Bogg's flight training, Buck lay stretched out on his back in his bunk for a buzz session.

Straddling his chair with his arms on the chair back, Jimmy Blake leaned forward. "Rumor has it that Commander Little spoke to President Roosevelt from his office the day before he went with you to talk with Boggs. Do you think the president is the one who gave the money for this program?"

"Yeah," said Luke. "I heered somethin' like that. Word I got wuz that Litt-ul got some extra money from the gov'ment."

"No kidding?" Buck said, his face turning red. "Aw, come on...you guys aren't serious...hey, cut it out guys."

"No, Buck," another said. "I think it's true...least that's whut ever'body's been sayin'."

Buck slid his legs over the bed's side and sat up.

"No wonder," Jake exclaimed, "You really did a job of brown-nosin' 'im."

"Hey, cut it Jake-head," Jimmie replied. He turned to Buck and said, "Thanks, Buck. You done a good thing for all of us."

A couple of the boys gave Buck a pat on the back. One gave him a soft punch on the shoulder as an accolade.

15. SOLO FLIGHT

OCTOBER, 1935, Dumfries, Virginia

In less than a month, Buck arrived at his eighth training session, and Boggs had him going through his paces in the air. He was the last of the five to go up that day, and they had flown a considerable distance from the landing field. At this point, Boggs had the controls. Suddenly, Buck heard the engine go idle.

"Uh-oh," Windy yelled above the noise of the wind. "Hey Buck. Do you know where there's an open field nearby?"

Buck glanced down at an extensive wooded area. "Hell, no. Are you serious?"

"Damned right. We're out of fuel."

"Holy shit, what now?" Buck knew plenty of barnstormers had crashed and died in foolhardy ways.

"Think fast, kid. We're losing altitude." Buck looked over the side and watched the trees coming closer. *Geez! I'm trapped in here. I can't jump out. Damn! I wish I had one of those parachutes...*

As they began skirting the treetops and houses, Buck grabbed the sides of the open cockpit, held his breath and felt his whole body tense. Then he heard the motor crank up. The plane started climbing again.

"Well what do you know?" Windy shouted back to him. "I must have accidentally turned off the engine." He laughed heartily.

Livid, Buck bit his lip to keep from blasting Boggs with swear words, his heart pounding from the scare. *You foxy bastard!*

As the plane gained altitude, Windy said, "I'm switching the controls back to you, Buck. Take it away. Let's go home."

Before landing, Windy had Buck go through some fancy moves. "Let's have you do a roll to the left."

Buck banked the plane and executed the move.

"Now let's see another roll...this time to the right...then take it up and do a loop. After that, take her around and put her down."

Again, Buck implemented Windy's instructions with precision. His landing was a little bumpy, but adequate.

On the ground, Windy put his hands on Bucky's shoulders and whispered to him privately, "I think you're ready for your solo flight. Stick around after the others leave and I'll have you take her back up alone. Do a decent job and I'll write out your flying certificate. The others have two more sessions to go, so keep this to yourself for the time being. You're the best of the bunch and deserve this."

Buck told the others he would stay behind to help Windy with a few things, and see them later when the camp truck came to pick them up.

"Okay," one of them said. "We'll hang out in town like usual. See ya later, Buck."

The plane, with Bucky at the controls, took to the air while Windy watched him disappear into the distant sky. He was back in twenty minutes to repeat some rolls and loops before landing. Bringing the plane to a halt on the ground, Buck bounded out and onto the ground.

"It's the biggest thrill of my life," he yelled to Windy. "Geez, what a blast when you're up there alone with the wind blowin' past you."

"Well, you did okay up there," Windy said. He handed him the signed paper certifying him to fly.

Staring at it, Buck exclaimed, "I can't believe it."

"You're almost ready to do your own barnstorming, Bucky."

Slightly built and only five-feet, three inches tall, Windy gasped and yelled, "Heyyy, wha...!" when Bucky picked him up bodily, spun around 180 degrees, and shouted, "Hot diggity-dog!"

Once on the ground, a flustered, red-faced Boggs gently pushed Buck back and said, "OK, take it easy. Now you must file an application for the pilot's license, and, after you receive it, you can fly legally...home free!"

"It's at the top of my list, Windy," Buck asserted

Afterwards, Buck hoofed back towards Dumfries to catch the camp truck. *Wait till I tell Emily and the folks back home I had my solo flight and finished my training. And K.O., too...he'll flip.*

As Buck meandered along, a shiny black car pulled up next to him. A friendly voice called out "Hey kid. Aren't you one of those CCC kids?"

"Yeah."

"I just happen to be going up to your camp. I have some business there. Hop in, kid. I'll give ya a ride."

People recognized enrollees from the CCC camps by their army issue clothes and their good behavior. The locals had high respect for these boys, so the man's hospitality did not surprise Bucky.

With Bucky inside the car, the man asked, "What's your name?"

"Bucky, sir."

"Okay, good. Listen. I have to take a little detour to run an errand before going to the camp. Do you mind? It won't take long."

Buck knew the camp truck was not due at Dumfries for some time, and considered a slight detour would still get him back before the others. Euphoric over his achievement, nothing fazed him.

"That sounds okay to me. I'd only be sitting in town for the rest of the afternoon waiting for the camp truck, anyway.

"What do you fellas do when you come to town? How come you're way out here with the cows?"

Buck jumped at the opportunity to tell him about Wendell Boggs and the flying lessons. The man seemed genuinely interested. Buck exuberantly announced he had gotten his flying certificate and showed it to him. The proud boy hardly noticed that they turned off the highway onto a narrow dirt road. It took them up a slight incline into a forest. As they progressed, they confronted twists and turns in the bumpy road. Buck realized this errand took them farther than he had expected, and he lost his sense of direction in this maze. At one point, another car came the other way, and they had to squeeze over to the side to let it pass. The heavy canopy of the woods cloaked the road in deep shade, making it appear later in the day under the setting sun. As they streaked through the forest, glimpses of sunlight between tree trunks and foliage appeared as lights flashing crazily. Buck found this repeated monotony almost hypnotic as he stared into the woods. In the darkening forest, Buck thought it unusual that his driver, who now had said little, kept his dark glasses on. From the back seat, Buck never had a clear view of the man with the hat and dark glasses.

"Where are we going?" he asked the driver.

289

The Boxcar Kid

"We're almost there."

A few moments later, they reached the top of a hill where the road took a bend to the left. After negotiating the turn, they came to a small clearing next to the road. The driver abruptly stopped.

Two men emerged from the woods and tore open Bucky's door. One grabbed him and yanked him from the car. Another held a rope in his hands. The driver came and helped them subdue their captor. Buck put up a fight, but the sudden surprise of the attack and their number proved too much for him. They wrestled him onto the ground and pulled a noose over his head and shoulders down to his waist. Two kept him pinned down while the third stood over him and putting his foot on the boy's abdomen for leverage, pulled the noose tight around his waist. Then they lifted him and stood him behind the car, still holding him fast. Buck shuddered as he watched them tie the other end of the rope to the rear bumper.

"What the hell are you guys doing? Let me go." He screamed for help, but no potential rescuer heard his cries. He tried again to break free. The vise-like grip clamped around his neck and body tightened. The men bent the hammerlock on Buck's arm upwards to the breaking point. Unable to move, choking and reeling from his pain, Buck abandoned his resistance.

Bucky's eyes shot to the side to see a man in the hooded garb of the Ku Klux Klan emerge from the woods. The white-robed hulk stepped forward and stood directly in front of the terrorized captive. Buck noticed immediately the hood had only one eyehole. With his brow wet with perspiration and his hair matted, Buck felt rivulets of sweat running down from his armpits.

Inches from Buck's face, the hooded man whispered in a sinister tone, "From Sky Ride to joy ride, my cocky little slugger."

Buck gasped. *Omigod! Crusher!*

Crusher watched Bucky's face blanch and the pupils of his wide-open brown eyes shrink into pinpoints. As he observed the petrified trembling of his captor, Crusher's unseen grin widened. *That's right, big shot smart ass, it's me...your old pal. I hope you're crapping in your pants.*

The driver, back in the car, impatiently pressed up and down on the pedal, racing the engine. The purpose of this moment dawned on Bucky. *This has nothing to do with the Klan. This isn't one of his henchmen, but the monster himself. I can never escape him. This is the end. God help me.*

The hooded villain grabbed Buck by his ears, pulled the paralyzed boy's face right up to the hood, and whispered again, "Crusher's back in town. Have a good trip, slugger."

Blind courage sparked by rage eclipsed Buck's fear. Sucking saliva to the front of his mouth, he spit it directly into Crusher's eyehole.

Jumping back, the tormentor roared, "You goddamned little prick! Take him away!"

The car jerked ahead, the rope lifted from the ground and snapped tight, yanking Buck forward. In the darkness, he took long strides over the rough ground running as fast as he could. He barely kept pace with the car, his feet tripping over rocks and bumps in the roadbed. He knew if the driver pushed the gas pedal to the floor, he'd be finished. Instead, the sadistic driver stomped on the brake. Buck hit the back of the car with a sickening thud, evoking loud laughter from the driver. Feeling as if he had been clobbered by a battering ram, and with the wind knocked out of him, Buck fell to the ground. In the split second allowed him, he took a long reach, and grabbed the rope closer to the bumper and pulled himself forward, providing some slack between his hands and body. Then the wheels spun again kicking out dirt and gravel from under them, propelling the car forward. Buck arched his neck to keep his head high. He felt his clothes ripping to shreds, the front of his body gouged by the unforgiving road. A bump in the road sent the car upwards along with the victim on the rope. Buck lost his grip, losing the slack in the rope. He hit the ground again. His head banged against something hard. Everything turned black.

•

Commander Little spoke to the men in the barracks. "It's past curfew and Bucky Ellis is not back. Have any of you boys seen him? What about those of you who are flying with Wendell Boggs? Do any of you know what happened to Ellis?"

Keith Little knew that enrollees who could not, or would not adjust to discipline and hard work along with the amenities of camp life might desert the camp without notice, but that would not have been the case with Bucky, whose reputation for commitment to the program was rock solid.

Jake, one of the trainees with Boggs, spoke up. "We were just talking about Buck and wondering where he was, sir. Last time I seen him, he was with Boggs. He wasn't on the truck with us coming back. We thought he was stayin' back in town and would hitchhike back."

"We sent someone back to Dumfries." Little said. "The place is deserted at night, but the few people we talked to haven't seen any trace of him, including Boggs, who said after talking to him briefly, Buck started walking back to town."

A state trooper walked through the barracks door and addressed Commander Little. "Are you supervisor here?" The commander nodded.

"May I speak with you, sir?"

"Yes. Is this about Bucky Ellis?"

"Yes, sir. Can we go somewhere private?"

Commander Little said to the group. "You have some time before lights out. Perhaps in the morning, I'll have more news to share with you."

•

The two men sat opposite one another across a table in the deserted dining room.

"We picked up your boy on a remote road into the woods north of town," the trooper said. "We sent him by ambulance to the hospital in Alexandria."

"Good Lord! What happened to him?"

"It looks like he was the victim of a brutal attack, but for whatever reason, we can't say. We found him unconscious. He had been tied to a car with a rope and dragged over a back road in the woods for some distance."

Commander Little started, a shocked look on his face. "Dragged through the woods? Good God! Why? How was he found?"

"It was lucky for him a forester was coming through the woods in the opposite direction on the same narrow road. He said he saw headlights light up a bend in the road ahead of him, and knew another car was approaching. We surmise the culprit in the car saw the forester's lights, stopped, turned off the motor and lights, and fled."

"What happened to Bucky? How is he?"

"He's got a concussion and has abrasions and cuts all over, including on his face. That's all I can tell you at this moment."

"Who would do this?".

"That's what I was going to ask you," the trooper replied. "Do you know anyone who wanted to hurt your boy?"

"No one," Keith said. "He was well liked by everyone."

"We don't know if this is the work of some local group or individual. We've never seen anything like this around here. Maybe some crazy is loose. Commander Little, you should caution your boys to be careful."

The following day at breakfast, Commander Little gave the boys a report. Beyond the news Bucky had been the victim of an unprovoked attack and was recovering in a hospital in Alexandria, he told them little else.

He also cautioned them, "I realize when you leave the campgrounds, you are pretty much on your own. Of course, it is expected you'll follow general guidelines of good behavior away from the camp. We expect you to be courteous and polite to everyone, but because of what happened to Bucky, we are issuing certain precautions. You may request permission to leave camp as usual. We advise you to avoid going anywhere alone. Stay with at least one companion or in groups. Use the camp truck to return from Dumfries. We are adding an additional truck and driver to the Sunday schedule to reduce the time you are standing around in Dumfries. Avoid hitchhiking whenever possible. Be cordial to strangers, but be on your guard."

16. ALEXANDRIA HOSPITAL

OCTOBER, 1935, Alexandria, Virginia

The following morning, Commander Little waited in his car for two passengers before heading for Alexandria Hospital. Little had selected two boys from Bucky's barracks to accompany him.

One of them was Kent Butler, one of the six arriving with Bucky from Norton. In the mountains, where the rowdy group had broken into the whiskey still, Kent had been the ringleader and the first to challenge Buck's authority by calling him "hotshot," and yelling, "how's y'r butt-hole for rats?" Though Kent started the slugfest, and Buck had to lay him out, they later became fast friends. Whenever they were horsing around, Kent would call Buck "Hotshot," and Buck would call Kent, "Butt-hole." The word went around and the nicknames stuck.

The other boy was Ted Staddler, one of the two boys who survived the firestorm by taking refuge in the cave with Buck. Ted and Buck had also become close friends ever since.

Once the three occupants were in the car, Little followed the road out of the camp, and headed north on their thirty-mile trek to Alexandria.

Arriving at the hospital that morning, Commander Little and the boys had opportunity to speak with Bucky's physician.

"He was in bad shape when they brought him in, but he's going to be all right. It could have been a lot worse than it was. Fortunately, someone came the other way on that road scaring the driver off. If not for that man, Buck's next stop might have been the morgue."

•

Ted felt a lump in his throat and swallowed hard. Kent just stood frozen in the face of this news.

"Just how bad is he?" Keith Little asked.

"Bad enough. He's in a lot of pain. We have him on morphine. We will wean him off it as the pain subsides. We put a cast on his broken leg and taped up his ribs, a few of which are fractured. He's suffered a concussion, but an examination of his visual and neurological signs indicate he should recover over time without any permanent effects. You'll see plenty of black and blue and swelling on his face. He has scrapes and bruises from his chest to his toes. We've cleaned him up and his vital signs are good. It will take some time, but kids are resilient, and I think he might be able to go back to camp in a week or two after we get him patched up."

"Can we see him now?" Little asked.

"Yes," the doctor said. "Come this way."

Buck was in a ward with three other patients. Commander Little had notified the Griffins immediately about the incident and kept in touch with them, and a bedside table next to Bucky's bed held a bouquet of flowers with a get well card that had just arrived from the family. A note on the card assured Buck, "Everyone at St. Bartholomew's is praying for you." Next to Emily's name, she had made three bold "X"s, knowing Bucky would know she held three kisses for him when he came home. Also on the table was a leaflet with prayers, Scripture and a hand written note from a local Episcopalian priest:

"Father Griffin contacted me and asked me to visit. I prayed for you while you slept, and our congregation is praying for you. I will continue to visit you while you are in the hospital. May God grant you full healing. - Father Daniel Pillar."

The boys gathered at the side of his bed. They stood in silence looking at the sleeping boy.

Kent said, "Hey, Hotshot, look who's here."

Buck's eyes opened into narrow slits. He said drowsily, "Is that you, Butt-hole?" Then they closed again.

Commander Little and the boys stood there with their heads bowed for several moments.

"Let me have the bag, Ted," Commander Little said.

Ted handed him a cloth bag filled with notes each boy at camp had written to wish the patient well. Commander Little took a few of the notes out of the bag and placed them on top of the bedside table. The rest he left in the bag and hung it from the knob of the table drawer. As they prepared to leave the room, Bucky became agitated in his drugged state. Emitting groans and some mumbled incoherent words, he then abruptly shouted, "No, Crusher...no...not you!" and then fell silent.

On the drive home, the boys recalled Bucky's words.

"'Crusher,' Is that what he said?" Commander Little asked.

"I think so," Ted answered.

Kent said, "He spoke so suddenly...I didn't get it. I'm not sure what he said."

"Any of you ever hear Bucky mention a 'Crusher' before?"

"No sir," each of them replied.

After another trip to Alexandria the following week, the three were once again on the way to visit Bucky.

"Commander Little," Kent said, "Doesn't it cost a lot to be in the hospital? How will Bucky pay for all that?"

"Kent," Little answered, "because he's a CCC enrollee, the government takes care of things like this. The hospital here has reduced Bucky's costs to one dollar a day, and whatever the total comes to will be covered by the US government."

"God bless the USA," Ted said.

As they drove onto Seminary Road, heading towards Alexandria Hospital, Little said to the boys, "The doctor reported Buck's progress has been impressive. He's on crutches and handling them well. The doctor told me, 'That kid's got a lot of spunk.' I think he may come back to camp soon.' Maybe we can take him back today."

17. DETECTIVE
DAN RUMSON

The story of Buck's abduction and abuse hit the front page of the local newspaper, as well as those of nearby larger cities. *The Alexandria Gazette* carried the banner headline: *CCC BOY ABDUCTED, DRAGGED BEHIND CAR*

The police set up a dragnet throughout the area on the lookout for a maniac suspect. People in the area started locking their doors at night, an unusual practice in this quiet suburb.

At police headquarters in Dumfries, Detective Dan Rumson and an investigative staff carefully examined a package left behind in the front seat of the abandoned car. The letters "C.T.I." identified the intended recipient of the carton. The specific mailing address listed a post office box in Chicago, Illinois. Investigators lifted clear fingerprints from two sides of the package. Upon opening it, Rumson recognized the contents immediately.

"It's packed with .45 caliber handguns," he said. "This certainly suggests the driver may have been part of a larger criminal organization. Billy, what did they pick up on the Chicago end?"

"The account was under 'C.T.I.', probably a phony organization that doesn't exist, but listen to this. Yesterday, somebody closed the P.O. Box. The transactions took place at the post office, so there's no other address available. I'm afraid we hit a dead end on that one."

"*Hmmm,*" Dan Rumson said. "News travels fast. This certainly seems well planned...almost premeditated."

The Boxcar Kid

A young police officer burst into the room. "Sir, an hour ago they found a body in the woods not far from the road where the kid got dragged."

"I wonder why it wasn't found when we scoured the woods earlier?"

"I don't know, sir. It wasn't hard to find. It was right out in the open. The gun was right next to him. It looks like the guy shot himself in the head. A full set of clear prints were on the gun."

Perhaps a little too clear, thought Rumson. *A trembling hand with a gun turned on oneself is likely to leave smudged prints.*

"They took the guy's prints and sent them to the lab."

"Did they get any results?" Dan asked.

"Yes. They match the ones on the box."

"Do they know who this guy is?"

"No. In fact, he had no identification...nothing on him at all."

A report on the incident appeared in local newspapers, but not as front-page news.

Notwithstanding Rumson's suspicion of a larger conspiracy, the Dumfries Police Department was eager to put the matter to rest, and concluded the victim was the target of a lone deranged killer who then took his own life. The police closed the case file.

Lingering questions troubled Dan Rumson. *How was the boy captured? The abductor must have had help to subdue him. A CCC boy would be able to defend himself. When I inspected the trail, markings of scuffling feet came to an abrupt end, and then a path of something dragged, no doubt marking the precise spot the victim fell to the ground. It seems implausible that the dead man alone could have trussed up the boy, tied him to the bumper, and driven the car without the victim breaking away. There also seems to be some hidden motive here beyond that of a deranged person gone wild.*

Dan deeply regretted his forced transfer from Alexandria to this Podunk town of Dumfries after he was caught shacking up with the police chief's daughter. Rumson's wife had divorced him and had custody of their two-year-old daughter, but he was clearly out of line and regretted what he did. *It was a dumb-ass thing for me to do. At 33, I should have had more sense.* It was of little comfort that she had come on to him, not vice versa. In following her seductive lead, he had ignored all reasonable boundaries when he laid her out on the boss's desk with the door unlocked and the chief still in the building. When the chief came into his office unexpectedly through a back door, he literally caught Dan Rumsen with his pants down.

Six-years later, Dan had learned his lesson. He kept his trousers on

298

even in the presence of the most provocative chicks.

With his prior indiscretions left behind and his increased maturity and experience, Dan Rumson now could not tolerate the ineptness of a police force of men who had the same relatives and lock-stepped to the theme of "The Good Old Boys." The department remained twenty years behind its counterpart in Alexandria in its hardware, forensics and investigative methods. *These hicks don't know their ass from a hole in the ground. This is what I get for playing around too much. Did anyone talk to the boy? The whole thing smacks of incompetence.*

Rumson brought his concerns to the attention of the chief.

"Look, Dan, the case is closed. Keep it that way. You'll only be letting yourself in for some trouble, believe me. Stay away from it."

"But don't you think it's odd…"

"Dan! Drop it, you hear? There are more important things for you to do around here."

To hell with you, chief. I'll follow up on my own time…and the first thing I'll do is talk with the Ellis kid.

18. THE THREAT

"Dan, this phone call...it's for you."

Seated at his desk, Dan glanced over his shoulder. "Who is it?"

"Didn't say," the clerk said as he pointed to the phone off its cradle a few desks away. Dan went to the unoccupied desk, sat down and put the phone to his ear.

"Detective Rumson here. How can I help you."

A raspy, sinister voice at the other end said, "Detective Daniel Rumson, listen carefully. You're a crack detective, but if you have any thoughts of conducting further investigation on the case of the boy dragged by a car through the woods, forget about it."

"Who is this? Who the hell are you?"

"That's no concern of yours. Just do as we say."

"We?" Who the hell are these people?

"Just as I suspected," Dan replied, "There's something more to this case than meets the eye."

"Shut up and listen. If you don't think we mean business, speak to your little daughter. Mindy has something to tell you. The case has been closed. Leave it that way and nothing more will happen."

"What the hell...who do you think you are? You think you can threaten me?"

"I wouldn't be impulsive, if I were you, Daniel. Think on it before you decide to take this further. Talk to your daughter. I think Mindy will be pretty convincing."

Dan yelled into the phone, "You son-of-a-bitch — if you've done anything to her, I'll—"

Dan heard the click at the other end. He slammed the phone piece onto its cradle.

Goddammit! He wasn't on the phone long enough to track its origin.

For a moment he sat transfixed, his stare fixed on open space. Then he picked the phone up again and called his ex-wife.

As soon as she heard his voice, she burst forth with a barrage of deep sobbing.

"June, what's wrong?"

"Oh, Dan, something terrible has happened. Chipper is dead."

"What?"

"Mindy is hysterical. Dan, can you come over? Please come at once. We need you."

"What happened to Chipper?"

"Someone slit the cat's throat. We found him on the front lawn."

Little doubt remained in Rumson's mind the man in the woods had been murdered, and Buck Ellis' abduction planned in advance. The invasion of the assassin into his personal life fanned the flames of Dan's decision to continue his search for the killer...or killers, as he more likely suspected. *This can't end here. I have to get to the Ellis boy and question him.*

Before leaving the station on Monday evening, Dan slipped into the Records Room and pilfered the file from the officially closed case.

The next morning, on his day off, he awakened with the dawn. Twenty minutes later, he sat at the kitchen table scribbling information he had gathered into his notebook, listing the inconsistencies of the case and the questions they raised. He ate the last piece of dry toast, downed his second cup of black coffee and took a final drag on his Camel cigarette. After grinding the butt into the saucer, he rose and placed the dirty dishes on top of the unwashed pileup in the sink. Grabbing the case file and his notebook, he stepped out the door.

Meeting the cool, fresh air, he breathed in deeply, and felt invigorated. The glistening lawn lay under a heavy blanket of early morning dew. Dan walked over the grass to his car leaving behind a pattern of imprints like single file ducklings crossing a pond behind their mother. *What a beautiful morning it is. I will get to the bottom of this and crack this case.*

Few vehicles traveled the narrow road to the CCC camp at this early hour, and the way was clear ahead of him. Patches of fog lingered wherever the road dipped. *So peaceful and pastoral in the early morning. Before long, the sun will be up to burn it off.*

He estimated he would arrive at the camp in about a half hour. The road snaked back and forth through the woods. Breaking out onto a straight stretch of road, his eye picked up in his rear view mirror a black sedan rapidly narrowing the space between them. In an instant, the car was on his tail.

What the hell...this guy in the black car is kissing my ass. What's the matter with him? He could see the face of his pursuer almost as though the man sat in the back seat. *No distinguishing marks...just a pair of dark glasses and a fedora on his head.* Dan coasted to slow down, cranked down the window and motioned for the impatient driver to pass. *The road is wide open. Why doesn't he pass?* Next, Dan tried to put some distance between them, pressing the gas pedal further. He was flying over the road, but the shadow directly behind him stuck like glue. Dan felt himself jolted back as the man behind him bashed his bumper. *Who is this bastard?* The car rammed Rumson a second time forcing a grunt from him. He looked at the speedometer. The needle was hovering around 50. *Got to stop! Got to stop!* He slammed his foot on the brake. It collapsed to the floorboard. *Omigod! No pressure! No brakes!*

Dan felt his white-knuckled, sweaty hands fused to the steering wheel. The car weaved erratically as he tried to keep it on the pavement. The driver behind him kept slamming Dan's bumper, shoving his car towards increased speed.

"You goddamn son-of -a-bitch. Stop! Stop it!" Dan pulled hard on the steering wheel to make a right-angled turn. Wheels on the passenger side lifted from the road as the car skidded sideways across the surface. One last strike from behind and his car catapulted off the road. Dan's eyes widened. The tree trunk was enormous. It shot forward at him. The bark—an instant snapshot in his mind of what looked like a three-mile-high aerial view of a mountain chain with its valleys and peaks...and then, *totally black.*

The police report indicated in part: "The driver's head broke through the windshield and he died instantly. A half-empty bottle of Jack Daniel's whiskey on the floor and the aroma of liquor on the deceased suggest the driver was intoxicated when he lost control of the car."

Of items recovered, there was no mention of any file or notebook.

19. TRAUMA

The staff at CCC Company 3383 announced the findings to the boys. They dismissed any suspicion about the events — except for one boy, who knew better. His body shuddered from head to toe when he heard that the police did not identify or capture the real perpetrator. At the same time, he felt relief he would not have to relate any of the happenings to anyone. The horrific resurfacing thought of Crusher's voice under that ghostly hood unnerved him, and he wanted to expel the whole experience from his mind forever.

For some time after his release from the hospital, Bucky suffered from mild depression. Trauma caused by Crusher's reappearance made him jumpy over sudden sounds and situations.

When Buck walked to his barracks one night and Kent "Butt-hole" Butler ran up to him from behind, Buck spun around to face him bent forward in a crouch with clenched fists.

"Hey, Hotshot, what the hell's buggin' ya? It's just me…Butt-hole. I was on cleanup in the kitchen an' just got finished."

Buck released pent up air from his lungs and relaxed. They turned and walked together to the barracks. Buck made no defense for his actions. He did not want to talk about it to anyone.

In addition to Bucky, still another person deplored the closing of the case. Dan Rumson's wife, June, had firm convictions about Dan's death. *Dan drank an occasional beer, but never touched whiskey. What he was doing and where he was going I don't know, but he damn well wasn't drunk. Someone forced him off the road. Someone deliberately killed him.*

June's first impulse was to go to the police, launch an angry complaint, and demand they reopen the case, but upon immediate reflection, she hesitated. Still traumatized by the deliberate killing of Mindy's cat, she feared reprisal from the killer if she told anyone her suspicions. She would not risk her life or that of her daughter.

Three months later, she and Mindy moved to Alexandria, where she hoped she would find closure for the grief and fear that never seemed to end.

20. A NEW RESOLVE

As a few weeks passed, Buck, with renewed determination, initiated a personal program of recovery. Rising before dawn each morning, he jumped rope and punched the practice bag. His routine included push-ups in the barracks and pull-ups using a branch of a sturdy oak tree. Several weeks of good food, hard work and a rigorous exercise regimen, toned his muscles and brought him back to his former healthy physical state.

Father Michael had never let him forget the benefits of spiritual health, so Buck continued his practice of reading from a small daily devotional booklet each morning. Along with most of the boys, he attended weekly religious services conducted by a local pastor on Wednesday nights. For some Jewish boys, a rabbi traveled from Alexandria to conduct holy day services and occasional Sabbath services.

•

Buck sprinted across the clearing. Throwing open the door without knocking, he burst into Commander Little's camp office. Two steps in he froze, realizing he had interrupted a conversation between the camp superintendent and a forestry official.

"Uh...sorry, Commander Little," he stammered. "I should have knocked."

"That's all right, Buck." Turning to the man next to him, Little said, "I think we're ready to wrap it up, Bill. Thanks for the help."

"Yes, Keith. Thank you. I'll take your suggestions under consideration and get back to you." The forestry official picked up a few papers from the desktop and left.

During the past few weeks, Commander Little witnessed the return of Bucky's confidence and spirit. *His rapport with the other kids is even better than it was. They respect him and like being around him.* The commander stood and motioned Buck to the chair. "Come on in, Buck, and sit down. Tell me what you're excited about."

Buck did not wait to sit down. "Look what came in today's mail." He waved his flier's license in front of Little's face and grinned.

"Well, well! Congratulations, Bucky." He matched his grin as he reached across the desk and put his hands firmly on Buck's shoulders. "It looks like we have our all-American boy back once more. Now all you need is a plane."

In the remaining days of autumn, Buck put time in as a relief pilot for Windy, who still received payment from customers and enjoyed time for himself. Buck felt gratified in giving back to his mentor while gaining more experience at the same time.

DECEMBER, 1935, St. Louis, Missouri

Home on furlough for Christmas, and alone with Emily, Buck felt a lump form in his throat as he held her close.

"Emily, I know she's not mine, but I want you to consider me the father of Michelle since her real father is a deadbeat and a rotten snake not fit to raise her. "

Emily welcomed his devotion and endorsed his proposal, but Buck's mention of "the real father" revived thoughts of Josh's sudden appearance and abuse last summer when he broke into the parsonage and threatened her and Michelle. *If you only knew, dearest. You weren't there when he assaulted and subdued me on the dining room floor. What if he should come back, as he said he would? He knows where we live. There were no surprises when you beat him up on the rails. But now...now you are unsuspecting in the face of danger. He could come in darkness...at night and murder us in our beds. Oh, God! What could he do? What would he do?*

Buck saw her avert her eyes away from him. Her stare seemed vacant, as if whisked away to another place...another time. He felt her trembling in his arms.

"What's wrong, Emily? Did I say something wrong? What's the matter?"

Emily stepped back away from him. She stood motionless, watching him with pleading eyes. Then she sprang forward, throwing herself into the safety of his arms. "Oh, Bucky, yes! Yes, I do want you to be Michelle's father. I want you to protect us. We need you to take care of us."

Her head on his shoulder, she let forth a flood of tears as she clung to him as though he were the last remnant of her life blown away by a gale force wind.

"Hey, hey," Buck said, stroking her back gently. "Everything's going to be fine. I won't let anything happen to you and Shelly...I promise." *Geeze...what got into her? Women! I'll never understand them. Hell, what difference does it make? Whatever caused her to grab me like that is turning me on. I can almost taste it...like honey in my mouth. I want this.*

Assigned to separate upstairs bedrooms, Buck sometimes switched rooms with Emily to be with Michelle, allowing Emily a night of quiet rest. On those occasions, Bucky would awaken and leave his bed and observe Michelle silently, often standing in wonder while the moonlight, streaming through a window, filled the room with a heavenly glow.

How beautiful she is. Dear God, I've got to see that no harm ever comes to her.

•

Sunday afternoon had come and everyone gathered in the parlor. Emily read a book, while Becky knitted a new blanket for Michelle. Bucky lay on his back on the floor, holding Shelly up in his outstretched hands, gently moving and shaking her and saying, "Wheeeee." Michelle showed her approval with giggly outbursts.

Father Michael left after Sunday afternoon dinner to go back to the church for a meeting. At the time, Buck thought it strange that he would conduct a meeting on Sunday afternoon, but he did not immediately question it.

"When's Father Michael coming back?" he asked.

"Oh, he should be home any minute," Becky said. "He had to go out to run some errands."

"I thought he said he was going to a meeting. What kind of meeting did he have on a Sunday?"

307

Becky did not answer Buck.

About ten minutes later, Buck heard some noise from the kitchen. Someone had come in the back door.

Michael walked briskly through the kitchen and dining room into the parlor. He greeted them with a broad smile.

"Look who I brought home," he said, then calling over his shoulder, "Come on in, kids."

Shelly played with blocks on the floor, and Buck still lay stretched out on his back. Rolling over on his side, he flashed a glance towards the dining room. He flinched and gasped at the sight before him. Making a grand entrance, K.O. and Estelle stood before him, an infant cradled in the muscled arms of the proud father. Everyone had a grin to match Michael's.

"What the..." Bucky said as he leaped to his feet and stretched out his arms to his old friends. "K.O.! Estelle! And who's that you got with you? What're you guys doin' here?"

"Hey, Champ, we just happened to get on a train in Chicago to Union Station here in St. Louie, and who should meet us on the platform, but the good Rev'rend." Laughter arose and filled the room. K.O. held up the child in his arms. "This here's Jason," K.O. said. "Estelle was carrying him, but I wanted to show him off to you myself."

"We call him 'Jay.' He's two months old," Estelle said.

"I can't believe you're a papa," Buck said, "and a proud one, at that! He's got your mug face. He's your kid for sure. Look at that nose. It's a boxer's nose."

"Yeah, but wit'out the scars," K.O. said.

"He has your soft, brown eyes, Estelle. They're beautiful," Emily said as she tickled Jay's ear and cooed at him.

At eight months, Michelle came creeping over to the group and tugged at her mother's dress. Emily lifted her into her arms. The child examined each of the strangers with curious eyes. Her gaze finally rested upon the smallest blanketed dark-skinned figure over which the others hovered, whispering soft words of admiration and praise.

"Well, don't just stand there," Becky said. "Take off your coats." Turning to Michael, she added, "Michael, take their coats and lay them on the beds upstairs."

K.O. gave Jay to Estelle, and grasped Bucky's extended hand. Buck gave a yank and pulled him into a bear hug. The two broke into a round of hearty laughter as they patted each other on the back.

"Aren't they something?" Estelle said. "Absolute bosom buddies."

"Yeah," Emily said. "I think I'm jealous."

Estelle looked at Michelle and smiled. Michelle, squeezing her arms more tightly around her mother's neck, returned a smile with her eyes sparkling with delight.

"Michelle, what a beautiful little girl you are. Why, you're the prettiest little girl I've ever seen." The babe retreated into a closer bond with Emily at these advances, as if she did not know what to make of it all.

Jay started to cry.

"Whatsamatta, little fella?" K.O. said.

Estelle took a whiff and declared, "Whew. I think he needs a changing."

"Come upstairs with me," Emily said, starting for the stairs with Michelle still in her arms. "We can change him there and talk. I couldn't wait to meet you. Bucky has already told me a lot about you."

"Excuse me, boys," Becky said. "I'll go to the kitchen and get some lunch together. K.O., what do you like?"

"How about Mulligan Stew?" Once again, they all laughed. "Anythin' fit to eat is fine."

Michael followed her into the kitchen, saying, "I'll give you a hand, dear."

"Buck, you look fantastic. The CCC must've done ya good."

"Yeah, it's really a great experience," Buck explained. "I'm finished, though, in March. Then I'm home for good. Say, you look damn good yourself, but how did you get that latest scar on your nose? It's a doozie."

"My nose got broke, but look," K.O. flashed his bright smile. "I still got all my pearly whites."

"What the hell...K.O., you been *boxing?*"

"Have I been boxing? Champ, let me tell ya!" He stepped back a little. "Buck, look at my belt buckle." He opened it and slipped off his belt, holding it up for a better look. On the front, it had a relief of two boxers. Buck took the buckle and read the inscription: *Chicago Tribune Intercity Championship Golden Gloves 1934.* He turned it over. Stamped on the backside were the words *Hickok* and *Sterling.*

"Geez. You been goin' to town, all right. That's really a handsome buckle."

"That's nothin'. Take a look at this." K.O. pulled from his pocket a small velvet covered box with a spring lid. He opened it carefully. A sparkle of light flashed before Buck's eyes. Inside the box rested a miniature solid gold boxing glove with a real diamond in its center. A loop at the top suggested it could be worn as a pendant.

"Geeze," Buck said. "You got this too?"

"Yeah, in the Golden Gloves Olympic Boxing Tournament. Champ, it's the greatest. It's really big time. They sell tickets and draw big crowds to see us at the Chicago Stadium. Golden Gloves started in Chicago about ten years ago, and now it's everywhere. I bet they have matches here in St. Louis. You oughta register and try it."

"Holy shit, K.O., you gotta show this to the others."

"Remember when you flattened that skunk in the woods on your first day out?"

"Yeah...those days were tough, but great..."

"How 'bout when the bulls caught us in Memphis and threw us in that jail with `Merciless?' "

"Geeze, yeah. And what about that sweet little girl and her mother in Lynchburg..."

"Mary Jane."

"Yeah...I wonder what she's doin' now?"

"What about the time when you got on your platform at the Chicago World's Fair and told the folks there would be boxin' on the Midway!"

"How did we ever get the nerve to do those things?"

"We were crazy kids back then..."

At lunch, Buck asked K.O. and Estelle how they came up with a plan to come to St. Louis.

"Mr. Gordon...you remember, Buck, how generous he was...he's the greatest employer you can find anywhere."

"He treats us like family," Estelle said.

"Yeah. Well, one day he asked about ya, Buck. He wanted to know if I knew what happened to ya, and what ya was doin'. So I told him how we got separated in Alabama, and how ya was here in St. Louis."

Becky and Estelle had returned and at this point, Becky chimed in.

"Mr. Gordon contacted us. We told him all about your experiences in the CCC and that you'd be here during the holidays."

Estelle continued the story. "The Gordons have this nice place north of Chicago on Lake Michigan, and they planned to go there for the holidays. Since they weren't going to be at home, they gave us the time off, and paid for the trip as a Christmas present for the two of us. They've always been very thoughtful towards Jeremiah and me."

It sounded strange for Buck to hear Estelle use K.O.'s given name.

"No one said anything to you," Michael Griffin added. "We all wanted it to be a surprise. Emily knew they were coming, but she didn't say a word to you about it."

"Oh, I get it. Holy smokes. You're all a bunch of sly foxes."

After Father Griffin offered a brief table prayer and a meditation, the men retreated to the living room while Becky, Estelle and Emily cleaned up the table and washed the dishes.

Bucky said to Michael, "I'm sure glad you picked them up at the railroad station. They might have had a hard time getting here otherwise."

"Yeah, I know," K.O. said. "St. Louis ain't no Chicago. I kin see they don't want colored folks around here."

21. EMILY'S HOMECOMING

MARCH, 1936, St. Louis, Missouri

Ending his stint in the CCC, Buck returned to St. Louis in time for Emily's seventeenth birthday and Michelle's first. To Buck, his new family projected a sense of "home" more than anything he had known since he left York. Emily was no passing fancy, but an inseparable part of his life. Now that Michelle had arrived, a sense of family, complete with stand-in grandparents, felt good. Family traditions, like birthday celebrations, became cherished memories, lending greater stability and strength to this growing community.

A few weeks later, Buck raised the topic with Emily of reuniting her with her family. She agreed they should discuss the matter with the Griffins.

On Sunday afternoons after services, the priest's agenda included a "Sabbath rest"—typically an opportunity for family interaction and conversation. In the parlor, Father Michael sat in his favorite chair reading the Sunday comics. Becky moved gently back and forth in the rocking chair knitting a blanket for the new baby. Emily had just entered the parlor after putting Michelle down for her nap.

"Father Michael, there's something we wanted to talk to you about," Bucky said.

The priest folded his newspaper while Becky put her knitting aside.

Showing immediate interest, they cast their eyes on Bucky.

Bucky began, "Both of you have taken us in and treated us like family, and we want to tell you how grateful we are."

"We already know that, Buck. Your presence in our lives has been a wonderful blessing from God to us," Michael said.

"Of course," Mrs. Griffin refrained. "There's no need to thank us," she said.

"But there is something else we wanted to say," Buck said in a serious tone.

"What is it, dear," Becky prompted.

"Emily and I love you both...and you could not have done more for us. But we...well...you see...our real parents—"

Emily broke in. "What Bucky is trying to say is that we both left our parents under terrible circumstances, and we feel awfully guilty for what we did to them."

Emily could see she had touched the Griffins' hearts.

"Actually," Emily continued, "Bucky convinced me a long time ago when we were riding the rails that I should consider returning to my family and confess...how...how...very sorry I am," she said, choking on her final words with her eyes turning misty.

"We'd like to go to Springfield, and see if we can find her father and mother and ask them to forgive Emily," Bucky said firmly. "We've talked about this a lot, but we want to ask you what you think about it. We know you will be able to tell us what would be the right thing for us to do."

After a brief moment in thought, Michael replied, "You're seeking our guidance, and we are so glad you are. We want you to trust us and turn to us for whatever you need. We love you both. It sounds like you've thought this out carefully, and it is always a good decision to want to mend broken relationships."

"Yes," Becky added, as she saw Michael glance her way to encourage a comment. "You both have our full support in your resolve to reunite with your parents, Emily."

Bucky released a relaxed sigh of relief over their understanding and support.

"And, Bucky, what about you and your parents? Have you thought about that?"

"Yes, I want to try and ask for forgiveness. But that will be for another time and place. Right now, I think the opportunity for Emily is the most important thing."

All agreed Buck and Emily should attempt a trip to Springfield, and they began to address details. Transportation and lodging loomed as a large issue, and to Father Griffin it seemed unsolvable.

"I just had a thought," Becky said. "Don't the Enders travel to Springfield occasionally to visit Martha's mother? I wonder if they would be willing to take Bucky and Emily with them. That would at least provide transportation."

"That's a good idea," Father Michael said, "It doesn't solve the problem of what happens once they get there, but it's a good starting point."

Becky and Michael offered to watch Michelle, but Emily expressed reluctance.

"I've never been away from Shelly before. It's not that I don't trust you with her, but as a mother, I'm afraid I'd be distracted much of the time thinking about her. I'd like to bring her with us. Besides, I think my parents will want to see her."

"She has a point, dear," Michael said to Becky.

"Perhaps we should contact the Enders before we make concrete plans," Mrs. Griffin advised. "We don't even know if we can get safe transportation much less if you both have someplace to stay."

"I'll telephone them," Father Michael offered. "We need to figure this out as soon as possible."

Father Griffin went to the phone.

When he finished his conversation, he returned to the family.

"I have good news. Not only are the Enders going to Springfield the weekend after next, but Mrs. Ender's mother lives in a large house and there are plenty of spare rooms for you. Her mother loves company and would be delighted to have you."

Buck and Emily gave each other glowing looks, and Becky was beaming, too.

"Emily, I found out something else when I went to call the Enders. I found that your parents have a telephone and a listing. I have an address, too. I could call them on your behalf and prepare them for your arrival."

"No!" Emily said abruptly. "I'm afraid what they might say. I need to talk to them directly. I'm sorry, Father Michael, but please don't call them."

"I think she's right," Mrs. Griffin affirmed.

"All right," Michael said. "Tomorrow we can start getting everything ready."

APRIL, 1936, Springfield, Illinois

From the address Father Griffin had obtained, Buck and Emily spotted the general area of the Bernard residence on a map of Springfield. The next morning, a bright and sunny spring day, Buck and Emily decided to walk the two-mile stretch to her family's home. Emily carried Shelly in her arms while Buck shouldered a bag containing items needed for the baby.

Large estate homes framed the tree-lined street of this established neighborhood. As they came upon the Bernard family residence, the couple stopped on the sidewalk and stared across a lush lawn with a manicured edge along each side of a central walk to the front door. Emily turned to Bucky with an apprehensive expression and squeezed his hand for support.

"The walk to the door seems so long," she said.

"Relax, Em. I'm right here by your side. Everything will turn out all right, you'll see. As soon as they see Shelly, their hearts will melt." The faint glimmer of an uncertain smile appeared on Emily's anxious face.

They began walking side by side toward the two-story brick English Tudor manor house with white wood trim. On their left, they passed a stately oak tree. On the lawn to their right, balancing the picture, stood an abundant red maple, its trunk caressed by groupings of blooming laurel and rhododendron.

At the front door, Emily paused a full minute before pressing the doorbell. She had given Michelle to Bucky, who held her in his arms as he remained at the foot of the front steps. Emily could feel her heart racing as she heard someone inside coming to the door.

The door opened, and Mrs. Bernard gasped at the sight of her daughter standing before her. "Emily!" Instantly, Emily's mother put her arms around her and hugged her.

"Mother, dear..."

"Emily...oh, Emily!"

At the sight of her mother's eyes releasing a torrent of tears down her cheeks, Emily felt her own eyes well up, and they each grasped at words to express their feelings.

"Oh, how I missed you," Mrs. Bernard said. "Are you all right? I died a thousand deaths thinking of what may have happened to you."

"Mama, Mama," Emily sobbed.

"I prayed for this day," Mrs. Bernard said.

At the foot of the steps, Buck, with Michelle in his arms, stood quietly, his eyes cast down.

Suddenly, Emily realized Buck's awkward situation. Taking her mother's hand, she brought her down the steps and said, "Mama, this is Bucky. He rescued me from some terrible situations and it was his idea and by his efforts that I am able to be here. "

Mrs. Bernard opened her mouth wide and looked at them in surprise.

Bucky turned the child in his arms to face her grandmother. "And this is Michelle, your grandchild."

Agnes Bernard moved close to Michelle. "Dear, dear child," she said, admiring her. Looking at Buck, she said, "And you are...Bucky! Thank you for bringing our baby home to us. Oh, I can't believe this is happening...so much, all at once. Now come inside and tell me everything!"

As they turned to go back up the steps, Emily could no longer contain herself. "Mama," she cried, "Mama, mama...I must tell you... I...I'm so sorry, Mama...sorry for running away...sorry for everything I did." Emily broke out crying as she and her mother put their arms around each other again. "Mama...can you and Papa ever forgive me?"

"There, there..."Emily's mother said. "Oh, my sweet child...of course we forgive you. You're home now and that's all that matters. Everything will be just as it was before."

Inside the house, Emily told her mother about their travels, the soup kitchen, and about the kindnesses of the Griffins.

Then Emily's mother spoke of Dr. Bernard's success at Memorial Hospital, and Nanette's progress in school. "Nanette will start her third year in high school this fall. She is getting good grades and is planning to go to college. Not many girls get to go that far," she said to Emily.

"Not this one," Emily answered with tears once more welling up in her eyes.

"Dear, dear, now don't start that," her mother said, stroking her daughter's hair. "Everything is going to work out fine for you...don't you worry."

"Where is my sister?" Emily asked.

"Nanette's at Grandma's house for the weekend. Grandma Bernard still lives in her house here in Springfield...do you remember? You last saw her when we visited in the summer of '33."

"Yes...the year after Grandpa died," Emily recalled.

Emily's mother said, "Since we moved to Springfield, my own home town, Nanette and Grandma have become the closest friends. Grandma will be so surprised and happy to see you, Emily."

"Does Nanette stay over at Grandma's often?"

"She has a babysitting job in Grandma's neighborhood. In fact, that is what she's doing tonight. It's convenient for Nanette to sleep at Grandma's after her babysitting and then she comes to church with Grandma in the morning, and after worship we bring Nanette home with us. Sometimes we have Sunday dinner together at Grandma's before coming home, and sometimes Grandma comes here and has dinner with us." Agnes Bernard chatted rapidly, bubbly with excitement. "I can't wait to see Nanette's face when she sees you. She cried so much when you left...she will be so happy when she sees you're home!"

Emily wanted to tell her mother all about Josh...things he did to her, and how Bucky intervened to rescue her on the rails, but she could not bring herself to speak of that now. *I will tell her and Daddy at another time...not now.*

Buck sat across from them in a chair amusing Michelle by tweaking her nose and playing with her fingers. He was elated over the warm reunion between Emily and her mother.

The two women continued their animated talk as Mrs. Bernard set extra places at the dinner table.

Dr. Bernard walked in.

Mrs. Bernard ran to tell him the good news. "Geoffy...Geoffy...look who came back to us! Our daughter has come home, and we have a grandchild! Isn't she beautiful? Her name is Michelle...and this is Bucky."

Bucky, holding Michelle, stood and extended his hand in a polite gesture.

"Bucky brought our little girl home," Mrs. Bernard continued.

Geoffrey Bernard, leaving Buck's hand extended, cut her short, lines of anger creasing his face. "A child? She has a child? She's just a girl. How could she have a child? How did this happen?" He looked at Emily. "Is this boy your husband?" he asked

"I'm...I'm not married, Daddy...I...I..." Emily fell silent.

Dr. Bernard turned and glared at Bucky with piercing eyes and lowered eyebrows. "You filthy son-of-a-bitch! You raped my daughter!"

"No, daddy, no! That's not how it was!" Emily interjected.

Bucky's jaw dropped open. He stood dumfounded before Emily's father. He could not believe his ears.

Michelle started to cry. "Agnes, take the child from him," Emily's father demanded.

Agnes dutifully went to take Michelle, who increased the volume of

The Boxcar Kid

her crying. Mrs. Bernard tried using her most soothing cooing tone of voice to quiet the child, but she could not restrain Michelle's loud wailing. With a look of desperation, Agnes Bernard handed the child back to Bucky. Shelly stopped her crying instantly and threw her arms around Bucky's neck, squeezing it with all her might.

"Sshh, sshh...it's all right, Shelly, it's all right," Buck said looking into her eyes.

Momentarily comforted with her head resting on Bucky's shoulder, she glimpsed her mother and quickly released her grip, stretching out her arms towards Emily.

Dr. Bernard clenched his teeth and tried to contain his fury. "Agnes, go upstairs and take Emily and the child with you."

Emily quickly went to Michelle and took her from Bucky, as Mrs. Bernard made a plaintive appeal to her husband.

"Geoffrey...please...why they only just arrived..."

His response came before she could finish. With a firm voice and a finger pointed towards the staircase, he said, "Bring them upstairs!"

Visibly shaken, Mrs. Bernard reluctantly took Emily's hand and led her to the stairs.

Carrying her child, Emily glanced back at Bucky. Her lips parted as if to speak in defense of Bucky...her champion, and as she now fully acknowledged, her beloved — but she said nothing, turned, lowered her head and proceeded up the stairs.

Alone in the room with Dr. Bernard, Buck watched as Emily's father turned and walked toward him. Dr. Bernard grabbed Bucky by his shirt and pulled the boy to him. With his full weight, Dr. Bernard pushed and slammed Bucky back against the wall so hard a protective glass from a decorative bracketed hurricane lamp shook loose, fell to the floor and shattered.

Bucky's heart pounded, the breath knocked out of him. He held his hands up to try to protect himself, but he dared not strike Emily's father.

"You're the one, aren't you, you bastard — you *raped* my little girl, didn't you? She would never have done such a thing unless you forced it."

Bucky, pinned to the wall by this enraged father, found no opportunity to give any defense.

Still holding him by his shirt, Emily's father pulled him to the door, ripping Buck's shirt, popping the buttons, yanking it loose from his pants, and throwing the boy down the front steps where he tumbled

318

onto the grass.

"You stay out of this house, you bum. Don't ever come back. If I ever see you again, I'll tear out your guts!"

Dr. Bernard slammed the door. A neighbor across the street heard the shouting and looked over at the ruckus. The man watched as Buck slowly raised himself up off the ground and stood with his head drooping.

•

Sunday evening, Michael Griffin went to answer the front door. "Sounds like the kids are home," he said to Becky.

He was surprised to see only Bucky, who walked straightway past him into the house. Michael immediately went to Mr. and Mrs. Ender, who remained in the car parked at the curb.

"There's been an unfortunate turn of events, Father Michael," Mr. Ender said. "It seems Emily's mother happily received them both, but when Emily's father came home, he jumped to the wrong conclusion and threw Bucky out of the house. He won't let the boy see his daughter or the child. It's been pretty rough on the boy. I'm sure he'll fill you in on the details when he feels up to it. I'm not sure he's ready right now."

"Would you both like to come inside? We have some tea brewing, and we could talk further."

"Thank you, Father Griffin, but it's been a long drive. Martha and I are anxious to get home. We feel sorry for the boy. We got to know him during our trip. He's a good boy. I think he got a raw deal. Let us know, Father, if we can be of further help."

"Thanks, Mr. Ender, for all you've done. We appreciate it."

When Father Michael returned to the house and saw the dark circles around the boy's sullen eyes and his unkempt hair and torn shirt, he put his arms around Buck and held him close. Bucky buried his face in Father Griffin's shirt, a lump in his throat, holding back tears.

Becky stepped closer to them and softly stroked Bucky's hair with her hand. "Oh, Buck, we're relieved that you're home. What happened?"

"Mr. Ender said Emily's father put Bucky out of the house." Bucky said nothing.

"Oh, Bucky," Becky said, her own eyes welling up. "How sorry we are. What can we do? Have you had anything to eat?"

Exhausted, Buck politely excused himself. "Thank you, Mrs. Griffin, but if you don't mind, I think I'd like to go right up to bed."

"Certainly, dear. You go right ahead. We'll talk in the morning."

Buck left the room and trudged up the stairs as if each foot weighed more than he could lift.

Michael and Becky heard the teapot brewing in the kitchen whistling loudly, demanding their attention. The couple retired to the kitchen where Becky poured out two cups and set them on the table. Before they could sit down and talk together, Becky's motherly instincts compelled her to go upstairs to check on Bucky. A moment later, she returned.

"Bucky is asleep. He looks exhausted. Oh, Michael, what are we going to do?"

"I don't know," Michael said. "It seems like things were coming together for them both. Now it doesn't look like there's a reconciliation in sight."

"Yes," Becky said, "And that goes for our hoped for wedding with the blessing of Emily's parents."

Michael put his teacup down and slid his hand across the table to hold Becky's hand. Becky understood and bowed her head.

"Lord, things have really soured. Something good has to happen, Lord. Please help us. Amen."

Becky broke the few moments of silence that followed.

"I can't imagine how they will get on without each other," Becky said.

"There's got to be a solution. We must find out in the morning exactly what happened. We must find a way to resolve this matter," Michael affirmed.

Before retiring, the cleric and his wife closed their day in the customary way. Busy days and late meetings sometimes necessitated the foregoing of this cherished tradition, but tonight they both strongly craved the encouragement and guidance their devotion could provide. Becky read the Bible verse, *1 Peter, 5:7: "Cast all your cares upon him; for he careth for you."*

The longer reading, from Genesis, highlighted Jacob's meeting with his brother, Esau, years after Jacob cheated Esau out of his rightful inheritance and his father's blessing. Upon hearing Esau was coming to meet him with a great band of men as Jacob returned home, Jacob was filled with dread. Turning to God, he confessed his unworthiness and asked for help. God guided Jacob through the events following to a comforting conclusion and a happy reuniting of the two brothers.(Genesis 33:1-9)

"That couldn't have been more providential," Michael said.

"Right to the point...and very comforting," Becky agreed.

"One door has closed, but we have hope that God will soon open another."

Michael reached across the table and put his hand on Becky's. They clasped their hands as Michael prayed again. "Dear God, restore your children, Buck and Emily, to each other. You love them so much, as we do. Mend our broken hearts, and especially bring Emily's father to an understanding that will soften his heart. Refresh us all with a good night's rest. We lay all this in your hands, Lord. Give us your peace in Jesus. Amen."

They stood and hugged each other before turning out the kitchen light and ascending the stairs to the bedroom, each pondering what the new day would bring.

JUNE, 1936, St. Louis, Missouri

For Bucky, the days after his rejection by Emily's father passed by as slowly as a camel in a desert sandstorm. His heart weighed heavily and he could not dispel a constant flood of memories of Emily and Michelle.

He found work at a local market unpacking boxes, cleaning and stacking the produce. It put a little spending money in his pocket. His dull stare and few smiles among his fellow workers evidenced his life had lost its zest. His most miserable experiences riding the rails had not depressed him like the feeling of loss harbored inside him now.

Letters arrived from Emily sporadically, but the expression of her own grief at their separation did not help Bucky's wilted morale, and her description of Michelle and the things she was learning to do made the ache in his heart intensify, and his longing for them grew more unbearable. One day as Bucky returned home after working at the soup kitchen, Father Michael greeted him saying, "There's something for you on your bed."

Without a word, Buck dragged himself up the stairs to his room. There on the bed lay an envelope addressed to him.

Michael Griffin had quietly followed him up the stairs and watched him through the doorway. "Aren't you going to open it?" he asked.

Buck picked up the envelope, turned it over several times, examining it before opening it.

The Boxcar Kid

Dear Buck,

First I must tell you that it's very difficult for me to write this letter. I'm a proud man, and it doesn't come easy for me to say I was wrong. But I have regretted my treatment of you since the moment I slammed the door on you.

The day after you left, I sat down with Emily and demanded she tell me everything, and she did. I realized the wrong I had done you.

She told me how you rescued her from unthinkable harm. She told me that you protected her and never violated her, but treated her with compassion and respect—"like a lady," she said. She told me how you stayed with her and promised to go with her to bring her back to us. She told me what a fine gentleman you are and since that day she has not stopped talking about your heroic exploits on her behalf. I guess you had it pretty rough yourself, and didn't need the manhandling I gave you. I was so terribly mistaken and hope you can forgive me.

I know Michelle is not your child, but you acted as her father and cared for her. I know the close bond you must have with my daughter and grandchild. I am not sure, but I think Emily is in love you. I must confess I am a bit jealous.

I am grateful to Father Griffin, as well as my own pastor, who counseled with me (the latter at my wife's promptings). I am lucky to have people who love me enough to set me straight when I make a fool of myself.

If you will permit it, I would like you to come to Springfield to spend some time with us. We are planning to engage a photographer to take a family picture. Will you join us in the picture? Emily says you have no picture of her or of Michelle.

Father Griffin has the details of proposed arrangements for your stay with us. At this time, we desire that Emily and Michelle remain with us, which is proper.

Exchanging letters and visits, of course, are in order. When you are here, we can speak together about what the future may hold for both of you.

Emily has written letters to you, and perhaps you have received some of them. I had forbidden her to have any contact with you, and whenever I saw envelopes addressed to you, I destroyed them. I wish now that I could recover them. I am sure she will be sending you letters on a regular basis and will do so with my heartfelt blessing.

Sincerely,
Geoffrey Bernard

Bucky's eyes were glowing, as he turned and looked at Father Michael. "I can't believe this! Is it really happening? Did he really write this to me?"

He caught sight of the grinning face of Father Michael.

"You!" he exclaimed. "You spoke with Emily's father? You did that?"

The priest answered modestly, averting his eyes. "Yes."

Buck leaped from the bed, ran to Michael Griffin and threw his arms around him. "Thank you...thank you...thank you!" he said.

For the first time in a while, Buck's spirit was buoyant. *Thanks, thanks, thanks, God! My life has finally turned a corner. Now I can make a fresh start. Hallelujah!*

"There's more, Buck. After he sent the letter he had another thought. He called me last night and said if you agree, they would like you to come and stay with them in Springfield. They have several spare rooms and you could take your pick. They think it would be good for you, Michelle and Emily to spend time together. Mrs. Griffin and I thought it over, and we tend to agree. We would miss you and hate to have you leave us, but since you reached your goal to find Emily's family, and you helped her in that, it seems that you belong with them, at least at the present time. What do you think?"

"Gosh...it's so sudden, I don't know what to think. I miss Emily and Shelly so much, but I don't want to leave you. Could we come back and visit and stay with you at times?"

"Most certainly, and Buck, there's more. This is not why he wants you to come, but he needs a helper for his groundskeeper. It's a job mowing the lawn, trimming the bushes and such, and he would pay you for it. You could earn some money, which would come in handy."

"If I went, when would I leave?"

"I have to be here on Sunday, but I think I could clear things to drive you up there on Wednesday, and I think Becky could come with us. Why don't you sleep on it and see what tomorrow brings?"

"I will," Buck said.

In the morning, Bucky said he wanted to talk to Emily before making a decision.

"That's a good idea, Bucky," Michael said. "You can use our phone to call."

A few minutes later, Bucky returned to the room where Michael and Becky waited. "Emily's super excited about it all. I'm going!"

22. KENNY

JULY, 1936, Springfield, Illinois

After a late night party, Kenny met The Mastermind's regional agent on the corner of Clear Lake and South McCreary Avenues in downtown Springfield. This sixteen-year-old was ambitious, and under the streetlight, the sparkle from his diamond cufflinks reflected his success in his service to The Mastermind. For almost two years, he abetted The Mastermind in some of his most important undertakings. In his petty thievery, he had the good fortune of procuring some highly valuable items, which he always included in his reported cache. For the most part, Crusher's stoolies learned greater benefits came from following the steps that brought rewards and recognition from The Mastermind, instead of attempting to dispose of the goods themselves, omit them from the report, and keep the cash. The accounts they all heard of the fate of those who crossed The Mastermind provided additional incentive to follow the rules.

The agent, who wore a hat with the brim tipped down over his face, pushed Kenny out of the light into the shadows. With steely gray eyes, he scanned this young upstart dressed in elegant pin stripes and bow tie.

In a cocky gesture, the boy pushed the agent back, brushed off his suit lapel where the agent had touched him and casually adjusted his sleeve, deliberately flaunting his jeweled cuff link. Then, from his pocket, he pulled a gold watch attached to a gold chain. Eyeing it, he said, "Hey, y'r right on the button. So y'r the big wheel operator in dis town, eh? Glad to meet ya." He stretched out his hand grasping another opportunity to flash his expensive taste.

"Shut up and listen, little twit. The Mastermind has an important assignment for you."

"*Ooo*...I git it...you're a big man on the ladder. But take it easy, Buster. You don't need to pull rank on me. So whut's da big man want me t' do? Spit it out. I'm list'nin'.."

"He wants you to keep a vigilant watch on a family here, recording details of each member's daily routines. The family head is a Dr. Geoffrey Bernard. His wife's name is Agnes. The young girl, Emily, is their daughter, who has a little girl, Michelle. Emily is unmarried, but her boyfriend...his name is Bucky...has been living with the family for a little more than a month."

"Is dere any udder directions?" the young operative asked. "Does the Mastermind want anythin' more dan keepin' m' eye out?" The good-looking boy with large brown eyes and a slicked down shiny auburn mane spoke with an air of smart-aleck confidence.

Having run across too many of these brash young hoodlums, the agent replied in a commanding tone, "And take notes for your report, twerp. Don't forget that. You'll be plenty busy tracking their moves."

"Whut d'ya t'ink Mastermind's up to?"

"I don't know what his purpose is, but he seems to have a vendetta against this family...especially the boy named Bucky. Supposedly, the boy is not the father of the child, but he adores her, nevertheless. Rumor has it this kid did something terrible to the Mastermind, but no one seems to know any details. Anyway, it ain't your business to ask such questions, numskull. Here's the home address and information." *These little hotshots always try to find some way to brown nose the Mastermind. I love the chance to take these bullshitters down a few pegs. It's the best part of this crappy job of keeping them in line.* "I'll see you again in one week at the same time right here at this corner. Have your report ready and don't mess up."

The agent disappeared and Kenny looked over the information. His ego did not seem deflated by any means. *So da Masterrmind wants t' make trouble f'r dis family, eh? Well dat's jist fine. Here's m' chance to git noticed. Mastermind wants t' stick it to dis here kid, Bucky. I bet all of dem go ga-ga over dat little girl.* A broad grin broke out on his face as his mind started spinning out a plan.

Dick Miller

23. LET THE GOOD
TIMES ROLL

For the first time since the Depression began, Bucky and Emily found a breath of fresh air blowing their way. They came to a turning point at which their lives had come together, bringing them a measure of peace and satisfaction.

The family was together. Michelle had advanced from the creeping stage and now kept everyone busy as she progressed from walking to running everywhere, investigating everything to mollify her insatiable curiosity. Family life took on a semblance of order as they became integrated into the traditional family patterns. They attended Sunday services at the Lutheran church with regularity, gathering afterwards at grandma's house for dinner. Nanette would be there, too, as she continued to baby-sit Saturday nights in grandma's neighborhood, staying over and coming to church with grandma on Sunday morning. Built-in babysitters were readily available with Agnes Bernard and Nanette close at hand. All this introduced a new and pleasant aspect into Emily and Bucky's life together: *dating*.

Now a welcome member of the Bernard household, Bucky drove the family car into the driveway, parked it in the garage, and took Emily's hand as they walked up the steps to the veranda and sat on the swinging bench on this balmy summer night.

"Did you like the picture show, Buck?"

"I was taken by the big screen and all the excitement of seeing a movie on it for the very first time. I thought the scenery was great."

"Didn't you love Jeanette MacDonald and Nelson Eddy in their singing duets? They are the perfect couple together."

"Well, yeah...that was good, but it seemed odd to me that a Canadian Royal Mountie would sing at the drop of a hat whenever Jeanette MacDonald came around. That seemed a little bit hard to believe."

"That's the way it is in motion pictures, Bucky. It's entertainment. It's life as everyone would like it to be. I kept imagining how handsome you'd look in the uniform of a Canadian Mounty."

"Well, maybe, but I don't think you'd like my singing." Bucky put his arm around Emily, as they gently swung back and forth on the swing.

"You know, Em, you look lovely tonight." He turned and kissed her, and she responded to his romantic inclinations by pressing her lips to his.

Sitting side by side gently swinging, Emily said, "Bucky, you know, Daddy has really taken a liking to you. Mamma and I have been talking, and she is excited, and wants to make plans with us right away. Now it seems the last leg of our efforts has been reached...we've united with my parents."

"You mean, Em...you mean...we can get..."

"Yes, Buck, yes. It's the right time for us to get married. I think this is the right time for you to ask daddy for my hand in marriage."

"Hot diggity! Lately, I've been thinking the same thing."

Buck slipped off the swing and knelt down in front of Emily in a gallant gesture. "Emily, will you marry me?"

"Of course, you idiot!"

They both laughed.

"Tomorrow...I'll ask him tomorrow."

Earlier, after the showing of the film, *Rose Marie*, people had left the theatre with happy faces over their shared experience of entertainment. There was one, however, who had been more interested in two particular theatergoers than the movie itself. Kenny had sat three rows behind Buck and Emily, but paid little attention to the picture show.

24. THE ABDUCTION

It was a balmy summer day, and Mrs. Bernard put a light cover over Michelle, asleep in her carriage in the back yard. She began hanging the laundry, starting with the small items, and then working her way through the laundry basket to the large bed sheets. Between her and baby Michelle, items on the line blocked Mrs. Bernard's view of the child. Humming a tune as she leisurely hung the laundry, she took the basket and the extra clothespins to the back door steps when finished.

A quick glance back over her shoulder to see the carriage prompted her to do a double take. She turned her face back to the spot and spied what her eyes passed over quickly in her first glance. *What is Michelle's blanket doing on the ground?* She walked towards the carriage. *Child, what did you do?* As the carriage and its contents came into full view, Agnes Bernard brought her hand to her mouth and gasped.

"Good Lord," she said, "The child is gone! Michelle!" she cried. "Michelle! Where are you?"

Her loud cries brought the other members of the household to the yard. Buck emerged first from the back door.

"What's the matter?" he said.

"It's Michelle," Agnes cried. "She was sound asleep in her carriage moments ago and now she's gone!"

"Omigod!" Emily cried, running to the empty carriage and staring into it. "I can't believe this. Where is she?"

She raced haphazardly towards the front yard calling Shelly 's name.

Buck searched through other parts of the property, calling, " Shelly, Shelly!"

A neighbor hearing them stepped outside to see what was going on.

"Did you see our little baby?" Emily said to the woman. "Someone has taken her."

Throwing her hands in the air in a gesture of futility, the neighbor shook her head.

"She couldn't get out of the carriage by herself," Dr. Bernard said. "I'm afraid someone has kidnapped her. I'm calling the police."

Within ten minutes, a uniformed policeman and a police detective arrived. The officer cased the outside property, while the detective went into the house to speak with the family.

The detective began, "I'm truly sorry this has happened, but we will do everything possible to find her. To do that, I need to ask you a few questions."

"Certainly," Dr. Bernard said.

"What is the child's name?"

"Michelle Rebecca Bernard," Emily answered.

"You're not married?"

"No," she said, adding nothing further.

"Does she answer to any nickname?"

"Yes, we call her 'Shelly'."

"How old is she?"

"A year and a half. She was born on March 18, 1935," Emily replied.

After gleaning further information, he asked, "Do you have any idea who may have taken the child?"

Emily said, "It was Josh."

She blurted it out with such firm and immediate conviction that the others turned towards her with startled faces.

As Emily pronounced her accusation, Bucky began to consider the possibility. *No one else had a stronger motive to kidnap Michelle.* "Yes," he said. "Josh. Of course…Michelle's father."

"Josh?" the detective repeated. "Does he have a last name? Where do we find him?"

"I don't know his full name," Emily answered. "Everyone just called him Josh. I don't know where he is now."

"He knows how to hop freight trains," Bucky added. "Maybe your men could check out the yards. Maybe he hasn't gotten out of town yet."

"When did you see him last?" the detective asked Emily.

She lowered her head and put her hands on her face.

In the midst of her anxiety, her father came to her aid, projecting an angry message with his eyes at the detective. "You don't have to tell him anything more, sweetheart."

"No daddy...I..." Emily stammered.

With soulful eyes, she looked at Bucky. "He showed up at the parsonage while you were in Virginia, Bucky. I was in the house alone with Michelle. Father Griffin and Becky were away at a conference. The door wasn't locked and he just snuck in and surprised me."

Bucky instantly rose to his feet, moved quickly to her chair and knelt down beside her clasping her hands. "The son-of-a bitch. Why didn't you tell me, Em? What did he do to you?"

"Nothing," Emily said, "...but he tried. Thank heaven a woman from the church stopped by, and he left out the back door in a hurry...but before he went, he said he would be back. Dear God...who would have thought..."

"If I find him, I'll bust his freaking head open!" Buck said.

25. THE REPORTER

"There's someone coming up the walk," Agnes Bernard said. "He's from the press. It's written on a card stuck in his hatband."

"How can we get rid of him? We don't want to talk to him." Dr. Bernard said.

The doorbell rang.

"Dr. Bernard," the detective said, "if the newspaper runs a story with a photo of Michelle, someone out there may have seen her and report it to us. That would be a great help."

"I don't trust those damn newspaper people. They love to dig up every piece of dirt they can find. I can just imagine what they'd say if they pried into Emily's background with this Josh character..."

"Oh, dear," Agnes said, putting a hand to her face.

Emily blushed, and Buck stared at Dr. Bernard, not knowing what to think.

"Emily," her father pleaded with a tender voice, "I think you are the most wonderful daughter in the world. You and Nanette are the light of my life. But the newspaper people don't know you, and I'm afraid of what they might say about you."

The doorbell rang a second time.

The detective offered a quick solution. "I see your concern, Dr. Bernard. Let me handle this for you. I'll speak to the reporter on your behalf. I'll tell him you're too upset for an interview at this time. I promise to tell him only what he needs to know and no more. I know the kind of questions these people ask. I think I can satisfy him with general information. Do you have a photograph of Michelle?"

"Yes," Agnes answered. "I'll get it and bring it to you. Go to the door and talk with the newsman."

"Yes, please," Emily's father said, motioning him to go to the door.

The detective stepped outside with the reporter, closing the door behind him.

The next day, the front-page story and photo of Michelle hit the streets. The story identified the child as the granddaughter of Dr. and Mrs. Geoffrey Bernard, and noted Dr. Bernard offered a $500 Reward for any information leading to the child's recovery and arrest of her abductor.

That same afternoon, Pastor Gary Messerschmidt from Trinity Lutheran Church visited the Bernard home. He was a good friend as well as their pastor, and they embraced him in greeting.

"We are all shocked by this awful situation," he said. "Members of the church have planned an all night prayer vigil on Michelle's behalf. Participants are signing up for different hours during the night to keep prayers going continuously. Our nearby sister congregations are joining us in including Michelle and your family in prayers at Sunday services. Geoffrey, you have many friends, and I've never seen such an immediate and widespread response on the part of our people. It's very gratifying."

"Pastor Messerschmidt, how could God let this happen?" Mrs. Bernard asked, her arms extended with palms up, her voice tremulous, worry lines etching her face. "She's just an innocent child."

"Misfortune occurs in this world and we cannot always explain it," the pastor answered, "but here are some certainties I believe about God. He did not will Shelly's kidnapping. Not everyone acts in accord with God's will. God promises to preserves us in times of trouble, sustain us and rescue us...even from death. When trouble comes, as it does to my own life, I remember God's promise in Romans 8:28 that he works 'all things together for the good for those who love Him.' That promise helps me to remain confident and to avoid capitulating to any bad circumstance that may come my way. God gives me strength to live above my circumstances and keep a steady course."

"It's so hard for me to understand, Pastor Messerschmitt," Agnes confessed.

"Yes, I know what you mean, Agnes. It *is* hard to see God's clear purpose when a crisis is upon us. Think of it as stepping into God's classroom and let your senses be alert to learn what God may reveal to us in such situations. Sometimes we learn things about ourselves that make us stronger. If we understand that God walks with us in such events, we can be patient as he consistently rolls out a picture of his grand plan of salvation, of which sacrifice, pain and suffering plays an important role."

A tear rolled down Agnes' cheek as she fixed her eyes on the pastor and listened intently to his words.

"God is faithful. He keeps his promises. He invites us to cast all our cares on him, for he cares for us."

Agnes put her hands on Pastor Messerschmidt's shoulders and looked up at him with eyes glistening, a gentle smile brightening her face, as if to say, "Those are just the words I needed to hear."

As Pastor Messerschmidt prepared to leave, he opened the family Bible and read Psalm 121 to the family:

> "I will lift up mine eyes unto the hills, from whence cometh my help. My help cometh from the LORD, which made heaven and earth. He will not suffer thy foot to be moved: he that keepeth thee will not slumber. Behold, he that keepeth Israel shall neither slumber nor sleep. The LORD is thy keeper: the LORD is thy shade upon thy right hand. The sun shall not smite thee by day, nor the moon by night. The LORD shall preserve thee from all evil: he shall preserve thy soul. The LORD shall preserve thy going out and thy coming in from this time forth, and even for evermore."

The pastor's tender response to their tragic circumstance stirred Emily to relate details of the choices that led her to run away from home to Josh's bed. Her involvement with Josh compounded her feelings of guilt over Michelle's disappearance. Her sincere expression of remorse stirred everyone, as the group surrounded and supported her. Her pleas continued as she wept. "I don't deserve my beautiful Michelle, and now God has taken her away from me."

"Sweet child," Pastor Messerschmidt said, "God is merciful. He forgives you and does not intend to punish you. He is always on your side. There is no denying that you made some bad choices in your life, but God has not abandoned you. He is always with you, especially in your time of need. You can never wander so far from God that you will be beyond his reach. When we stray like sheep, he is our good Shepherd and stands with open arms to welcome us home."

Putting out his arms to them, he said, "Come here to me."

They moved into a tight huddle, and the pastor prayed. *"Dearest Lord, you regard your people in need. You comfort the broken-hearted. You shepherd your people beside the still waters. We entrust Michelle to your tender care as we ask you to bring her back to us. Have mercy on us, Lord.*

"We pray as well for the person or persons who took her away. Turn their hearts toward repentance. By your love and mercy, melt the hearts of those who harbor evil desires towards others. Hear us for Jesus' sake. Amen."

After the prayer, Emily felt a deeper peace within her than anything she had experienced before. Some intruder snatched her child away in broad daylight, but her spirit remained confident and calm. *I will not let myself despair. I must be strong. Worry brings nothing. Whatever happens, God will see us through. I praise you heavenly Father. Please bring Shelly safely back to us.*

As the pastor took his leave, Geoffrey Bernard said, "We can't thank you enough for being with us, Pastor Messerschmidt. We could never get through this alone."

"Wait a minute," Buck said. "I'm going with you. I want to go to the church to join in that prayer vigil."

Dr. Bernard said, "I'll go with you."

"No," Pastor Messerschmidt advised. "One of you men should stay here with the women. You may be needed here, Dr. Bernard, if news about Michelle arrives."

"That makes sense," Dr. Barnard noted. "Go ahead, Bucky. I'll stay here."

"I'm going with Bucky, daddy," Emily said. "I want to be with those people, too."

"Okay, baby. Take care. How will you get home?"

"We'll walk, daddy. It will do us good."

At the church, people coming to the vigil found a table in the entranceway with Bibles, devotionals and prayer books to use for prayer guidance. The church elders also made available bookmarks imprinted with Scripture references, sent several months earlier from *Lutheran World Relief.* Highlighting God's mercy, the passages provided a fitting devotional for such an occasion.

Fifteen people sat scattered about the church when Buck and Emily arrived. The couple chose a book of prayers, a Bible and a bookmark before sitting in a pew. A few minutes into their readings, a woman saw and recognized them. She left her pew and directly approached them.

"Bucky and Emily. I'm so sorry for you, but glad you are here."

The woman slipped into the pew and sat next to Emily.

"You must be beside yourself. I have a two-year-old. I know how I'd feel if that happened to my child."

Others at the vigil left their seats and began to gravitate towards Bucky and Emily. In moments, all those in the sanctuary formed a cluster of supporters around the two. Emily felt her heart warmed by this demonstration of love and concern. After devotees offered expressions of comfort, they dispersed to return to their chosen places of solitude to continue in prayer and meditation.

People came and went. The group dwindled as the hours passed. Around 2 A.M., only Buck, Emily and another couple remained. Two police officers entered. Their late night shift had ended, and they decided to spend an hour in prayer at Trinity.

Weary from the day's events and the late hour, Bucky and Emily departed for home.

A full moon cast broad shadows under the canopy of leaves formed by majestic oak trees lining the deserted street as Buck and Emily walked together. Nearing home, they sat down on a wooden bench.

"Bucky, will we ever see our sweet Michelle again?"

"Em," he said, "We've done everything we can. A lot of people are praying, and the police are on the case. I don't know what more anyone can do."

"Bucky, earlier tonight I spoke of my regret of having run away from home, but if that had not happened, we would not have met. In that case, God chose to bless rather than punish. I guess what Pastor says is true...God brings good things out of bad circumstances. Why did I so quickly think of God punishing me when someone kidnapped Michelle, yet never thought to thank Him when He sent you to me?"

"I guess it's just human nature, Em," Buck said. "Maybe instead of blaming ourselves or others over things that happen, we should focus on trust in God's promise that he loves us, will forgive us and fix things when we mess up."

"God is awesome," Emily said. "Seeing all those stars above fills me with wonder."

"I know," Buck said. "Em, there are times when I wonder if he knows who I am. I feel so small in the universe...but not tonight. Tonight, when I see the night sky with you I get a sense of peace and assurance God knows what he's doing. I have confidence that he will bring Michelle back to us."

They paused and looked at each other in silence, deep in thought.

Then Buck said, "I'm grateful that God brought us together. Em, you are beautiful tonight."

"Oh, Bucky, I love you so much. Where would I be without you?"

26. CRUSHER'S RAGE

When Crusher's agent saw Michelle's picture on the front page of *The Springfield State Register*, he immediately notified sources who quickly brought this news to the Mastermind's attention.

Crusher felt the fire blazing in his eyes when he read the article. He slammed his fist down on the tabletop disrupting the objects on it, sending some scattering to the floor.

If Crusher himself had undertaken the deed, he might have relished in it, but the audacity of his abettor taking matters into his own hands was intolerable. The stoolie had too little experience to implement risky action that could alert the police and expose Crusher's whole operation.

Now Crusher felt the blood pumping through his veins and his nostrils flaring. He curled his lips in a twisted grimace and clenched his teeth. Glaring through his one narrowed eye, he paced back and forth murmuring vendettas against his operative and Bucky. "That jackass, Kenny! Why did he do this? I personally must be the one to execute justice against my enemy. I will lure that bastard, Ellis, into my clutches. He shall suffer the greatest of calamities under the veil of utter secrecy. I will do it...I alone. Never again will I leave the task to any subordinate. But now, the imbecile must be dealt with swiftly!"

He went to his desk and opened a desk drawer, pulled out a file, spread out its contents on the desk, then snapped the phone from its cradle. He made multiple calls to implement a plan designed to undo

Kenny's blunder and teach him a lesson that would remain imbedded on the boy's memory, like words chiseled out on a tombstone.

•

Kenny walked out of the grocery store onto the sidewalk. A firm hand clamped onto his arm and pulled him to the side.

"What the hell are you trying to pull?" Crusher's agent demanded.

"Whut...?" Kenny said.

"The Mastermind got the story on the kidnapping, you moron."

"Hey, hey!" Kenny laughed. "Was he impressed wit' whut I done?"

With both hands, the agent grabbed Kenny by the collar and lifted him a few inches, leaving the lackey's toes barely touching the sidewalk. "You bonehead! What were you thinking?"

"Whut da hell?" Kenny said. "I t'ought da big Mastermind would be happy. Da whole damn family is sick out of dere minds. Ain't dat whut da Mastermind wanted?"

The agent dropped Kenny who hit the sidewalk and stumbled a few steps backwards.

"Who told you that? I told you exactly what the Mastermind wanted from you. Your assignment was clear. It's too bad for you that you took matters into your own hands."

Kenny was silent.

"What have you done with the kid?" the agent asked.

"My doll's watchin' 'er. She likes da kid."

"I ought to bust you up good, you stupid punk. What did you plan to do with the kid, anyway?"

"I t'ought da Mastermind would know what to do," Kenny boasted.

"You're right about that. Here, take this.," The agent handed him a railroad ticket.

"Dis here's a ticket to Butte, Montana," Kenny complained. "I ain't goin' to Montana."

"Pipe down and listen up," the agent said. He pulled a black knitted cap from his pocket and pulled it down over Kenny's head. With his soulful, downcast look, Kenny looked like one of the *Three Stooges* caught in the act of doing something really stupid.

"Wear this when you get off the train. It will identify you to one of our agents who'll meet you there. Tell no one where you are going...not your 'doll'...no one. Lay low until you get word from the Mastermind."

"But..." Kenny protested.

"Shut up. You're damned lucky to be alive after what you did. If you ever decide to take action again without a directive from the top, you're a dead man."

"Whut if I jist stay under cover here for awhile? Whut'll happen if I don't go to Montana?" Kenny asked.

"He'll find you. The Mastermind has enough evidence of your criminal past to put you away for life."

"Okay," Kenny answered, "but whut about da baby?"

"Now listen carefully. If you mess up on this directive, you're finished. This is what you must do before you leave town..."

•

"Dr. Bernard, we have your granddaughter here at the station," said the police desk sergeant on the other end of the phone line.

Contacted at the hospital, Dr. Bernard interrupted his visitation rounds to race home, tell the family, and take them to the station.

When Agnes Bernard heard the news, she ran with hands raised high, shouting, "Praise God, Michelle has been found!"

Others in the house heard Geoffrey shout from the parlor, "They're holding her at the police station. Hurry, we're going to get her!"

In an instant, they all came together in the parlor, ready to go.

"Is she all right?" Emily asked.

"They told me she needed some cleaning up when they found her, but that she is fine," Bernard said. "That's about all they told me"

At the station, family members released a barrage of questions all at once to the desk sergeant.

"Where did you find her?"

"Did you get the person who took her? Was it Josh?"

"Was she crying?"

"Is she unharmed?"

"Where is she?"

"Whoa!" the desk sergeant said. "One question at a time. First, let me assure you she is all right. Early today, we got a call from Springfield Hospital that she was left there."

"The hospital? Was she injured?" Mrs. Bernard asked.

"Oh, no, not at all," the officer replied. "As I said, she is fine. She was left in a lavatory near the hospital entrance. No one noticed anyone going in or out. We found no clue to indicate who did this. It's puzzling. But the important thing is she is well and you have her back."

"I was at the hospital this morning making my rounds," Dr. Bernard remarked, amazed at the coincidence.

Standing, and stepping out from behind the desk, the sergeant said, "Come, I'll take you to her."

They entered a side room where Michelle sat on the floor with her back to them. A female clerk sat on the floor rolling a ball to the child. The ball bumped Michelle's foot and rolled to the side. As Michelle turned to follow it, she saw her family. Her face brightened and she made a fast turn, wobbled to her feet, stretched out her arms, and darted towards them as fast as her little feet would go. Emily met her halfway, and bending down, whisked her up into her arms.

"Wow!" Buck said. "I've never seen her move like that!"

The noise of chatter and laughter filled the room as everyone doted over the happy child.

•

The mystery of who took her and why lingered. Traumatic effects of the kidnapping remained, especially with Michelle, who was afraid to sleep for fear of an intruder coming to take her away. Michelle's crib sat in Emily's room, but Emily and Buck traded off sleeping in the room to reassure the child. During the day, family members stayed close to watch her, and, in turn, Michelle protested, crying, "Mama! Da-da!" if she found herself alone for a moment. Like lint clinging to a garment, the child stayed as close as possible, following Emily wherever she went.

Not long afterwards, the mood changed, as everyone turned their attention to a new and happy project — the wedding of Bucky and Emily!

As things calmed down, Bucky found the courage to approach Dr. Bernard to ask for Emily's hand.

"Bucky, as her father, I don't ever want to let her go," Mr. Bernard told him, "but if I have to give her away to anyone, it would be to you. You have my permission." He stood and shook Bucky's hand. "What took you so long, boy?"

Agnes Bernard threw herself into the project with passion.

"It will be one of the most wonderful weddings ever at our church... of course that's where you will be married...and we need to contact Pastor Messerschmidt...he'll want to counsel you before the wedding, I know that...and, of course, we need to select a date...to check the church's calendar...there's just so much to do...we shouldn't do it too soon...there's so many people we have to invite...you know, your father's a very prominent person in this community...we should see about reserving the church hall for your reception, as well...oh, I can't wait...it will be wonderful."

All this did not exactly meet with Emily's complete approval. She would have preferred a smaller, quieter gathering at the church, but the joy exuding from her mother constrained her to let her have her way. She would wait and make whatever changes she wanted as the project progressed.

Bucky later confessed to Emily his discomfort with the proceedings. "Emily, this is something I'm not used to...all these fancy frills and elaborate plans. As far as I'm concerned, I'd just as soon elope and get it over with, but I know how long we've been waiting for this day and what it means to you...and to your family, so I'll do whatever you want, but you may need to give me some help along the way.

Agnes Bernard's enthusiastic involvement with plans for the wedding, and her desire to find any excuse to pamper and care for her granddaughter's needs gave Bucky and Emily more free time to be together. After long exposure to danger, abuse, and hardship, Buck and Emily now enjoyed some of the happiest days of their lives.

Grandma Bernard put Michelle down for a nap and went to the kitchen to wash the lunch dishes. At the kitchen sink, she turned on the faucet and ran water into the basin. While it filled, she walked to the radio, turned it on and tuned in her favorite music station.

•

Meanwhile, Buck tended to his duties around the grounds. Dressed in a long sleeved unbuttoned white shirt over jeans, he raked weeds from the garden and cleared plants that had produced their full harvest by summer's end.

"Hey, Bucky, look what I found in the house!"

Buck looked up and saw Emily framed in the door to the back yard, her hands behind her back.

"What is it?"

She brought her hands forward and lifted what she held over her head. "It's a football!"

Winding up to throw the pigskin, she yelled, "Run out for a pass," and let the ball fly.

Seeing it headed high above him, he flung the rake aside, spun around and sprinted over the lawn, craning his neck to keep his eye on the ball. With a leap, he bounded up into the air, his arms stretching and his fingertips caressing the ball, bringing it down and cradling it to his chest. Running between two saplings, he flung the ball to the ground, jumped and shouted, "Touchdown!"

Emily laughed and clapped her hands.

"Where'd you learn to throw like that, Supergirl?"

"City parks have their advantages."

Buck picked up the ball and watched her, his one hand on his hip and the other with palm up, balancing the ball. She returned his gaze with her hands on her hips and a saucy stare. *Even in that cotton shirt and pleated skirt, she's a knock-out.* Having the resources to buy and wear new clothes, the good will clothing depots they had once frequented became a distant memory.

Buck grabbed the football and fingered the laces.

"O.K., now it's your turn. We'll see if you can catch as well as you can throw." Buck threw a pass as straight as a bullet at her. She ran a few steps, and reached, but the ball bounced off her fingers and landed on the ground behind her. Then she scooped it up and ran away from Bucky, looking back over her shoulder, laughing.

"Hey, come back here," Buck yelled. He took a few steps forward, saw her increase her speed, and started running after her. She entered a vacant field at the edge of their property and ran up a gradual incline. Buck gained ground, so she threw the ball aside and tried to run faster. She reached the crest of the hill and started down the other side. With a whoop and a holler, Bucky caught up to her, matched her pace and tackled her. Together, they rolled head over heels down the slope, laughing. At the bottom, Bucky ended up on top of her and kissed her. As she eagerly returned his kiss with passion, Buck felt the fireworks ignite. It was like the fourth of July!

•

In the kitchen, Agnes Bernard dried and put away the last clean plate as she hummed along with the radio to Leo Reisman's Orchestra and vocalist, Lou Levin, as he belted out the hit song, *Happy Days Are Here Again:*

> *Happy days are here again,*
> *The skies above are clear again,*
> *So let's sing a song of cheer again,*
> *Happy days are here again.*

EPILOGUE

Crusher had reached a stage of eminent success. His criminal network continued to spread, and he now amassed a huge fortune, which he stashed away in banking institutions all over the world. Not a man who favored refinements, he required little for himself.

Yet, his life was joyless. Loneliness ate away at him. Since his mother had died, no one remained who loved and cared for him. As the Mastermind, he delegated more and more of his operations to others, but remained aloof and kept his identity hidden from those who served him. Even so, pressing matters related to his expanding organization fell to him alone. Always, a fear of personal exposure filled his thoughts. He had taken extreme measures to distance himself from his crimes, even resorting to murder to cover his tracks.

•

On this rainy night in the French Quarter of New Orleans, the Mastermind dined at *Antoine's*, a world renowned restaurant established in 1840, with a labyrinth of fifteen themed dining rooms branching off from the front dining room. In his initial visits, Crusher chose to be served in the "Maison Verte" dining room on the second floor. Because of its more remote location, smaller dimensions, plush green carpeting and drapes with a black marble fireplace as its centerpiece, the room represented, in Crusher's mind, an isolated chamber of safety and seclusion. He soon learned, however, that these precise features attracted curious first time visitors who toured the maze of connected hallways in their quest to seek out the most hidden locations. At such places, they stopped, stared, gawked and whispered about the patrons who could afford the price to dine in rooms reserved for the privileged and the wealthy.

This time, Crusher dined at a small table by himself in the expansive and spacious front dining room where he blended anonymously into the crowd, and no such intrusions occurred.

To think that I, a master criminal, eat here, where American Presidents, celebrities and royal personages from around the world have dined. I come here but twice a year, yet they treat me as a king because I pay well, but none of them know me or give a damn about me. Money can't buy friends. If those who sit around me only knew what company they keep with me among them.

How many now, have I murdered? Let me think...countless puny runts on the rails...that doesn't count. They were lawbreakers. Who else? The old geezer who ratted on Ellis and told me they were going to the Chicago World's Fair. Then when we dragged the little prick through the woods and I had to kill Brutus, the driver...he knew too much, and I set him up as a suicidal maniac...and Josh...how could I forget that bastard, who stole me blind and now rots at the bottom of the Mississippi? And that nosy detective who wouldn't lay off...what was his name? Oh, yes...Rumson. He got pretty close...breathing down my neck...had to take care of him for sure. What trail remains uncovered? What evidence connected to my past have I overlooked? Is anything out there that someone might trace back to me? This thought haunts me.

St. Louis, Missouri

At a particular spot at the bottom of the Mississippi River, the slow moving current tugged at the human form fastened to its moorings. Partially submerged in the muddy riverbed at its feet, the body undulated like a waving flag in the breeze, as if struggling to free itself.

On the river above, a towed barge loaded with waste and heavy concrete floated placidly several hundred feet directly north of the spot. The intent of its owners, a St. Louis concrete company, became evident as they discharged these contents into the river. Beneath, the plunging debris caused a turbulence and an eruption of mud at the bottom which clouded the water, blotting out all visibility. After mud settled, dim shapes and forms reappeared. The riverbed had changed radically. The body was no longer anchored down, but had started drifting with the current.

Phillips County, Arkansas

At a rural area of Phillips County, Arkansas, Betty Crown, her 8 year old daughter, Ruth, and their dog, Misty, walked through a wooded area along a path a short distance from the river. Misty, accustomed to this walk and not prone to run far from her owners, ran free ahead of them.

Noise broke out quelling the quiet sounds of the forest.

"Mommy, Misty is barking!"

"I hear it, Ruthie. I wonder why she's barking?"

"She keeps on doing it, mommy."

"Maybe we better see what she's barking at," Betty said.

They left the path and walked into the woods.

"I can see her through the trees," Ruthie said. "She's down by the river."

Her mother, who had a taller vantage point than her daughter, could see the dog running in circles around an unidentifiable object on the ground. Betty hesitated.

"Dear, stay right here where I can see you. I want to go ahead and see what's happening."

"Why can't I come, mommy?"

"I want to see what it is first, sweetheart."

"All right, mommy."

Ruthie frowned as her mother drew near the thing. Betty Crown put her hand to her mouth and took a breath. Giving a quick glance back at Ruthie, her mother took a few cautious steps closer, her hands now covering her nose and mouth.

Ruthie's dog, Misty, shot glances back and forth from the thing on the ground and back at Ruthie's mother, wagging her tail, as if to say, "Look what I found!"

Her mother stiffly extended her arm and pointed a finger at Ruthie. "Go!" she said to Misty in a commanding voice.

The dog instantly ran back to the girl, with Ruthie's mother right behind her.

"Mommy, what did you see?"

"Something a child should never look at."

"Tell me, mommy, tell me!"

"It's a dead person," her mother said bluntly.

Ruthie said no more.

Betty bent down and quickly snapped the leash on Misty's collar. She carried it along as a precaution against any unexpected dangers. Then she grabbed Ruthie's hand and quickly led them away.

Such a disgusting sight...the body badly decomposed...must have washed up at the river's edge...whose body is it? How long has it been there? Good God! I must call the police immediately. She gagged as acidic bile from her stomach rose to scorch her throat.

Discussion Questions for Book Groups

Part One

Chapter One "The Burial"

What are your thoughts about Father Michael Griffin's act of giving a Christian burial to a woman who had an abortion?

Chapter Two "Farewell to Boyhood"

How did Bucky feel about leaving home?

Chapter Three "Lessons Begin"

How confident is Bucky with the decision he has made to ride the rails?

Chapter Four "Basic Training For a 'Gaycat',"

What effect would the circumstances in this chapter have on the relationship between Bucky and K.O.?

Chapter Five "A New and Useful Skill"

What characteristics describe the boy who gained a free breakfast in the diner?

What happens that tests the relationship between Bucky and K.O.?

What consensus is reached between the two?

Chapter Six "Caught"

What are your feelings towards each of the identified characters in the Shelby County jail?

Chapter Seven "Hard Times"

What kind of circumstance would have to occur in your life that would convince you to beg for food?

If you had no food for two days and you came to a ripe corn field with no one in sight, would you steal the product?

What distinction is made between "hobos" and "bums?"

Chapter Eight "Lessons In Survival"

How would you judge some of the "schemes" employed by hobos to survive? Dishonest? Manipulating? Necessary? Excusable? (See Matthew 12:1-8)

How do issues of justice and mercy come into play here?

When K.O. expressed his desire for revenge against those who took their money and beat him, how did Bucky counter his remarks?

Chapter Nine "The Homecoming"

What "covenant" did Bucky and K.O. make between them before they parted ways?

Chapter Ten "Nick"

Comment on Bucky's reaction to his father's grief.

Chapter Eleven "A Shocking Discovery"

Discuss Bucky's reaction to the surprise that he encountered in his family.

Chapter Twelve "Little Brother"

Who helped paint a different picture of Helen for Bucky than the one he imagined? How did Bucky feel after the testimony he heard?

Discuss your feelings about Helen as she wrote this letter.

Chapters Thirteen "A Fateful Encounter" and Fourteen "Crusher's Mother"

To what do you attribute the sudden appearance of the train Bucky caught that brought him back to the fracas just in time to save K.O.?

What was Bucky's immediate reaction to Crusher's accident?

How was Crusher's mother characterized in Chapter Thirteen, and what effect might his mother's character have had on Crusher?

Chapter Fifteen "A Lost Brother"

What did hobo's mean by "riding the rods?"

How did Officer Mark Brady react to some tactics of his co-workers from up the line? What relationship influenced him in his assessment?

Chapters Sixteen "Crusher's Expanding Syndicate" and Seventeen "Injury in the Yards" and Eighteen "The Ticking Clock"

What danger threatened those who rode in a gondola car loaded with large pipes stacked on one another?

What opinion did Willie Higgins have of the railroad bulls?

What kind of dangers did railroad workers face?

In what ways did Bucky and Willie Higgins demonstrate a caring concern for others in these chapters?

Chapter Nineteen "The Wallet"

What temptations in this situation did Bucky face?

What motives came into play in the frenzied response of the hospital administrator and staff?

Chapter Twenty "Tanoa"

What qualities describe Tanoa's character?

Chapter Twenty-One "Hard Questions and a Generous Act"

How did Bucky confront Mr. Lockingham on hospital policies?

How did the administrator react?

Chapter Twenty-Two "Life in the Jungle"

What issue angered K.O. and resulted in an argument?

As the argument progressed, we read, "In his mind, Bucky began to realize K.O. had a point, but he wasn't going to back down now." Why was Bucky unwilling to stop arguing even after he felt he may have been wrong?

Initially, the argument was about Bucky's failure to accept the money Tanoa offered. How did the issue of the argument shift as it grew more intense?

How was the argument resolved?

Who "won" in this situation?

Chapter Twenty-Three "The Mysterious Stranger"

How did hobos in this camp who knew Bucky regard him?

To what lengths was Crusher willing to go in pursuit of his prey?

Chapter Twenty-Four "'Century of Progress' World's Fair"

What risky act of courage did Bucky perform after he was hired by the World's Fair management?

How much are "hobo nickels" worth today? (Check the internet)

Buck and K.O. reflected on the benefits they had gained at the World's Fair:

"You know, Buck, this life ain't half bad. Maybe we can make somethin' of ourselves. At least we got a good place to sleep in hay in the elephant tent."

"Yeah, and the lake's a pretty big bath tub for the both of us," Buck said. "We've been getting good and honest money and plenty to eat."

What one desire did they mention that had not yet been satisfied?

Chapter Twenty-Five "At the Gordon Estate"

List three adjectives that describe each character in this episode:

    a) Clarence Gordon

    b) K.O.

    c) Bucky

    d) Estelle

Discuss reasons why the promotion of Fascism failed to attract America's youth in contrast to Germany's youth who passionately embraced it.

Chapters Twenty-Six "A New Event on the Midway" and Twenty-seven "An Unexpected Surprise"

Launched during the Depression, the 1933 Chicago Century of Progress World's Fair was the only financially successful of all World's Fairs. What do you think contributed to this?

If you have a personal story about someone who attended the 1933-34 World's Fair or lived in Chicago at this time, share it with the group.

Chapter Twenty-Eight "Out of the Shadows"

What was the condition of the custodial staff Supervisor?

Who tried to act as an advocate of a more reasonable approach to the situation (cite examples)?

How much influential success did this person have?

What uncharacteristic reaction did Bucky display during the police interrogation? What prompted this?

Chapter Twenty-Nine "Jailbirds" and Chapter Thirty "New Evidence"

Back on the job, how did Bucky feel about himself in the restroom before Crusher's action?

Chapter Thirty-One "Crusher Savors a Victory"

What kind of spirit characterized Crusher as he walked the path to the hotel after buying the newspaper?

Chapter Thirty-Two "The Chicago Fair Revisited"

What fortunate circumstance in the elephants' response to the gunshot spared Buck and K.O. from being instantly trampled?

Chapter Thirty-Three "Harlem Y.M.C.A."

What boyhood experience prepared Bucky to help in a crisis situation?

Contrast Bucky's reaction to Clyde's predicament with that of the other onlookers.

Who good fortune resulted from this incident?

The Boxcar Kid

Chapter Thirty-Four "229 West 43rd Street"

How did Bucky regard the good fortune of acquiring a job with the *New York Times*?

What unpleasant side effects did the job bring?

What did he think about living in New York City?

Chapter Thirty-Five "In the Dead of Night"

What factors led Bucky to conclude the man asking for him was an emissary of Crusher?

How did the fact that the man gave chase effect Bucky's thinking and emotions?

How did K.O. express his anger and disappointment walking along the street?

How did they get out of the city?

Chapter Thirty-Six "The Bernard Sisters"

At this stage of her life, what was Emily's biggest annoyance?

What had become her biggest attraction?

What rude discovery followed her brief reverie?

What comes to light regarding what happened in Chapter Thirty-five?

What assumption may be drawn by the reader when he learns in Chapter Thirty-One that Crusher knew his prey was n New York City??

Do you think Crusher may have come to New York and had been shadowing Bucky?

If you were Crusher, what would you be planning?

Chapter Thirty-Seven "Emily and Josh"

As a character who is quick to reap vengeance against those who wrong him, what prevented Crusher from immediate search and seizure action?

What lessons could Crusher learn from this incident?

Chapter Thirty-Eight "Hospital Board Meeting

Who provided information that led the Hospital Board to reach its decision?

Chapter Thirty-Nine "Runaway"

Was there ever a time when you considered running away from home?

How do you feel towards Josh's character?

Chapter Forty "Disowned"

What does the term "zero tolerance" mean? What do you think of this principle?

Read Matthew 18:21, 22 and discuss in the light of this chapter.

Consider the behavior of Emily's father and that of the father in Luke 15:11-32. How are they similar? Different?

How do issues of justice and mercy apply to the older son's response?

Chapter Forty-One "Sex For Sale" and Chapter Forty-Two ""All the Way"

"What happened *inside him* that launched Bucky into immediate action against Josh?"

In what way did this experience change Bucky's life?

What new purpose became the chief priority for him?

A promise is a commitment. It can be made without any expectation of payback, or it can be conditional; kept only if certain stated obligations are met. Promises in the Bible are often called "Covenants." Compare the promise Bucky made to Emily with the promise God made to Abraham in Genesis 15.

Who makes the promise in each covenant? What conditions are set for the one receiving the promise?

In what way are these promises similar? Different?

Chapter Forty-Three "A Painful Separation" and Chapter Forty-Four "Bucky and Emily"

Read John 15:13. Love that puts others before self is sacrificial. Sometimes it involves taking a risk. Identify sacrificial acts in these chapters that demonstrate love. Who performs each of them?

Chapter Forty-Five "St. Barthomew's Soup Kitchen"

In response to the diatribe of the woman who pointed her finger at Bucky, he says, *"What does she know about God...about anything?"* From the woman's comments, what attributes does *her* God possess?

How would you characterize the woman? How do you think her husband may have felt?

What differences are apparent in Emily's and Bucky's behavior at the wash basin?

Chapter Forty-Six "Intersecting Pathways"

Do you think this meeting of Bucky and Father Michael Griffin is

    a) implausible
    b) could have happened by coincidence

c) might be part of God's plan of intervention
d) a serendipitous event

Chapter Forty-Seven "Safe Harbor"

Discuss Becky Griffin's comment, "We always have enough. The Lord always provides for us," in light of the previous paragraph.

What factor may influence why some are satisfied and others not in similar circumstances?

In John 10:10, Jesus speaks of abundant life (translated in some versions as "life to the full"). How would you characterize the life that Jesus promises?

a) Wealth and Power
b) Inner peace, contentment and satisfaction is every circumstance of life
c) Having the most "toys"
d) Freedom from pain and suffering
e) Other

Chapter Forty-Eight "Bucky and Butch"

What was the cause of Butch's complete turn around in his attitude towards the deaf man?

What attribute in Bucky is recognized by Father Michael in this situation?

Chapter Forty-Nine "A Defining Moment"

What makes this experience a "defining moment" for Bucky?

How would you answer Father Griffin's questions to the congregation?

What impact does this chapter have on you?

Chapter Fifty "Pressing Concerns"

What "pressing concerns" do Buck, Emily and the Griffins have in this chapter?

How would you advise them in each case?

Chapter Fifty-One "A Christmas to Remember"

What holiday traditions did you follow as a child?

What subject matter in a Christmas sermon might have you going home afterwards with an uplifted heart?

What is "good" about this news announced to the shepherds?

Is this news intended exclusively for the shepherds?

Chapter Fifty-Two "Stirrings"

In this chapter, all the characters have marriage on their minds. Summarize and discuss the thoughts of each of the characters about marriage between Bucky and Emily:

- Bucky
- Emily
- Becky Griffin
- Father Michael Griffin

Chapter Fifty-Three "Decisions"

What negative reactions about the marriage issue does Father Griffin anticipate from the members of his congregation?

How would you characterize those who raised these opinions?

What strategy does the priest employ in this situation?

Do you think Father Griffin, as a Christian pastor, should think ahead and strategize to respond to varying opinions, or he should he remain passive and trust God to take care of anticipated problems?

Chapter Fifty-Four "A Disquieting Intrusion"

List as many choices you can think of (good and bad) for Bucky to respond to the news he received about his father.

Speculate on the consequences of each response you listed.

Chapter Fifty-Five "Back On the Rails"

Why did Bucky choose such a dangerous place to ride the train?

What consequence of his choice did he not anticipate?

What other troubling consequences arose in this chapter?

Review the choices and consequences you listed in chapter 55. Would you deem any consequences listed to be better than the one he chose in the light of this development?

What part did God play in all of this (if any)? Are there any signs of God's intervention here?

Chapter Fifty-Six "The Trial"

When Bucky began to tell his story, what did his attorney direct him to withhold from him? Why?

You are a member of the jury. Forget that you know what happened and why. On the basis of the arguments raised at the trial alone, how would you have responded?

Chapter Fifty-Seven "The Attorney's Letter" and Chapter Fifty-Eight "Some Pieces Come Together" and Chapter Fifty-Nine "Homeward Bound"

What prospects appear in these chapters suggest that Bucky is making headway in finding a more productive future?

What threat looms over the horizon?

Part Two

Chapter One "Welcome Home"

Speculate on why you think the attorneys responsible for delivering Queen Salote's letter could not be found.

Chapter Two "Michelle Rebecca Bernard"

Do you know the ages of your parents when they married?

Of those in your group, whose parents were the youngest when they married? Whose were the oldest?

How many siblings did you have, if any?

Where were you in the line-up (youngest, middle, oldest)?

Chapter Three "The Civilian Conservation Corps (CCC)"

How were other nations faring during the Depression?

What answers did youth in other nations find to address their condition?

What feelings about the USA might the restoration programs of the FDR administration raise in those who participated in them?

The CCC was primarily directed at helping:

____ children
____ homeless people
____ families with teens and older boys
____ the elderly

What plans did the members of the Griffin household postpone because of a qualification for Bucky's entrance into the CCC?

Chapter Four "Mc Dowell County Courthouse"

What tactic did the forestry supervisor use to strengthen the muscles of enrollees?

How old were you when you had your first taste of liquor or beer?

How did it taste to you then?

What did Bucky expect to hear when he was called to the superintendent's quarters?

Chapter Five "Fire!"

What conditions prevailed when the fire raged?

How many days did it take to put it out?

How did Bucky and his fellow enrollees get trapped in the flaming inferno?

Chapter Six "The Noose Tightens"

By what title was Crusher known by those who worked under him?

How did Crusher keep his identity hidden?

Chapter Seven "Barroom Brawl"

What was the chief recreation for the men of the Twelfth Street Erecting Shop?

What mistaken notion about Chuck and Helen did Lucky have?

As Chuck's feelings and behavior come to the fore as the story progresses, what image do you have of him?

The Boxcar Kid

Chapter Eight "Life In a Coal Mining Town"

What was Chuck Ellis' intent in seeking work in the mines?

What kind of feelings do you have toward Bud?

What did you think of Lily's disclosure of Bud's behavior to his father?

How did she feel when he was whipped?

Chapter Nine "Aunt Helen's Letter"

What kind of feelings surfaced as you read Aunt Helen's letter?

Chapter Ten "The Cunning Thief"

What special ability would you attribute to the young operative? In what kind of legitimate vocation might he prosper?

Conjecture how the story might have progressed if the letter had been sent and received.

Chapter Eleven "A Visit From Josh"

How did Josh find Emily's location?

Why didn't Emily cry out for help?

How much interest does Josh demonstrate in his own child?

Another "what if" question. How might the story develop if Josh had his way with Emily?

Did Emily speak to anyone after Josh and the women were gone? If so, who?

Chapter Twelve "Murder At the Parsonage"

Did it occur to you before the identity of the victim was revealed that Bucky could not have been in St. Louis?

Chapters Thirteen "Franklin Delano Roosevelt"

Were you alive when FDR was president? If so, how old were you?

Do you remember who you, or your parents voted for when he was elected?

What were some of the prevailing political opinions expressed at that time?

How would you characterize Eleanor Roosevelt's political stance?

What circumstances and ideas from the Great Depression are similar to those prevailing today?

Chapter Fourteen "Company Commander Keith Little"

How much flexibility did CCC supervisors have in selecting programs and activities for their enrollees?

What do we learn about Windy from the plans he proposed for training?

Chapter Fifteen "Solo Flight"

Of all the characters in the story, who is the one you root for the most? The least?

Chapter Seventeen "Detective Dan Rumson"

Do you think the chief had a hidden agenda in his strong objection to Dan's desire for further investigation?

Chapter Eighteen "The Threat"

What affect did the phone call have on Rumson?

Chapter Nineteen "Trauma"

How do you view the trauma that grips Bucky?

Is this a "chink" in his armor?

What is your assessment of Bucky's character in this chapter?

Chapter Twenty "A New Resolve"

What did Bucky do to restore his confidence?

When Bucky spoke of his determination to adopt Michelle after he and Emily married, what did Emily fear?

Chapter Twenty-One "Emily's Homecoming"

What decisions did Emily and Bucky and the Griffins adopt?

What kind of reception did Emily and Bucky receive from Emily's mother in Springfield?

In what kind of spirit did Emily approach her mother?

Discuss Dr. Bernard's assumption and reaction to Bucky.

Chapter Twenty-Two "Kenny"

What status did Kenny assume he had in the Mastermind's eyes?

What opinion did the St. Louis regional agent have of him?

Chapter Twenty-Three "Let the Good Times Roll"

When Emily said to Buck, "Now it seems the last leg of our efforts has been reached...we've united with my parents," he responded, "You mean, Em...you mean...we can get..." What was the unsaid word he had in mind?

Why was he hesitant to say it openly?

Chapter Twenty-five "The Reporter"

How did Pastor Messerschmitt help the distraught family?

In what ways did Bucky support and comfort Emily?

Chapters Twenty-Six "Crusher's Rage"

How did each member of the household respond to the revival of marriage plans?

What did you think about the story's ending?

The Epilogue

Comments?

Author's Note

Thank you for reading my novel and using it as a study guide. I hope that every reader came away with something of benefit...and perhaps for some, a greater personal sense of God's love, mercy and grace for all people.

Dick Miller

Coming in 2009

The Boxcar Kid II: Glamour Boys

The next book in this poignant series chronicles the origin of Bucky's aspiration to be a pilot, and his path to secure the position of an ace fighter pilot in WWII.

More than a documentary, *Glamour Boys* focuses on personal harrowing experiences of the characters in the context of the military events.

This story focuses on Bucky's spiritual maturing and the issues of conscience he encounters throughout the series.

Laced with intrusions of Crusher's vengeful activity, the book moves to a chilling confrontation between Bucky and his nemesis.

Statue pictured is featured at the Naval Aviation Museum, Pensacola, FL
Original life-sized statue by Artist, Captain Robert L. Rassmussen,
USN (Ret), Museum Director

LaVergne, TN USA
06 October 2010
199705LV00004B/7/P